The **MOHAWK TRILOGY**

Sky Walker

Tehawennihárhos
and the
Battle *of* Vinegar Hill

DRAGON
HILL

S. Minsos

The Publisher: Dragon Hill Publishing Ltd.

Library and Archives Canada Cataloguing in Publication

Minsos, Susan Felicity, 1944-

    The Mohawk trilogy : Sky Walker: Tehawennihárhos and the battle of
    Vinegar Hill / Susan Minsos.

ISBN 978-1-896124-53-7

    I. Title.

PS8626.I685S678 2012   C813'.6   C2012-902579-8

Project Director: Gary Whyte
Project Editor: Kathy van Denderen
Cover Image: Photos.com
Image Credit: Sugarbush Road © Michael Swanson (pp. 16, 41, 307, 325. 363),
reproduced with permission of Michael Swanson
Map Credits: Sidney E. Morse and Samuel Breese, Clerks Office of the
Southern District of New York, 1845 (p. 11); Library and Archives Canada
(pp. 12–13); Ontario Ministry of Natural Resources, Queen's Printer for
Ontario, 1986 (p. 481).

Produced with the assistance of the Government of Alberta,   **Government**
Alberta Multimedia Development Fund   **of Alberta** ■

PC: 1

Dedication

~

To Juliette, Émilie and Matt

Acknowledgements

~

My thanks and deep appreciation go to Dragon Hill Publishing and the people who have made this book possible. Thanks, also, to the close readers, commentators, literary and history aficionados who have read manuscripts, queried the history and supported the project focusing on the Grand River. In alphabetical order, they are Janine Brodie, Lesley Clarke, Lisa Davis, Dianne Gillespie, Bruce Hill, Mel Hurtig, Anita Jenkins, Franklin Miller, Laraine Orthlieb, Malinda Smith, Michael Swanson, Kathy van Denderen and Sally Williams. Thanks to my immediate and extended family for our communal knowing and caring about Brooklea, where, for us, the story was incubated. The heart and soul of my own narrative belongs to Ove Minsos, father of our precious troupe, the children who mean the world to us and for whom this saga is written.

Note to Reader

~

Although I have researched the era and tried to absorb the flavour of the 1840s, I may have faltered from time to time. I ask you please to note all mistakes are mine and the novel is fiction. Characters, if real, are fictionalized.

–SM

Prologue

~

There once was an old man who took up wild land to farm. He lived on the oxbow of a gleaming river near the swarthy village. It was where he belonged.

For many years the old man's son and later his daughter-in-law helped him. They cleared the brush. They built the fences. They tilled the land. Others helped too. The villagers from the swarthy village helped each other in times of trouble, in times of need and in times of construction. It was their mysterious sacred bond.

One day the old man from the swarthy village caught a dreadful disease. He died. It was a sad time. It was sadder still because the old man's son caught the same disease and he also died, leaving his wife alone, a poor widow with five children. Naturally the widow feared the terrible evil disease and was afraid it would kill her or her innocent children. The doctor from the neighbouring swampy village told her to stay away from the cabin. And so the poor widow and her five fatherless children abandoned the site to allow fresh healing air to purge the evil spirit. She retreated from the farmhouse, leaving the furniture and the potatoes, corn and oats.

Of course the poor widow planned to return to her husband's homestead to reclaim her goods and property. This she did after some months. She and her five children and her brother came back to the cabin but things had gone terribly wrong. A greedy woman had taken possession of the farm. The poor widow's winter stores had been eaten, eaten to the last crumb. The poor widow was frantic and at last the greedy woman, seeing the harm she was doing to the fatherless children, agreed to vacate the cabin and to hand it back to the rightful owner. That was a good thing but alas the poor widow's troubles were not over.

Less than two hours after the poor widow's return there was a whooping and a hollering outside her door. Many men from the swarthy village armed with knives and a pistol barged into the cabin. The children were terrified. They cried. They screamed to their mother. They said the evil spirit was back, and in a way it was. Men from the swarthy village had descended upon them like wolves. They chased the poor widow and her frightened brother and the fatherless children right out the door and through the woods and far away from the oxbow and far away from the family farm. The men from the swarthy village were armed with knives and a pistol and they called the poor widow and her five young children bad names, names like beggarlegs and half-breed. They said the poor widow and the fatherless children did not belong in the swarthy village. Finally the men gave up the chase and turned back to set fire to the cabin.

Through some miracle the poor widow and her family survived.

The poor widow kept with her the three youngest children and she worked in service for a man in the swampy village. Kind relatives took the two older boys. The eldest fatherless son went to live with the poor widow's frightened brother.

The second fatherless son went to live with the fat grandmother, Aughguaga Polly, the cranky one, the one who was a renowned healer. In time the second fatherless son grew into a brave, intelligent, compassionate man, but footloose and wandering. He never forgot the day the men from the swarthy village armed with knives and a pistol had driven the family away from their home and he felt his mysterious sacred bond with the village had been sorely tried.

Dramatis Personae, in Order of Appearance

On the Crazy River

Lawrence "Lawrie" Filkin, visitor to Dumfries House, Brantford, from New Glasgow, Nova Scotia, brother-in-law of Octavius Millburn Sr.

Octavius (O.G.) Millburn Sr., owner of the village emporium and a wealthy land jobber

Walter Winter, "Whiskers," Tory politician, a village gossip

Tacks, an ubiquitous gossip

Fannie Filkin Millburn, wife of Octavius Millburn, sister of Lawrence Filkin

Mrs. Hart, reporter for the *Brantford Courier*

Seeum Johnston, editor of *Brantford Courier*

Squire Tehawennihárhos Davis, Wolf clan, called variously the Mohawk or Sky Walker, son of the late Peter Davis (Mohawk) and Margaret Riley (unknown lineage)

David Shagohawineghtha, Oneida, adopted father of Squire Davis, and son of Aughguaga Polly

Jedidiah Golden, ("Jeddah," a.k.a., the "Snowman") from Appalachia, descended from a Butler's Ranger, owns a horse stock farm in Uxbridge

Peter Johnson, African Frenchman, and formerly Pierre Beauchemin from Detroit, married to runaway Georgia slave Sarah

Barton Farr, "old Fox," an old friend of Squire's late father, owns a stage stop and tavern in Canboro

Pomeroy Munny, "Pommie," an Irish starveling

Chrisinny Munny, Pomeroy's sister

Chief Thomas Davis, cousin to Joseph Thayendanegea Brant, Methodist instructor at Davisville

Bride Munny, Irish Catholic immigrant, Pommie and Chrisinny's mother

Missus Lucille Oihwanéhégwaht Goosay, a Cayuga woman with excellent sons

Alfie Williams, "Cook," works for Nellah Golden at the Cave Tavern and the Cyclops Inn

Ann Bergin, maid, works for Nellah

Margaret Magdalene "Maggie" Walker, Mohawk, Turtle clan, wants to marry Squire Davis

Aughguaga Polly, Oneida, Turtle clan, healer, "the fat grandmother," reared Squire

Mahlon Joe, Delaware barber on Vinegar Hill

Nathaniel Burr, from Burwick, Vaughan, Markham and later Brantford. Nathaniel and his wife Margaret Burr are Reformers. Nathaniel is brother to the prominent Reformer Rowland Burr and uncle to Robert Burr, the leader of the Markham Gang

Luscious and Westonbury Fowler, "Cockers," own a travelling cockfight

Mr. Peel, from Cavan, Canada West, Irish Protestant, gambler

Patrick "Paddy" Connelly, Irish Shiner

Nellah Blaize Golden, sometimes called "Teacher," first cousin to Jedidiah Golden, mother of Pearl, co-owner of the Cave Tavern, owner of the Cyclops Inn

Lizzie Bosson, maid, pregnant with the child of Meatface, works for Nellah

Flash Dunlop, remittance man

Elias (Reba) and Fink (Franz) families, Mennonites

Lieutenant Horatio Needles, British military, Royal Canadian Rifle Regiment (RCRR)

Sergeant Jimmy Nelson, RCRR

Corporal Bing, RCRR

Richard Boynton "Boy" Hewson, Anglo-Irish, cohort of the Warriors

Jake Hearenhodoh Venti, Mohawk, Warrior, boyhood friend of Squire

Danielle O'Herlihy, Millburns' new maid

In Uxbridge

The Fergusons, Jennet, Rebecca and William and their parents, William and Mary (Graham), immigrated to Canada from Cummertrees, Scotland, in 1832 and arrived in Uxbridge, Upper Canada in 1834 to run a stock farm

Asahel Filbert, Free Kirk, visiting Presbyterian minister from Toronto

Pinky Filbert, Asahel's wife

Ann Auld, Fergusons' young Ulster maid

On Vinegar Hill

Charles Murray Cathcart, 2nd Earl Cathcart. In January 1846, he was chief administrator and acting Governor General of the United Province of Canada; he was appointed Governor General on April 24, 1846.

Julia Katoserotha' Good, a dissipated woman

Paulus "Bobby" John, cousin to Squire Tehawennihárhos Davis, leader of the Warriors, descendant of chiefs Joseph Thayendanegea Brant and John Deserontyon John

Darius Davis, younger brother of Squire Davis

Central Canada West, 1845

Grand River Map, 1828

Plan of the Grand River & Location of 6 Nations of Indians, as found settled by the Rev.d R. Lugger, February 20.th 1828

Any deviation by a public man [sic] from the straight and narrow path of disinterested public service, any abuse of public office for private advantage, high salaries and exorbitant fees, any undue private gain from public measures were venal acts, which should be denounced and exposed for the public good. Above all, the people's representative must not only do no evil, he [sic] must avoid the appearance of evil by refusing public office or association with private interests, which might benefit from public policy.

–R.A. Mackay. "The Political Ideas of
W. L. Mackenzie," *Canadian Journal of Economics
and Political Science*, January 1937, p. 1.

⁓

Lo, what an entertaining sight,
Those friendly brethren prove

Jad kah thoh ji ni shon gwa wi,
Ne n'yon gwe ti yo se

–Peter Hill's Hymnal, Tuscarora County: 1896
Kanyengeiiaga Kaweanondahkoga,
For those who speak the Mohawk language
Ottawa: Government Printing Bureau.
Printed for The Six Nations, 1892

Communication is a more-or-less matter, seeking a fair
estimate of what the other person said and has in mind.
A reasonable speculation is that we tacitly assume that
the other person is identical to us, then [we introduce]
modifications as needed, largely reflexively, beyond the
level of consciousness.

–Noam Chomsky. *Language and Thought.*
The Frick Collection, Anshen Transdisciplinary
Lectureships in Art, Science and the Philosophy of
Culture. Monograph Three, Rhode Island, 1993, p. 21

⌒

Old School Assembly, Minutes 1845, p. 18

Resolved, 1. That the general assembly of the Presbyte-
rian Church in the United States was originally orga-
nized, and has since continued the bond of union in the
church, upon the conceded principle that the existence of
domestic slavery, under the circumstances in which it is
found in the Southern portion of the country, is no bar to
Christian communion.

–Harriet Beecher Stowe. *Dred: Tale of the Great Dismal*
Swamp. Appendix, p. vii, Brantford: A. Hudson, 1856

⌒

We must take this matter of names seriously; the
Murchisons always did.

–Sara Jeannette Duncan. *The Imperialist.* Thomas E.
Tausky (Ed.), Ottawa: Tecumseh Press, 1988, Chapter 1

PART I

THE BAFFLED KING

THE VILLAGE OF BRANTFORD
1845
OCTOBER

CHAPTER
one

I t was all about fitting in, thought Lawrence Filkin.

Who fit in? Who did not? Take O.G., for instance. That was Octavius George Millburn Sr., the husband of Filkin's sister, Fannie. The brother-in-law. The troglodyte.

O.G. Millburn on the Grand River was rich.

Except for G.T. Dennison on the Humber River, Millburn was about the richest man in the Gore and Home Districts but it did not matter. He did not fit in, certainly not with so-called ordinary Brantfordites. He didn't have to, though, did he? Outside the larger municipalities there was no law and nothing to stop or control him. Millburn had land. He had money. He could do what he wanted but Filkin said O.G. was a king without loyal subjects and without loyal subjects, really, whom did one rule? Millburn said he was an island. Filkin said he wasn't. Millburn said he did not give a goddam fig for Filkin and the social fandango in the village but no one believed him. O.G. was a businessman. He cared about his followers. When it came to fitting in, an active businessman had to care.

Fannie Millburn attended Mr. John Wilkes' Puritan church. She joined the Congregational women's group, even signed up for the potholder circle, thanks to the encouragement and guidance of dear Reverend Thomas Baker. Lawrie Filkin wished his sister well with the potholders but he could not get over her husband.

He regarded O.G. Millburn with resentment, not because Millburn had made a fortune. No, that wasn't it. Filkin enjoyed the offshoots of wealth, notably the genteel ethos of Dumfries House. Money did not whip up Filkin's envy.

It was Millburn's satisfaction. Millburn was happy even though he longed to be popular. Millburn had asked Filkin the seminal question. What could he, O.G Millburn Sr., do to win approval in the village? Filkin protested he did not have a clue. Filkin had studied his own reflection. He knew who he was. He was slight. He was fawn-coloured: hair, eyes, eyelashes, quill-shaped body and the soft remains of the fuzz over his ears, all plain. His fingers were long and double-jointed. That was something.

With his old-fashioned French-fork beard and imported black silk-waistcoat, Millburn, though deaf as a doorjamb, loved life. He loved the opportunities on the colonial frontier. He was satisfied. Self-satisfied. That is what Filkin resented, the self-satisfaction of types like Octavius George Millburn and the irritating self-satisfied smugness of the wealthiest residents. Filkin hated Canada West. He hated the smugness of wealth. He did not hate wealth; he hated the way wealthy smugglers ran things.

Lawrence Filkin despised his smug brother-in-law. Even more, he despised Millburn's smug business partner, black-skinned Nellah Golden. He could kill the bitch. Poof, if he could, he would make her disappear from the village. And good riddance.

CHAPTER
two

Lawrence Filkin, late of New Glasgow, Nova Scotia, hankered for sugar-coated nuts and he was an expert on nuts and, immodest as he was, on sugarcoating. He said, "You have done very well for yourself, O.G. Your fine silk waistcoat does you credit. Still—"

"Still?" said Millburn.

"Come now, sir." Filkin gave a little huff. "The swamp is hardly the place to bring a decent girl, is it?"

"You mean Fannie?"

"Mmm-mmm, poor Fannie." Mouth full of pink sugared almonds, his favourites, Filkin said, "Bloody goose poop. There's shit everywhere, O.G. It is positively disgusting. On the plank walkways people actually slide on the stuff." Filkin's hands were spidery and he nipped another almond with his pincers.

"So what?" Millburn was otiose. Yawned. His beard rose and fell in a hairy wave.

Filkin was no fool. Of late, the brother-in-law seemed bored with him.

Millburn opened a weary eye. "Shit's customary. Aint you a fusspot."

"Big fines for the goose poop." Filkin ignored the fusspot. "Ten pounds. Harsh treatment. Gaol time for repeaters." Thinking of cracks, Filkin saw a big one. In the plaster, there was a crack shaped like a willow tree, over the window sash. It had rained with intensity for three days and the crack's willow branches on the wall were wet, dark and blurred. It was a bushy, natural tree but an imperfection nonetheless and Filkin took note. "Poopers pay the price."

"Your sister aint hard done by, you know." Millburn yawned again. "Lotta undercover going on but this here village aint yet seen fifteen years. You can't stick a goose in a gaolhouse."

"Ha, ha."

"Unless it's on a platter."

"Ha, again," Filkin said. His thin hand scratched his cheek. His tone abandoned censure and turned to blandishment. "Did you know, O.G., they are girdling trees up and down the Hamilton road?"

Millburn shot Filkin a look. "It's for clearing the forest. For arable land. Why would anyone suffer in this God-forsaken place without land? Here." He pushed the hand-painted gold-and-red ceramic candy bowl toward his brother-in-law.

"Thanks. Don't mind if I do. Say, O.G., there is a lot auction happening next week. Are you buying?"

Seated next to Millburn, Filkin felt as small as a brown spider. He sat on a footstool whereas the brother-in-law sat like a monarch butterfly in his wine-coloured Moroccan leather reading chair, which dominated the library like a throne.

Octavius Millburn crossed his thick limbs and he dropped a grey cashmere sleeve on the padded armrest and let the lead crystal snifter dangle sketchily in the delicate air above the indigo whorls of the Wilton carpet. He wore impeccable Egyptian cotton high-collar shirts, silk dickeys, fine cashmere double-breasted jackets, narrow, button-fly tweed trousers and tan suede riding boots. People said he wanted to add distinction to the proceedings at the O.G. Millburn Sr. Emporium and Merchants' Exchange. That he did. Millburn needed occasional help at the emporium. From time to time, Filkin worked for his brother-in-law. First-hand, he saw the truth of the matter: Fannie's husband was a paragon of fashion. He changed his gloves on the hour and he had seven coats: four morning coats, a Prince Albert frockcoat, a dress tailcoat and a new fur-lined navy overcoat.

Villagers knew it. A darn dandy. They narrowed their eyes. "Where does that darn Octavius Millburn think he lives? Montréal?" Filkin wondered the same thing but he sat as low as Miss Muffet. He picked at a yellow thread. "Who is your tailor, O.G.?"

"None of your business."

As for style, Filkin was not in the least dandified. It was just for his private entertainment that he had asked Octavius for the name of his tailor. Filkin knew, of course.

It was Miz Nellah Blaize Golden.

"Teacher," the villagers called her.

Some time ago a certain village gossip, the stealthy Tacks had told him about the black seamstress on Vinegar Hill and her rebellion, her ambition, her vitality, her sinfulness and the felicity of her seams. Lawrence Filkin despised her and her growing pocketbook but, like the almonds, he kept his presentation sugar-coated.

Yes, I could jolly well kill her, he thought.

She did not belong in the village, any village.

She might die a stranger in a strange land. By the rivers of Babylon, let the willow weep for the likes of Nellah Golden. He would not. Filkin suspected Millburn had not heard about it yet but two men, Filkin (himself) and Mr. James Wilkes, had started a petition for the removal of coloureds from Brantford, which they intended to submit to the Governor General upon the collection of the appropriate number of signatures. It was just a matter of time, thought Filkin. Goodbye to coloureds. Men of Progress would sign the petition. He would see to that. The coloureds would leave for Queen's Bush, the Wild West.

Those who do not fit in will be removed, Filkin thought. He cracked his fingers both backwards and forwards and was amused by his uncommon flexibility.

~

Filkin did not know why it happened but the Queen's horses crossed his mind as soon as he and Millburn had repaired to the library. It was the Castle Fyvie. Yes, it must have been. The painting hung over a mantle of brass monstrosities. The castle's ghost seemed to moan like the wind in the creek willows, "You are welcome, sirs, to Upper Canada."

Millburn and Filkin had a routine.

Millburn respected the routine but Filkin knew O.G. could be a man of surprises. It was Fannie who was stuck in the glue. High tea came first. That was Fannie's calf-head cheese, hash and scrambled eggs. Dreadful. The hash deserved special mention. Filkin had a sensitive stomach. Digestion period took place in private, often in the outdoor convenience. After a rather lengthy digestion period, it was their custom to return to the library, where Octavius discussed mercantile opportunities.

Could Millburn buy the Queen's horses? Lawrie Filkin wondered. How many horses, as it were? How much stuff did the man want for the emporium and for himself? What Filkin wanted now was closer to hand. Imported comfits. Millburn was on the nod. Filkin looked at the almonds. He wanted O.G. to stay awake to keep passing them.

"Good heavens—" Filkin rose to his feet with a rattling glass and he poured himself an extra dram of Glen Grant. He had the habit of asking Millburn passionate questions, hoping his host did not notice the frequent refills. "More land. Can you afford it?"

"Prices are holding. A lot or two, I expect. An investment, you know." Millburn looked affronted because Filkin had asked whether he *could afford it* but the old man passed the ceramic bowl anyway.

Millburn had aged early and his looks had stayed put.

Overnight, his beard turned steel grey.

His hearing was as bad today as it had been yesterday. A tin ear trumpet was to hand although he hated to use it and Filkin, for one, had learned to speak up in O.G.'s presence. In any case, it was just coincidence Millburn's eyes and beard were the same shade. A few of the clients at the emporium had noted the steel in the grey when O.G. traded rum for furs or baskets.

"I do not mind if I do, O.G." Filkin pinched a fancy sugared almond with an arachnid's delicacy, as though the almond were a fly he feared to squeeze. Filkin had such a sweet tooth. He stared at the sugar-coated confection, studying the pleasure of it. He thought often about Nellah Golden, the seamstress. The whore. The witch of Vinegar Hill. She co-owned the Cave tavern with Millburn and she managed it and she owned the Cyclops Inn that was attached. The Cave was a drinking hole, far too grotty for Filkin's taste. Everyone was welcome, women, Indians, Africans. He squeezed the almond hard, as though it were a ripe runner bean, ready to pop open. Drink in hand, he sat hunkered down on his three-legged footstool. The fur on the stool was shabby, worn to the parchment and, as he had told Fannie more than once, the seat was a disgrace to the household.

Filkin said, "A petition is in the planning stages. Soon the village will be a town. A mayor makes by-laws, O.G. No more shit on the streets." There was the other petition in the works, of course, the one about the clearance of Africans from the village, but on that particular paper he stayed mum because he colluded with James Wilkes, and Wilkes had made him promise to keep his mouth shut.

Millburn helped himself to the nuts. "Um. Not to rush. Them black boots of yours can tip-toe through the goose poop for a while yet." This time for some reason he did not pass the nuts and Filkin was annoyed. Filkin knew Millburn wanted to buy, beg or steal as much land as he could but what Filkin wanted was an almond. He liked to suck them, one at a time, until the sugar coat had melted.

"What's to be gained in delay, O.G.?"

"Indian lands, young fellow. What else?"

The Millburns lived in Dumfries House, a three-storey yellow-brick dwelling with a single veranda, white-columned. Ivy vines crept up the walls. The house was on Dumfries Street. They had built the house on reclaimed swampland and had landscaped it with English touches. The garden was a masterpiece. Fannie Millburn eradicated coneflowers, wintergreens and squirrel corn and pulled up every stubborn trillium that tried to hide its tripletail white-and-purple bracts in the bog and she imported wagonloads of clean dirt and planted hybrid roses and hedgerows. The Millburn estate housed grounds the poor lonely immigrant could love. Everyone in the potholder circle thought so and offered compliments to Mrs. Millburn. They scolded her for not sharing her seeds and gardening secrets with them. Fannie Millburn, showing in full her half-set of European teeth, was charmed. She started a botanical association for the import of English seedlings to the outreaches of Empire. Dumfries House provided a hideaway for an upper-class gentleman like Lawrence Filkin and he simply loved sugared almonds. Sugar was boredom's anodyne.

"The pink ones. Those, right there. Yes, there. They're the best," Millburn said with a hint of impatience. "Say, d'ya know anything about James Higginson?" Millburn regarded the ceiling like he expected an answer from above.

"No," said Filkin from below.

"But the Filkins and the Cathcarts are cousins. On good terms, are they, eh?"

"Mmmm. Yes. Amiable, as far as I know."

"Perhaps I'll write to our cousin General Charles Murray Cathcart in Montréal. Ask him to visit us. Show him the pleasures of the bush country."

"Mother will make introductions." Filkin's stare never wavered off the dish. He willed O.G. to pass the sweets.

"Excellent," said Millburn. He scooped another nut. He did not pass the bowl to Filkin, whose mouth was watering.

Millburn started his evening rant.

Filkin had trouble listening. His feared his eyes were getting as glossed as the ceramic bowl. Here we go, he thought. Land is plentiful. For miles and miles on either side of the Grand River, the lands of the Six Nations are unimproved. Land entices smart capitalists. Grab a parcel, make improvements, *or say so*, and you win. Sure, sure. Filkin knew the speech. He did not worry about Indian lands and he didn't say improvements meant things were working out for the best. Not like Millburn. O.G. told himself such lies, thought Filkin. Filkin, for one, recognized devilishness. He saw a justice system to suit the occasion. Colonials fought against ancient Indigenous landholders. Indians got screwed. So what? The ghost of Castle Fyvie whispered in his brain. Goats and monkeys were welcome to the place.

Filkin cared about Nellah Golden, though. But it was not a nice caring.

Her success bothered him.

An African. Black skinned, she was.

Yes, there were improvements on Vinegar Hill, if you could call them that. Nellah's brick house was solid enough to withstand the world at the door. The shady Louis Burwell had surveyed the village and the question remained. Did Nellah hold a quit-claim deed?

Surely not. She was on Indian land. Did she hold a patent from the Crown? Unlikely. Filkin buffed his tapered nails. He sucked on white and pink almonds, almonds as rosy as his cheeks. He hated liquorice pipes and orange jujubes and it bothered him something fierce that Octavius and Nellah were business partners and sexual partners.

Their partnership was supposed to be a secret.

Secret from whom?

A secret from Fannie Millburn, of course.

Don't tell Fannie, Millburn had said.

Poor Fannie.

Lawrie Filkin understood familial duty.

He seized opportunities to turn Nellah's virtues to pitch.

He said the strumpet could sew a fine shroud for the Archangel Gabriel for all he cared. Filkin and James Wilkes, the ambitious son of John, wanted Nellah's property for a Christian organization, a men's country-and-sporting club. For Fannie's sake, Filkin must hurry. Immediately, he was to survey the villagers and collect signatures for a petition of clearance; the petition would read, *that all coloured persons should be cleared out of the village of Brantford and moved to the Queen's bush.* On the matter, James Wilkes had set the parameters. He was bold and aggressive. He had wasted no time. He had staked a land claim next to Nellah's property and built a white mill and pond at the foot of Vinegar Hill.

But for the sound of Octavius Millburn's munching nuts, the library had settled down. O.G. ate sweets by the handful and muttered under his breath about putting dear Aunt Filkin to good use with people of influence, in particular the Cathcarts. Filkin was feeling resentful. Simply no one in the village could look more sullen.

So Millburn deigned to be agreeable. "Here, brother-in-law, have some sugar." Millburn had an absent expression and hummed

"Tippecanoe." "I think Charles Cathcart—the Queen's Commander-in-Chief—should come."

"Commander-in-Chief? Come where? Here?"

"Yes, here, my friend. General Cathcart is the very man I need. He is the man to help me. Keep me in a piece."

Bully for you. Your wife finds out about you and the Golden woman, why, all the Queen's horses and all the Queen's men won't keep you in a piece, mused Filkin, sucking glaze and sipping spirits.

"Enough," Millburn said, picking up his tin ear and hefting himself out of the armchair. He turned this way and that and ended up setting his crystal glass down beside the burl-wood magazine rack, which would annoy Fannie, who had cried and begged her boys to be tidy, otherwise they would have to hire *a girl*, in all events an Irish girl. His last drops of single malt whisky spilled on the "Affairs of Honour" page of *The Sporting Magazine*.

Milburn yawned and his open mouth was as wide as the last cut of the Brantford canal. "To bed, Lawrie. The malt you're pouring down your throat is too dear to swig, eh?"

CHAPTER
three

Paulus "Bobby" John and Richard Boynton Hewson raped and robbed Nellah Golden, the first lady of Vinegar Hill. They stole her silver coins, her markers and her Wedgwood tea set. They nearly killed her and her unborn child.

News travels fast.

Bad news has a first-class ticket.

On Tuesday, 30 September, the day after a midnight dinner in Nellah's great dining room on Vinegar Hill, a Six Nations Mohawk, one Bobby John (the great-grandson of the late chiefs Joseph Thayendanegea Brant and John Deserontyon John), and his white cohort, "Boy" Hewson, violated Teacher. The Queen of the night.

The Warriors, who knew how many of them there were, had discovered Nellah was rich.

They had knocked her senseless.

They had stolen her Wedgwood.

"Hear ye," went up the hue and cry. "Hear ye. Hear all about it." Walter Winter, the Tory, had heard all about it. He had heard the news because the stealthy, ubiquitous gossip, one ever ready Tacks, had been on the scene.

Tacks had told Mr. Winter.

Mr. Winter knew how things worked, he often said, and he planned to get busy spreading the news. He, who had enjoyed many a meal at Nellah's expense, told Tacks he was surprised. Not over the attack. She must have had that coming to her.

But she was rich? Nellah? Teacher?

Winter shivered in his big-collared navy-blue greatcoat. He did not want to play the fool. "You sure? You very sure?"

The sly Tacks had said to Mr. Winter, yes, he was sure. It was Indian Bobby John and the Englishman Boy Hewson. They stole her riches. Everything.

Winter's whisker-chops covered his astonishment. "Rich? Well, I never. Tacks, my man, you do have news. Aint that a caution?"

Tacks agreed it was a caution and the two men shrugged at the world's folly. A Negro woman with wealth? And now, certain of his news, Winter set out to rake the muck.

On the same autumn evening, just as ribbons of rain-empty clouds turned lemony in front of a setting sun, Mr. O.G. Millburn met Mr. Winter. Mr. Millburn was strolling along the wet and glistening plank sidewalk on Dumfries Street. Winter told Millburn what terrors had just befallen poor Miz Nellah Golden, why, she'd had her head split open, "cracked open like a ripe conker, yessir, a ripe conker," a concussion for sure, and "she were raped and beat up" and it looked like her silver coin and American dollars and all her due bills was stolen and what was bad was the loss of her precious mulberry-leaf Wedgwood tea set, and it happened not six hours back, at the brick house on the crest of Vinegar Hill. Nellah was rich, did ya know? Old Oneida woman Aughguaga Polly was there, attending her. Baby was born too. A girl. Winter had a tic in his left eyelid and a melody in his voice like a heaving water pump. "Can ya get over it there, Octavius? Nellah has money!"

She might not live.

Octavius was stunned.

He whispered over and over what Winter told him, "Nellah has money. Nellah has money." No. No. No. He'd warned her, goddam it. He'd warned her right from the get-go. He warned her to keep quiet about her money. The man she would listen to was her cousin, white Jedidiah Golden, but even then she chirped at him. In the early days, though, Octavius Millburn was cocksure about business and he had had sexual clout. Millburn bade Nellah to keep her mouth shut about the Cave's co-ownership. The midnight dinners, Hell's spinning bells, they'd best be secret. Her midnight salon must be as exclusive as their old saloon was not. There was no good to come, Octavius had often said, in her babbling like a brook about success. Timid, squeamish village folks did not need to learn about her. Her lineage was African. She made money. If people knew she had a genius with fabric and she made money, why, she'd make herself a target. That was as sure as shooting. She wasn't in a state of Grace, not with her skin. Who the devil among the Protestants of Brantford would condescend to greet her when they learned about her commercial acumen and penchant for tailored clothes?

Nellah had scoffed. Grace? No. A Disgrace. Who among them looked upon her at all?

"Well, you can forget your hopes of fitting in," Millburn had said one day, long ago, when he had stopped into the Cave for a drink. Nellah leaned over the polished bar. To Octavius, she was beautiful, glorious, and the best thing about the whole of Vinegar Hill. Her dimples were deep whenever she felt friendly but she was not friendly, she was listening and weighing her options, which were few, oh my yes, a precious few. Millburn sat on a high splintery bar stool and scolded like a magpie. The black-and-white "No Tippling" sign was crooked and it drooped over Nellah's head, slung up there by fishing gut. Millburn chomped on a delectable tartlet, a flaky quarter of salted pigeon-wing pie, and he quaffed his ale and talked about truisms and the dangers of obvious wealth in uppity folks.

"Trick is to be ignored, Nellah. Forgotten. Don't market yourself. No flag-waving. I warn you," he said and he used his fork to tong up the pigeon-pie pastry crumbs, "Make yourself known and it's a target you'll be.

"Besides," and here he leaned over the counter and with smart taps targeted a crocheted rose on the bodice of Nellah's dress with his greasy fork, "it'll do neither of us no good if the partnership comes out. Your business is fine, as is. Hear me now, Nellah. It's the way to survive. As far as folks know, you're poor as a tinker. You have no money."

It was harsh but Octavius was her partner, in the bed, on the ledger and in the Cave. Thank goodness for the Cyclops Inn, which was hers alone, Nellah thought, and she agreed. She would present herself as poor. For ten years, the secret midnight dinners turned out as smooth as Cook's blancmange puddings, and intelligence about the village-hill partnership never found itself greasing squeaky tongues.

Back on Dumfries Street, in the fresh moonlight, Millburn's mind and mouth had locked in memory. "You're poor, Nellah," he was repeating to himself just as he'd told her on that one day, long ago, "You're poor. In their minds, you must stay poor. Our business needs you poor. Don't you forget it! Your poverty is our friend. In the village, anyways."

That was then.

Word was out.

Nellah had money.

She had made herself a goddammed target.

CHAPTER
four

Walter Winter was unleashed.

On and on Winter went, describing Nellah's weakened state and giving intimate bloody details, some true, some not, until, as Octavius acknowledged to Filkin much after the fact, he could have screamed. Within minutes, Millburn held up his hand. Stop. The emporium's owner told Mr. Winter's bobbing whisker chops, told them direct, that he, Octavius, was too upset to say anything. Let alone anything sufficient to the offence.

Winter was disappointed not to get a quotable quote. He felt the irresistible urge to move on to spread the word, and with a quick backwards glance he drifted away and moseyed toward the rickety bridge and Colborne Street. He walked and he stopped and told all and sundry about the attempted murder of Queen Nellah. An innocent with a ministering chipper air, he had no idea whatsoever of the effect his gossip had had on his last quarry.

Millburn had turned as white as a winter hare. Fright had kicked him a good one. He hastened home to have a late supper with Fannie. The couple supped on headcheese, hash and eggs. The meal was never palatable but tonight it tasted like punk. The fright lasted. His teeth ached. Millburn felt palpitations. He had a fever. He told his wife that he needed a shot of ardent spirits. He kept a bottle in the bedroom. He had several bottles in the library and a very good bottle in the parlour, on the table beside the tea wagon.

CHAPTER
five

Mr. Millburn, the paterfamilias, quite under his own volition, or so Filkin heard, wandered about Dumfries House in search of a wee dram. Oh, my. That was the wrong thing for O.G. to do, Mrs. Millburn told Filkin. Yes, she said, wrong was the right word.

She explained to her younger brother what had happened.

Filkin's plain face swelled up. His pink cheek was like a sugared almond. He listened. He blushed, even pinker, with the satisfaction of the news. Fannie wore the latest, most modern costumes, brought to America by Algerines, and she burped in a delicate fashion. She held a diaphanous hankie over her mouth and whispered that her husband Mr. Millburn should have stayed well clear of the parlour *and the harlot* if he'd known what was good for him.

"And what do you think happened, Lawrence?" said Mrs. Millburn. "No, do not answer. I shall tell you, my dear brother. Octavius made a discovery."

"Truly, sister? Come, let me guess."

"Oh, of course." Fannie Millburn curtseyed with one arm forward, a Russian ballerina.

Filkin rubbed his hands together. "Octavius has discovered it. The Wedgwood. Yes, I know. Nellah Golden's tea service."

Fannie fanned her fingers into a maple leaf and clapped the mounds of her hands. Her plain face, so like her dear young brother's face with similar unremarkable features, was aglow. She said, "You win."

"Where did he find it?" Filkin could not keep approval from seeping into his tone.

Executing an arabesque, she turned toward the front door and the parlour. "Follow me."

The woman led the way into a dusty space, jam-packed with the doodahs. They needed a maid, Filkin thought. They really did. They loved trinkets as much as they loved Wedgwood but who was there to quibble? Lawrie admired his elder sister. She was such a middling kind of person. She was fifteen years older than he and fifteen years younger than her husband. She was not one to do anyone any kindness; she was the first one at the trough when kindness was being served up but such was her entitlement. One could only aspire to it; Fannie's self-regard had colossal proportions.

"Here," she said. She pointed down. "Octavius found it here. On the tea wagon. See, the potpourri dish sits with my own Wedgwood pieces."

Filkin saw it all with his own eyes. The potpourri dish and Nellah Golden's tea set, in leaf-and-pearl-patina glory. Someone had positioned them with quiet assurance on the walnut trolley. In a cracking voice, Fannie told Lawrie how she had 'fessed up to her husband. She had stolen the Wedgwood, she'd said, because of his traffic with Nellah. The real shock was to come. Finally Fannie admitted her secret. She had asked the Warriors and Boy Hewson to call on her at Dumfries House.

Filkin was amazed. "You invited the Warriors here? You paid them to rob Nellah?"

Yes, yes, she had.

And she wanted Octavius to know what she had done. During the Reverend Baker's recent sermon to the pilgrims at the Congregational Church, Fannie had felt the hand of Divine Intervention. Octavius should hear about it. She was the mastermind. She had arranged the robbery. She had plotted out the whole thing.

"Well, well," Filkin said, offering felicitation. "You? My sister? Fannie Millburn? The robbery's mastermind?"

"Yes, I am too." Fannie blushed with pride. "I must say, Octavius did not peep."

And why should her husband peep, anyway?

Mrs. Millburn pointed out the obvious. Her husband had had Nellah Golden in his bed but he did not want the whole village to know about it. And no one would take the word of Injun Bobby John against hers even if he shouted the truth from the rooftops. The Warriors' violence against Nellah was not Fannie's fault. Fannie had not told the men to hurt Nellah. Of course, she had not told them not to, either. Anyway, where was the harm? Teacher was still alive.

"The cost was high," Fannie said. She clasped her hands to her breast and let loose a burst of pent-up air. "I paid a small fortune to Bobby and Boy. In coin. In gold coin."

The cost was high?

Filkin believed her.

He was thinking of the spider and the fly, *oh no, no, said the little fly, to ask me is in vain, for who goes up your winding stair, can ne'er come down again.* And then with a sour expression he thought, bah, not high enough.

The bitch lived yet on Vinegar Hill.

CHAPTER
six

And so it happened that in a fit of conscience the day after the tragedy, Mrs. Millburn, acting on her brother's advice, picked up her brand-new red parasol and tucked it under her arm and set out for the corner of King and Dalhousie streets and the offices of the popular local newspaper. She felt pressed to explain her role in the current crisis on Vinegar Hill and she picked Mrs. Hart, the best journalist at the *Courier*.

Mrs. Hart wrote a newsy column, "Hart to Heart," but Mrs. Millburn had serious reporting in mind, not social titbits. To be fair to Mrs. Hart, Mrs. Millburn gave a plausible rendering of the previous day's events. Might Seeum Johnston write up the story? Mrs. Millburn certainly hoped so. Mrs. Millburn told Mrs. Hart savages had invaded her home, mid-day, and she was alone. They wanted to rob her of her silver coins, jewellery and fine goods. They wanted her very own precious mulberry Wedgwood collection. Over their married years, Octavius had given her the Wedgwood, Fannie said with her dark eyes glowing, and her voice, waspish. The thought of that, swear to God Almighty, was the final straw and the reason she had sent the beasts to bother the wealthy whore on Vinegar Hill.

It was her female weakness.

She had panicked.

Yes, that was it, Fannie said; she had panicked something terrible. She never otherwise would have thought of doing such a terrible thing, never, never. She would admit it. She had sent the thieves to Miz Golden's house. She knew nothing special about that wicked Nellah Golden, who lived on Vinegar Hill. Goodness no. Didn't everybody know the harlot owned a tavern on the outskirts? It was just a wild guess that she might have valuables lying around.

No, she told Mrs. Hart, she could not imagine why a strumpet like Nellah had Wedgwood that matched Mrs. Millburn's own pattern.

No, she had no idea why Nellah would have truck with men of poor character. Surely those speculations were best left to Mrs. Hart, ace reporter, to figure out.

Mrs. Hart's ace instincts were affronted. Who was she to speculate about a certain African woman's fundamental character?

You're the reporter, dear.

Right. Mrs. Hart bobbed her pencil between her fingers. She gave the yellow ties on her bonnet a smart flap and dove into the story. She said the rape was a tragedy. She commented on the simple fact of Nellah and Fannie's matching Wedgwood patterns. Why was that again?

Yes, Mrs. Millburn agreed, a tear rolling down her cheek, the patterns were the same. She was mystified but nothing would be gained in collapsing the distinction. A coincidence.

Mrs. Hart nodded and again she tossed the ties of her bonnet. Yes, indeed. It was. Same gifting source, perhaps?

Mrs. Millburn encouraged the tears to roll.

Of course not.

There were two women, Mrs. Millburn said, so different in character, she added, each with the same set of Wedgwood. A coincidence. Nellah Golden's got stolen, though. Pity.

Mrs. Hart wrote down the gist of the story and gave the by-line to Seeum Johnston.

On Saturday next, Octavius Millburn read it in the *Courier.*

He told everybody he found Seeum Johnston's version of events convincing.

Villagers agreed. They believed it too. Bamboozled most of the time, they believed anything in print. Bobby John was a devious trickster. How devious, readers asked? Was Bobby John as devious as Rumpelstiltskin, who got so mad at the Queen after his tricks were discovered that he flew out the window of the Castle Fyvie on a cooking ladle? Yes indeed, Bobby John was every bit as devious as Rumpelstiltskin. Never mind that Rumpelstiltskin had a contract because he had saved the Queen's sorry arse.

Poor Fannie.

She got gobs of sympathy. Everyone was worried about her. Without question citizens concurred with the Wild West headline, "Savages on Warpath. Innocent Villagers Next."

CHAPTER
seven

Octavius was loopy and Fannie was in denial.

Filkin believed they had lost their minds. His sister and her husband knew the truth about Fannie's involvement in the robbery and yet they bought into the newspaper story. Millburn was enjoying high status in the community and he was a jolly man but Filkin remained cautious. Someone's outing the truth about the robbery would be catastrophic. To Filkin, it was as clear as day. Details about Fannie's role in masterminding the robbery at Nellah's place were best never known, let alone forgotten.

In a follow-up story the *Courier* reported that Octavius Millburn had offered a hundred-pound reward for the capture, dead or alive, of Bobby John but most citizens knew about the reward already, right from Tuesday, the day after Nellah's assault. They knew because Filkin hastily posted *Wanted Dead or Alive* bills on every inch of available space on the village square. Naturally, Filkin was the man in charge of handing out the money.

The reward was a tidy sum, but why? Filkin wondered. Why did he do it?

Filkin guessed why. Millburn's motivation must be fear.

The reward was guilt money. To hide the Millburns' culpability for Nellah's unhappy situation, well, one hundred pounds ought to do the trick. There was nothing like a splodge of fear to grease a purse with a rusty clasp and Millburn's offering a reward was clever.

In a million years, Millburn told Lawrie Filkin, he might never have dreamed that such a sorry business could have a happy conclusion.

Citizens loved O.G. Millburn. He was king.

Hosanna.

Millburn and the local citizenry were one. He appeared to look after the concerns of the villagers and they were grateful. Being one with the villagers caused Octavius Millburn, crusader for peace and order, to swell his chest with pride and pain. He was a Napoleon who kept slipping his hand inside his shirt to pat his heart.

One night in the library a few days after the *Courier*'s second story, while Millburn talked in general terms about land and trees and undesirables and business opportunisms, Filkin brushed a stray speck of dandruff from the shoulder of his beige jacket and reviewed the situation. As usual Millburn droned on. This time Filkin was silent. He allowed himself the opportunity to think and took a good long look at Millburn.

Yes, he thought, you old bastard, you are damned lucky.

Fannie was safe. So far.

But they were not out of the woods. Not yet.

But there was good news too, Filkin mused. The good news was that he, Lawrie Filkin, had collected almost enough signatures for the petition of clearance. Put Octavius Millburn's name on the paper and Filkin would make quota. He wanted to get Millburn's name down, in ink, and get Nellah Golden out of Brantford before some-one-in-the-know spoke to the *Courier*'s Mrs. Hart to set the record straight. After all it was Filkin's bitter sister who had masterminded the Wedgwood affair and her admiring brother desperately wanted her to get away with it.

PART II

THE HUNT FOR BOBBY JOHN
AND BOY HEWSON

WANTED

FOR THE ROBBERY AND RAPE OF
NELLAH GOLDEN

INDIAN, PAULUS "BOBBY" JOHN
DEAD OR ALIVE

100 POUNDS REWARD
WITH AN OFFICIAL CERTIFICATE OF DEATH OR
INCARCERATION IN HAND, PLEASE SEE
MR. LAWRENCE FILKIN,
DUMFRIES HOUSE, VILLAGE OF BRANTFORD

There was no mention of a reward for the capture of a certain male, one Richard Boynton "Boy" Hewson.

CHAPTER
eight

Friday, October 3, four days after Nellah's Monday dinner and three days after the incident on Vinegar Hill

Four horsemen, rougher than Butler's Rangers, left Brantford just before midnight three days after the incident at Nellah's home. They were after bounty. On a manhunt.

Mohawk Squire Tehawennihárhos Davis, adopted son of David Shagohawineghtha and biological son of Peter Davis, was on the magnificent Canadian stallion, Cap'n.

Jedidiah Golden, his friends called him Jeddah, rode Joker's Breezy, a snooty Appaloosa.

The African Frenchman Peter Johnson rode the enormous draft, Diablo, and Barton Farr of Canboro rode Jennet Ferguson's sweet-tempered Canadian mare, Poco.

The horsemen sought Mohawk Bobby John, and for redress or perhaps redemption they sought Boy Hewson. They planned to bring order to Canada West, however it came.

Jeddah Golden rode quiet, which was not his custom. Worry pinched the lines on his face and smudged the skin under his eyes. Jeddah wanted peace. That was all he wanted. Peace in the vale. Peace on the hilltop. Peace on Earth. Getting justice for his first cousin Nellah Golden, the mother of his newborn child and the enduring love of his life, was a misery. No one quite understood how it was possible for Nellah to be dark skinned and Jeddah to be white skinned but nature has her ways and the two clever, charismatic Goldens, born of the same lineage but growing up with different hides, had to make do with the anomaly. Justice, like life itself, caused a commotion but Golden's multi-hued family deserved justice as much as anyone on the frontier. To see justice done, the "Snowman," as Jennet and Rebecca Ferguson of Uxbridge had tagged him, why, he would damn the peace he longed for.

As for Peter Johnson, or Pierre Beauchemin as he was known stateside, he said he would not miss a chance to stamp out sin but he could not bring himself to come clean and admit to a personal interest in the matter. Nellah had been his lover before he had met Sarah, his wife. Peter wanted to help Nellah because he felt he owed her a favour from times past but he was on edge. He wanted to get away with something. He had committed a serious crime. A murder. Not two weeks ago. The manhunt for Bobby John might bring him trouble, a brush with the law, a constable or a soldier, and he would not want that, goddam *sûr*. Johnson was cultured. A wine aficionado. He knew his Amontillado. He had wanted to kill old Ziggy, the slave-snatcher, and kill him with impunity. So far, so good. No one chased Peter yet.

The third man was Barton Farr. Farr realized the posse needed to be savvy as well as determined, and just because he felt like it he rode with them. Farr, the old Fox, used excitement to get his blood up and, as he admitted to Jeddah, chasing down a couple of marble-hearted desperados was a risky business. Fair enough. He could abandon his commercial inn and stage-stop operations in Canboro to enjoy the manhunt for a few days but only a few. For a certain Barton Farr, risk was the spice of life.

Squire Davis did not want to be there. His grandmother, Aughguaga Polly, *she*, who watched over the healing of Nellah and tended to the new baby, *she*, who was angry at her grandson, *she* made his life a goddam misery. Polly's list of complaints was long and irritating and lately they had all started with Margaret Magdalene Walker, "Maggie," the woman whom *she* wanted Squire to marry. Polly hated the very idea of Squire's chosen one. White Eyes. A Scotchwoman. Jennet Ferguson.

The four men rode from Vinegar Hill out of the village of Brantford and Squire's expression was icy. Farr complained about it to Peter. A glance from Tehawennihárhos was enough to freeze the knobs off a brass monkey.

For Squire, leaving with the posse meant leaving Jennet Ferguson back at the Cyclops Inn and he, for one, was not all that enthusiastic about hunting down an Indian, his cousin yet. Less noble than the actual manhunt was his desire for money. Snaring Bobby John would put coin in his purse. He needed money. He needed it to buy land and he needed it to court Jennie. He wanted to feel like a whole man, not a qualified, hyphenated man, not a red man or a half-breed. He wanted to find a dynamic community and live there and move ahead with his life. After the horsemen brought Bobby John and Boy Hewson to account, Squire would look for a place for Jennie and him, a place where folks overlooked trivial human differences, like skin colour. Of all the horsemen, the Mohawk wanted the most out of life, more even than Golden, who wanted merely Peace on Earth.

The posse would ride night and day until they found the outlaws that had abused and beaten poor Nellah and robbed her household of silver and gold coins, her pearls and a rare mulberry-leaf Wedgwood tea service with a matching potpourri vase.

Before they left, Golden had made arrangements for the tavern and inn. He had charged three individuals with tending to Nellah's business. They were Miss Jennet Ferguson of Uxbridge, Mr. Alfie Williams, "Cook," as he was known, and the boy, "Meatface," whom

Lizzie Bosson, Nellah's sweet-smelling, teenaged maid, called Adolphus. The three stood on guard for the security of Vinegar Hill and safety of the Hill people.

It was a time of love and hate, violence and intimacy. Squire was sweet on Jennet. Meatface was sweet on Lizzie. Peter Johnson had killed Ziggy, and Meatface had been Ziggy's young confederate. Meatface was a slave-snatcher too, a "trapper," he had told Lizzie, and he was the pa of Lizzie's forthcoming child.

The Mohawk did not trust Meatface as far as he could throw a five-fathom canoe but Johnson and Golden had listened to Lizzie and her defence of the troublesome kid. Golden had decided to give the youth some goldern responsibility. He had offered Meatface a chance to prove his mettle while they were away looking for Bobby John. Squire was jumpy about it. Squire had caught the stink of mischief at Nellah's house and he warned his beloved Jennet to keep clear of Lizzie's Meatface. The Niña, the Pinta and the Santa Maria left Palos with less guilt than Squire felt on that very October night when he left Jennie.

CHAPTER
nine

Mohawk. *Kanata, Kahnyen'kehàka*.

Mohawk, the derelict village of the Mohawk nation, was not up to much if you liked a tidy appearance, and Squire had had to convince a dubious Jeddah Golden they should hole up there. They might find a gossipy squatter, someone, anyone, who would talk to them and maybe give away secrets. Octavius Millburn had posted the large reward for Bobby John, captured dead or alive. Nellah had told Jeddah that, yes, Bobby John had been there all right, but her assailant was Boy Hewson. The capture of Bobby John would pay the horsemen money. The capture of Boy Hewson would be satisfying in another way. But the abandoned village on the Grand River seemed to make a poor start for the manhunt.

Nothing was impressive about Mohawk.

"Shite clumper eh, Squire?"

Golden pronounced *Squire* the same way as Alfie Williams, Nellah's Liverpudlian Cook.

Sounded like *Square*.

Squire was too tired to correct the pronunciation. He tried instead to convince Golden they were right to try Mohawk. He said the original villagers were gone downstream but the posse might find a few hangers-on. Always plenty of camps here and there along the crazy river and as for getting a tip about Bobby John, well, Squire owned up that it was a hunch. Many people blamed the poverty of the Six Nations on vilified Chief Joseph Thayendanegea Brant. Bobby John was Joseph Brant and John Deserontyon's great-grandson and you could count on it, a few bitter souls of the Longhouse had put the hex on the Brant and John families. They would talk against a Brant, turn in a John.

Farr was a wiry old guy. He was uneasy about the semi-deserted village and cast his eyes into the distance. He dismounted and walked Poco to the river. He smacked his hat on Poco's rump to get her to move ahead in the line-up to water. The old Fox said he felt as skittish as the mare and he put his hat back on his close-cropped head. His mystic blue eyes peeped out from under the brim. "I see rotting carcasses. There. And over there. Proves it. Mohawk's a goddam hodgepodge. Ghosts."

Golden said, "Jayzus, Bart."

Farr squinted. "Over yonder, is that a horse cart?"

Without turning, Squire said, "Yup."

"Nobody's tending to things."

Squire and Golden did not respond.

The two men dismounted and led Cap'n and Joker's Breezy to the edge of the still water, which was a polished mirror as sleek as glass and a few degrees above freezing. The horses lapped up a cold drink. Manes' shaking, they made a great spray.

The men looked about and wondered where to bunk.

Daylight on the crazy river, about seventy yards broad, reflected lapis lazuli. On this October night the river was patently black. The air was humid and the stars were as bright as diamond buttons on a shearling. Moonlight had painted silver streaks on the ghostly buildings. There was nothing left, nothing more than falling-down shacks. No warm, welcoming lanterns in windows.

No joyous, clever rafts or ingenious paper-birch canoes resting nearby. Nobody shouted *Sekoh orye* or *Hey-oh* when the horsemen rode in. The wind had died down but the night air was heavy and you could hardly see across the river.

Farr wanted to avoid causing Squire hurt feelings but he could not stop himself from expressing disdain. He pointed to the remnants of a home. He singled out a cabin with a collapsed roof. "Damn. What an upheaval." He picked a stalk of prairie grass and scooped off the seedy part between his thumb and forefinger and stuck the wet end in his mouth and sighed. "Who knew?" He spit. He turned to Squire. "I aint been around here in a month of Sundays."

The Mohawk was not set to argue. "Brother, it is changed. We get over it."

Farr said. "No soul-bird."

Over his shoulder, Squire frowned. "Eh? Soul-bird?"

Farr said, "Rebirth. Rejuvenation. Ah, something like that. Maria's expression." Maria Burnham Farr, Barton Farr's long-suffering wife, was Onondaga, related to Chief Kaneahintwaghte.

"You mean raven?" Squire said.

Farr made out that he was mystified and he scratched his head and shrugged. "Dunno. Yeah, I expect so. Anyways, I mean dump."

~

Bart Farr rode as straight as a sprite on Jennie's Poco but Peter Johnson was anything but a sprite. Johnson was not in the least elfin. He was the opposite of Farr, a colossus. Broad shoul-dered, muscled torso, Johnson could have made his living in the boxing ring but he was no rider, that was sure. He rode drag and not by choice. He had been well behind the rest of the posse and endured Farr's wagon-horse, Diablo, but in a temper. The gelding had the stallion's exotic markings and the Belgian mare's lumpiness. Old critter was a swayback. With a long dark head.

Two eyes rolling in a giant zucchini. Squire knew Farr's draft horse gave Johnson a jagged ride, as jagged as a cow, and he hid amusement.

Johnson's unhappy face was contorted. The Frenchman looked as though an enemy had speared his guts and he was reluctant to admit he was exhausted but wanted to know, where were they going to bunk down? *"Je déteste les chevaux."*

"Huh?" Farr chewed on the stalk. "What's the problem with Diablo, Pete?"

"Ouah! Don't like the horses."

Squire, the best horseman in the bunch, was letting Cap'n drink at the river. He looked up at Johnson, "You get accustomed, my friend."

Farr picked another grass stalk. "Ah, you can't get mad at old Diablo." He patted the horse's neck. "Fine hunk of horseflesh, this one here. He's as nice a feller as you'll ever find."

Rankled, Johnson smacked the rump of Diablo. "You ride him. I take Poco, eh?"

Farr chewed harder. He said, "No sir. No siree. No trade—" Johnson turned away and he rubbed his thigh.

Farr added, "—and pretty Jennet Ferguson wouldn't like it, would she?"

Golden was not listening to their banter. He had spoken little that night. Not like him. Finally he had wandered off because he admitted he was in no mood to kibbutz. He said he would poke around the village to find for a place for them to bunk.

Squire was listening to the exchange, though. He thought, no, Jennie wouldn't, and me neither. He had more or less gifted Poco to the Fergusons and Jennet took up the horse as her own. "You take care, Bart, to treat Poco good."

With a moan, Johnson dismounted. "Diablo is the devil."

Farr was getting chirpy. The old Fox did not have much patience. "No, Diablo aint the devil. You're too big for Poco. You would kill her."

The giant Johnson stood on the riverbank and he rubbed his backside and bent over and straightened. "I kill both of you."

Farr wasn't up to pretending to be amused. "Coming from you, Pete, after we all helped you bury the bounty hunter, that aint altogether funny."

"Bre'r Renard. You have no humour."

Farr said, "Not in the middle of the night, I don't." He took his hat and used it as a pointer and said his piece yet again. "Aint this a pigsty, Squire?"

"Yeah, yeah. I get it. Tsitsho, a pigsty," Squire said. It pained him to recall the busy comings and goings of yesteryear at Mohawk and to see nothing here but ruins. He remembered a swirl of colour and activity, the proud men and the broadcloth leggings. The way the women had sewed them, hours upon hours, with abstract patterns of white beads. And the blue and green tie strings they wore for belts. And the pewter gorgets and silver beauty pins. He imagined he could see the twirling triple-turkey-feather headdress worn by his father. He imagined he saw the grotesque expression of the Doorkeeper in the ghost wood. He remembered as a child he had been scared of the false-faces. False-faces and ashes were for chasing away disease but he hadn't known quite what they were. Squire grew up with Jake Venti and the Beaver kids and old Missus Beaver used to tell them whoppers. She said Hagondes the Longnose would steal them from the village if they were not good boys. Missus Beaver was a character. Tonight, travelling the road, he had thought he had heard the song of the Doorkeeper. He had heard the past and felt the ancestors' sorrow. "A dump," he said.

Golden bellowed at them. He waved. He told them to leave the riverside and climb up the sandbank. The three trudged up the bank, sliding on the dunes.

Just as well to get going. Squire was glum; nothing made him feel more miserable than seeing precision-crafted, hand-hewn canoes left to rot. Europeans had invaded the county by the thousands. The Six Nations had no power to stop land grabs on a vast scale and the chiefs had done what they felt was necessary and surrendered more territory. The people had shifted downstream and with resignation they had moved their barn-sided shanties and log cabins to other villages and tried to forget the disruption at Mohawk.

Golden had found what his men needed. A sizable vacant structure next to a corral where they could put the horses. The building had been a river way station. Villagers had collected, tagged and stored various commodities, like corn and wheat, for river transportation. The three men approached Golden and the way station, and in the wood knots of the station door, Squire traced the outline of an impotent Doorkeeper, the one who should stand guard. He cursed the thing. He kicked in the lopsided door and felt irrational in blaming it and one by one the four horsemen stumbled through the doorway and entered the single room.

The station was windowless.

It had a skylight covered in cracked lambskin.

The building had been a fine structure, once, but mellow walls sagged under an uneven roof. There were five plank beds on square homemade frames in the single room. The furnishings were meagre but the men did not want luxuries. They wanted sleep.

From a steel washtub beside the hearth, logs poked out splayed ends. Golden said, "Goldern. Them logs require a-splittin'."

Johnson said, "*Non, monsieur.* Dry. See? They crumble." Johnson borrowed Squire's flint, steel and punk and built a fire. The intensity of the smoke-filled room encouraged them to surrender vigilance and Johnson yawned. Squire thought he could see right down to Johnson's belly. Golden said he appreciated their sticking with him and he brewed some weak sugar-tea. The tea was English. Not smuggled from America. Which meant that Golden had paid a hefty price for it and they drank it, acting all delicate and ginger-fingered, and agreed it was better than the other stuff. They picked out their plank beds and crashed. Their heads were on their saddles and in their bedrolls they lay curled up like babies.

Squire was slumbering deep.

The child needed a minute to roust him.

"Mister, mister, wake up."

CHAPTER
ten

The boy shook the man's arm and pulled hard at a rip on the leather jacket and he puffed up and yelled into his ear. That did it. The man jolted, gave a jerk, like he was sitting on the end of a seesaw and the other guy had jumped off.

The boy said, "Mister, git up."

Squire was reluctant but he obliged and looked around the room to see whether the others were sleeping, the way he should be. Male snoring in various frequencies rattled the carved wooden candlestick holder on a triangular table. Squire had no idea how long he had been unconscious and he glared at the intruder and snorted at the kid's audacity.

The kid's shuffling was annoying. Bugger it. He started to lie down.

"Mister, you foller me, please?"

The kid's limbs were as long and thin as lily stems. He was dressed in rags and wore no shoes. His lips were the colour of ripe plums and he had unwashed sticky-looking red hair and bore the general aspect of the famished people in Indian Territory. No, thought Squire. Kid was not from the people. Looks were often deceiving but the boy didn't speak like the people and his eyes were as dense as blue stones. Irish. Squire took it all in but did not comment. He stretched. He sighed and further narrowed his eyes and

·beetled his black brows at the quaking urchin but he did not say anything because, as groggy as he was, he could tell the boy was dancing with news, just itching to tell him something, maybe something about Bobby John.

The boy persisted. "Mister—"

Squire yawned. At last he said, "Yeah. What is it?

"Mister, Chrisinny's up tree."

"Who? What? What do you mean 'up tree'?"

The boy nodded. "Yessir. Yessir."

Squire said, "Go home."

The boy said, "No."

"You kid me, sonny. Right?"

"I aint. Sister's stuck. She's gonna die!"

Unwilling and almost unable to hurry, Squire rolled to the edge of the bed and stood. He towered over the mite but the kid was not afraid of losing his scalp and, unlike many of his Irish countrymen, he didn't fear meeting a gruff longhaired heathen savage.

The Mohawk said, "Yeah. All right. Show me."

The boy belted out the cabin door. In bare feet.

Squire saw the bruised and swollen feet and he felt a bolt of pain score his instep. *Iothó:re.* The icy-cold dew droplets on the grass must have been numbing to the child's naked soles but the boy seemed to pay no mind. He barrelled into the night and ran until darkness swallowed him up. Squire grabbed the rope coiled on his saddle horn and he sprinted toward St. Paul's. He remembered the village and its twists. He'd guessed right. In two minutes he saw the kid scrabbling down the incline and heading in the direction of the chapel.

The boy turned back to yell at the man running after him. "Over t'ere," he said, and he pointed to a primeval black oak parked like an open-winged thunderbird near the lane-side of the church. The tree was fifty feet high if an inch and the branches started low to the ground.

The youngster hopped up to the stone rim of the well, which also stood low, only about two feet off the ground

He teetered there like a trapeze artist. "Oy. Oy. Chrisinny! Kin you hear me?"

"Yes, sure an' I hear you, Pommie."

The girl's voice was weedy.

Christ! Squire couldn't quite digest it.

What he saw and heard made him sick. "What's your name, sonny?" Squire stood beside the youngster and he did his best to sound easy but found his breath in his throat when he looked into the oak tree's tight-woven branches, fabric far darker than the night, and imagined a child was up at the top, freezing, clinging to the cumbersome trunk like *anèntaks*, porcupine, and still with the courage to answer her brother.

"Name's Pomeroy Munny."

To Squire's ear, the boy seemed to say Pommie. He said, "All right, Pommie. And the girl, Chrisinny, she is your sister?"

The boy nodded.

Squire touched Pommie's head.

He did not grimace at the gumminess and, discreet, wiped his hand a few times on his pants. "My own sister is named Chrisinny."

"We share somat, then, mister. Kin you help her? Kin you git her down? I tried. Not strong enough. Kin you git her out of tree?"

"Sure." Squire rubbed his chin. He made small talk. "Sure, sure, that can be done. Uh, how old are you?" He debated whether he should carry the girl down or lower her by rope.

"We was playin' hide and seek an' Chrisinny got the jump and climbt to top."

"Little brother, do you call her down?"

"Course I do. She likes furries an' magic and she kin climb like lord's monkey. Better'n me. I am nine, ya see. Ten, next birthday. December. She is five, actchully, five and a half."

"*Rawenniyo*. God. Nine? A brave lad for nine."

Magic? Furries? Fairies? Ah, yes. Squire remembered. The Fergusons' *girl*. Ann Auld. She was from Ulster. Twelve or thirteen. Give her two seconds of conversation and she mentioned fairies and Fairyland. Squire had wondered what on earth Ann was going on about. He had seen her peeking under bushes and searching for pots of gold and he'd thought she was nuts. Squire had inquired about fairies. What were they? Mrs. Ferguson had laughed and explained that fairies were tiny beings and they were like flowers with wings and they could perform magic spells and worked in the employ of Titania. "Peaseblossom, hobgoblin and leprechaun are Ann's escape. Poor wee gel saw churchmen inflict horrors on unmarried women back home," Mrs. Ferguson had said in whispers. Squire had kept his own counsel on churchmen but he thought about a few glimmers of sameness in the Celtic world and his own.

Magic was the flashpoint.

To the agitated starveling, who was by now dancing at his side, Squire said, "Furries. Magic, eh? Right. We see what we can do."

"Yessir."

"So you help me, eh? You whistle, Pommie?"

The Mohawk whistled cheerio, the birdsong of dawn, and asked Pommie to try. "Little brother, ho there, pay me mind. Stop dancing. Whistling tells your sister you are around and you keep her awake. You tell her I get her and you do your best to whistle like a robin. She's gotta stay awake. You do that, Pommie?"

"Yes, sir. Do trill again. Kin you give me it? I kin jiggy about and trill, sir."

Squire nodded. He whistled and Pommie got it.

Pommie called up to Chrisinny and he recited the plan and, with another flush of worry, hopped around, birdlike, under the oak. "See, Chrisinny, it is like so. In a minute or two, this here fella's gonna climb to gitcha. You be fine if you kin 'ear us whistling. Listen."

The boy did a breathy but tuneful cheerio.

Another robin on a cloud answered, "I hear ye."

Squire shut his eyes and hoped the spirit of the great Seneca prophet, Handsome Lake, would guide him and he would be able to do what he had promised and be snappy. The night was damp. Child could seize up, let go of her moorings and tumble through the branches and he would have no chance to get her. He looked at the rope. It had frayed sections. It was no good for this venture, pure and simple.

"Say, I take over whistling. Run to men. I need rope."

Pommie stepped back and readied himself to do what the man said but there was already another on the scene. Jedidiah Golden was beside them. The Snowman was puffing like a fugitive. He leaned on the bark of the oak, peered up into its mass, removed his wide-brimmed hat and scratched the bristles on his head. "You left back there in some goldern noisy hurry, Squire. I reckoned I heard a fuss. Whatcha got? Sometin' climbt up t'beanstalk?"

"Forty, maybe fifty feet. Girl. She is five."

Golden stood straight and he put his hands in his pockets. "You are a-shittin' me."

"Yeah. Well, no. It's true. Pommie says she's five. She climbs trees like a monkey. Up, fine. Getting down, not fine."

"Goldern."

"Brother, I need a good rope."

"Unh-huh. Fer sure that thing aint no good." Golden fingered the end of it. He said, "Yer danged rope's old as the chapel."

Squire said, "I go up."

"What?"

"I climb up. Now. This instant."

"Wait a minute." Golden ran his index finger along the bark. His fingernail scraped a ribbon of white. "Hoarfrost. Mornin' will do."

"No!" Pommie shrieked. "Git 'er down. She bin up there all night." He hopped about and whistled with gusto, like a dervish.

Golden furrowed a deep-lined brow and muttered about his own girls and that he'd best inhale his calculations for all their good but he could not resist a chivvy. "This here would be a good lesson, Squire. New line of rope be handy when youns out a-huntin'."

Squire snorted and was about to mouth off about a rich man's expectations but Golden cut him off with a wave and spoke to Pommie. "Where be the folks, kiddie?"

The boy did not like being called "kiddie" and chirruped an objection. He said, "Name's Pomeroy Munny, sir. Me pa's Ginger Sorley Munny. He has gone to village. Brantford. Yessir. He's gone t'Brantford. For supplies. Yes, gone, gone t'Brantford market. And me ma's sleeping in her cot, riverside yonder."

Golden was measuring the old hemp rope and he spoke to the boy but did not look up. "This rope will have to do. Unh-huh. Shoo. Best be off to get her, kiddie."

Pommie hummed and havered. He hopped and whistled in distress. "Can't. Can *not*."

Golden snapped the rope again. "Pert, aintcha? Yer ma would be a-wantin' to help. Bring blankets and water. Lotsa water, unh?"

Pommie had held himself to a high standard but he was once again teetering on the well's rim and the edge of endurance. He was weepy. "I saw the old way station with your men in it, mister, an' I woke this fella here. He helps us. That's what yer man said. I swear."

Squire was not happy being called Jeddah Golden's "man" but he let it slide because he saw the boy was beyond coping. "Jeddah, he—"

Impatient, Golden said, "Jehoshaphat! Run! Git yer ma."

Pommie was mutinous. He started to scream and jump. "Can't, can't, can't! Can *not*!"

Golden hunkered down, grabbed the boy's shoulders, held him tight and put his face close. "What is wrong with yown head?"

"Ma's knackered. I tried ter wake her during the day. Then I towl her to get her rest an' I'd watch over Chrisinny but Chrisinny climbed into tree this mornin' an' I tried real hard ter wake Ma an' I even yelled out me lungs but she don't move a muscle. She stays put. I can't get her to come with me. She just lay there. Stiff. Like a board. She's blue and she aint movin'."

The apparent state of Pommie's ma gave Squire a shock, like taking a punch in the gut from his old boyhood friend Jake Venti. The Mohawk and the Snowman gave each other a steady look sparked with concern.

Golden said, "Stay put then, kiddie. Relax, unh?"

There was a sudden, dead quiet. Breaking the silence, Golden said in a soft voice, "Huh. Me man, I fear situation would require a recalibratin'. Reckon it be best you do not wait, Squire."

Pommie did not catch the significance of the change in tone. He looked at the Mohawk. "Your name's Squire then."

"Yup, sonny, that's right. This here's Mister Golden and them fellas hurrying down the hill is Monsieur Johnson and Mister Farr and we are wasting valuable time. Girl must come down, Jeddah. Pretty fast."

Squire started to whistle the robin's song and Pommie joined in and Golden shook his head at the frenzied kid who was making so much noise in the minutes before the dawn.

The boy felt compelled to inform Jeddah the mountain man that he was well occupied in ensuring the safety of his sister. He whistled to help her. After the Snowman, the boy told Farr and Johnson the same thing.

Farr was pleased. "There's a brave lad. Pommie, do you say?" The old Fox dusted his pants with his hat. "Pommie, you jest keep a-whistling then. Tehawennihárhos will git her."

Pommie said, "Who? Uh? Him?"

Farr said, "Yup. Him. The Mohawk. Squire."

"You sure, mister? He's a wild Indian?"

Peter Johnson swooped up the boy with his left arm and he held him like he weighed less than Bart's hat and cooed. "Oooee. Indian. *Oui.* Not too wild, eh?"

Pommie said, "Can the Mohawk get her?"

Johnson nodded. "You picked the right guy. He will climb up. *Oui,* he is Mohawk." He raised his other arm. "The Mohawk. They're sky walkers."

"What's that?"

Johnson said, "Sky walkers?"

"Yeah. What is sky walkers?"

"It is just what it sounds. Mohawks have the big reputation. They like heights. They see the world with the bird's eye. He is the right man for you, *chou chou.*"

Pommie fought the tears. He said, "They came on s'strong. The feelings, that is. On the holy saints, I saw you ride in, mister. I knew your man there was one to help."

Johnson said, sure thing. He set Pommie down.

Pommie, clasping his hands behind his back, got into non-stop whistling. Every other minute he shouted to Chrisinny while the men planned the rescue and Golden measured the line.

Farr was worried and he said he wanted to measure the rope. Again. He squinted one eye and drew his gaze low along the ground as though he saw wee bugs in a terrestrial scope. "How long's the rope, Jeddah?"

"Longern yown." Golden was arch, even at a time like this.

With thin lips, Farr sniffed. "Funny."

Golden laughed. "Unh-huh."

That was enough. Farr was full on ornery, snaky as the frayed hemp, and he beat his hat against the oak a couple of times.

"Yessir, aint you the funny one. And since you aint about to chance your life and climb to the top of a fifty-foot tree on hoar-fuckinfrost, how long?"

Golden slapped Farr on the back. "Settle yourself, Bart. Do not a-get all het up, hear."

But Farr was all het up. He took his hat. He beat his knees. He beat his arms. "A man's gotta be loco to go up in that tree and not just up, way up."

Golden shrugged. It was not his fault. "Unh-huh. Reckon so." He bit his full, pink lower lip. He said, "I calculate the Mohawk's a-gonna drop the kiddie down to ground real easy. Rope is 'bout fifty feet. Leastways, that is what our optymistic friend Squire do reckon. He surely did not figure on a rumpus like this here."

Johnson said, "You have enough, *Monsieur*. Rope, I mean."

"Name's Jeddah, Pete."

Johnson said, "Yes. Jeddah. *D'accord*. Squire's idea is the best one. Tie rope seat around her. Lower her. It's the clear drop over here. Few branches. It's the safe way, I think. Poor petite is fatigued. The Mohawk is able to carry her down but he could slip. They die."

⌒

Squire listened to the others as they planned and he feared they looked set to palaver all day. He went ahead and tied one end of the rope into an Appalachian sliding double-loop like Golden suggested and took the other end and tied it tight around his waist and coiled the rest around his shoulder and started up the oak tree. A bridge of leaden-coloured clouds spanned the horizon. The cockeyed fading moon was mocking and the old oak tree was as dense as a corn-husk basket but the sun's rays shot bolts over the ancient plain and would burn off the mists to improve chances of sighting the girl. Mohawk village was a landscape with a greater range open to the eye than usual along the river and morning radiance shone on the black soil, which was cupped as neat as a patty-cake in a clay mould, and the light burned birch-bark transparencies into the walls of the ghost houses.

Got rid of that worthless Doorkeeper.

Squire was wriggling and hauling himself up the giant tree, already halfway, and rays of sunlight splintered the branches and captured him, and the men below could follow his progress.

Each move was intentional but he slipped anyway. He missed his footing on the slick bark a couple of times and just caught himself. He might as well have been rock climbing. Moccasins were pliable and easy to wear but they were polished from use and demanded extra caution for a sure foothold. Sun torched still greater visibility into the branches. Squire inched up the glass tree, crack and crevasse, and he whistled all the while he climbed. Autumn wood, some pieces dead and brittle, creaked under his weight and yellow oak leaves, shaped like frog's feet, fluttered down, aimless and indifferent.

Chrisinny must be as slight as her brother, Squire thought. A little red cat. She had climbed to the top of the tree without snapping a twig. After more manoeuvring, concentrated and hesitant, Squire looked up. He saw her.

Her calves were skin-and-bone and they dangled over a rough branch and she was hanging for good and all to the tree trunk. She wore a dirty sweater, more loops and whorls and dropped ends than wool knitted together, and she had worn-out laced boots on her feet, with no socks. She wasn't dressed right. Not for the chill. Not for anything. Her eyes were closed and her lips had turned white and the skin above her lips was blue.

Squire stopped whistling. "You awake? Do you hear me, Chrisinny?" He threw the rope over the branch she was sitting on and reached for her. He picked her up with his right arm. She was bone and sinew. She weighed next to nothing, a fairy-weight.

He carried her down a foot or so and crawled back out on a lower, heftier branch, went as far out on it as he dared, far enough to get a clear view of the ground. He wound one end of the rope around the branch, made a rope seat from the double loops, and fastened it around her. All she had to do was hang on to the rope's taut cord and he could lower her down nice and easy. Could she hang on? It all depended on that. She'd have to hang on tight. The child's hands looked frozen stiff, too stiff to pinch a moth. Squire could feel his heart juddering in his chest because he was nervous, scared for her, and he hated to ask anything of her soft-boned fingers but it was the right moment. He inhaled and touched her back.

He said again, "You hear me, Chrisinny?"

The girl snuffled and she wiped her nose on her shoulder and hiccoughed. "Yes. I towl you I kin 'ear you, mister."

"Good."

"I'm cold."

"We get you warm. Real quick."

"Quick?"

"Yup. Quick. Ready?" he said.

She made no answer.

"Ready?" he said. "You swing down, Chrisinny."

No answer.

"This here looks like a hemp rope. It aint. It is corn silk."

Nothing.

"I hear fairies like the corn silk." He was frightened. He tried to sound enthusiastic. "Ahhh, see? The corn silk. It's magic."

Nothing. Not a word.

"You float like a fairy. Fun, eh?"

Still nothing.

He spoke soft and made her look far, to the horizon. "Look there. Beautiful sight. You want to fly like a fairy, little one?"

Chrisinny had glued her eyes to the horizon.

A hollow voice with a faint croak agreed. "Yes."

"Here, see it, here is just the thing. You will fly like the best fairy in the woods. You have a corn-silk rope, right here. Can you hang on tight?"

"Yes."

"Good girl, Chrisinny. You can do it. Ready?"

"Ready. Yes. I kin do it."

Pommie had picked the right man for the job.

Peter Johnson nodded. He knew it.

And Jeddah Golden, he knew it.

The Mohawk got to the girl and the men shouted and whistled to him and they said he was the one; the hero of the day, and the rescue was a sure thing. Accolades that came his way were rare. Catching a modest applause because you could climb a tree, heck, that was better than a kick in the pants. He felt the joy. He hadn't had the feeling for some months. Not since last summer. On the Fergusons' farm, being around Jennie Ferguson. Near her, he had been preposterous, too happy for his own good. Life seemed fair. He lowered the girl. Chrisinny swung downward. It was not fair Chrisinny was born to this. Other little girls had enough to eat and warm clothes. Where, he wondered, where did we get the concept of fair? Were you born knowing what was fair? At the Institute, Jake Venti used to say old man Gillen was not fair because he gave Squire a corncake with leering sanction and he only gave Jake a corncake. No approving smile for him. Was Jake right? Was Gillen unfair? Was Squire hypersensitive to fairness? He was not in a position to judge because Chrisinny doubtless thought there was fairness in staying alive. She zipped down through the autumn leaves. She was quick and smart, as quick and smart and red as a strung cranberry. With Squire's help, she avoided the wizard-fingered branches of the oak and she landed in the arms of Golden as gentle as a summer bee floats to an aster. She broke into a grin. Maybe she wanted to try the long swing again. She was a tiny tree climber. Her two front teeth were missing.

In the end, the girl had floated to the ground like she believed she held a rope of corn silk and magic wishes. Squire thought that was a fair measure of what she needed. She was an immigrant Irish child, a starving kitten, a blue-cold, white-lipped, raggedy-assed, mother-less fairy. Was her mother dead? How unfair was that?

CHAPTER
eleven

Methodists preached against the evils of vigilantism and asked the people to support the laws of the land. Well and good. It was fine to support the laws of the land but whose laws, Squire mused, and whose land?

Where were the enforcers for these laws of the land? Where was the constabulary? Lawmen were scarce. For Europeans, surveyed territory in the upper country was less than fifty years old and public policing services were urban organizations and not in place in the towns and villages, not so's you'd notice, and yet the question remained. Could a posse bent on revenge be a good thing? Methodists said no. Anglicans had the British military. Longhouse religion was equivocal about European ideas of justice, being more or less outraged by the white man's assumptions about land. Squire picked his teeth with a willow twig, mulled it over, and rationalized some Christian good in a manhunt.

Peter Johnson had removed his Shetland jumper; the warm one Nellah had knitted for him because he was riding shotgun on the Van Barnum stagecoach. He had pulled the scratchy goliath sweater over the two children. Sooty rosehip heads peeped out from the huge neck hole. Pommie and Chrisinny, with itchy chins, reeled in warmth and freedom. *Yonehrakwat.* Children were surprising. Squire would not have imagined it. Hearing them laugh was almost as impossible as the playfulness of Farr and Johnson, who had teased the youngsters and, better yet, promised them sweets. The two men swore they had frosty cakes in their saddlebags. They said they felt peckish. Wanted to eat them cakes, eat them all right up. They would eat them all and not share a crumb, they teased.

Squire and Golden watched the games but they did not participate.

They had nothing to say. No jokes to make. No tricks to add. They were prudent and unhurried and lingered in the cool morning shadows because they were unwilling to visit the Munnys' cabin while the children remained outside laughing and dancing around in a giant sweater of knotty tufts and woody prickles. The way Pommie had described his mother's condition played with their imaginations. Likely, untimely death had paid a call. They wanted the youngsters kept busy inside and, in solitude, they would set out to look. Farr and Johnson understood they would be the distractions. They must keep the children busy while Squire and Golden investigated the state of the Munny woman. Farr waved for the children to come into the way station. "Git in here, you kids." He shouted he had found the cakes.

Johnson herded the starvelings into the building and the Mohawk and the Snowman walked downstream, away from the way station.

Jedidiah Golden was well over six feet, maybe six-foot-two. Pleasant looking. Outsized in very feature. He was a fair-skinned, fair-faced, fair-haired Appalachian mountain man with deep-set, shrewd and sometimes twinkling black eyes. He had an African mother and a Scandinavian father and he was tough, almost to the point of being careless. He wore a wide-brim hat and a cattle-baron's sheepskin coat and he marched along the riverbank with heavy here-I-am steps. Rusty sumac tuques trembled. Their sumac brains must have thought Golden was the beanstalk's ogre, come to earth.

Squire Tehawennihárhos Davis was a few inches shorter than Golden. The Mohawk's adopted father had trained his son different. Squire was quiet. He was also dark-eyed, copper-skinned, slim, keen-sighted and a creature of the bush. He swung beside the Snowman as silent as air and as observant of plant and tree and river as the circling, omnipresent turkey vulture. The two men made curious enforcers in an unsettled land where nothing but vigilantism and revenge kept the peace.

~

At Pommie's order, Squire and Golden had headed south, to the edge of the crazy river. They found the squat hut as the boy described it.

A lean-to. No doorway.

One carved hole in the pumpkin. Askew.

A bent stovepipe tippled over as though it too could feel gloom, aware of its own uselessness. The sorry affair looked like the crooked house of the crooked old white man and Squire felt scorn for the dirty Irishwoman, she who brought her kids to live in squalor. Broken shovel handles and splintered boards were tossed around. The mess was depressing, as though the Munnys refused to work. The path needed a cornhusk broom to take a good swipe or two at the raccoon scat.

Golden must have thought the same thing because he was muttering aloud, why? Why were they not holed up yonder? In way station?

Squire was feeling that maybe he did not resent Jeddah Golden. Not like before. Not like when the Snowman had shamed him in front of Jennie. Shamed him with the promise of reward. Golden, may the devil take him, used money to get Squire to take up the manhunt and, brother, he said to himself making the little snort, hadn't the bait worked just fine? Here he was. Octavius Millburn had posted a reward to remember. Dead or Alive. One hundred pounds.

Squire was honest.

Without beating himself up with illusions and false hopes, he knew the truth. He would buy property and register it under the British system. The promise of reward had provided him with a powerful incentive to join the posse, although, at first, he had resisted. He consoled himself: he had hesitated. He had not trusted the mountain man and he sure did not want to hunt down a man of the people. That was big trouble. The inner circle of the councils at Ohsweken and Onondaga and Chief George Henry Martin Johnson would revile him and they would be open about it. They would find a way to get even. Tehawennihárhos, son of David Shago-hawineghtha and grandson of the old medicine woman Aughguaga Polly, knew very well that justice for Nellah Golden would come at a high price and he hoped he could find a way to pay it because the Grand River settlement would never see itself in error and say, by the code of Handsome Lake, you're right, young man, our Bobby John is a scoundrel and a drunk and he should be locked away in the white man's gaol. The Six Nations Anglican establishment would believe Squire was acting out against the people. Maybe he was trying to get back at Smoke Johnson for the Oxbow property he stole from the Peter Davis family thirteen years earlier. Who knew? Maybe he was.

CHAPTER
twelve

Bobby John had crossed the evil line.

Lots of Europeans had gone wrong. Look at Boy Hewson. Why couldn't an Indian?

Golden had said it, good cow kin have bad calf.

Paulus Bobby John and Squire Tehawennihárhos Davis were cousins. Bobby John was not always a scoundrel. Squire had liked him. The cousins were near the same age and they had learned English together. Chief Thomas Tehowagherengaraghkwen Davis, the uncle, taught them. On one fine day, the lesson the boys took home was unexpected, a lesson in humiliation. A government regulator had appeared at Davisville, midsummer, and he had heaped scorn on the head of Chief Thomas and shown him his place, right in front of the kids. According to the government regulator, the chief was a primeval person and not the boss of himself or his property. Squire remembered the terrible white man, the man with the black curls on his chin who tapped his fingertips together and made his hands into a plains tipi. The man had a face like a bat. Little pointed teeth. Pointed ears. Mottled complexion. Pug nose. The black curls of his beard curled around his wide snout.

At the time Squire was Pommie's age. Almost ten.

Bobby John was thirteen.

The children were supposed to be serious, trying to acquire a language was hard work, but it had been a warm friendly sunny day until the man with the curly beard rode in. He rode down the winding trail and right up to the learning circle on the river's bank and the students had stopped what they were doing. Uncle Thomas stood to greet the bat-faced one and, quick as you please, with no nod of respect, the man sat down in the old one's canvas-backed chair and started to scold the chief. On and on he scolded and he made the tent with his fingers while he talked and he did not notice the children, or if he did, he paid no attention to them but they knew who was the boss. It was the government man.

"I am embarrassed for Uncle," Bobby John had said to Squire in Mohawk.

Bobby John spoke in Mohawk because his English was still at the primer level. In fact, Claus' *A Primer for the Use of Mohawk Children* was open and lying across Bobby John's knees. Chief Thomas could speak English but the bat-faced one would not understand Bobby if he spoke in Mohawk. Uncle did not think the students were invisible. He might hear chattering and that was trouble. Children kept their voices soft, below the men's hearing. They knew what would happen if they caught Uncle's eye or he heard them whispering because he had told them to remain respectful. Uncle said good Methodist behaviour would impress the official visitor. Squire spoke back to Bobby but in a manner not very Methodist. "Bible trembles in our chief's hand. Do you see?"

Uncle was a big tall man and he was very old but he stood as straight as a forest pine. The younger man in the chair was not impressed. He was emphatic. The bat-faced one's voice rose but his hands on the finger-tent were composed.

Joseph Davis, the chief's son, sat in the learning circle. Joseph spoke good English. He translated for Squire. In a few minutes, Squire told Bobby John what Joseph had told him.

Bat face: "No, sir. You may not do it, Chief. You simply may not. You may not will any part of your land to Mister Seth Crawford. Your land is not your land, don't you know? John Johnson and the Lower Mohawk, they'll stop you. They don't like your estate plans. The Great Mother, she don't like 'em much neither. Your cousin Joseph Brant was dead wrong. Indians are not British allies. They are not British subjects. They are wards, y'see? There will be no sovereignty within sovereignty around these parts. The land hereabouts is Crown. You people own no country. You Upper Mohawk are primitives, well, compared to us anyway."

Squire was Lower Mohawk. He thought the bat-faced one would not like his people either. "Lower" referred to the Mohawk people originally from Fort Hunter in the Mohawk Valley. Smoke Johnson was Lower Mohawk. A shameful man.

Tehawennihárhos looked at Bobby John. He knew there would be an explosion.

He was right.

"That interfering bastard," Bobby John said. Bobby was Upper Mohawk, like Joseph Brant and Thomas Davis. Their people came from Canajoharie, upstream on the Mohawk River, and they were quite proud of the fact, especially young Bobby.

"The white man is rude to Uncle," Squire said, wanting to see how upset Bobby would get. No one among the Six Nations dared to speak to Joseph Brant's cousin, Thomas, in such a manner and it was not just a brief smartness but a whole conversation laced with officiousness and forced patience. Bobby fumed about it for days.

Squire had never forgotten the meeting between Uncle and the bat-faced one at Davisville. He believed Bobby John had not forgotten either.

So it was. Bobby John had refused to swallow colonial humiliation. Since boyhood, he had harassed white officials and he had got himself and a few other boys into all kinds of trouble. Bobby and his gang of Warriors liked the demon rum and that only made bad matters worse.

Squire decided his cousin had gone too far. He had turned villainous. Jeddah Golden had seen right through Squire's hesitation to join the posse to track Bobby John and a minute before the horsemen had taken off he had said he understood the difficulty. Squire was a bouncing ball rebounding between the walls of two societies. Squire had rolled his eyes in a mute plea. Shuddup. The Snowman had not shut up. He had said that, like it or not, Squire belonged to Six Nations. But, he added, the right sort of fella was not afraid to set hisself to a higher benchmark than he would expect from the group. Justice for a clan was one thing and justice for the individual ought to be more choicy. Squire had waved him off. The Snowman had an infestation of homilies worse than a Methodist saddlebag preacher had ticks.

Right now, he and Golden would investigate the rickety lean-to. They would see what was up with Pommie's ma.

Squire, well, he figured he knew what was up.

They had found the Munnys' place.

They would find within the hut a white woman.

Cold as a wagon tire.

Dead as a stoat.

CHAPTER
thirteen

No mode of life in Europe can seem pitiable after one has seen Ireland.

−J.G. Kohl, *Travels in Ireland,* 1844

Inside the lean-to, the topsy-turvy pantry shelf was bare except for a dinted tin of peas. The lean-to leaned toward the river. Jeezus, the Snowman said, pushing the tin of peas back to the wall from its precarious perch at the edge of the shelf.

A bundle of dirty tatters, none would call the thing a blanket, lay heaped against the wall. No food. No firewood. No candles. The family could have put a roof over a ditch or lived in a bog and they would have been less uncomfortable.

Squire thought Aughguaga Polly was as poor as a dark-eyed junco but Handsome Lake knew Polly was smart and took sustenance from the land. He suspected the dead one here was feeble. Clueless. She had not known what to eat and what not to eat in the little garden growing around her. No beans, no berries, no nuts, no corn.

Golden removed his hat. "Scarce-hipped, gal. Towhead."

Squire said, "What is towhead?"

"White blonde. Lookit them curls."

"Irish is carrots."

"Some Irish would be dubh, dark. Some towhead. Boy Hewson, see, he would be a towhead, like her. Kiddies yonder would be carrots, a-course."

"She had beautiful face. *Yakotiwen*."

"Uh?"

"She is thin, all right."

"Lost soul."

"Brother, them kids are lost."

"Unh-huh." Golden twisted his head to look at the woman. "Fish-belly white. Skelyton would be as neckid a-goin' as a-comin'."

All at once exhausted, Squire snapped. "Come downstream, Jeddah. I show you skeletons. Lots."

"Pur angel. Taint right."

"No." Squire had had warm feelings floating inside of him since the rescue of Chrisinny Munny. No more. Happiness was too light to last and it had flown into the ether like the chaff on a grain of rice. He was gloomy and out of whack. Like the stovepipe. "You say it, brother. Starving aint right."

With a yeoman's deference to the manor born, Golden removed his hat before the thin corpse. "Tsk. Young-un, too."

Eyebrows crumpled in disgust, Squire said. "Brother, there are dozens of women. Lying in villages along the river. They are Indians, eh, and they starve to death and good for them. Indians die and are doing what we are supposed to do and white people get land. They starve us. Or chase us away. Mind what happens to Martin last year. Burned out. It is chaos in our territory. Dangerous as hell."

Golden coughed and looked up.

Squire took up the dispute. "You think I don't got the right?"

Golden shoved his free hand in his trouser pocket. He was as relaxed as Squire was annoyed and that was more annoying.

"Pile on the agony," Golden said. "It would be all yown, son—"

"Thanks."

"But do not get callous. Who kin tally misery? Aint no contest for pain. You would not want t'win it, leastways."

Squire scoffed. "I see you. You're a mush-hole moralist."

Golden shrugged. "We have a misunderstandin', is all."

"Sure, sure. Where's the fatherly advice?"

Golden was deliberate and he surveyed the bleak prospects of the shack and looked down. "Lookit pore womern, Squire. She would be entitled."

"Brother, she is one person. Think of a people. A whole society. A nation of people."

"Tiz same for Irish."

"My people are cheated. The Irish are cheated? Not like us."

"Reckon so, Squire. Irish suffer."

"Then the Irish don't forget neither."

"Unh?"

"Brother, it's a fact. It disturbs my sleep. Once I lived in a hole like this, just like this here. You get hurt, you don't forget."

"No. Reckon not."

"Soon it gets to be all you can think about. You hear the crying of your mother and you can't get it out of your head."

"Unh-huh. A pity. What would you expect, Squire? Folks a-throwin' morning-glory petals at yown feet? What would be eatin' you?"

CHAPTER
fourteen

Enhatkahtho. He will see.

What was it about Jeddah Golden?

Squire started to sound off and could not stop, not even on account of the shock he felt, or maybe because of it. He ranted like an old fart on a soapbox and he wondered what hell had possessed him because in his right mind he was not all that demonstrative. Most days he was a stoic, tighter with emotions than a Scotchman.

It was Golden.

Goddam Golden.

Golden made him talk. Explain. Curse. What did he want the older man to understand? Squire did not know but he could not shut himself up and complained to the Snowman about the evils he saw in Indian Territory. He complained about the discrimination in the villages. He complained about the way the Lower Mohawk had pushed around his own family and, goddam, they were Lower Mohawk. He complained to the Snowman as though Golden were God Almighty. Squire spat on the Indian Department and David Thompson and William Hamilton Merritt and the Grand River Navigation Company. The people lived with conflict and crooked deals and corruption and children suffered, sometimes in ways too horrible to imagine. The Navigation, which the Compact had promised to them as the white man's redemption, was the perfect fraud. Land jobbers flooded in. Why were the Irish Munnys hanging around here at the abandoned village? What would happen to the kids? Who would save them?

fifteen

G olden was attentive to the outburst.

He nodded. He grunted when he agreed.

He shrugged when he could not get het up about it. He listened and he waited and waited, he frowned, he waited some more, without a doubt hoping to catch a glimpse of the thread weaving Squire's painful tapestry together.

The Snowman held up his hand.

"Jehoshaphat," he said. "What is this all about?"

Squire said, "What d'ya mean?"

"Never heard you take on like this. Youns see'd a ghost?"

"A ghost? Why not? A haunted village, anyway. Haunted by the past."

Golden said, "Unh-huh. In life, change would be a for sure but Farr's idea of reincarnation is nuts. Tsk. Old Barton Farkle. Too mysticle." He tapped his temple. He spit out the window hole. He said he was ready to go back to the way station to get the other men to see what they could do about the body but, indicating with a wind-up hand, a go-on gesture, he said he was listening. He was still holding his wide-brim in a show of respect.

Golden was trying to perk him up.

Squire said, "Brother, I am sorry. For Pommie."

"Unh-huh. I do not differ."

"My mother runs into trouble."

Golden shifted feet but he pressed, "Cause?"

Squire felt the urge to argue switch off. He did not want to fight. The pines were whispering. What did they know? They whispered sympathy. Sympathy. He wanted sympathy. Someone to take his side. Someone to tell him his life was worthwhile. He put one hand on his hip and thought of Johnson on Diablo and he stretched his back to let go of tension. The past was past. He was calm. He was young. His voice was steady. He was regained. The shock of finding the woman was wearing down. "Cause our men are dead. My father. My grandfather. Cholera kills them. Doctor Gilpin tells us to leave our farm. We come back. Lower Mohawk kick us out. My mother has some white blood in her. Pah. She aint 'real' like them. They take our cleared land. Our work. Our food. We hide. In a hole like this. Worse maybe. Why would a mother bring kids to something like this?"

"Caint answer y'all that." Golden used the rolling motion again to rewind. "Go on. What happened? Indians chase your family off your own property? Because your ma would be partial white? Smoke Johnson?"

"Yeah. Chief George Henry Martin Johnson's father. John Shakoyen₪waráhton, that's Smoke Johnson." Squire hesitated. "Say, Jeddah, you know the Johnsons?"

"Smoke and George. I kin say I know'd 'em both, actually. I run into them a coupla times in the—ah, the regulatin' business. Biggity fellers. Johnson boys are United Empire Loyalists."

"Hucksters."

"Mebbe so. Say, 'bout yer ma, Squire, youns ought to know old Fox a tol' me a'ready."

"Yeah. Farr knew my father, Peter Davis, back in the old days. Bart Farr and my pa, they were good friends."

"Unh-huh. What happened? After Smoke?"

"Brother, we go hungry. Nothing new. Our mother works for a man named Jacob Decker, who lets her keep my sister, Christina—Chrisinny. Aughguaga Polly, she is the mother of David Shagohawineghtha, well, she takes me. Afterwards, my mother marries David. He adopts Peter Davis' kids. She lives at Whiteman's Creek. I live in Oneida village with Polly but I'm with Uncle Tehowagherengaraghkwen in summer. At Davisville."

"That would be who?"

"Uncle. Thomas Davis."

"Colonial life would be hard on your uncle, I 'spect. Would he be yown uncle?"

"Don't let me say how bad Thomas was treated. Yown? Real uncle? I dunno what's real or who's real, Jeddah. Clan uncle for sure. Wolf clan."

"Right." Golden grinned and moved to the pantry shelf to pick up and examine the tin of peas. "Past is past, son. Youns would be a healer. Reckon Polly done a fair to middlin' job a-rearin' y'all."

Unenthusiastic, Squire said, "I suppose. The fat grandmother. She is tough lady. Torturer. Yeah, yeah, and healer."

Golden put the peas back. He said, "She taught y'all one or two tricks." He waved toward the Munny woman. "But no tricks will help her. We gotta see her buried."

Squire looked at the raggedy stack. "Brother, I agree, but in a garment. We cannot bury her so. Talk about disrespectful."

The Snowman inhaled to his boots, ah, t'hell his expression read, and he spoke to the younger man and took the liberty of patting his back, friendly-like. "Some folks do not get lotta options in life, Tehawennihárhos. Live in moment, see? Share resources. Join in with the world. Quit your innards gazin'. Folks pray to God fer he'p fer today or fer tomorrow, never you mind yestiday. Yestiday's done."

"I hear you, brother." Squire pretended to agree, as though the advice were some damn good to him. Who gazed at their innards?

Golden held his hat in both hands and respected the body one last time. Squire was willing to bear witness. He dipped his head and allowed himself to stand in honour for the dead one. He was in the goddam moment. He let himself see her. The crazy river ran off in all directions, the same as always, but for a minute, two men, not much more than strangers, stood together, side by side, and they recognized change and respected the body's will to live. They bowed and acted civil. Woman had tried to make a go of it in this vale of tears but she had had rotten luck because she was born in Ireland at a bad time and her home country had fallen down, economically, going from hard times to worse times to famine. She had survived a coffin ship crossing to Grosse Isle only to die in squalor in Mohawk.

Golden said he hated it. Every young death was appalling. "Grand River aint the Perath but it would be no place to peg out."

How to prepare the body for burial?

CHAPTER
sixteen

Tekenera'ks. Mistake.

The poor young woman was blue-naked, half-covered by a moth-eaten goatskin, her brown nipples and whey breasts were revealed. Squire squatted to take a closer look at her but from a natural reverence and distaste of the macabre he did not touch her flesh and pulled the goatskin over her waist to cover the bony nakedness.

Golden said, "A cause? Starved, a course."

"Yeah. I aint certain but—"

Golden said, "But what?"

"Other things. Maybe starvation's not—"

"Squire." Golden was anxious to get a move on. "She be filthy dirty and holler as a reed. Aint it obvious?"

Squire pointed to her neck. "Yeah, yeah. I see. Holler as a reed. I see bruising too. Look. Both sides. Here. And here."

"Shit."

"Sure," Squire said. "Some man beat her good."

"Strangled her to death?"

"Could be. Choked her, that's a fact."

Jeddah pointed to her neck. "What would be the shiny spot, d'ya reckon? Looks like grease. Mebbe wax."

Squire squatted down and from his high moccasin he slid out his *àshare*, the precious Missouri toothpick. He scratched off a seed and rubbed it between his fingers. "It is. Wax."

"Hunh. Where would be the pa?"

"Pommie says the man goes to village," Squire said. There was a pause. He stood up and reached for the pipe tucked in his belt beside the squirrel pouch. He wanted a smoke but put the pipe back in his belt instead. "Brother, I dunno. That don't ring true."

Golden shook his head. "Sure as hell do not. I'll have a word with the kids. Get to the bottom of it."

"Not the wee one." For all of Chrisinny's agility, she was tiny and Squire remembered how light she was. "Too much, I think."

The Snowman conceded. "Unh-huh. I support you. Pommie's line about his pa's a-gettin' supplies t'aint entirely real, I 'spect."

Squire said, "Brother, there's no one else. Pa's gone."

"Reckon so." Golden slapped the Mohawk on the back in a way that spoke *we're finished*. "Directly we kin bind her in rags yonder."

"We can try. Rags aint clean, though. I hate to see them on her. I know she's under layers of mud and grease already, but—" Squire said. "Need be, Farr and Johnson both carry extra blankets."

"That would be so. We may need one."

The men turned away from Miz Munny, poor blue creature, and wandered to the wall of the lean-to. They hesitated. Their backs were to the body. They were in no hurry to touch the tatters piled in the corner to see whether any of the filthy shreds would be useful for binding a corpse and, in private reflection, each man had drawn the line at what was tolerable and had decided to get a clean blanket.

"I am getting up, sir."

Golden muttered, "Say what?"

Squire did not turn around. He shrugged. "Eh?" he said. "Nothing. I don't say nothing."

85

*Shon gwa thon dats nay a gyon hek O ya nok o ya joh se
rat.* Yet doth He us in mercy spare another and
another year.

Miz Bride Munny sat bolt upright on her plank bed and Squire
would say with no word of a lie she looked dead. Her aura was as
vaporous as Bart Farr's putative vision but the truth was clear and
it was a humdinger. The men had made a grievous error. The woman's sudden resuscitation hammered on dry-rot sensibilities like
a spring woodpecker. She was alive. For God's sake, they had prayed
over her. Squire felt sick. Christ, they might have buried her.

The Mohawk felt his skin crawl as though maggots nibbled
on him.

Golden did not stop to offer apologies.

He had roared like a grizzly and swept up the nude woman and
marched her over to the way station. Squire sprinted ahead
and secured a blanket from Farr and, as it turned out, Miz Munny
entered the hearth-warmed way station like a royal personage and
there she presented herself to her children with all the dignity of
a proper mother.

She wore a mantle wrapped around her, Indian style, and
whined like a guttersnipe, Irish style. She bristled against her fecking husband, Ginger Sorley Munny, even as she commended her
brother, the darling man. She did not hide her destitute condition
because it was not in her nature to lie, she said. She wanted money,
though. She had to get her hands on some. Ginger Sorley Munny
had better hand over something for kids. That was all she wanted.
Her brother, the darling man, would find the miserly Sorley, somewheres near Welland Canal looking for work and make him pay up.
Sorley and his friends had joined up with Catholic Irishmen from
Cork and they fought with them fellers from Connaught and lived in
a shantytown on the canal bank, occupying a mud hut or a burrowed
hole in the sand-hills, pilfering flour, firewood, murphies, money,

pigs and whatever else they could lay their hands on, so's they could survive, cause there were no proper jobs left for digging Brantford canal. She wouldn't get so much in hard cash, she figured, because the labourers were paid in truck more often than not.

Bride Munny sniffed.

Conditions were worse in the Irish shantytowns than in the Mohawk village, she could fecking promise them that.

Squire and Golden nodded but Squire knew each was wondering how conditions in the canal shantytowns could be worse than here.

Bride Munny was mostly cheerful, all things considered. She said she would be proper fulsome except for Sorley Munny's jiggery-pokery.

So Squire was right.

Bride Munny's husband was gone. Permanent.

"He were Shiner but no more. He is canaller," the wraith said.

She was hungry. She ate pumpkin seeds and hickory nuts and dried currents and squash strips and hardtack biscuits and looked congenial, maybe even full of contrition, but the pleasure of food did not reach the lines around her eyes, and she kept a-chewing. The four men were prepared to be lenient with the pitiable soul and she must have felt it because she was free with them. She talked about her man. Cutting trees and digging canals. Maybe some quarrying too. There were few ways for a poor Irish lad to earn a nickel. Irish labourers were flooding into Boston, Savannah, Montréal and Toronto. Miz Munny was self-deprecating. Irish immigrants were like head lice, she said. Irish were in your hair everywhere. Even with thousands upon thousands in competition, that Sorley Munny were up for a job, Miz Munny declared. "Yes, kind sirs, you heard me. My own Ginger Munny does toot horn and he says he has turned a corner, the bugger. He says he's a canaller. For the bastard Merritt. He were tree cutter. Peter Aylen's man."

Whoever Sorley Munny was, Squire thought, he was not Bride Munny's man. He had skedaddled last week.

Might he return?

No, she said. Never, she said. Over her dead body!

At that, there was a nervous little titter.

The canallers' camp was some distance from St. Catharine's but to say where, in precise terms, that she could not do. It was of no consequence to her, anyhow, because all would be well. Her brother would find a certain Mr. Ginger Sorley Munny, of that joyous fact she had no doubt. Wouldn't her dear kinsman read the Riot Act to Ginger Munny? Oh, yes. And if the bugger had cash, or anything a'tall worthwhile, why, Miz Munny's kinsman, the darling man, he would get it. Mr. Munny couldn't hide from her kinsman. Not even.

CHAPTER
seventeen

Last night the horsemen had arrived at the phantom village on the crazy river and, for every step forward, the raven had shown them folks in trouble and seen fit to beak them back twenty paces. It was a frustrating game and required their forbearance.

The Munny woman was perched on the end of the table situated under the grainy skylight, which allowed a morning ray to hit her on the head. She was seated on a prisoner's bench and it was her last chance to evade the hangman. Pommie and Chrisinny had assured Barton Farr they had the faith. Their ma would show up. She always did.

The children were eating hardtack biscuits dipped in whipped maple syrup and they were delighted to include her in the party but Chrisinny was not delighted to share the maple cream and she circled around the tin bowl and spooned it up in gobs. She fingered her way around the last belt. She wanted no part of speeches or excuses or sharing food and, quite done, pulled Pommie toward the door.

Pommie had been as reluctant as Chrisinny to hand over a biscuit to his ma but the boy had something temperate. He had grace. The men warmed to it.

As his sister tugged on his arm, Pommie said, "Chrisinny and me, we thankee. We was peckish, sirs. We gone at your grub like we was Yorkshire hogs."

With gritty, sticky hands Chrisinny stretched the arm of Peter Johnson's sweater but Johnson grinned. It was all right. He had no doubt either his friend Nellah Golden or his wife Sarah would knit him another one, even itchier. The Munny kids giggled at the teasing. They wanted to play on the riverbank and left the men to figure out what to do with their ma.

Such was the children's faith.

Johnson half filled a cup with a double tot of rum. Squire saw him hesitate before he handed it to Bride. Johnson told her to drink it slow. No doubt the Frenchman had debated about giving her a mug of hot tea but had decided against it because, as he said to the men later, English tea was too good for a guzzler. There was American tea for that.

Squire got the point.

Miz Munny was a guzzler. Why shouldn't she be? She was starving.

Her white-blonde curls were stringy and greasy-dirty. Dried tears had left sooty tracks on her cheeks but she had no means to wipe her face. She had a mole high on her cheekbone under her left eye and it was an attractive feature but damn if the mark did not make her look wretched. The woman did not seem to have any possessions, not in the vicinity, and the horsemen sat there like bumps on a log and felt bad.

They did not want to ask where her clothes were or whether they could fetch them for her but Squire figured he wasn't the only person to wonder how it was possible to have nothing to wear and manage to get 'round and about. It was autumn, October not July. The men wanted to be on their way to hunt down their prey but there was this here Miz Bride Munny. They were stoic and faced up to their fate.

They were held up.

They could not get out of it and gave into it and chewed the fat with Bride Munny and asked polite questions and watched her eat up all their supplies, the biscuits and maple syrup, the salt pork, the pumpkin seeds, the dried squash strips, the corn cakes and the tea-sugar, the rum, the beans and molasses, the potato skins. They had packed provisions for two weeks but the poor starving lady, appealing as she was, why, she sure did know how to chew the fat and knock back a drink, no problem, and she ate and drank it all up.

In the end, she did not leave so much as a corn crumb in Farr's maplewood bowl or a spit of rum in Johnson's flask or a ha'penny's worth of commodity in the entire way station.

And her story was not half told.

eighteen

Out of Miz Munny's line of vision Squire's eyes made the unhurried gesture to catch Golden's eye and the Mohawk took the opportunity, aside, to remark about the danger of sharing resources with Bride Munny. Golden laughed pretty hard and said maybe her ma should have named her Birdie instead of Bride because she'd ate her weight by sunset. With everybody watching, Golden sobered. He dropped the laugh and altered his tune. Golden was sorely pissed with Sorley Munny and he stated the obvious because, he said, he was just that pissed. "Someone has a gotta warsh and feed these here crawdads."

Farr nodded. Yeah, what about the kids? "Oh, by the way, Miz Munny, what's a Shiner?"

The old Fox removed his hat and scratched his head. He pointed the hat at the youngsters outside. Maybe he did not mean to be harsh but he curled his lip. "Is a Shiner some feller who runs out and leaves his wife high and dry with no food for her belly? Or theirs? Why, no clothes a'tall? That a Shiner?"

"*Chêneur?*" Johnson's melodiousness tempered Farr's scorn. He did not understand "Shiner." "What is that? Oak man?"

Miz Munny turned her attention to Peter Johnson. "Oak man? Maybe, sir, but kinsman tells me tis Shiners—"

It was Squire who identified them. He had travelled around the province in the company of road builders. He had served a couple of go-rounds laying out the plank roads north of Toronto in Reach and Scott and Uxbridge townships and the ferocity of the Ottawa lumberjacks was the talk of the road camps and the pathmasters, no slouches themselves when it came to making trouble. Shiners were legend. They were Irish choppers. Hardnosed brawlers. Squire was familiar with the reputation of the crooked timber baron Peter Aylen. Aylen and his louts were the privileged ones along the Gatineau. Sawdust nobility. "Shiners is tough." Squire idly turned to Farr and said, "Tough as your hardtack, Tsitsho."

"Awful," Golden said.

Johnson's wide grin bobbed.

Farr waved off the kidding and set a final biscuit on Bride Munny's plate with unnecessary encouragement.

"Shiners take it to French Canadians," Squire told the men with a turn-away frown. "Take it to them good. Murdering aint rare."

Bride Munny dipped her cheek and said, why certain, Squire were right. Some Shiners, her brother had told her, were indeed murderers. Aylen, their king, why, he were a regular stinker. Except for Miz Munny's dear brother, the darling man, the Irish raftsmen were mostly gasconading skunks. Loggers floated into Bytown on the fresh waters of a new logging season and they affrighted Bytown's fine folk, yessir, a-scared 'em shitless. Them Shiners was unforgiving of slights, a body shuddered to think about the nasty tricks, and the return of good weather was such as to welcome home the black flies and raftsmen and the entire Ottawa Valley had come to fear break-up but even Sorley Munny were a proper keener when it came to hating Canadian choppers. It was certain that no woman wanted to waltz with a French logger. Too dangerous. Irish Shiners would like to throw the Canadian into the kettle, ah, the whirlpool, pardon, and end his miseries. Poor Canadian. He should never mess with a Shiner, she said.

That is what the lady told them and, almost against their will, everyone in the station turned to Peter Johnson. What did the Frenchman Johnson think about experienced and reliable French Canadian axemen taking a shellacking at the hands of the Shiners?

Johnson waved it off.

It was nothing.

Johnson was French from Detroit, not Canada East, and he wanted to move his wife and forthcoming child to Montréal, not the Gatineau. Montréal was Shangri-La. The *chêneur* or Shiner who spent his time booting French Canadians from one end of the Ottawa valley to the other, why he held no fear for Johnson, who seemed unafraid of anything. "Too bad, Madame. But they are far away, no?"

Miz Munny shook her head to disagree. She made the bent-spoon mouth and she raised a finger and leaned over to touch with gentle strokes the hem of the Mohawk's coat.

She spoke to Squire.

She said, "They're for sawn timber, not only square timber, and Shiners is on the move, sir. They done their worst in Bytown. They've split up and moved, sir, now their king has gone law-ful. They are gone from Bytown."

Squire was silent.

He moved away from her.

Bart Farr said, "So, Miz Munny, you say your husband aint a wood chopper no more?"

Bride Munny waved off the idea. "Lumberin's too much river work for my old man. He is five-foot high. He'd bloody ruther stay put and dig. Like a ferret, he is, that lickspittle Ginger Sorely Munny. My kinsman is the only Shiner now."

"Is?" Farr said. "What's with 'is'? You said Shiners was over. They had broke up."

"Shiners is about. I can say that, sir."

Everyone seemed to feel the presence of the village ghost.

Squire said, "Here?"

"Yes, sir. I believe the Shiners have something in mind, sir. Something bad. They steal timber. They smuggle. Bad for the Indian Territory of the Six Nations. They hook up with Warriors. And poachers. And smugglers."

Squire used a deliberate so-what gesture but it was unconvincing because he could not help but give her a steady look and he paused and spoke in low tones, "So. Now. What? What do you say? Miz Munny, what is this? What do Warriors have in mind for this valley?"

"Lumber prices is falling, sir. Falling fast. Warriors and Shiners have it in mind to chop the old growth along river. Yes, take timber. For free. Steal it. Why not? David Thompson does it. Steals timber, that is. Them Shiners take what's there and go for profit. Sneak logs out. Float them like rafts down the river to Dunnville. And you know what, sirs? The British Army's deserters get a ride to freedom for their pains. Off to Sandusky or Buffalo. You chooses your poison and you takes your pick." Bride Munny sat back, apparently satisfied with the reaction she got. That bit of intelligence had stopped them cold.

Squire regarded her with a tinge of revulsion, as one tends to do when the messenger reports some unpleasant news. He was tired of listening to her.

~

Bride Munny was calm.

She thought the Mohawk glared at her as though he would reach down her throat to grab her last pumpkin seed but never mind. She figured that was a natural reaction to hearing the tale of further woe in Indian country and she declared she understood. She repaid their charity with bad news. Poachers and moonshiners and smugglers and deserters were moving into Grand River Country and they were ready to steal not just lumber but also land and to do it in exchange for white lightning. Before long the Six Nations would feel it, new losses and more drunkenness.

Miz Munny said she felt it was useful for her saviours to know the truth. With forewarning, they may prevent problems. She said she would settle the score with them and her Messiah and she had. She had returned the concern the kind sirs had bestowed upon her. She said she had reached into Pandora's urn and she could give her liberator, Squire, the Mohawk (he was her liberator after she had heard about the tree-climbing stunt), she could give the fine-looking, straight-featured man with the pointy eyebrow and, speaking of it, the sudden white-lightnin' grin, a grin what wouldn't shame an Irishman, why she would give him a peek into his darling future. "Shiners have joined up with a gang of Warriors and they are fixed on poaching lumber and smuggling out British military deserters, sir. I tell you they'll pay for it all with liquor."

Farr said, "You positive?"

"Am too. They aim to take a thousand sticks from your valley before freeze-up. The bad Indians, them Warriors, they move deserters over Erie to Sandusky, regular. And Buffalo City's a destination too, sir. American army takes in deserters. British military sends loyal Indian runners to Sandusky and Buffalo to spy and check out deserters and report to commanders on the whereabouts of the bad Indian smugglers. My kinsman tells me so. Yessir. My darling kinsman says ardent spirits fuel the comin's and goin's of timber poachers."

Farr growled about the wooden shipbuilding industry and the way imperial bleeding England with its shifting imperial bleeding mercantile policies favoured imperial bleeding England, what couldn't get enough square timber and hadn't the Crown already taken a walloping amount of tall-mast lumber from Canada? The old Fox looked at Golden with accusing eyes because, wouldn't you know it, them poachers, why, course they'd use "white lightnin'" for temptation. Appalachian moonshine.

Golden could not demur. He rubbed his eyes and half-laughed. "Unh-huh. Pink ellyphants and blue johnnies."

The news had upset Farr. Apprehensive and grey-faced on account of yet another unseen menace, he said, "Confiscate the moonshine and stop the timber poaching, sure. But by God, Indians aint smuggling. Aint smugglers neither. Traders. Always have traded, always will. Trade routes run north-south, y'know. Lumber's for locals' benefit. By golly, I hope authorities regulate them Shiners."

Johnson had a few loose tea leaves bothering the tip of his tongue and he spat outside. He said, "You have the hope, Bart? Hope? What authorities? British mercenaries? Ouah, I ask you, old Fox. What hope?"

The questions were rhetorical but Miz Munny chose to answer in her aspen-leaf trembling voice. "I don't know, sir. I leave hope to you, sir."

Farr's eyes had not moved off the woman for a tenth of a second but Bride Munny had more to say to her liberator. She turned to Squire. "See here, sir, Shiners choked me. Two nights ago. I have marks to prove it."

The bruises Squire had noticed on her neck were merging into a greenish blob. A man's thick-shafted fingers had squeezed tight.

"Me darling brother's upalong somewheres, gone to seek out Sorley Munny. Else I'd a-bin looked after. Shiners took me to Brantford. They say we go to a fine party. I say, all right, and I promise to pay the murderous viper Lucille Goosay, old lady who lives over yonder, for watching my kids. The Shiners have wicked parties, sir, and this time they give me gin. Bathtub gin. Poison, it is, sir. They take off the clothes I own and throw them over the riverbank. They strip me starkers. Some men do impose on a girl, present company excluded, sirs, and drunken Shiners are the worst.

Me and another poor lady, one Miss Lewis, we two are caught cold. There are witnesses. They see us. View our shame. Worst of it is, sir, I get no coin from it and I owe that murderous Missus Lucille Goosay cash money. All's I got is me candle. They scrape me backside with oyster shells. They make me parade up and down Colborne Street near the bridge. I am lighted up like a firefly. I aint got no money and I owe the Goosay woman."

Squire said, "Miz Munny, I am sorry for you. But tell me, madam, who is the murderous Missus Goosay?"

~

"The murderous Missus Goosay wants to kill me. Kill me dead." To Farr, with a tremolo in her voice and eyelids, Bride said, "Yessir. I am scraped raw. Shiners do a proper job. I am paraded around. Lighted up like a firefly."

Farr donned the mystic expression.

He was a blowfish, puffed to indignation.

Farr's indignation was palpable.

Golden gave Farr an "Aw, nuts," but it did no good.

Squire saw the exchange and felt Farr's resistance. Farr made the Mohawk laugh but he felt edgy. Farr stuck his grey face right close to Bride Munny's nose and donned the matching mystic voice. "Firefly, you say? I am told fireflies are ancient beldames of a hated race. They were brimstones, with fire in their hearts. Doomed to be firebugs, story goes, as warning to the fair sex. You carry fire in your tail, madam?"

Bride was bemused. "Sir? I carry fire in my tail?"

Squire was set to change the uncomfortable subject of Bride and fire in her tail. "You find your way back from Colborne Street to here but how, I wonder? Shiners are violent. They do not have much in the way of charity. I think maybe they aint going to help you."

"Ahh." Halfhearted, reluctant, Bride turned her head away from the liberating Mohawk and she put her hand over her mouth and, uncertain where to turn, after a full look-see at everyone, she eyed Barton Farr. "Shiners brought me back. I leave Pommie and Chrisinny in care of Lucille Goosay, who is an avaricious and murderous type, as I have presently told you. Shiners know about the children, sir, and they know how it is that I have no husband hereabouts. And they know my brother, sir. He would kill 'em all, one by one, if they didn't bring me back. My darling kinsman will find Ginger Sorley Munny in St. Catharine's or my name's not Bride Munny. My real fear is the murderous Missus Lucille Goosay. I owe her."

Squire grunted.

Story did not seem to hang.

Bart Farr wanted to get back to fireflies but Golden cut him off. The Snowman's tone was chilly. "C'mon Bart, wind 'er up. Mind be a-wandrin'. Leave 'er be." Golden turned to Bride Munny. He said, "What about the murderous Missus Lucille Goosay, Miz Munny? Precisely what sum would she be a'spectin?"

"As much as I kin save, sir. She thinks I'll earn fifteen maybe twenty shillings for going to the party in Brantford and being nice and pleasant to all and sundry in the village."

Golden's lips were folded thin and his black eyes glowed. "Unh-huh. I see. I see. That would be fifteen shillin's which youns aint a got?"

Miz Munny whispered. "Yes, sir. No, sir. I aint but rubbing along. I aint got nothing, sir, nothing but the can o' peas."

"Fergit it then. Womern caint get what you aint got. I reckon she do not need yown peas."

"Tiz not a joke, sir. I pay the murderous Missus Goosay and my debt is done. I care about my kids. They mustn't see me murdered. I aint a bad mother, sir."

Farr interrupted. He was pleasant. He was, he said, quite sure he for one had never said she was not a good mother. As gracious as the Pontiff granting a selection of indulgences, he bowed. "You are a good mother. Your children would agree."

"Sir." Bride Munny slipped to the floor and she fell to her knees and folded her hands like a convert at the gate. She begged Farr. "Take me away. Take me away from the likes of the murderous Lucille Goosay. She takes nothing but coin, just for minding kids. I stay here in this place and Lord knows what will happen. Missus Lucille Goosay means business. I do mean it, sir. She will murder me in my bed if I don't give her the coin she's owed. Yessir, I rightly believe it. Missus Lucille Goosay wants me dead. I am almost glad the valley is done for. Shiners will clear her out. Goddam old firefly is Missus goddam Lucille Goosay. Help me get a position, sir. Please, Mister Farr. I need to give her money. Else she'll do me in."

A wavy ray from the skylight shone down on Bride Munny and gave her the look of a plaster saint. With sooty points. Nose, finger-tips, mouth. Squire thought it was an eerie happening, the way she entreated Bart Farr to help her find a job and her being startled and afire from the efflorescence of the skylight and all of it happening not half an hour after her death and she had come back to life so unexpected and so forceful. This was a dreary business and he was happy to think about Jennie Ferguson in every spare minute.

Barton Farr was all sympathy. "Tut, tut, my dear. Forget that Goosay woman. What do you have in mind? For work?" Farr tipped his head and leaned down to help the woman to her feet. "Please don't kneel. Stand up, for heaven's sakes. What is it you want? I can help."

"A lady's maid, perhaps," she said. "'The Widow exclaims and clasps/The shivering Orphans around her knee.' I recite poem, sir, because it is noteworthy on account of my dreadful and hopeless situation. I must have a position. Before it snows." She got to her feet and, standing in the shadows very close to the old Fox, she held the plain grey woollen blanket a tad looser over her warming white shoulders and looked at him from under half-closed lids and touched her hair. "I could work in service, sir. If I had the proper clothes, a course." Bride laughed but straightaway it occurred to her to disclaim, "Nobody wants to see me naked, sir."

Farr said, "That aint true, I—"

Golden barked. "Jehoshaphat! Bart! Old turpin, youns git a-hold of yown self." He rubbed his high forehead and went to the door and he whistled for the kiddies and over his shoulder he said to the woman, "My Nellie would be the queen of extry duds, missy. Youns will get the proper attire for service."

The Snowman came back to the table. He put his right boot on the bench. The heavy-soled pegged boot was the size of a three-fathom canoe.

Squire had noticed that boot once before.

Never had he seen a bigger boot in his life. That boot had sat like a cinder block in the middle of a certain liveryman's back. That was when Squire had fought with the arsehole, Norby by name, and the Snowman had intervened and maybe stopped a killing. A hundred years ago. Squire had forgotten about Norby until just now but he did not mention the incident because Golden was thinking.

Squire felt his blood rise at the memory of all the year's happenings and at the same time, a swell of fatigue rolled over him and nearly flattened him. His eyelids were lead sinkers.

Golden's boot was on the bench. His hat was hooked on a wall spike. He curled his round stubbly blond head into both hands, thinking, and he sighed and rubbed his stubbier beard. In less than a minute, he got up and put his boots firm on the floor. The Door-keeper, thought Squire. The Doorkeeper is disinclined. But he is home. Golden put his hands on his hips. He faced the group and he did not circle the issues anymore. He had regained himself, was clear-headed, ready to lead, ready to get going. "Y'all, it'd be like this." To a soul, the people in the way station held their arms frozen in mid-air and waited for old Chiron to tell them what they ought to do to get to the other side of the problem.

"Caint be a-leavin' them Munnys. We know'd it. I figure this. We would be takin' them. To Vinegar Hill. To Nellah's—"

Miz Munny was near to fainting with the pure relief of it but in a heartbeat her grubby little face jiggled with anxiety. "Hooo hooo. Mister. What about the murderous Missus Goosay?"

"Goosay? I do not give diddly squat fer Lucille Goo—"

Tearing out her hair, Miz Munny screeched and kicked the wall. "That old Indian woman will murrrrder me!"

Ears were ringing and Golden raised a hand to stop the howling. "But I will have a word, I 'spect." From annoyance and in the habit of Bart Farr, Golden picked up his hat from the spike and banged the hat on the doorframe. "Just a word. Mebbe give her a coin. For a-buyin' peace. Jehoshaphat, you kin a-holler, gal. I aint a-happy about seein' Missus Goosay."

"Thank you, sir. I will pay you back, sir."

"Well," Golden scowled at his boots like they were rats. "See you do, missy. Nimble sixpence would be worth a lazy shillin'."

Johnson said, "We are out of supplies, Jeddah. We need to go back to Vinegar Hill for more food but, me, I do not prefer it."

"Aint my druthers neither, Pete, but we would be down from slim t'nothin' on choices."

That was it.

They would turn back.

They would take the Munnys. To the Hill. Done deal.

"Yes." Johnson finished packing the saddlebags, his own and the bags of everyone. He rolled up the last bedroll. He started out the door. "*Allez*. Let's go. To the inn. We waste time."

Squire did not *allez*. He let the wall hold him up. He spent long minutes in the mind's cloudy place, seconds before sleep, to marvel at fate and to thank his lucky stars. He wondered whether Golden could imagine how pleased he was to have to return to the inn and the crappy tavern and Nellah's solid red-brick house with the white railing and the creaky plank veranda and white front door and tinkling bell chimes. Jennet Ferguson was there. Waiting for him.

CHAPTER
nineteen

Without a doubt, Squire was the one out of three who was pleased with Golden's revised directions. Returning to Neilah's place on Vinegar Hill was as good as putting in your thumb and pulling out a plum from Becky Ferguson's missionary cake. He thought about plums and cakes and sighed in his dozy state. Jennet Ferguson was there. She would be thrilled to see him. Glad he was fine. She would want to check out his body to make sure he was in one piece. He would let her. The satisfaction grew and his eyes stayed closed. A naked Jennie made a fine dream but who else was pleased about returning to Nellah's? No one. Golden was a-skairt he would find his dear cousin Miz Nellah Blaize Golden and her baby girl, their baby girl, in a noticeable decline. Barton Farr wanted to proceed downstream to the stage stop at Canboro. He believed he was supporting the manhunting enterprise with the money he was losing by not collecting byway tolls but, shucks, he had to go to the Cyclops Inn anyways, to pick up pretty, pregnant Maggie Walker and take her back to Farr's Tavern and Stage Stop where Maggie worked as a barmaid. Peter Johnson had his own troubles. He, for one, did not want to return to the Cyclops Inn, not now, not ever. For a few youthful transgressions, which he kept to himself and refused to discuss even though the other horsemen knew everything about him and his ex-lover Nellah, Johnson wanted to avoid the inn and, especially, the young slave-snatcher, Meatface. Johnson was strong, stronger than Meatface. Meatface was strong enough, though, being built like a man of wire, but a bigger man, someone like Johnson, why that man could twist Meatface into an ice auger. The Frenchman was tired and he wanted to get the manhunt done and over and, goddam *sûr*, he said he did not want to have to kill the slave-snatcher, the teenaged Meatface, which he might do if they met up and Meatface had more slave-snatching in mind. Johnson wanted home, hearth. He wanted a way to try to make peace with his wife Sarah, the magpie, the runaway Georgia slave.

But back to the Cyclops Inn, they all would go.

Exceptional news but Squire was almost done in. He continued to lean against the barn-board wall, standing next to the plank bed where he had tried to slumber before Pommie had awakened him, and he kept his eyes lowered and said nothing. It wouldn't do for the Mohawk to look as contented as a full-bellied bear in the middle of a salmon run. From the heart, Squire knew it. Going back to the Cyclops Inn was a setback for the posse but he didn't care. He figured the posse wouldn't dawdle, though. They would get what they needed and set back out on the trail. They would secure the Munnys at the inn. They would buy supplies at the O.G. Millburn Emporium and Merchants' Exchange and visit Vinegar Hill's bathhouse.

The bathhouse belonged to Delaware Mahlon Joe and his brothers. Sign read: "Mahlon Joe's Hot and Cold Baths 25 Cents" and, underneath, "Mahlon Joe's Indian Scalp Treatment."

Joe might have a sense of humour.

Squire wasn't sure. He had never bothered with the Indian scalp treatment in case it burned out his hair roots and he often wondered about the poor condition of a scalp that would require Joe's treatment. Joe promised that everything was on the up and up. He swore he possessed essences and elixirs. Essences and elixirs provided wonderful relief. From dandruff and other ills of the scalp. In any case, the horsemen needed a wash.

Early this morning Farr had declared it. A wash was necessary. Nellah had a showerbath but it was ladies only. The men planned to bathe in Joe's newfangled tubs, have a shave and a buff-up and partake in a bit of Joe's patter. Get the news.

Better than a broadsheet, Joe's place was.

Squire and Jennie would not have much occasion to spend together before the horsemen set out again but he would at least see her and be with her and the thought of it was almost unbearable and pleasurable and he caught himself on the verge of getting distracted instead of staying on the alert and going to the corral to saddle Cap'n and the other horses so's they could get the hell out of this dodgy place. The sliver in the ointment was always the same. Aughguaga Polly, the fat grandmother. Polly wanted him to hook up with Onondaga Magdalena Margaret Walker of the Turtle clan. The fat grandmother had little use for white folks, dim-witted creatures, and she had even less use for the fiendish Jennet Ferguson with her undisciplined flyaway brown hair and her passionate sea-green eyes.

Ridiculous eyes, Polly had said. Scary.

In reality, for about a minute Squire was asleep. On his feet. Back to the wall. Head falling forward to his chest. Cyclops Inn. Aughguaga Polly. Mahlon Joe's Hot and Cold Baths. Jennie. Squire dozed but Farr was vigilant and as cranky as a butter churn. Golden and Johnson were ready to depart the way station but Farr could not let the shame die. Miz Munny hated the murderous Missus Goosay, and Farr, such a kind gentleman he was, as Bride had said to her new saviour, he hated her being paraded, starkers, up and down Colborne Street.

~

Bart Farr wiped the back of his hand across his mouth.

He sounded as though he were a Shiner swallowing a frosty cake made of sawdust. "Miz Munny. So tell me. It's true? You are the whore?"

Squire was dozing off pretty good but his subconscious had sucked up Farr's question and registered the cheek of it, the kids were nearby, and the Mohawk came to life like he had been stuck with a hot poker. He was tempted to put his finger in his ear to give his head a shake to make sure he had heard right. The old Fox was as crazy as the crazy river and someone should rein him in. Farr was European. A European should stop him. Squire looked to Golden.

The Snowman was there. He yanked hard at Farr's sleeve. Shuddup, Bart. We wanna tree our coon and youns would be a pure distraction.

The Frenchman had heard *whore*.

He had returned from carting a couple of saddles outside and he made a low sound in his throat and turned back to look behind him and to speak to the kids, who were on the verge of traipsing into the station. Johnson shooed away Pommie and Chrisinny and told them to stay by the corral. He fair barked at them to gather the riparian green at the river's edge to feed Diablo.

Miz Munny touched her bruised neck. "Oh sir, please allow me some respect. You don't know trouble, sir. No picnic, my life."

Farr summoned his battered hat and whipped his trousers; thousands of pellucid flecks of dust and straw hung like firebugs in the pale light and scattered and drifted to the floor. "Pardon, Miz Munny, pardon. I got no call to ask you that."

With open eyes, a protean Bride Munny shifted her posture and she accepted the apology and excused herself. "I make no trade with the serpent, sir. My courses come regular. I do what I do with a pure heart. I have my honour, sir."

"Yes, ma'am. You do. I dunno what come over me. I apologize."

"An ordinary gal now, sir. See? I am just ordinary. No different than anyone else."

The coral dawn of frigid morning welcomed a warmer day but a fast-moving and low-hanging cloud had fogged over the plain and covered the sun. It had started to drizzle outside. October invited certain inclemency. It rained a great deal and the Grand River valley bloomed into a dying and intense and colourful autumn mosaic. Adjacent to the great plain were the woods. A shiny solidity of vertical stands and various barks, grey, black, large-pored, shaggy and smooth. Trees got messed up with leaves, a falling, floating, flying carpet of red and yellow. Squire wished he were in the cool mist where it smelled fresh. The silence in the room was claustrophobic. The Mohawk wanted to go outside but he felt pinned to the wall and had to imagine the fresh air and freedom. Wet wood. Pine. Maple-seed twirlers. Sweet sage. Even the tangy smell of the rotting leaves would be better than the male stench in here. Let him be anywhere but here, listening to Bart Farr.

Farr was tired. That was the problem.

They all were. Squire had got to bed around two o'clock and Pommie had had him up at six and he'd felt his heart quivering with anxiety every waking moment. He could sleep for a hundred years. He noticed that he had cut his wrist in the climb. Little bubbles of clear gunk exploded through the fiery scratch. Throbbing from the bloodless wound had not bothered him until this very second. Salve was in his saddlebag. Johnson had packed it. Goddam Farr. Squire wished the old Fox would belt up. Squire should move and ease out of the station but it was awkward and he could not bring himself to disrupt Farr and Bride who were staring at each other wondering where and how far to take their florid intercourse.

Farr beat his hat on his thigh about four or five times. "Ya see. It's like this. Them Shiners bother me some, Miz Munny."

Miz Munny sought to stir up Farr's sympathy with bravado. "The murderous Missus Lucille Goosay is worse. I handle them Shiners, sir."

"I dunno, Miz Munny. Parading and candling is terrible."

"Shiners kick us out of way station. Send us to lean-to."

"Terrible. A gal like you. The risks you've taken to get here. You need good wages, eh?"

"Oh yes, sir. I need good wages."

"You're a hardworking gal."

"Oh yes, sir. Yes." Bride summoned her strength in an inhalation the people across the river might have heard. "What I have suffered woulda killed you, sir. Holy nuns kept me, sir. Nuns who have never known the pollution of a single wicked thought; nuns, whose virgin bosoms have never been crossed by the shadow of sin; nuns, breathing purity, innocence and grace, they kept me, whose breath is the very pestilence of burning hell. Do you think I would fuck a Shiner for free?"

Jeddah Golden pulled himself to full height and he glared at Farr and shoved the old Fox through the doorway. "Jeezus. Bart. Leave 'er be. Nothin' further, uh? Youns act dumber than an empty coal bucket."

For once, Squire noted with relief, Bart Farr took heed, backed down, stayed out and kept his big mystic, lover-man trap shut.

In melodious tones, Jeddah Golden spoke to the woman. "Miz Munny, uh, Bride, I will take care of Missus Goosay, I surely will, but, say, lookee here. If'n youns would be s'kind, the darling brother of yown self, now—"

"Yes?"

"Might I axe your kinsman's name?"

"You might well, sir," Bride Munny said, glowing. "Our mother was a Pomeroy. She was from Ballyshannon. That's where I mostly grew up. I went to a Magdalene laundry when I got pregnant with Pomeroy. Ginger Munny and I got married after Chrisinny was born. My father was from London. Hewson. Henry Hewson. Never saw much of him."

"And?"

"Me brother's name is Richard Boynton Hewson. Pomeroy and Chrisinny and me, we calls him Boy."

CHAPTER
twenty

B ride said she had no more to tell the men about her brother
except to repeat that her darlin' kinsman was *upalong somewheres.* For a few minutes, no one spoke. Everyone but
Golden and the woman appeared stunned. Bride Munny was Boy
Hewson's sister? Squire said poor Nellah Golden was not going to
be happy to hear about that development. Jehoshaphat, Golden had
turned and pointed to each one in turn, in particular the angelic
Bride, Jehoshaphat, he said again, *Nellah had better not hear about it
then.* Bride asked, hear about what? Johnson took the matter in hand.
He was brief and polite and circumspect and explained to Bride
about Nellah's injuries, until Golden, who could not bear to listen to
him describe the assault, interrupted and ordered Johnson and Farr
to stay in the way station with Bride and the kids. The kids were
already playful and ready to be amused. Sex assault carried no
meaning for them. Golden nodded to Squire. *Let's get out of here.*

The Mohawk, for one, was happy to leave the five of them arguing over some kind of a password game and he left the building with
Golden following hard on his heels.

Outside, Squire sucked in the morning air and thought about
the murderous Missus Goosay. Pommie had said the men should pay
her a visit. Missus Lucille Goosay, according to Pommie, was
a woman of note. She knew a great deal about a great deal and she

might even know something about villains. The child made no direct mention of Uncle Boy but Missus Goosay might, Pommie had offered with a sweet expression, know the whereabouts of the Warrior Bobby John. Missus Goosay, why, she were a mysterious old lady and she hated to see the sun set on a glorious past. Pommie explained it to Squire and he seemed to choose his words with care. Old Missus Goosay, she were fixed in the past. She didn't like people or places to vanish. Perhaps she might know whether Bobby had vanished. And if he had, whereto he might have got hisself. Perhaps Missus Goosay's excellent sons might know something as to the whereabouts of Bobby John.

That was more or less what Squire repeated to Golden.

A formal visit was called for and Squire said he was prepared to find the woman's camp but Golden stopped him. He said if Squire were going on a useless trek, well then, he was going too. He had the money to pay her off, after all.

Squire tipped his moccasin in the cool sand outside the door and he made a clockwise circle and, for amusement, swirled his foot counter clockwise. He stopped the swirling and looked into the silver sky. "Yeah. Right. I'd say it's worth a trip to see the lady."

Golden remained sceptical. He did feckin' hope so, was what he said. "To get that howlin' female offa my back." The Snowman shook a small brown leather drawstring purse while he talked, yup, he would be the man to take care of Missus Goosay. Few coins would buy peace. All he wanted was peace. A bit of coin was worth the price.

Squire said, "Brother, you are arrogant."

Golden coughed and choked at the same time. "Huh? Zat so?"

"You think you take care of everything. Take care of everyone. Me, Bride and the kids. You are all set for taking care. It's a bad habit, you got there. And Nellah. Yeah, Nellah. Why, Teacher, I bet she don't even like your worryin' about her."

The Snowman paused to make sure he heard right. "Nellah aint a-wantin' it. That would be why I like her s'much." Golden laughed outright. "What be a-pricklin' y'all this time, son?"

Squire took his flask from his belt and he poured gulps of fresh-drawn well water down his throat and spoke his piece. "Brother, why do you think you have to be the one to set everything to rights? Why you gotta be the man to protect everybody? And everything." He took another long gulp. "The farm in Uxbridge. The Cyclops Inn. Justice in the upper country. The vigilante musket. Why you?"

Between his front teeth, Squire spit an arc of water into the nearby sumac bush, which someone had long ago transplanted in the spirit of hope. The spray caught the light. It was like a rainbow. It pleased him. He spoke like a pleasant man, as though he said, *hey, nice rainbow*, instead of, "Yup. I believe it, brother. You are arrogant."

"Arrogant?" Golden scratched his day-old beard. He tucked his thumbs in his belt. "So's the Almighty but I caint help it."

"Almighty? You aint God."

"Nope. Am not. Neither would be Bobby John's great-granddaddy."

"Huh?"

"Thayendanegey."

Squire spit again. "What are you onto now?"

"I reckon if the old Mohawk were alive and a-kickin' today, there would be plenty of people who say they hate Joseph Brant. Them same folks would be a-bangin' on his door to axe for his help. Why? Cause the man would try his best to do right by them, arrogant or no."

Squire was feeling smug. The last spit made a huge bow, the best one yet. "I hear Brant made mistakes. Bad ones."

"Unh-huh. Miscalculations. Made in expectation of a sovereignty."

"He was like you, eh? Yeah. More arrogant than God."

"Mebbe so. I figure the Almighty fashioned us all after his own image and it would be arrogant to question. Leastways, I do not sit around with my thumb up my arse, diddlin' my life away and philosophizin'."

"Fuck you."

"That is my boy. Philosopher. Feckin' genius."

"Huh, you change subjects. We don't speak about Joseph Brant. We speak about you."

"'Bout me, uh? Well, doggone. Aint that somethin'. I reckoned we was a-speakin' about you, son. Same as always."

Squire could not hear himself think because of Golden's rocket of a laugh. An amused Snowman was galling and he wondered why their relationship was so damn prickly but he had no time for cogitating because he had Pommie's bidding to do. He had to meet the murderous Missus Lucille Goosay and get information from her about the whereabouts of Bobby John.

Golden sighed, maybe Squire was not amusing him anymore, and he said he would get the horses from the corral, and saddle them, and he turned over his shoulder to bark out another order. "Whistle inside for the kiddie, son. We need him to show us the way to ol' Goosay's place over yonder rise."

CHAPTER
twenty-one

O ld Missus Goosay, Pommie said, she were but a teenaged girl when she watched Segenauck drown. In *Karegnondi*, Lake of the Hurons.

Squire listened. Pommie prattled on. They were walking toward the home site of the violence-prone Missus Goosay who lived, Pommie said, about a half-mile upstream.

In summer, Missus Goosay had told Pommie, the great Huron Lake had vicious three-day blows. Storms came up in a mighty wave. Undertow as bad as the ocean, caught you unawares, an' like that, in a snap, 'specially when you wasn't paying proper mind, you was gone. A lesson there. Pay mind if'n you're swimming in *Karegnondi*. Anyway, Segenauck was a grand wife, certain. Pommie nodded with understanding. She was paddling a small canoe coming home from gathering whitefish, most of which, Pommie said, had been left behind, up-coast. Segenauck and another woman ran into one of the blows and they tried to navigate a sloosh. Women did their best. They tossed overboard the fish they had. No good. They were weighted down. Could not float no more. Not like the duck over the waves. Husband of Segenauck, he watched from the shore-line. He jumped into his own canoe and he paddled out. He tried to save her. He could not prevent the tragedy. The canoe capsized. The woman drown'ded.

"Too bad."

"Yeah. That's so. But she didn't just sink down to bottom and vanish. It weren't the end of her, mister."

Squire squinted through the trees. *How far was Goosay's place?* "No? It was not?"

"No, mister. Not at all. Wouldn't you know it, Squire, it aint the end? The spirit of Segenauck has wandered into this here abandoned spot. Here she stays. Stays put."

"Why is that?" Squire reassured the soft muzzle of Cap'n and half-listened to Pommie. Squire and Pommie and Cap'n walked on a tight path through sacred white pines and sugar maples. They followed a trail through puddles and squishy mud and they advanced toward the bluff overlooking the crazy river, a fair distance north. Golden was on foot too. He was leading his camel-faced Appaloosa. Golden held the reins but Joker's Breezy walked, head up, looking around with disdain, certain that flight scents would sweep down on him. Golden and Breezy were twenty paces ahead and Pommie wanted to tell Squire some more things about the murderous Missus Goosay. Sky Walker ought to know the lady weren't a monster. Far from it. She were a pleasing sort of person. She did keep an eye on the children when their ma weren't around. "And truth to tell, mister, Ma aint never around."

Squire did not speak but he nodded to let Pommie know he had taken note and in a silent vow he promised he would buy boots for the youngster even if he had to chase Bobby John all the way to China.

As for Boy Hewson, Miz Bride Munny knew more than she was saying. Squire knew it. Golden too. The Mohawk had read the dramatic full-flourish of the disingenuous Snowman and the butter-wouldn't-melt sweetness on Golden's dimpled puss when he had asked her the name and then the whereabouts of her brother.

Squire knew he and Golden were of a mind on the considerable fabricating of Miz Munny but at least she had come clean on her kinsman, Boy Hewson.

After that bit of news, Squire and Golden had filed out of the way station. They left fast, heads down, so as not to give the game away. In the event, Squire should have scoffed when Bride claimed Shiners carried her back from the village to Mohawk. No doubt Boy had dumped his sister in the mud shanty and left her to die. Her darling kinsman did not care a stack of road apples about the kids, let alone one five-year-old who had gone and got herself stuck up a thunderbird oak.

"She looks for her poll."

"Huh?" Squire said, "Sorry, Pommie. What?"

"Segenauck. She looks for her lost head."

"Is that so?"

"Yes, mister. I towl ya." Pommie enunciated his words, as though he were speaking to a deaf man. Segenauck loses her head in the drowning incident and she looks for her missing part round and about old Indian villages where she did once live out her life here on earth."

"That's quite the tale."

"Missus Goosay takes us on a picnic hereabouts, up and down summer hills, into these woods. We hear warblers and flycatchers and we follow the crik for fun and we three, we goes a-seekin' Segenauck. We looks for her head. To help her git herself together."

Squire laughed. "Sounds like a treasure hunt, little brother."

"Tiz a super time we had, Squire."

"Do you find the poor lady's head?"

"Ah, no. Magic will happen when we do find it. One day, before we come on over to Missus Goosay's place, the ghost of Segenauck did visit Missus Goosay. Ghost says she plans to leave next morning but, now, listen 'ere, Squire, that morning never did come! Missus Goosay says, 'We cannot never quit. We take our picnic with us. We keep looking because she is our headless guest,' and when Segenauck do get herself put back together, she leaves a gift. Tiz a scary story, uh?"

"Yep, yep. Very scary. Disturb you t'all?"

"Ah, no. Like I says, Missus Goosay aint a monster, sir. She is quite comical herself. She plays sports and takes us on hunts and tells us stories about the trait'rous English."

Ah yes, Squire thought. Perfect. The traitorous English. The breakthrough. Someone who hated the traitorous English was not about to like Captain Joseph Brant.

Pommie said, "Missus Goosay, she do scold us like she were our ma. She bothers and fusses. Course, our own ma do hate 'er."

Squire nodded. "That right, eh? So, Pommie. This here murderous Missus Goosay, she aint fooled so easy?"

"Not even," Pommie said kicking a square stone off the path with his bare toes. "She is old but I figure she has her wits."

A companionable silence caught up with them but Pommie was working himself into a confession and he was fidgety and picked up a flat blue stone and threw it into the trees. Squire and Cap'n moseyed along, easy. Squire let Pommie take whatever time he needed. In less than thirty paces, Pommie stopped short and he took a breath and for a minute, man and boy looked direct at each other until one would give way but neither one did until Pommie broke.

He lowered his eyes.

He patted Cap'n's soft muzzle and poured out his heart. "Missus Goosay, she says do-gooders are on the prowl. They swoops in and takes me and Chrisinny. We could vanish faster than Segenauck."

"Do-gooders, eh? Who are they?"

"Maybe the Congregationalists."

"Never heard of—"

"Yup. They're do-gooders. Them religious do-gooders takes Indian kids, y'know."

"That I do know. I remember Anglicans."

"They takes them and sometimes the kids never comes t'ome again. Missus Goosay tells me. It is true, mister."

"Ah-ha, Pommie. I understand. I see the problem. You afraid this's gonna happen to you, you and Chrisinny?"

"Yes sir, Sky Walker. I am so. Missus Goosay, she do fear it. We get ourselfs taken to a nether school and we never again sees our ma." Pommie was serious and not tearful but he clung to the man's jacket and finally grabbed Squire's hand to make his petition. "It happened to Missus Goosay's own excellent sons. They was stolen but she stole 'em back." Pommie's voice broke into a squeak but he was not done. "Don't let it happen. I'm beggin' you, mister. I'm beggin' you, Sky Walker, I need my poll. Keep your eye on us so's we don't disappear and get drown'ded and sink to bottom and turn up headless like poor old Segenauck."

CHAPTER
twenty-two

They passed an overturned birch-bark canoe resting on the pebbly beach. Pine gum made the joints watertight. The bark was yellowish and even textured, an indication that the trees had been found far inland.

As for the wigwam just ahead, Squire had never seen the like.

He had been up and down and around the crazy river and from what he could tell, the Cayuga and Tuscarora people never built them. His zest for the cone-shaped hut was infectious. Pommie saw it about every day and he had thought nothing of it. Jeddah Golden was committed to doing a duty and getting to Vinegar Hill and setting out again on the Onondaga trail and he had ignored it until Squire's passion for the structure demanded their respect.

In admiration they stood still a moment.

The fourteen-foot staves for the house were tented so as to allow for a sizeable air intake and the birch bark, the miraculous wood, was cut into two-foot pieces, and the pieces were rolled and sewn and overlapped to prevent leaks. The structure was tall, over six feet, and about ten feet in diameter and someone had fixed the doorway, just so, for wind protection, and they had adjusted the chimney hole to the willow trees to keep out rain. Clever people had made it. The excellent sons perhaps.

The hut was perched on the elevated part of the riverbank. The solitude was palpable. Peaceful. Perfect. It was a superb location, hidden from the trail, but with good sightlines and a breathtaking view of the river. Through the fog and hollowed-out space you could see the slim distant curve of the water upstream. The enormous sweep of green riverbank and the flaming trees took you by surprise.

The shadowy wigwam on the river filled Squire with awe and he felt a powerful link to the ancients and the intensity of the moment pounded in his ears, about enough to knock him over, but he was able to collect himself to tilt his head to Lucille Goosay in recognition of their bond in the customs and laws of the Six Nations and the Longhouse, *Kanonhsehsneha*.

Missus Goosay greeted her visitors as though she had expected them. She was elderly and dignified, certainly discretely murderous, and she wore a huge white apron. She was pleased to explain the singular wigwam. Her two excellent sons had indeed made it for her. They were gone. The boys were busy. They hunted game near the Chippewa Creek and Missus Goosay expected them back, yes, any minute now. They were excellent sons, yes, excellent canoe men and portagers. Excellent construction workers too. Missus Goosay's sons had talents but she said she was modest about them. It would take her excellent sons three days to travel home but they would return to the crazy river laughing and pleased with themselves and they would bring meat for winter and right away they would pack up their poor old mother, she said this with the tiniest moue to indicate she felt neither poor nor old, and they would bundle up her goods and bind them over their four-fathom canoe and shift her and her small canoe to their winter lodgings.

For four months the three Goosays would join her sister's family. The sister lived in a three-room log cabin on the river between York and Cayuga. The birch-bark *kanonhsa* she lived in now may not survive the winter but it had made a fine home for the summer.

Missus Goosay explained that she spoke excellent English, as they must have noticed, because she had rubbed elbows with local hostelries. As a young woman she had left the Indian settlement for a time and worked in service at Mansfield's Inn at Cayuga Heights, close up the hill, and she could not help but mention the fact to her guests to ease their curiosity since even her employers had praised her quick ear also. The old lady insisted that she was their host. She must have them enter her humble dwelling to share, she was sure, an even humbler but delicious cup of pine-needle infusion.

Squire bowed. *"Hen'en.* Yes." They would be honoured. It would be rude to refuse her invitation and ruder still to eyeball the woman and see into her soul like you would a dog.

Golden bowed, too, and he kept his eyes averted.

Pommie had no notion of any society's protocol and he bounced through the doorway ahead of everyone and he gave the woman a hug and plunked down by the fire.

He was at home.

Missus Goosay did not appear displeased.

CHAPTER
twenty-three

Introductions were made.

Missus Lucille Oihwanéhégwaht Goosay, Squire Tehawenni-hárhos Davis, Jedidiah Golden and, holding his own because he was that loveable, a certain almost ten-year-old, tall for his age, Pomeroy Munny. Everyone sat cross-legged on the tight-woven cornhusk floor mats. Missus Goosay's self-assurance made the men courteous. Wordless, she pulled a deerskin over Pommie's limbs and Squire suspected the Cayuga woman had read his mind and she also hated to see the child's bitten, purple, mud-caked, bootless feet.

They sat near a stone-banked fire pit.

An oak-wood fire burned hot but low.

Embers glowed beneath white ash. Humidity slowed the upward draw and smoke made a couple of stinging swoops over their eyes before rising in melancholy curls through the chimney hole. The air in the house was thick but the place was as neat as a pin and it was stocked with provisions and utensils. The low birch table held elm-bark spoons and basswood bowls. The higher table held sifting baskets and washing baskets and a couple of flat stones for cracking nuts and beside them, a ferocious-looking corn-husking pin. A digging stick leaned on the wall. Milkweed flowers, burr-oak acorns and a bowl of wild rice were visible but, best of all, Missus Goosay set down a maplewood container of brown honey beside them and she scooped honey into the maplewood cups and poured the steeped liquid from the kettle into the cups.

Squire thought of Aughguaga Polly.

Polly would do much the same. Grumpy as hell, though, and chewing tobacco. Honey was the special treat for guests and a main-stay in their former household. A cure-all. Miraculous for burns. At the way station, Chrisinny had near devoured a jug of maple cream. He imagined how a glimpse of the golden honey would spur the little girl to new heights and his catching the image of Chrisinny climbing to new heights was amusing but climbing tall trees was not tops on Aughguaga Polly's list of worthy undertakings. The fat grandmother was a miserable taskmaster and getting stuck in an oak was worth a sound licking and no honey.

Lucille Goosay appeared more delicate than Polly, less inclined to offer hourly whippings. She fed the Munny children and she fed them often, and she did not whip them with a stinging willow branch or save a tin of peas for that particular rainy day, already long gone. Missus Goosay's food supplies, fresh and local and sim-ple enough, must have seemed bountiful to small hungry bellies and the Cayuga lady did not appear to be in the least grudging.

The small company sat at ease. They drank citrusy pine-needle tea from their wooden cups and chatted like old companions and said some grave things about the deteriorating state of the Munny house-hold. They acted as though Pommie could not hear. Keeping up the pretence, Pommie ignored them and twirled a toy bone buzzer, which must have belonged to one of Missus Goosay's excellent sons.

"There's some consideration for me," Missus Goosay said. It was a question of time. Her excellent sons were expected any second.

The thing was, hours were short.

The Cayuga woman was glad to see the young horsemen ride in. She needed help. She needed the help of humane strangers. Someone must grab hold of the bad situation yonder. The Munny kids' ma was purely insufficient. That was Missus Goosay's opinion. The Cayuga woman suffered qualms as hurtful as knives, she said. She needed the horsemen to relieve her of her duties, not that she was responsible for the little ones, you see, but she felt responsible. She gave the expressive hand-flutter. Poor starvelings. She believed they might have died without her. Pommie could not help it. He nodded. Missus Goosay rapped his arm for proper respect and she continued. She needed relief in case there was no change forthcoming on the road ahead. Conditions stayed as they were and she had to leave for the winter, soon, maybe even today, and she might just have had to turn the children over to white do-gooders. A terrible pity. Do-gooders, and here she admitted she was the sombre voice of experience; they would as soon whip your backside and starve you dead as look at you.

Pommie shuddered and he nodded again.

He used an I-told-you-so eyebrow raise, similar to Squire's own feature, and Squire was ready to laugh but the threat was critical. The Mohawk had once been the object of a whipping so bad it had made the grandmother's lickings seem like love-taps. His face fell. Squire assured Missus Goosay she wasn't to worry. On this very day the Munnys would find a new home. In Brantford. The cousin of Mr. Golden here ran an establishment, ahhhh, well, a hostelry of sorts. The cousin was seriously ill, which was a terrible concern, and she could not do much to help the kids right away but there were good people at the inn and they would welcome the Munnys and do their best for them, certainly for the time being. Who knew? Perhaps food and clothes might bring the children to a new plateau and planning for their future could take place? Best they could offer, Auntie, and it would keep the little ones away from religious do-gooders.

In a rich, almost hypnotizing and rhythmic intonation, Missus Goosay said, "I hear it. I hear the sound of your place. You are

Mohawk. You are Grand River, I say. People of the Oxbow? The beautiful Oxbow?"

"Was," Squire said. "Now I guess I am from all over."

"A bad time for us."

"Yes."

Outside, mist beads had turned into a waterfall.

The rat-a-tat hammering sound of a heavy October rain hitting the wood roof made it difficult for them to hear each other but there were no leaks in the house. It was dry and warm and no one wanted to move, let alone go outside.

What must be, must be. Rather too loud and deliberate, Golden said, "Pardon, missus." He got to his feet and peered out and whistled and tsk-ed. A sheet of wet had unfurled. The silver river had melted into its silver banks and you could not distinguish the shore from the offing.

The woman spoke. "The horses?"

Missus Goosay seemed alert to suffering.

Golden was gracious and he bowed in the woman's direction and explained his concern. "No, ma'am. Horses would be fine, I reckon. Saddles what would be a bother. Wet leather, most particular. Makes for a nasty ride."

"You will find shelter to the east. A strapped wood-pole overhang. Back, ahh, thirty paces. Venison hangar. Until it lets up."

"Thankee, Miz Goosay. Much obliged for pine-needle tea."

Golden tipped his hat to her and he dropped his arms and hiked up his belt in readiness to run out. "Youns be done, Squire and, say, look 'ere, we would a-meet y'all back at station." He tossed over a pouch to the Mohawk. It was the drawstring purse. Golden gave him a last meaningful look and dashed outside. Pommie's head drooped with fatigue and Squire knew the feeling because the same wave had rolled over him not even an hour ago. He had had no time to enjoy it and that was too bad but it was a fact. He had a job to do.

It was up to Squire and the Cayuga woman to fill in an information gap. Where was Bobby John?

Squire knew what Golden expected of him.

Get intelligence or get out. It was that clear on Jeddah's face. Information was their whole basis for setting here a spell and the wretched Munnys ought not to distract the horsemen from their rightful job. Information would be mighty helpful. The horsemen could skedaddle back to the Hill and they could pick up supplies and get right back on the trail.

No doubt Farr and Johnson were doing their best to entertain Chrisinny and Bride and they were likely raring to go, to have the tiresome ride over and done. Squire sighed. What would get Missus Goosay to share her secrets? She seemed as sharp as her husking pin but she was lonely and lonely people talked much. Aughguaga Polly was a case in point. It was hard to break away from Polly when she was on fire and yelling at you.

A long polite conversation with Missus Goosay would waste precious time. How could he reach her, heart-to-heart?

Squire was not the honey-man sort.

Not like Bart Farr.

The direct approach was impossible. Very impolite. The way of the people was slow and indirect and the Mohawk had no choice but to comply.

~

Squire drank pine-needle tea until he was fit to burst. He felt he could float like a corked jug but he did not dare disrupt the intimate mood to excuse himself. He had considered how he could best lead the old woman into a relevant conversation without giving offence and causing her to clam up or, of course, murder him.

He had settled on an agreeable issue.

They felt united on it.

Indian territory. Land. In particular, land theft. Land surrenders. Land patents.

He spoke in Oneida and Cayuga Lucille Oihwanéhégwaht Goosay responded likewise. She recognized the diplomacy of his gesture and was willing, as with English, to show fluency, on account of her quick ear.

Yes, land was the key.

And squatters. The deserving kind.

He said, "Auntie, it's an inexhaustible quarrel. With whites."

"Yes," she said. "Tehawennihárhos, I say so, but they don't see it. Quarrels happen between equals. Indians, I say, are merely quarrelsome, 'specially over land surrenders."

"How's that?"

"The whites' opinion. How can we quarrel when we don't get it? That's what they think. We do not get it."

"Ah." Squire nodded, a wise soul. But, feeling thick, he had to ask. "What don't we get?"

"You can't guess?" Scorn darted into her every syllable. "In the opinion of the English, Six Nations people are quail-brained. We are primitives. We wander about clucking like idiots and we tell people we own the grass and the sky. That's what whites think. They would very much like to believe we are too exotic to understand governance and land ownership. Yes. I say it. Don't look at me so. We created the Great Law of the Longhouse. Whites say Indians don't understand property rights and nationhood and how can we even begin to notice land theft and dispossession? Apparently, our simplicity is our ruin."

"Ah-ha. Who says?"

"I say Francis Bond Head says. None other."

"Ah. So. Really? He did?"

"Yes. So, what quarrel? What quarrel can there be? How dumb are we, Tehawennihárhos?"

"Oy, not that dumb, I hope, Missus Goosay."

"Too dumb to recognize a power play?" Missus Goosay had a red cardinal's smart expression and she filled Squire's cup and patted his shoulder. She was a handsome old woman, as slim and directed as a stave. She sat straight. She held her spine to account. She wore her salty hair in a bun not a braid. She was square-jawed and bright-eyed and not in the least dumb. She was even a bit of a jokester. "Skin doesn't have colour. It has attitude, mister." Missus Goosay smiled broader. She enjoyed her own company.

She held centre stage and hugged herself.

Tracing the dots of the deep scratch on his hand with his finger, Squire said, "We seem unable to stop the land jobbers. I know this. Not all jobbers are white. Even the people steal."

She agreed. "Tehawennihárhos, in times of scarcity and confusion, the people get mean. Anglicans hate the Longhouse religion. They quarrel. I have seen strange things too, you know. My sister and her neighbours used to hunt together for food but not anymore. Last winter the two families fought over a rabbit. A rabbit! That bad. How could it get that bad?"

"Auntie, whites say it's because our Pine Tree Chief Joseph Thayendanegea Brant picked the wrong side. You know, in the American rebellion. Some of our people say it. Some say, 'Pine Tree Chief Joseph Brant took too much on himself. He was too great a man.'"

"Who says it?" Missus Goosay wrinkled her straight nose. "People stateside, I suppose."

"And others. Right here on the river. You say it too. Longhouse people hate Anglicans. Some of the people loathe the Brants. That is what I have heard. They curse Captain Joseph."

"Fools accuse Thayendanegea."

"Fools? Really?" *Damn.*

"The killing fields of Europe came to his doorstep."

"If I am to understand you, Auntie, I think you don't agree he's the cause of our problems." *Please let him be the cause of our problems.* Shit, this was bad. He had not counted on this. What had Pommie told him? She hated the traitorous English? He would have to try another tack. It was a disappointing turn of events. The horsemen were stuck if he did not winkle out information but she did not hate Brant and she was not going to rat out Bobby John. A waste of time, this was. His bladder was bloated. He had to pee. Enough with the American rebellion. He had to figure out how to move her ahead about sixty years. He would give it one more try.

"So you don't blame Joseph Brant then? Who do you blame?"

Missus Goosay slapped her thigh in anger. "Hell no! Not Brant. Brant was a genius. Whites do not say he was too dumb to understand."

The lady's flag was up.

Squire was surprised. He regarded her with respect tinged with amazement. How had he managed in a few short minutes to get the jokester Missus Goosay ready for the murderous warpath? To feel where the trail led, he asked, "Red Jacket, now, he was ready to puff things up and everyone knew he was jelly, like Brant."

"Tehawennihárhos, stop. You, you are too young."

"What's that, Auntie?"

"Forget Red Jacket. I am telling you the truth. War is complicated. Trust is simple. Joseph Thayendanegea Brant trusted William Johnson and he wanted to trust England because it was John Bull that cried, 'Fight with us! Please, fight with us. You fight with us and we promise you your country. An Indian country will exist somewhere within our claim.' Tehawennihárhos, you know it! The Six Nations Territory was bigger than the whole thirteen colonies."

"Still the people should have stayed out of it. The American rebellion was a civil war—"

"Not possible to stay out. No fight, no status. No hand to sue for peace. The Crown enticed Indians to join. Sweet promises. Sweet, like the honey."

The ebullient Missus Goosay turned as pale as his worn moccasins. She was over-excited and she swayed and stood up, put a tall basket half-full of tamarack needles upside down on her head, and waved her arms like a frantic person. A person wearing a thistle-down wig. Pommie was fast asleep under the deerskin and he was missing the show. That was a shame because he would have loved to see Missus Goosay wearing a basket on her head. What boy wouldn't? She was mercurial. She looked funny and made you feel good. She was a fun companion and a natural storyteller.

Missus Goosay said, "Americans took the Indian land for themselves. At the time, English Crown made the better offer: an Indian country in the upper province. Whom do you trust? Greedy, land-hungry American patriots and their regulators? Or John Bull, the English King? Thayendanegea chose the English but the clever Pine Trees chief was first and foremost loyal to the people."

The basket came off and Squire wondered whether the woman had a looking glass somewhere. She might be bothered to learn that the damp, golden tamarack needles had clumped together. It looked like a bird's nest. Squire whistled like a robin under his breath. He shook Pommie. The Munnys must sleep deeply. Too bad. The goddess Missus Munny had a store of theatrics. Pommie would have been amused.

Missus Goosay picked up the crusty digging stick and twirled it like the young warrior goddess Onatah. She said, "Americans were greedy. If they wanted Indians as allies, they should have stopped moving their frontier. They went too far over the line."

It was Squire's fault for starting the dialogue on an obsolete note but how was he going to finish the tales of the past and coax the energetic woman into the present? He was running out of time and he needed to bring her on side so that the trip to the Mohawk village was not a big waste. What he really wanted was to prove to Jeddah Golden that he and Pommie had been right to seek out the woman. Pommie had said Missus Goosay might know where Bobby John was hiding. What would get her going? Move her to the point?

"I still say Brant was wrong to trust anyone," Squire said, and he tried to imagine a likely way to squeeze Bobby John into the American rebellion without appearing direct. "Some say Brant was corrupt. He sold hunks off the grant. Maybe he kept the money."

"Without Thayendanegea, there would be no Haldimand Grant, nephew. No Grand River Settlement. Not here. Not now. Not ever."

"Hunh. I never thought of that."

"Well, think about it. Without Joseph Brant, we would be in America, dispersed all over the eastern United States. Even into Wisconsin." Missus Goosay looked sad, maybe disappointed. "Kept the money? What evidence do you show me? You are too cynical for a youth. Trust is a fine quality in an ally."

"Ah-ha. Cynical? Me? I shall try to do better." Squire sipped at his tea. He wondered what utter madness made him put more fluid into his bursting bladder and shuddered in irritation.

Missus Goosay did not notice his wriggling or, if she did, she gave no sign. "Six Nations played fair. Of course, Samuel Kirkland's Oneida must go their own way and it's Wisconsin for them. And the trail of tears. Never mind that, though, Tehawennihárhos. We keep our promises to fight as allies. English play us false."

"Well, Auntie, that is too bad. Hey, what do you say, what do you do if a man of the people don't play fair? In our time."

"Sixty years ago. It was the end of an ancient era. No more strong allies. The great betrayal. The great treachery."

"Yes, yes, sure it was, Auntie. Sixty years ago. Say, what about now? What about another betrayal? What if one of the people was treacherous? Six days ago?"

"England dumped the Iroquois as allies and that was it. You can pinpoint the exact moment, Tehawennihárhos. The Confederacy stumbled and could not recover. *Treaty of Paris*. England does not say a single solitary word about us when she makes a treaty with America. Right then. Right there. That was it. Over. Done. Stabbed in the back. Over our land. England is a traitor. English are disloyal. To us! No covenant chain. No two-row wampum. The enemy of the people. The great betrayal. I curse England. I curse Anglicans."

Jeez, the woman was a fossil. "Auntie, there are enemies all over. What would you think if a great betrayal happened last week?"

~

Squire was growing weary, no, wearier. The woman was beside herself. Their talk stimulated her and brought sudden depth to her whisky-coloured eyes and made her jump up and down but it exhausted him because he could feel himself slipping from the goal, drowning in the blood of the ancients, weeping with them in frustration.

Jeddah Golden had counselled Squire to cope with time present and the exhausted Mohawk saw the infinite wisdom. He was firm, "Please, now you listen, Lucille Oihwanéhégwaht Goosay. Times change. Enemies shift. Allegiances form. You speak true but sixty years past is sixty years past. In sixty years, the crummy American colonies have grown up and Indian land is still on their minds."

Missus Goosay hunkered down next to Pommie and she repositioned the deerskin, which he had sloughed off in his sleep, and snorted. "So? So? Tell me something new, I say."

"Their incoming president, Mister Polk, agrees with John Louis O'Sullivan. O'Sullivan claims Americans have a *manifest destiny* and their destiny is to own the whole territory of North America. United States steals Indian lands bigger than the size of Europe. It is their destiny, I guess. And ours."

"The crummy Americans?"

"Yes. The crummy Americans. Our people like the colonies' resistance because we hate the States and the Indian Removal Act. It don't pay us to curse too loud about deserving squatters in our own territory. North of the border, we figure to stay loyal, Auntie, and we wave our loyalty in Polk's face."

"The Americans will have a President *Poke*?"

"Yes, Auntie, yes. You may know it very well that England does not polish the covenant chain but I have more bad news for you."

"President *Poke*? I say, sure, Tehawennihárhos? Poke!"

"Sure I am sure. President Polk. 'Young Hickory,' the *Globe* calls him. I can read, Auntie." Squire grabbed his mug tightly so he would not bang her with it. "'James Knox Polk is from the back-country. Descended from North-Britain's purple vein.' Scratch away at Young Hickory and what, Auntie? Yup. English."

Missus Goosay slumped.

Squire had her on the run. "Polk has an agenda. It is territorial. The enemy wears an American uniform. The enemy swallows up Indian country. Miles of it." Squire threw up his arms, the maple-wood cup in his left hand, and he did not spill a drop. He claimed he was not sure about anything except the rise of a counterbalancing colonial loyalism, likely to combat the possibility of Polk's manifest destiny gobbling up the whole of North America. Squire said he wished he could give more intelligence to the respected elder. A smart woman like her needed to know things. He tried to explain. "Look, Auntie, town markets crawl with loyalists. You must know that. Orange and Papist. Go to Toronto or London or Hamilton or the village yonder. Not just Tories. Not Protestants. Not moderates. Everybody loves Queen Victoria. It's a mania. It is the street talk. People on the street say England gets tired. The famine over there is bad. They say Britain's colonies will get strong but not yet. America is the strongest. America has a plan. America has a manifest destiny.

The united Canadas, why, they want a plan. A destiny, just like Polk says America has, but different. Royal. Loyal. I dunno, Auntie. The settlers around here are mixed-up crazy. Like the river."

"Not us. Surely, not us! Not the people. Not the Six Nations."

The Mohawk blew out his cheeks. "You seen George Johnson, huh? He dresses like a British Napoleon." He made an effort not to sound impatient but tapped his finger on the angry scratch. "Yes, of course, it has infected us too."

"Don't make me sick."

"Sorry to make you sick, Auntie. Loyal totems are everywhere."

"What totems, Tehawennihárhos?"

"Empire totems. Let's see, what? Union Jack. Rule Britannia. Ah-ha, the new Victoria Day. George Johnson's uniform. Loyal signs? Toronto is right smug with 'em."

"Why? Why? Why? What has come over us?"

"I tell you, Auntie. It's likely America."

"No."

"Yes."

"But why?"

"Dunno. We know the enemy. The enemy has a destiny."

"That's it?"

"Please. No more. I read the *Globe*. Tell you straight. Loyalty is the trend. It's kind of a stunt. No, don't ask me to pin it down. I tell you what I read. I tell you what I hear. We are loyal. Loyal to the traitorous kingdom."

Missus Goosay was pained and raised her shoulders. "Where does this leave us?"

Speaking of leaving, Squire begged her indulgence. He summoned his strength and hopped up and sprinted out of the wigwam and into the rain and pissed like Joker's Breezy. He came back in two minutes to hear her still raving like a fanatic against fanaticisms as though he had been sitting there beside her.

What could he possibly do to start her talking about Bobby John?

She said, "Indians are public enemy number one. I say this, yes, I do. Enemy number one! We have land. Squatters steal it. To hide rapaciousness and guilt, the squabbling white morons agree on something other than their loyalty, I say. Mark me well."

Squire sighed. He sat down. He had to hurry but he could not take the chance of hurting her. "What, Auntie? What do you say? What do the squabbling white morons agree on?"

Missus Goosay narrowed her whisky eyes and coiled her tongue and wet her lips. "Us. They agree on us. Indians are dogs and we do not deserve our land. I say to them, Bah! We know the value of our losses. So, my friend. We end up where we started."

"What do you mean?"

"Whites say Indians are dumb. Too dumb to know what happens. The Six Nations' joining with settlers and having loyalty to the English *is* dumb. Honestly. I say the English are not loyal to us."

"No."

"And neither are the settlers."

"No."

"I put a hex on the English."

"The British, Auntie. You must say the *British*. No more *English*."

"Fine. Fine. I put a hex on the British. The Six Nations are loyal to the British but even so they write in their colonial newspapers that our caste goes extinct." A gleaming tear as perfect as a rain droplet wobbled on the rim of her eyelid. "Nobody has brains, I say."

Squire felt guilty for shoving her down memory lane. Here she was, a kind Auntie, after all, and so upset. He teased her. "Tut, tut. For a nice lady, you are too cynical."

"Tehawennihárhos," Missus Goosay said, her shoulders coming down to earth. "You're hurt. Have some salve for your hand."

She reached for a small wooden bowl of grease that smelled of goose and pine sap and applied it to the cut. She apologized for not having witch hazel. She had used her bark-and-leaf decoction on the children's cuts and their insect-bitten feet and must collect more seeds. "Tehawennihárhos, let us never mind about the great British disloyalty. Let us move along, I say. Who acted false last week?"

For a slow-spoken and thoughtful man, he was quick to answer. "Paulus Bobby John."

"Great-grandson of Catharine Adonwentishon Croghan."

"Yes."

"I am sorry. What do the whites say he did?"

"Golden's cousin, Nellah, she was robbed."

"Hmmm." Lucille Goosay squinted and she put away the small goose-grease bowl in a niche in the wooden wall and made her shrug dismissive. He had best come up with a better crime because she was not going to tie herself in a knot over it. A robbery was just getting even.

"Nellah tried to protect herself and she got her head cracked open. With a hearth rock. The grandmother, Aughguaga Polly, says Nellah was interfered with. Nellah's baby comes early. Polly cuts her belly and takes the baby. Baby and Nellah are doing their best."

Missus Goosay nodded. That was it. Treachery enough to move her. She said, "Bobby John is in Oneida village near the new Caledonia. In the bush. At his sister's house."

"How—"

"Tehawennihárhos, I beat the trail a fair bit. And I paddle up and down the crazy river. You see I live here. Alone, most of the time. So I get to visit with folks. I get news. People tell the lonely woman things because they think maybe I got no one else. At camps along the riverfront many talk. They make excuses. For Bobby John. He feeds them. He is a Warrior. No mention of injuries. No mention of President Poke either."

"About Nellah, I tell you true."

"Yes, I say so."

"Auntie, there was another."

"Another what?"

"Another robber, Auntie. Uh? Do you know this?"

She twirled and unwound her apron ties and wrapped a tie around her finger. "Tehawennihárhos, I believe I do."

"Well?"

"Maybe. I say, maybe I heard as much."

They turned their heads and checked to see whether Pommie was insensible. The child was breathing even, sleeping as sound as a pup on his master's bed and Squire envied him but he must press the lady to tell him what she knew from her travels on the river. He didn't hold back. He said, "I tell you. Pommie Munny's uncle is Boy Hewson. We are out for him, Auntie. We bring him in. Do you know where he is? Do you know where Boy Hewson is?"

"Hmmm." Lucille Goosay frowned and looked around as though trying to recall where she had left her argyle socks. There was a silence between them. It was the proper moment for Squire to mention the fears of Miz Bride Munny and offer the second solution for ending a sea of troubles. Money. Golden's drawstring purse.

"Auntie, you should know it. Bride Munny thinks you want to kill her. She says you will 'do her in' if she don't pay you. She says you are the murderous Missus Goosay."

"Tehawennihárhos, what do you say? I say Bride Munny tells lies. That's what I say. I wouldn't know her from a, a digging stick."

"Hmm. I doubt that, somehow." The crooked grin returned to take away the sting. "Does Miz Munny hold debts with you, Auntie?"

"No. No. I don't ask the children for anything. Bride Munny is never around. She is gone, Pommie says. To village, he says. For days I don't see kids until Pommie shows up. With you."

The murderous Missus Goosay, hah.

Squire chuckled. "So, you aren't going to murder her?"

Shoulders rallied again, right up to her neck.

"Where is this story coming from that I am a murderer?"

Squire chafed his chin and he laughed with certain insight and pointed to the sleeping form. Pommie. The Mohawk had been considering the issue of a murderous Missus Goosay and had a little speech at the ready. He touched the child's sore foot with affection and complimented his youthful ingenuity. "Him, I believe. This one. Pomeroy Munny. You have helped the boy protect Chrisinny. Fed them. Taken them on picnics and treasure hunts. Told them scary ghost stories around the fire. Got them warm, allowed them peaceful sleep. I believe he wants you to have something for your troubles. It is clear to me his mother flips coins and markers to a procurer. The best way to prompt her into squirreling away a coin or two is to scare her. So, see? Now you are a murderer, uh? The murderous Missus Goosay. Pommie loves that. It worked too. Miz Munny was scared. She is one scared lady. Everything scares her. Including her brother, I'm guessing. Pommie here gets less than nothing from his ma but he tried to get something for you. He wouldn't let his ma leave without giving you a gift. He understands the meaning of presents."

Squire held up the drawstring purse to her and she held up her hands, nay, and shook her head to refuse.

"Auntie, the coin is from Mister Golden. He is pretty wealthy. He understands your value." And the value of peace and quiet on the trail. "You must take it. Pommie has risked his uncle's wrath and ma's displeasure to make everything right between you two."

The woman relented. "Tehawennihárhos, you say well. I accept the purse. There is not much at my sister's. I pay my way."

"Auntie, I know that."

"Tehawennihárhos, I have given you a gift. I have told you where to find Bobby John."

"There is more I must hear, Auntie. What about the other one? What about Boy?"

Missus Goosay sagged. "Boy Hewson. Ah-ha. Richard Boynton Hewson is the other one. It is true. I have heard it. He's English, I say. All right. All right. He is *British*."

"Can't jail a man for that."

"Evil."

"Ah-ha. Why?"

"He has wealth but neglects children. From what I hear, he abuses their mother. In the bad way. He is not Irish exactly but he claims he is a Shiner. He uses the woman Bride and he sells her to Shiners. In Brantford. In Hamilton. Tehawennihárhos, I say he is a, he is—"

"Yes? What? Where is he?"

"He is close, I say. Oh, I worry."

"I worry too, Auntie. Him, I want in gaol. Where is he? Nearby? Is he around here?"

"Close, I say. You have already laid the trap. You take his sister. You don't chase him. You take his sister and, my young friend, oh yes, you can count on it—"

"What do I count on?"

"You haven't heard the last of him."

"Good. I'll be ready."

"It is very bad for you, Tehawennihárhos."

"Why?"

"He is ready to fight, fight to the death. Looking for it. Any excuse. Boy Hewson is not a chucklehead like Bobby John. Boy Hewson is devious. He has connections. Family Compact, maybe. Military too. Yes, nephew. Connections. High up. He does things for people in high places. He will never go to jail, not to stay. That's what I say."

"What do you know, Auntie?"

"Boy Hewson is like sticky winter ice on the crazy river, Tehawennihárhos. More trouble than he looks. Nothing much to see in him, I say, but he is terrible mean. He maims horses."

"Horses? You sure? That's ridiculous."

"He does it for hire. For coins."

"I don't get it."

"He hires himself out, I say."

"Who wants him?"

"Feuding Irish. English soldiers. Family Compact. Reformer gangs. Anyone who needs a fire set. Anyone who needs information and doesn't care how he gets it. I hear the colonial government hires him."

"Why is that our business, Auntie?"

"Tehawennihárhos, don't you be ridiculous. He's mean. I say he goes after horses. He cuts out a tongue. Chops an ear. Slits a sheath. No, young man, don't look at me. He is wanton."

"I hear you. A woman is nothing to him, then."

"Nothing. Less than nothing. I say he's mean. Mean enough to kill. Vindictive too. That's what I tell you. Do you see now?"

"What, Auntie? Tears? Do I see tears? What's the problem?"

"I say this, Tehawennihárhos, you are a fine man. You are no match. Not even. I would almost have you abandon the Munnys but it would mean death. You're no more than a child—"

"I take care of myself." He sat motionless. He was upset and sounded pitiful to his own ears, trembling, like Bride.

"Mmmm. Nephew, I hope so. You better look sharp, I say. Pay mind to the trail."

"I will."

"Good. Cagey is the way to beat him."

"Auntie, I will be cagey."

"Poke him first. Poke him hard."

"I will do that."

A cascade of tamarack tumbled down in a flurry, from her crown to her draped lap, but she was upset and did not seem to notice or care. She stood and walked to the doorway. She shook her gingham dress outside and she flattened her apron. She returned to the taller of the two tables, reached behind a stack of bowls and retrieved a pair of deerskin moccasins, worked in red and gold beads, with corded ties. A thousand times better for a boy than pegged boots. "Give these to Pommie," she said. "Tell him Segenauck made them. The ghost found her head. She leaves here. Tell him— she goes with him."

Squire hauled himself to his feet. He was glad to stand and stretched and in due course accepted the moccasins with another bow of respect. He was tired of sitting and his knees felt creaky. He was done here but sorry to leave her. "I will, Auntie."

They were quiet. Glad to think they had met and not wanting to say as much.

They exchanged formal wishes for safe journeys and safe returns and Squire promised to look in on her and he tucked the superb moccasins into his corded belt.

He asked the Cayuga woman to please pack up her belongings and food. She must be ready for the trip downstream. No delays. She should hop into the canoe and paddle away the very minute her excellent sons arrived home. Best done within the day. Missus Goosay nodded. Bits of the bird's nest trickled from her head. Soon, she said, perhaps even within the hour. They would pack up and leave the village in a snap. Out of Boy Hewson's way. She had no desire to face off with Irish Shiners or English traitors. She swore she would not breathe a word about the Munnys. Munnys? Who were they?

Squire gathered up a sleeping Pommie, the other Munny fairy-weight. He expected the youngster to wake up while he was moving him but no. Squire breathed long and hard and he did the one thing he could and hoisted him up like an offering to the river. Pommie was slung out like a bolster over both of Squire's arms and the Mohawk prepared to carry him to the river station, figuring Golden had taken both Cap'n and Joker's Breezy back there.

Proud Missus Lucille Goosay bowed to them. She looked at the sleeping Pommie to remember his face. Squire understood. He paused to give her a last look as much as he wanted to hightail it to the way station.

Most unladylike, she hollered at the Mohawk's departing shoulders right at the moment his foot hit the path. "I say Boy Hewson bites like a boggy rattler. Do not corner him. He is meaner than you. I say, never corner anyone meaner than you."

Squire advanced into the bush but he was not out of earshot. He heard her fading words because the waves of her low singsong came paddled on the wind. "And you tell Pommie you'll keep an eye on him and Chrisinny. You see to it, Tehawennihárhos. Promise. You mind them. They do not vanish, I say. Not like Segenauck. No do-gooders. Save these children from harm."

CHAPTER
twenty-four

Jennet Ferguson was not waiting for Squire on Vinegar Hill. She was on her way back home to Uxbridge. She had left the Hill not ten hours after the posse had set out to find Bobby John and Boy Hewson. In the space of twelve hours, there had been a murder and a betrayal. Meatface was dead.

Squire was overwhelmed. Alfie Williams, Nellah's man, the cook, and Nellah's two young helper girls, little Ann Bergin and weeping Lizzie Bosson, they had troubles, what with Nellah's being under the weather and all. People were busy, too busy running an inn and a tavern to chat with Squire about the nature of things and the trials of the heart. He took off for the barn where he could brush down Cap'n. He could sulk and fume at the same time, in private, before he had to face his own people, Aughguaga Polly and Maggie Walker.

twenty-five

Cook, Alfie Williams, had been astonished to see the four horsemen back at the Cyclops Inn. They had not even got half started on the manhunt and there they were again with more folks and more folks meant more food. That was problem enough and Cook was set to grumble to Golden about extra mouths to feed but more trouble was on the horizon. Bart Farr and Peter Johnson had gathered collateral. Them Munnys.

The horror show began.

Nellah Golden ran an establishment of village and country. It was a mixture of up-to-the-minute and down-to-the-earth. The village part was Nellah's six-year-old red-brick house with its spindle-rail veranda and Mallory-glass windows. Not a big home by Brantford's standards but it was solid and it had a large, welcoming great dining room with a stone hearth and wooden mantle and numerous detailed features that warranted inspection, like the front-door chime.

Countryside, in contrast, was the Cyclops Inn.

It was unadorned, a weathered and creaky frame structure with nothing to recommend it. It was bare, a pewter-sided wooden box with six-foot front and back doors and a few small white-trimmed wooden-sash windows. There was no upper balcony for escape in case of emergency. In an emergency, if either a fire or an infidelity had erupted, it was certain you were on your own.

Nellah had built the brick house forward, toward the circular dirt lane, and the barn-board inn had a pushed-back appearance, as though it were loping toward the bush. The path to the rear of the inn took you to Nellah's dining-room door or, if you veered left, you were ready to climb the bare wood steps to the tavern, the Cave. Everybody in the village knew about the Cave and everybody drank there or partied there at one time or another. Seeum Johnston of the *Courier* called it a resort for dissolute people.

Seeum Johnston had a point.

But people drank there anyway.

In the clearing between house and inn there was a murky space, a half-cobbled yard that sprouted wild-grass and weeds. Nellah tried to plant a flower garden in the corner but she had no time to tend it, after minding the tavern and the inn.

Not all was lost. Cook, one Alfie Williams, built an outdoor showerbath for her and the ladies. The water barrel was full on most days and the showerbath worked as well as any old whisky still. The rain barrel sat on the flat roof of the inn and it caught the water. Pipes ran from it, up and down and around, and into a funnel and the funnel had a door and a seal and a spring and when you pulled the cord the splash from the funnel was an honest soaker.

A showerbath was sufficient to take Nellah's mind off a garden.

Ann Bergin and Lizzie Bosson and even Nellah herself, when she was not feeling so poorly, took showerbaths at female-satisfying intervals, more times in a week than Cook required for bathing himself, but the women had never emptied the barrel. A shower-bath. Great idea. No trouble. No trouble until them Munny kids arrived. Squire, Farr, Johnson, Golden and that thin white-haired woman and her pea-pickin' brood descended on Cook. Before he said "soaker," the rain barrel was empty. What a to-do.

At first, it had been hell on earth to dip the kids underneath the showerbath funnel. The barrel was full up and spilling, perfect and ready for them two tykes that badly wanted water and lye soap and a wash-up but them Munnys hated getting wet.

Farr wasn't going to fight about it. "No sir," he said.

"Oh, yes, sir." Ann Bergin shook a small clenched fist at the old Fox. "You are going to fight about it. Get them to the showerbath." They needed a cleaning. Ann was positive. She was not about to let the children march into Nellah's house and up to the bedroom area otherwise. The children's ma, Brydee, she called herself, was not interested in any rub-a-dub, neither. She preferred to eat out the entire pantry. Farr had got mad at Ann for being pernickety, he quit trying to lend her a hand, and he meant it. He stormed off to Mahlon Joe's Hot and Cold Baths 25 Cents. Ann was near frenzied because she was all for scrubbing kids but she was standing guard over the eggs and trying to chase Miz Munny out of the pantry.

Woll, Cook said, that was bad enough but it wasn't the most awful part. Tykes got used to the cold water and they decided the showerbath was fun and they wanted more soakers and that was after they hadn't wanted any water at all in the first place. Water spilled from the platform and trickled over the side, ran into the mud and made soapy puddles. Puddles were fun. Kids plopped right into them. They needed another shower. Down came the soaker. Up on the platform for another shower. On and on. Ann screamed she'd wring their necks like stew hens if they did it again. They must have believed her because they wrapped the flannel towels around their skin and bones and spun a murky trail into the house like inky ants. They had no decent clothes, of course.

Ann put them naked on straw pallets upstairs and she threatened them with a lacing if they so much as breathed.

In a flash they were abed.

Lizzie Bosson was abed too. She of course was feeling too poorly to help anybody since her boyfriend, Meatface, the pa of her forthcoming child, had been carted off to the undertaker's. Lizzie, redolent in Guerlain, cried, and everybody wondered what would help her depression.

Time alone, most like.

Poor Annie Bergin. She had to handle the entire influx.

Golden was upstairs with Nellah. He was holding baby Pearl, sitting and rocking in the chair in Nellah's bedroom. Nellah was not so feverish no more and she appeared stronger, like she was going to make it. Thanks to Aughguaga Polly, there was no contamination in her wounds. Not yet, anyways. Baby was set up for nursing. The Snowman was pleased about his family but he had clouded up some after Alfie Williams had got his hands on him to ask for money. Snowman said he warn't the lord of the manor but Alfie sez he 'as to pay up anyways. Woll, Alfie had an obligation to Nellah, didn't he? Woman couldn't pay for such goings-on, not after robbery. Cook had mouths to feed. Golden shelled out the money. Golden told Johnson to get supplies. Pick up warm clothes for kiddies. Nellah had duds enough for poor old Miz Munny.

twenty-six

Meatface was dead? How?

"Je ne sais pas." Peter Johnson said he was mystified.

Squire had spent an hour or more rubbing down the horses. The kids and their tomfoolery with the showerbath had happened without his knowing until Johnson stormed into Diablo's stall and grabbed a saddle from the crib. Squire had said, "Going some place?"

Peter Johnson had grunted.

He had glared at Diablo and sworn. The gelding had been willing enough to start out again and he moved with docile steps out of the stall and, after all, the poor beast had as much right as the Frenchman to feel sore. Diablo had to carry the Frenchman's considerable weight.

Complaining rights were a toss-up.

Squire had complaining rights.

Where was Jennet Ferguson?

For his part, Johnson had given the Mohawk a quick look and then a fair run-down on the waterlogged Munnys but he had said he didn't know anything too much about Mademoiselle Ferguson. He was to go for supplies. And to get fresh garments for the children. So the horsemen could get the hell away from Vinegar Hill to catch Bobby John and Boy Hewson, if they could. Johnson had snapped on the bridle.

Squire said, "You pick up a sheet of paper, Peter, will ya?"

"*Oui*. I need paper. I write Sarah. I have stayed in the cause of Nellah too long. Sarah does not want me home, not now, not at this point. She manages. That is what she says, *Au revoir pour toujours*."

"You should go home, brother. Talk it out."

"No. I commence this thing. I finish it." Johnson mounted the lumpy Diablo and he joggled like a sack of beans on the back of the huge paint horse and headed down the ramp and out of the barn.

Squire sought Cook to get the whole story but, of course, there was trouble, just waiting, just longing to accost him. Maggie Walker and Aughguaga Polly were standing in the open-aired, downstairs veranda next to the front steps, each tapping an angry moccasin, and Alfie Williams was sitting on the steps. The women were eager to tell all, and tell it to their advantage.

CHAPTER
twenty-seven

"She is bad. She makes bad wife. Her family is cursed. The black swan will crumple to see her. People will cry. She stinks. She murders the spotted one. *Àshare* sticks him. Arghhh. Blood drips."

Squire stood at the bottom of the steps and Maggie Walker performed the death scene of Meatface on her porch stage. It was a murder scene. The murderous Missus Goosay was forgotten, lost in the sands of time, because, like Maggie said, Jennet Ferguson, why, she was a real murderer. Maggie had a candid expression, just like Tehawennihárhos, and the same straight nose, same pointy black brows, same white teeth. She was very attractive and, when the two were young, some folks had claimed that Maggie looked a lot like Squire, the only man she had ever loved, but they had usually added she had none of his depth. She was one-dimensional. She wanted to wait on him. Not much of a life, they had said, waiting on a man.

Squire listened to Maggie and he did not say a thing.

What could he say?

Maggie acted out the murder of Meatface and Jennie's part and the whole death scene with the enthusiasm of Miss Ince. The *Globe*'s man had castigated the unfortunate Miss Ince. She had starred in a catchpenny performance of *Barbarossa: The Siege of Algiers,* and the melodrama at the Theatre Royal and Miss Ince's wild gestures had affronted the *Globe*'s reviewer. The reviewer should catch this performance, Squire thought. Sweet little Maggie scolded, harangued and accused Jennet Ferguson of multiple crimes of perversion, including cold-blooded murder.

In normal times, Squire and Maggie got along all right. She was nice. Lissome. Glossy hair. A tiny woman. Girlish voice, pitched high to make you feel you had to look after her. She had none of Jennet Ferguson's restless, fiery vitality. Jennet was smart and capable and her energy sparked like sun on water or a flint on stone. Maggie was vague. Limp. Wet. Not fixed. That was what some folks said.

She was pregnant and plenty upset with Squire for not coming to her rescue but she must have known her condition was outside his medicine and not his fault and he was not for her. He could not help her. As a couple they were no good. He cared about her, though, and hated to see her distraught and tried to dismiss her acting, which struck him as entertaining. At some primal level, he understood the worst thing to do would be to laugh. Anyway, he, the only man she had ever loved, was not the father of her baby and he was not her protector and could not make her soul fierce or her wits less gullible.

Aughguaga Polly was not gullible.

She was a tobacco-chewing thug.

A renowned healer among the people.

Hah. They should know it.

She could pinch you purple and call it a fix.

Polly was not so sure that Jennet Ferguson was a murderer. The white-eyed one may be worse. A stinking bully, maybe. Dirty. Too thin. Too bossy. Too loud.

Squire thought of someone else he knew who felt like Polly about hilarity and noise. Polly and Jennet's father, William, were one under the skin.

In English, Polly said, "White Eyes is hit, Tehawennihárhos. A little hit. Not even a big hit. A tap. Meatface gives your Jennet a tap. She honks. *Onahsakenra*." Polly waggled her finger, this way, that way, and her gurning face shook like headcheese. "She makes bad wife."

Stinking. Dirty. Bad wife. On that note, Polly and Maggie chirruped from the same hymnal. They waggled their fingers and swayed like gospel singers on the veranda.

"*She* runs out on you."

Like choristers, "We told you so."

He listened to the tale of Jennie's betrayal and her departure and he tried to separate the kernel of truth from the shell but Aughguaga Polly was not having things any way but her way. "Pah. It don't matter no more. *She* is gone. *She* runs out on you."

Polly had the words to pierce his heart and she knew it.

She hawked a chaw over the white railing. Not satisfied, she pierced deeper. "*She* leaves. Mister *Big Shot* takes her. *You* can't catch her."

The torturer of small boys favoured him with a tobacco-stained smirk and he knew from long, sad experience she never curled the corners of her mouth to be nice. She grinned when she had you. Anymore, Tehawennihárhos was too old to whip but so what? The fat grandmother had her style. She could ladle out the tortuous medicine by the barrel when she felt he deserved it. He was supposed to marry Onondaga Maggie Walker of the Turtle clan. He was supposed to forget the white howler with the scary eyes. The goose. *Onahsakenra*. All in all, he really was overwhelmed. He was numb.

~

Cayuga Lucille Goosay dwelled on the past but Aughguaga Polly was an uncanny bellwether. She rammed her way through the barrier of current trends. She knew what was up-to-the-minute in the noxious British colony. She knew whites. She knew their tricks. Pound for pound, Polly was a powerful woman and she had a trickster totem and, say what you would, in this world, you had better get up early and watch your steps because you did not fool her. Polly recognized competition. She did not give the mouse a chance to nibble at the runner bean. She snapped first. Snapped hard. Gave the hex.

That was it. The reason Jennet had left. Polly had hexed her. Jennet was helpless.

Squire felt better. He would write to Jennet.

Actually, no, he would not write. Why should he?

She did not leave him a note. Not a word. He hated himself for wanting her. He was lovesick. He hated the whole lovesick business. It was a gaping hurt like a mammoth toothache. Something he had never before experienced. An alliance with a white settler? What had he been smoking? Pah. Polly was right. He was as crazy as the crazy river. Why on earth did he want to marry a Scotchwoman? It made no sense.

"Gone, she is. *You* can't catch her," Polly repeated. "And aint that too bad for *you*."

"Nathaniel Burr. 'E's from Mark'am, so 'e sayz. He is the one. Feller wi' the terpshiner came ter take 'er round ter place."

That piece of the puzzle came from Cook. The man in white. He peeled murphies. He put them in a huge cast-iron pot. He counted them, thought for a moment, and doubled the number out of the burlap sack. He sat on Nellah's top step and added his farthing's worth to the overall destruction of Squire's soul. The Cave was filling with drinking patrons. It all cost money. Cook watched the pennies. With Nellah ill someone had to. Cook fretted. Nellah was broke in so many ways. Squire's problems were more like irritants.

Squire rubbed his hands until they warmed. "So, Nathaniel Burr takes Jennet to home? Home, where? To Uxbridge?"

Alfie said, "Ay-yah. Yis. Misti Burr and Jennie. They do 'ry ter kep the coach. Jump on tergether, maybe one 'n 'alf, mebbe two, mebbe t'ree hours pas'."

Squire had an ally in the old Scouser and he trusted him a whole lot more than he understood him. "Alf, tell me. What happened?"

"Right. Woll, yer Jennie is cryin'."

"Why? Do you know why? How bad is she hurt?"

"Woll, she is ragged, I can say 'at. Meatface, he 'its 'er awright, square on da kisser." Alfie twitched to see Aughguaga Polly frowning and waving her turtle rattle aimed at his kisser. No sympathy for Jennet Ferguson there. Cook shrugged. Lingo aside, Alfie Williams always said he felt he was an open book, but Polly, like most women, was hard to make out. Alfie said he was into explaining because that was what his old friend Squire wanted. An explanation. "Girl's cheek was swoll up like a trout bladder. Beun some kinda tragedy, Squire. In Uxbridge, Death, I 'ear. Missy 'as to 'ead up tee 'ome. 'Er pa, he says so. Gewd chap, Cornelius, 'e collects 'er whotnots at Smith's Corner."

"Who dies in Uxbridge?"

"Dunno 'at."

"Alfie, did Jennet murder Meatface?" Maggie's performance loomed large and fresh in his mind. Perhaps she had.

"Na-ow." Cook flung a spud into the pot with enough force to rock the caldron. "Na-ow, Squire. T'was me. I done it. T'umped ter bugger with me ol' fry pan. 'E fell flat ahead, mug down." Alfie went on and on and he blamed himself for the pitiful end of Meatface and he defended Jennie and put into words to the best of his ability the reason for her leaving—she was summoned, she had to go, and he kept talking and revolving the story around and around in his kind, unintelligible idiom until Polly was so angry she exploded. Squire knew she could not understand Alfie, not a word, but it was obvious she had felt his concern.

155

She leaned over the rail and clomped him. She got him on the back of the head.

Alfie glowered but stopped talking. He had nothing more to say.

There they were.

The four of them.

Under intense eyelids, they intermittently peered at each other and turned and peered and turned. What next?

The women pressed their mouths into a thin line.

They waited and hoped for Squire to rail against Jennie and they waited and hoped in vain because Squire, goddam, he sure had nothing to say. He tapped the bottom step with his moccasin, sniffed the air and wondered aloud whether they would get rain.

It was misty. Dark.

Time to go.

Meatface was a slave-snatcher and he was dead. The ugly one had had a second chance because Lizzie loved him but it had not worked out. Squire could not understand, though, why Jennie had run out without a word. Had Maggie said something direct to her? Or Polly? Who would break the silence?

The fat grandmother at long last gave in. She spoke. Speaking in Mohawk, and not Oneida—this was to mollify him as well he knew—Aughguaga Polly grabbed the floundering moment and took command. "My grandson, come now, it's over. The spotted boy is dead and buried. The goose has flown. You have no hope with pale eyes. *Kahnyen'kehàka*. Your nation is best choice for your children. No white people. Get it? Here. Look. Beautiful Maggie. *Ononta'kehàka*. She waits. Child comes. The people rejoice. A baby for Tehawennihárhos. You accept the baby. You are big hero. Like your adopted father, my son, David Shagohawineghtha. You forget this Jennet. Get it?"

He got it.

Polly tried to basket him like a cornered trout but Squire was not swimming her way. She tried harder and he stayed firm but through it he felt sorry for Maggie. He could have taken a second look at the girl to spite Jennie but he knew he would not. He had done that before and it was not worth it. He had enough sense to realize he was not a fair man to treat Maggie as his ally because she was familiar and attractive. The fat grandmother was pushy and she did not understand it but pushiness made it easier for him to resist Maggie and stick to the chaste path on Vinegar Hill, which was a joke. Vinegar Hill was anything but chaste. He felt down and out and he was not Maggie's man. He wondered about the father of her child but had no claim to ask. He would learn the truth soon enough and, if he did not, he could live. Overhead, a V-formation of robust grain-fed geese headed southward and they honked like dumb *onahsakenra* to make him more miserable. Proof positive. Polly nodded. Her symbols were endless. She pointed. She had the virtuous look. See. Get it?

Squire saw. Yep. He got it.

There was Alfie, sitting on the top step, self-conscious but detached, peeling spuds.

There were the women, Maggie and Polly, elbows on the rail, fingers pointed heavenward, armed and ready with fresh scowls to fire down if he said a single thing to rile them. In less than twelve hours, everything had changed.

A man was dead.

There was no Jennie. That was all he knew.

That was all he cared about.

Polly had no hold on him.

He was positive Jennie wanted him.

Perhaps the tragedy at her home was truly serious enough to draw her away from him. He whistled for Cap'n, who nibbled at grass bouquets on the edge of the dirt pathway. Squire threw

himself up on the horse and, with no smart retort to the fat grandmother, as much as she deserved it, he turned from Nellah's establishment and galloped down the chunked-out trail through the
swamp cedars and maple trees and beechnut grove. He thought
that maybe he would go to Mahlon Joe's after all. Join Bart. Get
the scalp treatment. Try the miracle elixirs. Cure his dandruff.
Get something for a headache. Those women could try the
patience of an Irish saint. He had taken Missus Goosay's advice,
though. He had not cornered Aughguaga Polly. She was mean,
meaner than him, meaner than anyone. Her razor tongue could
have torn strips off him and she could have fed his heart and liver
to the turkey vultures and not broken a sweat but, for all that, he
wondered. He wondered about what Polly had said. Maybe she
was right.

Jennie had run off.

She could have stayed.

She should have stayed.

A thought was there and made a getaway. What was it? Ah. He
knew. The hex. Polly had hexed Jennie. The fat grandmother was
sensitive to challenges. She was possessive. Squire was her appren-
tice in the healing arts. She lorded control over him. She was
tough, old Polly. He wondered whether Jennet Ferguson were just
as tough.

CHAPTER
twenty-eight

Squire arrived late at Mahlon Joe's. Bart Farr had gone. The bathhouse was not busy, six or seven customers, and Joe took his time with the Mohawk. Crunched in a tin tub, Squire had his back scrubbed. The languor from hurt feelings made him sore-jointed and he stayed put. He sat in the water until his skin cockled. He dressed again in his dirty stuff, which bothered him, but there was no help for it. He had no other clothing. The Delaware barber massaged and anointed his scalp and he used up gobs of lavender and citrusy essences and spirituous elixirs and gentle emollients and expressed his high hopes for success.

Success?

Squire was too shy to ask what success Joe had in mind but, after the scalp massaging was over, Joe's special client was as cool as the heather. Squire tied back his trimmed hair with a thong and he nodded his thanks for the effort and paid up and got out before Joe could make an announcement to the other patrons to advertise his incredible skills, as practised on the wild Indian there.

With a cleansed body and a troubled soul, Squire rode home. He eased up on Cap'n. He did not feel like pounding over the ground with the normal reckless speed and let the stallion fall into a canter back to the Cyclops. A large black rodent scuttled across the trail. It ran direct. It made a line from cedar to cedar, right in front of

Cap'n, and the horse almost trampled it. The Hanover rat. A recent gift to the upper country. Brought on one of the Navigation's steamers. Big rat was seeking a barn or a mill, Squire figured. Shit. Europeans were generous. They shared their honeybees, earthworms and vermin. They shared smallpox and typhoid. The horse balked a step or two at the slithering rat but the Mohawk barely noticed because bigger rats gnawed at him. He was lonely, *flâné*, the Frenchman had said, and he felt very, very sorry for himself.

CHAPTER
twenty-nine

A mizzling rain sharpened to pin-tips. Black, dreary beech-nut trees linked angular branches overhead. A burnt-leaf canopy protected Squire and Cap'n and they avoided the worst of the downpour but the Mohawk suffered, even in the touch of the wind. Horse and rider rode past Nellah's clearing, they headed for her commodious barn, over a hundred yards behind the house and almost out of sight of it. Squire had tightened his jaw; he was holding his breath, he realized it and inhaled to his toes. What was going on?

It sounded like a cockfight. Uncle Pat Riley called a cockfight the *exquisite debauchery*.

There were dozens of people milling about under the overhang of the shack and some men had hitched their horses to tree trunks or as faraway as the rail leading to the Cave. The tavern was not full of people, though. Most were in the barn.

Squire had been gone from Nellah's for a couple of hours and in the intervening time a travelling pitchman had arrived with game-cocks and had set up inside the stable, where Teacher's mud-base floor was swept and waiting, ideal for a pit. The flailing of mad roosters in the ring and the encouragement of the frantic betters who were leaning over the boards blasted his ears. It was louder than the rain, which had started to come down in buckets, like

Cook's showerbath. The din was awesome. It was raining Irish cloggers on the roof and it was all commotion and jollity and fowl murder on the floor. Humans and hens shook the rafters. Flapping, squawking, running, shouting. In the midst of it, Squire sat high on Cap'n. A spectacle, he thought. Like coming upon an anthill, he felt the marvelling sensation of a Gulliver gazing down on Lilliputian industry. Too conspicuous, he dismounted. He headed for the cribs at the far end of the barn, though they were narrow.

"Yay, Blackhen!"

"Go, Marcher!"

The volume boomed up as a sturdy little Shamo gamecock won his fight and slashed his aged rival, a regal Old English Game. A great squawking arose like screams of torture.

"Atta boy, Cummins!"

"C'mon, Darrig!" Another winner.

Towheaded Bride Munny wandered about in the middle of the melee dressed in a black skirt and a ruffled, feathered wrap. He was sure it was Bride. Took another look. Yeah, it was. She was clean. He almost did not recognize her. Her chemise had drooping cape-shoulders. She wore the modern elegant dipped bodice and she was clinging to a pomaded Barton Farr, the way a telltale blonde hair clings to the vest. It seemed that Miz Munny had met up with a nubbin of soap. Her side-knot was as shiny as the rising sun. Farr did not look to be doing much betting. Doesn't want to lose his hard-earned coin in front of the Munny woman, Squire thought, and, away from home, the old Fox must have believed he was a free man. The couple riffled among the men and Farr was the cockiest. Bride saw to it. She nattered into his ear. Farr did not seem to care. He swaggered and was hen-pecked and the paradox appeared to make him happy. He steered her away from the gamblers.

The eyes of a fair-haired young man burned over the crowd.

The man wore a plain-cut buff coat and high black boots.

His gaze stalked Farr and Bride.

Squire remembered him from Nellah's last midnight dinner. It was Filkin. Lawrence Filkin. The Nova Scotian from New Glasgow. Squire and Filkin had met at Nellah's dinner party, late September. Filkin was the man who held Millburn's reward money. Filkin had a cat's eye with a yellow, gleaming focus. He did not lose sight of the Munny-Farr duo as they strolled about the floor. Squire felt a bolt of pain in his instep. The pain was from an old injury. And it alerted him to trouble. It was as though the mere willpower of Filkin could hammer the couple into the dust. Even at a distance, Squire sensed Filkin's aggression. The Mohawk paused to follow the pantomime. From across the room Filkin suggested to Farr that Miz Munny might have base origins and whoring predilections but Farr shrugged him off.

Farr was amazing tonight. He remained guarded and avoided making contacts.

The couple rambled to the corner opposite.

Squire snorted to himself. The old Fox was not going to surrender his prize on the strength of an insult. Farr saw himself as a defender of the lady on his arm and he seemed to sense Miz Munny's furbelow had room for one hero and the man to whom she clung was the man to whom she appealed. Farr waved off Filkin's crude jibes. He must have chalked up the young man's invective to jealousy and for a man like Farr, jealousy was all right. Perfectly understandable, you might say. Squire could hear Farr justifying the situation and nearly laughed. The old Fox would crow. The gamblers were rowdy. Filkin meant to create a disruption but it was not working. No one felt disrupted and one or two Irish frowned at the little fop, telling him to stop pissing into the wind.

Not Squire, though. He did not tell Filkin or anybody anything.

For *Kanien'kehá:ka* in the chicken coop, a low profile was best. He guided Cap'n toward a narrow stall. Discord was afoot and he speculated it was only a matter of time before it knocked a few heads. He would duck. Avoid trouble.

"Hallo, Chucks."

"Hey," he said. The woman who spoke was an absurdity. She had a shaved bald head, a long purple nose and a tight-laced, feather-dusted bodice, with great foul petticoats twittering underneath the hem of her skirt. She greeted the Mohawk, nice and sociable. He was interested in the woman's head and wanted to know something about it. All in good time. Vinegar Hill was a select population and soon everyone would know about the cockfight, and Mahlon Joe, the shaved-scalp expert, would show up and Joe might broach the subject with her because he was in the business. Joe might even tell the woman she should have kept a Mohawk topknot.

Squire said, "Who's the fellow taking the bets?"

"Wagers? My West, Westonbury. I'm on a tea-break, Chucks."

"Your West owns the gamecocks?"

"Why, yes sir, he does. Westonbury Fowler, he is. I'm the mis-sus. Luscious Fowler. Folks call me Lush." She indicated her shape. "I'm a party—" she jiggled her bosoms, licentious puffballs squeezed into a too small corset, "—in a package. And your name is?"

"Squire."

"You're wet, Squire."

"My coins are dry."

The lady with the shaved head and purple nose screamed with laughter. She pounded him on the back. "I'd bet on that, Chucks."

Squire gave her a weak look and he continued to the back of the barn and felt bothered.

She followed him. She trotted behind him like an obedient crit-ter. He did not stop to ask why she was after him and clucked at Cap'n to get in the stall and the three of them crowded their way in. She pressed herself flat against the man and he had nowhere, north or south of her, to squeeze away without making his distaste evi-dent. A snoot full of the fumes from an old rum butt was less raw than her breath. She was born for the pitch. She was like wallpaper. You could not peel her. Damn her. Damn his own self for wanting to gamble. He needed a drink.

CHAPTER
thirty

Vinegar Hill had several suppliers of ardent spirits.

For moonshine, buy local, Nellah always said. There was less chance of getting cat piss and if you did get a bad barrel, you knew where you got it. Teacher had tucked barrels of moonshine and a tin dipper in the loft of the barn and it seemed that Westonbury Fowler had found the best of it. The private stash. From Toronto. Gooderham and Worts. West had popped the bung on a thirty-five-gallon barrel and the travelling husband and wife team were ready to let the good times roll.

Lush had helped herself largely.

She was tottering on her feet standing still and she had Squire's chest for support but never mind. She was game. She wasn't fading into the slurs. Her speech was as lucid as her body was tippling. West and Lush, why they were parched in the throat from travelling far and wide with chickens and they felt they were entitled to the hosteller's largesse. Lush had a look of entitlement about her, no doubt about it. Coy as a boa, she said, "Mister, you smell fresh picked. Like lavender and lemons."

The Mohawk answered more civil than he felt. "Lush, you getting started or quitting? Gambling, I mean. I rub Cap'n down and join you. Place a few bets, maybe."

Lush said, "A rub down? Huh. Lucky horse. You know what, Squire? There's a little kid running about. He helps the men, so he says. He can look after your horse. But no worries. It's all fine and dandy for you, anyways. Take your time. West and me have birds a-plenty. Hey. Hide your saddlebags. Kid'll rob you blind."

"Right. Ah, what kid?" *When had Nellah hired a stable boy?*

"Him."

Purple nose and bony finger pointed down.

A redhead nudged into view.

Sliding between the loose boards of the adjoining stall, the full child emerged. He had no room to move either but he was a wiggly worm and wriggled to face them. He was dressed in a brand-new woollen cap, a navy-blue jacket with a row of wooden buttons running down each side under his lapels, a brand-new pair of broadcloth pants and, finally, wonderfully, a pair of magnificent beaded moccasins.

Pommie. Red hair, two shades lighter.

Pommie, dressed to the nines. "Squire. Hey."

Squire said, "Hey, to you, Pommie."

"I'm helpin' with horses."

"I see. Where's your little sister?"

"She is in pore l'il Lizzie Bosson's space. Up at old brick house. She lies on truckle under weepin' Lizzie's bed."

Squire couldn't help himself. "You should be abed too."

"Na-ow, mister. Not even. I am big now. Look 'ere. Yer man brung me garmints. These here are me own vety-ments, Monsieur says."

"Who says?" Lush cried, harsh. She said to Squire she feared the kid was a little scofflaw. She had seen many in her day. "Who says, I say!"

"Monsieur Peter. And it's him you kin ask." Pommie pointed to Squire.

Lush said, "We're late from the Toronto circus and, believe you me, we trust no rotten hobbledehoy. We know country folk and you are country folk. Dressed some fine there. Maybe you've some explaining—"

Leaning in for an inspection of the wooden buttons, Squire said to Pommie, "Mmm-mmm. Nice. You are the gentleman. Like your friend Mister Golden. I fetch him, if you want."

Lush was not used to feeling left out of any conversation but the mention of the Golden name changed her tune. Her faced cleared. "Pretty as the Blue Boy. Yes, sir." Hell, a boy were as honest as all that, she said, and she'd be the first to take note and congratulate him for not stealing like others of the immigrant persuasion.

In tight quarters, Squire and Pommie shuffled. They nodded at Lush, with charity, a bit forced. Squire was thinking that when it came to thieving, Lush might want to take note of the barrel she and West had bunged but, no sir, he wasn't for starting a commotion with such a lively woman, not in a room full of folks with wild eyes and wager tickets who were enjoying Teacher's unheralded generosity and more than ready to mob a wet Indian blanket for suggesting a whole barrel of whisky wasn't on the house. Nellah would drop, though. She would faint dead away at the sight of the squandering but Nellah wasn't there and how he could stop it anyway? Take more than Cook's old fry pan to bring order to a frolic like this. It would require Golden and the flintlock but who needed that? A bitter cure for a little fun. There'd be no trouble, not of Squire's making. Of the four horsemen, Squire and Farr were in the barn but Farr would be no good at stopping the shenanigans because the old Fox wanted to make love not war, or so Squire assumed, not feeling very clever.

With an expression of sheer fascination, Pommie gaped at Miz Fowler. His round blue-stone eyes were focused on her head. His gawk was firm and unwavering, like Filkin's gaze had been on Bride

Munny, but the child did not address Lush. He spoke to Squire. "Be s'kind, mister, as not t'allow me dear ma t'spy on me. She will fuss o'er me and ask me whether tiz a lickin' I'm after. Promise you won't? She'll be mad."

Squire thought not. It was the gods' grace the mouth did not have to say what the mind was thinking, which was, your ma aint looking for you, kid. "Right," he said, "I promise. I don't tell on you and you help me. Rub Cap'n down, right, Pommie?"

"Right, Sky Walker."

The Mohawk reached out to pat the boy's shoulder and the boy leaned into the gesture, clearly proud of his new friend, proud to be of useful service and ready to groom the best horse he said he'd ever seen.

Pommie was a good lad. He deserved a kindness.

Squire said, "Listen here. I get winners and you get York shillings. There's another promise, sonny."

"T'anks, mister. You do keep an eye on us."

Lush backed out of the stall. "T'anks, indeed. Come'n see me, mister! Mister fine-looking Squire. Find your way to me when you are done giving instructions to Pommie here. Winners you will have. The best you've ever known." The puffballs jiggled and the woman was delighted to catch a glimpse of them in action. "Saucy milksops, they are—"

"I like that, Lush."

"Of course you do. So does every man."

The Mohawk cleared his throat. "I mean I like to have the winners."

He grinned and hated her.

"Ho, ho. There's a brave look. You sure will," the woman said. "A couple of winners for you, Tecumseh, I promise." She retreated from the stall and returned to the fracas at the front. Her long purple nose turned to the right and to the left and she checked out who was betting. She pointed to Westonbury to warn him to watch out for one odd fellow. Men in their cups needed prodding. Stimulation and stupor rode the fine line between profits and expenses.

Pommie sighed. "Caint talk to her, Squire, not with that bald poll. Never seen a bald poll to equal that one."

Squire said, "She is hypnotic. Like a rattler. I guess we mind our manners. Staring aint so polite neither, Pommie."

"No? Why?"

With an off-hand shrug, Squire said, "Starin's for fights. And other contests." Lush and her saucy milksops disgusted and aroused him. He was reluctant but admitted it. With despair. Bart Farr and his prospects with Bride had made him envious. It was not the woman, though; it was the sex, pure and simple. Squire was a twenty-year-old male. With no Jennie. He was a disappointed man. Squire handed the body brush to Pommie, toed a stool over. "Here. You need this." The Mohawk backed himself out of the stall and he meant to follow Luscious Fowler to the cockpit and the betting area and, for sure, keep the watch out for a certain Lawrence Filkin but Pommie grabbed his arm.

"Squire, answer me this. Did old Missus Goosay sew them moccasins for me?"

"Segenauck made them."

"Oy. C'mon, mister. You kin tell me true."

"I tell you true, sonny. Missus Goosay believes you ought to know the ghost of Segenauck follows you and watches over you. A blessing, I say—" Pommie laughed at the mimicry and Squire joined in. "I say, Missus Goosay wants you to know the story of Segenauck is, uh, for the general satisfaction of Pomeroy Munny."

"There's a bit o' joy in Segenauck. In spite of she's a ghost. I git skairt. I do git a bit lonely, only sometimes, you know."

"Mmm. Know what you mean, little brother."

"Cayuga woman now, Missus Goosay, she—"

"Yeah?"

Pommie took a deep breath to make his admission. His eyes slid, first to Squire and then to the floor. "She aint directly kin, I know it. But she is me own dear granny. That's what I say."

How did the boy come by such a kind heart?

In Pommie's squalid life, where was the gentleness? Where was the fairness? How was it possible to care about anyone after the things he had seen? Squire thought he would be damned before he got involved with the Munny kids but Pommie and Chrisinny were hard to resist. With grave admiration for the boy's feelings, Squire said, "Missus Goosay knows it, Pommie. She worries about you." He felt the boy's anguish. "I say, Missus Goosay sees you hanging out in a cockpit, why, she fusses about you being here and she scolds you good—"

Lush interrupted.

The cocker's wife bellowed like a monger in Portobello Road. "Squire, mister, come on. C'mon over, Chucks. Have a drink, Tecumseh. On the house."

~

Squire tossed back another shot of Nellah's whisky and he placed his bet. A certain Mr. Peel, teetering next to his elbow, was receiving travel tips from Lush. "Niagara Falls is glorious. Measurements have been made, Mister Peel. Yes, sir, measurements. The cataract of Niagara is enormous. It exceeds in power, by forty fold, or so they say, the whole mechanical and steam force in all of Great Britain. Do not doubt me, sir. A wondrous scene. Not rainy, as you may think. Waterfall is what sprays you, Mister Peel."

The travelling Fowlers were natural hucksters. Everything on earth could be bought and sold. Everything had a price. If in the extreme off-chance you weren't a buyer for Lush and her wares or she weren't a buyer for yours, why, she would say it to you directly or indirectly as the case may be, "Piss off."

Squire saw men milling about the huckster's platform who did not realize what kind of woman they had encountered. Men like saggy Mr. Peel.

Rude, impatient, Lush Fowler listened to the smallish man with curly hair and a jaw with an estimable under-bite, an Anglo-Irish bulldog. The bulldog was affable but confused and not in carnal mode. He was spinning on his feet and his ticket was a winner, which was all that could be said for Mr. Peel, who clapped his hands over his ears to keep out the hubbub, even as he declared he wished to be amiable. Peel said, "Shhhee Niagara and die." He handed over his stub.

Lush paid him. "There you are, Mister Peel. Run along."

"Thank you, my love. I am vishiting my friend in the village of Brantford, one O.G. Millburn. Know him?"

"No."

"But, my blossom, you must. We're staying at Dumfries House."

"Is that right?"

"Yesh, my angel." Squire thought Peel was hearty. Peel was getting the brush-off and kept trying to step forward. "I'm from up Peterborough way."

"Well, Mister Peel, see Niagara and die—" A too pregnant pause. Lush added, "Before you return home."

"Say, did I tell you about Québec City?"

"No. Never did." Lush raised a heavy shoulder. She had no time to waste with the ugly effete. Betting was active and she and her husband hated travelogues in any case. They had been everywhere in the upper and lower country and she complained that travelling was all they did and she wanted to hear no more. "Listen here, Mister Peel, no more aimless jawin'."

Westonbury worked the pit and he set up the fights but Lush took the bets and she designed the odds with her own special opaque system and, with enormous confidence, she ran chalk through a number and paid out the money. It was a good arrangement, she confided to Squire. Lead the frolic in binge drinking and start the wild betting. Get gamblers drunk and drunker and at last there would be a delicious state of affairs. Lush, alone, as sober as the green salamander fresh from the flames, was ready to help you with a deal, special, just for you.

Men got blind drunk. Squire included.

Lush had the sight. She was clear-headed, the one to trust. She never made an error. That's how she reassured the customers. Hush boy, listen up. She had a special deal for the Mohawk. She had pointy canines. She licked her grinning lips.

The Mohawk tweeted back like a silly mouse, he complimented Miz Fowler and applauded her cleverness and placed his bet. He hated himself and could not help but wonder whether the mathematical genius, William Ferguson, Jennet's young brother, might have a word about Lush's competence in figuring the odds but there were no Fergusons here. No painful thoughts, either. He was the loneliest man in the world. The dog-woman sniffed his trail and he had to be on the alert. Miz Fowler had offered her special full-body deal but the Mohawk was a realist. What he really wanted was money.

He wanted to depart richer than he had come in. He had set himself quite the task. Winning money and losing her. He made another bet. Last one, he promised.

All the while, West raked fowl remains into the corner of the barn. He removed a precious steel gaff from the leg of one loser, poor old Kilmartin, moulting too much to fight, and he flung the bleeding, dubbed and wattle-less bird on a growing pile of dead or dying chickens and rubbed his hands on a bloody cloth.

"Lotsa stew for Teacher's pot, Lush. Enough for cock's army."

"Pays our spiriting bill." Lush yawned.

They were an intuitive couple. Late in the evening, as it now was, Lush was serious, stony serious, and the Ulsterman, Mr. Peel, seemed determined to be boring. Lush's eyes were for the Mohawk and she sought him out wherever he turned.

Squire tried to make himself scarce but it was getting more difficult to avoid both her and Filkin. Filkin's smell was as pervasive as sulphur. Lush was always on the lookout for Squire and ready to grab his arse or rub his leg or put her hand up his shirt and for a while he had dodged her. The Mohawk looped in and around the men who surrounded the ring. In a lumpy, dogged way, Mr. Peel was as dexterous. Lush followed Squire. Mr. Peel followed Lush. Mr. Peel caught them up as they reeled on the floor in the unconventional dance. The bulldog had taken time to pocket his coins but he jingled them, ready to remove them for re-analysis. Round and round they went.

Mr. Peel said, "Haruspex readsh guts."

Lush was nasty. "Oooh. Spittle. Haruspex, eh? Can you say that again, sir? Without spitting?" She was loud and clear and she smacked the sialoquent bulldog on the face, not very hard, but she spoke mean and quick and used her tone, *Get lost*.

The spitting, breathless fellow was slow to react but he did finally take the hint and he moseyed over to the boards to have a word with his host at Dumfries House, the plain Mr. Filkin. The bulldog held out his ticket stub and he fished around in his pocket and pulled out the coins to show them to Filkin.

Peel was disgruntled about the betting.

Squire was sure it was a useless complaint to the likes of Lawrence Filkin, who didn't care, but a familiar scene to most hucksters. Lush seemed to think so. She copped another feel up Squire's shirt and shrugged off Peel's grumbles. "See you later, Chucks. We'll have a time."

Not unlike Pommie, Squire gave her a dumfounded stare but the purple-nosed, bald, cockamamie woman missed it because she was up on her soapbox platform and back in business. She had grabbed her dirty underskirts in tight fists and climbed on the overseer's apple crates to survey the goings on. Her head shone like a beacon over the crowd. Squire was losing the battle and he had failed to steer clear of her, and Filkin, and cursed her for appearing tonight, of all nights. Her ogling tore his ratty clothes off his back. A good Methodist, Uncle Thomas Davis had told him that gambling was a sin. Lush was old Scratch. Drunk, she was funny. Sober, she was hideous. His imagination battled the image of the enticing milksops. He made himself see smelly, hairy legs under many filthy petticoats and he shrank before her. Worse, there was Filkin, standing nearby, shoulder-to-shoulder.

Filkin sneered.

Squire sneered.

It was difficult to keep avoiding the Nova Scotian and that was bad. Too much sneering was stupid and Squire had no time for it and he wondered what would happen now that Mr. Peel had shared his concerns about the game's honesty with Filkin. But no volcano erupted. Not yet. Everyone reeled and turned and danced and moved around and around the action.

CHAPTER
thirty-one

Lawrence Filkin appeared unimpressed with Mr. Peel's coins and ticket stubs and he looked more disgusted than before with the poor man, who was staying at his sister's place, the Millburns' refined and ever so lovely Dumfries House.

The bulldog scowled and he lurched after Squire and called to him, the man who wanted to melt into the night. Squire thought getting a few coins into your poke shouldn't be this hard. Finally, the Ulsterman shuffled to the crib boards and leaned on them. The poor man prepared to study, one last time, the entrails of the birds. With his biceps taut, the bulldog firmed the slats that were shaking under his armpits. He chewed his lip and he was altogether sickish looking, as though he had sailed the seven seas.

"I'll tell you the future. There's gonna be one helluva cockfight, West, my dear."

West looked up from the floor with weary cynicism, mouthed *sure thing*, and wandered over to the cages to count the non-molting cocks, penned for tomorrow's fights, to see whether he had enough. He tried to whip up the crowd's sympathy but no one, intoxicated or teetotal, could observe the growing mess of dead and wounded fowl in the corner of the barn and work up a bead of sympathy for a cocker's troubles. West said he was full tired. Squire thought West was full of shit and his feeling seemed suddenly contagious.

Everyone copied Filkin. Men sneered. Maybe West should leave the chicken business, they shouted, or control his wife. Get better cocks.

West Fowler sighed, bit his lip and freed the last two birds. His manner was agreeable but Squire suspected old West was anything but agreeable. "Last fight. Here's Ace, son of Darrig," West said. "And t'other fella, this fella, what's-his-name? Lush, what's his name?"

"Name's Marion."

West was tall. Not fat but heavy. He had a stiff spine. He walked tipped forward with his elbows pushed back. His arms were like the bent-backward limbs of a locust. The travelling life wasn't easy, he complained, but the wife did not mind. She liked meeting new people. West looked at Squire. West said he didn't have the energy to go out on a purchasing spree tonight. West and Lush were pastoralists but the flock was chickens, not wistful sheep, and the melodious birds didn't sing madrigals, they crowed. Who cared about cockers? West asked anyone who would listen. So what, he answered himself when nobody would. Farmers cared. Some farmers near the Hill raised birds and they held onto a few rummy males and took the chance that the likes of Fowler might wander down their lanes. Buyers such as West bought up aggressive cocks. Rural people were glad to sell. Chicken farmers couldn't keep the damn roosters in the yard because the birds fought with everything in sight and crowed a racket at sunrise, as if dawn was the resurrection, and most farms couldn't be bothered to run a game. It was a risky business and wagering attracted louts and canallers, if not worse: Christians.

Christians were everywhere. They interfered with local economies. West could tell you that supply and demand was the best policy. The free market benefitted all, didn't you know? Gamers bought cocks and farmers made a pound.

Squire willed West to shut up. What was there to complain about? It was a lucrative show. For the pitchman. The pit won. Taking a cut from the top, the Fowlers came out ahead of any gambler, someone like him, or Mr. Peel. Pitchmen didn't care who won bets. They won all the same, all the time.

What kind of fool was Squire to keep at it?

He was done. He started to leave but he stopped as he heard the final fight was up on the board. Everyone was jeering at West and his complaining about the hard life. Both cocks wore metal spurs but Ace had a proud strut, unlike Marion what's-his-name, and the sporting Miz Fowler had a hard time to check the surge of inured gamblers who knew the score by now and wanted to bet on Ace, never mind the odds. "New one is Marion. From the Morrison farm," she said to Westonbury one more time. "Ace is the old cock."

For Squire, it was a notion, betting on Ace, but he decided to pass. Odds were lousy. He was tired, more tired than West.

The pitman upset him. So did the bulldog, Mr. Peel.

So did Lush.

She bothered him because she was mostly fascinating, as predators are. Gamecocks did not throw fights but Lush was a good guesser and Squire was a good reader. She understood chicken hearts and the kind of gaffs and bracelets they wore. Squire noted her shifting about on the stacked apple crates, as she twitched a purple nose here or a waggled her baldness there, and he managed to do all right on his bets, even earning decent returns on a few. From her platform, Lush had winked at him and she had pressed her bodice with her right hand and splayed her hand under her breasts. She was eager to make a connection and the best way to keep her out of his bed was simple and ancient. She would seek; he would hide.

Squire intended to return to the inn, slip into his room, lock the door and hit the hay. He'd won a few extra foreign coins in the mix but nothing much, some York shillings for Pommie and some American dollars. He had more money than before but the barn was whirling from left to right. His brain did not collect the scene into one frame and he was drunk on another planet trying to figure out which was left and which was right.

Farr and Bride had disappeared.

Pommie too.

Time to call it a night.

He thought he had hustled to the edge of the action and he thought he had been stealthy and he had moved to the open door, all set to run through the rain and the muck to reach the safety of his room in the inn, away from the barn, but Mr. Peel had seen him and grabbed his arm. "Why d'we bet anywaysh?" The bulldog held on to Squire and held out his other paw. "Look here. I won fights and I've lesh than what I started with."

The man was in a bad way.

He coughed and sprayed saliva all over Squire, who wobbled to avoid contagion.

The Mohawk was mild and he patiently endured Peel but raised his arm. "Brother, I never see your stubs."

Bulldog lowered his head, his bulging eyes stared at his hand, and he counted and re-counted his money. Brain-addled with more drink than he could have handled in twenty lifetimes, the man kept repeating his numbers. He was resolute. It was a serious matter, he said, and he knew something was rotten. The gaze came up, wanting to seek a source for blame. Bulldog's jaw further protruded to show he was truculent, not afraid, and the hand of fate tapped the shoulder of a certain fellow, one hearty, ill-favoured Shiner named Patrick Connelly. Everyone knew Paddy was a Shiner from the Gatineau.

"Paddy. Yeth, I mean you, my jewel." Mr. Peel was cuckoo and swayed like a pendulum. "D'ye have your proper stubs or have you stolen mine? So? Have you?"

Paddy Connelly was in his usual state of high dudgeon. "So shut yer gob, Mister Cavan blazin' Orange Peel." He took Peel by the lapels and shook him. "Check your own bitty stub."

Squire bobbed under bulldog's sightlines and he backed to the barn ramp and reasoned he could make a run for it and he almost did but he didn't, not quite, because trouble had truly arrived. Ardent spirits had played havoc with Paddy Connelly's judgment and he'd said something ill-advised to poor Mr. Peel, who was weak-limbed and harmless despite his under-bite and his perpetual whining. It wasn't fair. Men shuffled their eyebrows and raised their feet. Unfair. Unfair. Nerves had frayed.

Lawrence Filkin saw his chance and he grabbed it.

Filkin was excited. He shouted, "It is the savage, boys! Over there. He cheats." A pale Neo-Glaswegian digit pointed first to Lush and then to Squire.

"Who cheats?" An outraged voice asked.

"The Indian," Filkin said. "I saw it. I saw her signalling him. The cheating Hottentot. Do not allow him to get away with it."

"Cheatin'? That aint right, chief."

Filkin was juiced. He warbled, "Get the mongrel. Bring down the gaming house of the black whore. Get them."

An echo. "Get the whore. Get the redskin."

Someone else cried, "I sees 'em too. Yessir. I seen 'em. They's all in cahoots. Even them ol' cocks take the fall."

Another shouted, "Where's the skinny blonde gal with the purdy face? I'd cheat fer her."

The murmur of drunks grew loud.

Was Lush a cheater?

Was Lush a cheater hired by Teacher to rob them of their hard-earned pay packets? Was the game fixed? In the event, no one sought his better self to ask how. How easy was it to put in the fix with a bunch of chickens? Which farmer's cock took the fall? Nobody cared for nothing, neither for reason nor intuition. An accusation with the innocuous poof of a wee ladyfinger firecracker had started it because drinkers had spent the night oiling their screaming throats and, to top it off, the purple-nosed woman who had figured the long odds, the one who had pushed her sleazy puff-balls into every conversation and into every face all night long, well, what was she? A cheat? Was it true? Was she a cheat?

Irishmen were not milksops.

They were pugilists. Ready to be whipped into a frenzy and, lo! It was like fair day at Toomyvara. Knives, a knave, a bunged barrel and there was the mix for a frolic.

The Haruspex won her wager.

There was a brawl. A doozy. Squire was caught. He had not been quick enough to escape the eruption. Should he run now, every man Jack of them would take him for a coward, and he was not a coward. Reluctant. Aloof. A wanderer. A drunk, maybe. Yeah, very, very drunk. But not a coward. Not when it came to fighting the likes of Filkin. Tehawennihárhos hated the Glaswegian's boarding-school accent. There was no Jeddah Golden loitering around to save the day but goddam the Snowman and his three-fathom musket, well, goddam them all, and he didn't need Jeddah. Not this time. In his bleary state Squire vowed to go at it alone. The cocks had at it. Ace wasn't in the pit. Neither was what's-his-name, Marion. He could hear the Snowman a-sayin' it, life is hard but being stupid makes it harder.

In the pit fighting for his life was Squire Tehawennihárhos.

CHAPTER
thirty-two

Special brew.

Just for you.

Squire was dreaming. He had fallen asleep in his chair. He had a vision about chickens and geese. The chickens were dead, floating and whirling, like a lady's feather boa. They floated on the surface of a dark and rippled crazy river. He was in the river with the chickens. Next thing, geese pulled him into the night sky. He had swum underwater and he'd tied a cedar-bark rope around his wrist and around the feet of the geese but had had to come up for air. Ahhhh. He had startled the wild birds. They took off and pulled him along. In a V-formation. Up and away. His wrist could not hold the rope and the knot came undone and he fell back into the water. He fell into the mess of chickens. Luscious Fowler was there, treading water, waiting, waiting. "Hello, Chucks," she cried. "Come thither, turdy guts." In a jiggle, Lush was swimming. She used bold strokes. She was gaining. Inexplicably, he felt the rope tighten around his wrist. His wrist hurt and his instep pounded but he tried to make himself swim faster so she would not catch him but he could not do it and he struggled, unable to move. He ached. He couldn't swim.

Someone had hooked him like a bigmouth bass.

"Sky Walker! Wake up." Pommie woke him, yelling from the doorway.

"Unhhhh?"

"Your granny Polly, she wants you to drink t'special brew, Squire, right this minute. Tiz a splendid cure, she says. Cook sends it in his very own cup." Pommie added, with hope on his face, "Hey, Squire, you ate ham 'n eggs for breakie?"

"I ate like a Yorkshire hog."

Pommie was tickled and he laughed and moved gingerly into the screened room. The latest treat was in a thick-rimmed and gaudy purple teacup and matching saucer. Squire had seen Alfie's cup hanging on a clipped nail in the pantry cupboard and he wondered why the Cook's own china was in use. The youngster inched forward with care. He took baby steps with pains not to spill because the drink was hot. A steam cloud rose to make him walk slower.

"Tiz them twinges she's all for fixing. Bad, uh?" Pommie's face was far too sympathetic to be comforting.

Squire grunted.

"Polly says, 'Drink it!'"

"She's—imperious. You too."

"Best to drink, anyhow, mister. You skairt us some, y'know. You have bin conked out on and off. For a whole week. Coz of pain."

Squire sniffed the liquid. Dried raspberry leaves. White-willow bark. Feverfew leaves. Honey. Lots of honey. Something else, echinacea root. Bound to cure the worst hangover. Or tonsillitis. A week? With shivering bravado, Squire said, "What pain?"

He sipped and Pommie hovered by the invalid's chair. "You punched back at them bowsies." He showed Squire the fighting boxer's stance and air boxed and jumped around the screened porch. "You decked a couple, I think."

"Little brother, thank God for that."

"But there's a certain cheeky gobshite, looks like he's got pink fard on his kisser, and he took it to you, mister, he took it to you proper. He were kicking you." Pommie was distressed and he declared he felt some awful bad about it. "You tried, anyways."

Squire assessed the feeble commendation. He had tried. He nodded. There were dozens of Irish. They were smashed and they were riled about things, things unfathomable, feuds from the old country and feuds from this one. There were Blackfeet and White-feet. Blackfeet were scabs. They collaborated with mine owners back in Ireland and got their feet dirty with coal dust, and their opponents, well, they were Whitefeet. They were mad at each other. And there were the Tipperary factions. They were just mad. Not to be overlooked were the Dublin Catholics and Ulster Protestants and they were mad as hell.

He was one lone half-assed Anglican of the *Kahnyen'kehàka*.

Pommie affirmed the obvious. "Was waaay too many, Squire, and nobody on your side." The youngster found expression by giving a quick pat to the wool blanket that was covering Squire's knees. He said it was the one-sidedness that had shocked him, by gully, and that was a for certain. "Mister Jeddah says bettin' odds of thirty-to-one is goldern nuts. Mister Farr agrees. Meself, I'm for wishing you hadn't bin hurt so grave."

"Me too."

"Keep drinkin'. Tea'll fix pain. C'mon, drink 'er up. Down the hatch."

Squire finished the last bit of Polly's intriguing bittersweet blend. His right wrist was in a splint and wrapped tight in strips of unbleached mill cotton. He was forced to balance the chinaware in his left hand and he passed cup and saucer to Pommie and sought to act unruffled, especially about having to take the grandmother's medicine as though he were a cooing, paleface namby-pamby, but the cup teetered on the precarious saucer. He spoke out. "Hup." He stretched out his arm. "Careful, Pommie. It's Alfie's cup. It's hard to figure but he's annoyed with us if I break it." In reaching to balance his body and the china, Squire jostled his ribs. It took a second to catch his breath. A shriek of horror cut into his chest and an uncommon bleat escaped. "Ah!" he said. He grimaced. "That pain."

Pommie said, "Yeah, mister. That pain. Sprained wrist. Wee guts bruised. You're injured up and down left side. You broke coupla ribs where the yeller gobshite with them black boots kicked you. He kicked you fifteen maybe twenty times. He kicked you till Mister Golden ran in and offered to shoot him between the horns. That slowed kickin' to a smart halt."

"Mister Golden? Where does Mister Golden come from to save the day? Uh, Pommie? Tell me that."

"I fetched him up from Miz Nellah's room. I fetched him and Mister Farr and Alfie Williams. Mister Farr is up at t'inn. Me ma is in room with him but I reckon she don't want to see the likes of me. Anyways, Mister Farr yanks up his trousers so's he kin help us out and Alfie runs up to t'barn with his fry pan. Monsieur, well, monsieur is a bruiser, eh? He hears the fuss. He comes a-gallopin' like big old Diablo, runnin' over from Cave and afore you know'd it, all's there. Everybody's fightin'."

"Little brother, what about the Fowlers?"

"Gone, Squire. Gone." Pommie seemed appalled to have to say it. "Gone as soon as fight starts. I 'ate 'em."

"Do you see them go?"

"Yup, mister, sure an' I do. I sleep in stall next to Cap'n. I wakes up sudden and watches 'em two packin' it up. They shove t'cocks in cages. They steals the whisky barrel. 'Whot?' I says to 'em. 'You stoppit, now!' Bald cow jumps over t'crates and on t'chicken wagon and they skedaddles. Wagon beats it down lane yonder. T'rew mud, even. To somewheres safe." Pommie jumped twice in recognition of their cowardice. "Ha! I bet you that's true. Squire, Ann says old Lush do shave her head on account of wee lousies."

Lousies. Lice. Squire was sore but grateful because Lush Fowler and her wretched milksops were gone. Ribs notwithstanding, he could breathe. "Lousies, eh?"

"Unh-huh, and Cook and Mister Golden and Mister Farr and Missus Polly, oh yeah, and Monsieur Peter, they stop t'brouhaha. Mister Golden brings his old long rifle. Cook bangs his fry pan like a steeple clanger. Irish go from fightin' you into fightin' one t'other. Monsieur Peter, he is in t'middle of them and waves his huge fists and his knife. Mister, the Frenchman brings a bowie knife, this big!" Pommie demonstrated by making a fisherman's exaggerated spread with his hands. He laughed at himself. He narrowed his hands some.

"And Polly brings what? Her tongue? A willow switch?"

"Yessir. And a pitchfork. After gobshite stops kickin' you, Missus Polly does poke him good and hard in his arse." Pommie laughed. "Maggie's fussin'. She cries and cries. She and Lizzie. They cries in pantry."

"Ah."

Pommie was saddened by the outcome. "Our men hoick you to your bed and give you over to Missus Polly."

"Mmm. Little brother—"

"Yeah?"

"The—gobshite, he kicks me till I am dead?"

"I reckon he would of."

"He would kill me?"

"So I 'spect. Not just me, Squire. Mister Golden and Mister Farr, they 'spects it too. I kin tell from their looks but I hear—"

"What do you hear?"

"Fight's done and your men carts you back to inn." Pommie leaned in close to his ear. No one else was around to hear him but Squire caught the significance, a boy's overhearing one adult's low conversation to another adult about something profane. Tinged with the melodrama of a Miss Ince, Pommie said, "Mister Jeddah, he says to Mister Farr—" Pommie growled down in his throat to imitate the Snowman, "'Jayzus, Bart.'" Pommie coughed but started up again, his voice even lower. "'Fuckin' whoreson meant bizness. He were a-hell-bent on a-murderin' the kid. That refined sonofabitch better watch hisself.'"

"And what does Mister Farr say?"

"He says—" Here, Pommie raised his tone. "'I hear you. Two more boots to the noggin and wham. It's all done and over. Tehawen-nihárhos floats his way skyward to chat with his pa.'"

The Mohawk and the boy looked at each other and they pondered the violent incident and did it along individual lines, one sorry to be beaten up and one planning a revenge.

Kicking a fallen one took a forceful mentality and a careful husbanding of energy at every step, so to speak. Squire wondered what kind of rage incited a man to kick another man to death, to kill a stranger whom he didn't actually know, except by sight.

For his part, Pommie murmured about a plan. What kind of saw-toothed, deep-pit, clever and devious booby trap might he dig? Right outside the Cyclops to ambush the yeller gobshite if he ever dared to show his face again at Teacher's establishment.

"You save my life, young Pommie. You are a brave boy for almost ten. Thank you, Pomeroy Munny."

"Welcome, Sky Walker. I'll bring you s'more of t'special brew. Hope you git better soon, mister. You lookin' better, eh?"

Pommie edged away from Squire.

Once past the chair, the boy travelled lickety-split to the door and opened it with a great show of caution and went out. He had a firm grasp on the cup and saucer and he was bold and grinned and, without a sound, he waved the china at the Mohawk to play pretend catch. Oops. Might drop it.

A little boy lived inside there after all, thought Squire.

Where were the others, though?

A jade and leafy maple branch, which was a precious sight and a green holdout against dry leaves, scratched against the window screen.

Squire was in the brick house, in the upstairs veranda off Nellah's bedroom.

After breakfast Polly had made him get up from his bed in the Cyclops Inn to walk through the yard, up the stairs, and through Nellah's russet room to the stuffed armchair on the porch. Polly had propped up Nellah and the baby in Nellah's bed because the infant was nursing but there was no stopping to chat. Polly shoved him through the bedroom and outside to the screened porch.

He had wanted to sleep. He had wanted to sleep forever.

Polly would not have it.

Mahlon Joe had brought him marijuana. Joe had brought plenty. Squire remembered mixing it and putting in his pipe and smoking it.

No more, said Polly.

He had to deal with the pain and there was no time like the present. She got him out of the stuffy small-window room at the inn and she brought him here to enjoy the sunshine and fresh air at Teacher's house where she could keep a closer eye on both of her patients. She had covered the Mohawk's knees like he was an ancient one but he had no strength to tell her how much he hated it and, anyway, she threatened more broken ribs if he moved an inch. He had obliged, fallen asleep and dreamed about geese.

The arrival of the merciful Pommie had arrested the terrible dream.

He was content to visit with Pommie and he almost fell asleep again after the boy left but at the last second he was conscious of something. Even in those hours Squire had saturated the pain by smoking weed he had wondered why he had seen neither hide nor hair of the horsemen.

They knew where Bobby John was.

Missus Goosay had told him and he had told them. Goddam. Now they would collect the reward without him.

Every decision he had made stunk to high heaven and, although he was sure that was what had happened, he had to check it out.

~

He got up from the chair.

He walked as stiff as a zombie.

He wanted to avoid unnecessary exertion and tried not to put pressure on the old rib cage and he walked from the porch outside Nellah's bedroom and tapped with a light touch on her door. He waited a minute to hear a faint, "C'mon in," and he peered through the open door and, casual-like, leaned back on the doorframe.

Nellah was lying in bed and yet, being Teacher, she was busy embroidering red holly-berry clutches, green-leaf beads and white curlicue pearls on the bodice of a navy woollen skating outfit. The costume was for a villager, one Miss Permelia Wilkes, who had promised to pay Nellah a handsome sum for facilitating some fashionable skating on the pond. Woollen fabrics were Nellah's choice today. A white woollen bed-cape and woollen blankets cocooned her. Squire recognized Polly's bundling. Nellah's sole nod to fashion was a multi-coloured silk scarf. She had wrapped it around her hair and tied it tight, many times, like a turban. The scarf covered her injuries and her hair, which she said she had not straightened with them agonizing hot irons since the attack and, she'd offered, maybe she never would use them awful things ever again. Restored to a tolerable state, though thinner in the face than she had been before she met them brave Warriors, Nellah smiled at Squire and he appreciated the sarcasm. Every time he saw the woman, he paused to appreciate her beauty.

Her skin was clear and transparent, like maple syrup.

Teacher pointed to a baby sleeping in a drawer and made her voice into a murmuring chanson. "Squire. Whoaa. Lookit them bruises on your head, hon."

Squire nodded. He stated the obvious and kept his eyes averted. "From the fight."

"The trouncin'."

Ah, yes. Teacher. Beautiful but direct. Always direct.

Squire said, "That is what I hear."

"You would be all dishraggy, bless your heart."

He laughed and groaned, modest. She had no call to worry about him. "Not done yet."

"Lord of mercy, we was worried."

Squire would have laughed off her comment but his ribs hurt. "You don't fuss, ma'am. You gotta get strong yourself."

"Why, goldern, hon. We would be tough'uns, unh?"

"So it seems. At least, you are. A tough'un for sure." His ribs were shrieking and he gritted his teeth. "Baby Pearl is well?"

"Yup. Young'un's well. Be like sugah. Sweet thing."

"Well, then—I intrude."

Nellah waved off the mere idea. "Fiddle-faddle. You would be welcome, Squire. Always welcome. And you brung me Aughguaga Polly."

"Ah, the grandmother. I am happy she helps."

"I calculate she he'ped us both."

That was over the top. "Mmmm." He should sound more gracious. Polly was family. "Yup, she does have her healing ways, Nellah."

He shifted his weight to stop his wrist from throbbing. "One question, if you'd be so kind? I have not seen the men."

"Unh-huh."

"Where is Jeddah?"

"Who? Where?"

"Yes. Jeddah. Where are the men, Nellah?"

The dark-skinned Virginia-born Teacher was refined in appearance and intonation, by far more refined than her kinsman, the fair-skinned, fair-haired, har-haring Jeddah Golden, and she would tell you that she was cottoning on to gentility real fast and she hardly ever dropped the haitch in "help" or added ns's to "you" anymore but she had the exact same shilling-sized dimples as her cousin. Against the rumour, Appalachian dimples, unlike Irish eyes, were not forever smiling. It took a minute of deep-dimpled concentration to finish the mother of pearl beads on a delicate curlicue and even then Nellah paused too long.

She said, "Where? Unh-huh. Well, I reckon they would be 'round here somewheres."

"Try again." Squire waited. Nothing. "Please tell me the truth, will you?"

Nellah pursed her lips. "Truth? Unh-huh. I will tell you, Squire." She looked up at him. "You aint a-gonna like it, I expect. You told our Jeddah that Bobby John were hidin' out in Oneida village near Caledonia. At his sister's place?"

"Yes."

"You said Bobby would be a-stayin' there with her. In the bush."

"Yeah." Certain realization. "No." Just so. They were gone. He had feared it.

"Unh-huh. Jeddah and Peter, gone yesterday. First off, two days back, Farr took Maggie home to tavern in Canboro and, the others, they would be a-plannin' to meet up at Farr's so's Peter kin have a day or two with Sarah and try to persuade her to take him back and let him come home again and then, when they all get together, they would be a-settin' out after your cousin."

"They leave me here?" His voice rose.

Nellah put her finger over her lips and pointed to the drawer. "Baby. *Shhh-shhhht.*"

The turban slipped to the left. She put down her complicated embroidery to fix her hair. She tucked in stray strands and secured them tightly under the silky cover. Squire tactfully backed off. He had the sense to button his lip because his situation, bad to him, had nothing to do with an injured Nellah. He turned to hobble back to the old armchair on the screened veranda and muttered to himself, feeling pissed at the deep pains in his ribs for cutting off his breath and pissed at the men for the sake of his empty purse. "Yeah. Shhhhit all right."

∼

He picked up the blanket to put over his knees and sat down. He shivered. Anyone would shiver. The sunshine was brilliant but the air inside the porch was bone-chilling and fifty pounds of English sterling had just upped and flown out the screen window. A wayward breeze blew by, altogether too cheerful, and again the green leaves bowed and rasped at the screen, reminding him of what had flown out.

Squire should never have repeated to the Snowman what Missus Goosay had told him about Bobby's whereabouts. He cursed again. The horsemen had saved his life and they put him down on his bed, forgot all about him, and left without him. What good was that?

He was all right to ride.

Why didn't anyone bother to wait for him?

He leaned forward and his aching ribs reminded him to rest back and quit complaining. He couldn't ride the stuffed armchair let alone sit on Cap'n. Squire sniffed his pits. He smelled sick. He wasn't lavendery. Or citrusy. He did not have the scent of elixirs. He sniffed again. Poultice, sweat and blood. Polly must have rubbed his cuts and bruises with what she called stinky Davis, wild strawberry, ginseng and coneflower salve, and he knew he needed a showerbath but he did not have the energy to face it and, for the first time in a long time, he turned away from the healing waters of the crazy river. The thought of a fat drop of cold water on his hide made him quake like a lily.

He must have a fever. He was thirsty.

In a minute or two he would steal down to the kitchen to chew the fat with Cook and maybe get the real story about the fight and the gobshite.

Pommie was clever.

He had seen right through the likes of Lawrence Filkin, that was sure.

Golden also knew Filkin for what he was. The buff fella from New Glasgow and the killer intent of the black riding boot upset Squire just as much as the missing posse. What a mess.

Polly's revolting tisane was effective, though, and he finished another cup of the brew that Pommie had just sneaked into his room, special, just for him, and drifted on the wayward breeze to the land of Dekanahwida. Nose in the cold air, the rest of him hibernated under the woollen blanket. Awful throbbing in his head, his wrist, his ribs. He had problems. Big problems. But he fell asleep and never found his way downstairs to talk to Cook.

thirty-three

Three long weeks in October

He was stuck, physically, in the present during his convalescence; moreover it seemed as though his days of wandering were numbered. It was a pause in his life, a period to reflect on the past, to turn the clock backwards, to seek out hints from a remembered time to help him plan the future but nothing brilliant struck him. Fact was, he was bored to death.

The summer Squire turned fifteen, he had left home. For five years, he had lived a nomad's life. He was footloose in the Canadas. Europeans, who would flip arse over kettle-pot at someone's calling them nomads, because they were "explorers," were everywhere in the upper country and they stuffed their pockets and saddlebags with mechanical aids for plotting and more or less stumbled all over each other even as they calculated the lay of the land.

Uncle Pat had sneered.

Pat used to clench his clay pipe in his teeth and squeeze or bend the poker cards and blow white rings to the ceiling and, half-amused and half-angry, he'd say that white men had shit for brains. Simple logic, he'd reckon. If Europeans weren't fucking nomads, well, by God, what were they doing here? Why hadn't they stayed put in their medieval villages, over there, wherever over there was? Explorers? Pah. Nomads. They were nomads. Nomads or not, Europeans drew their maps with painstaking effort. They had no talent. They were not possessed of the natural mapmaker's recollection.

Tehawennihárhos had memorized the landscape. He knew where he was, easy, like he had grown a map unit in his head but he never explained his talent to uncomprehending minds, who had never thought to ask him anyway. Good thing they didn't ask because he wouldn't know what to say to inept people. It was just like Uncle Pat said about the strangers. They were nomads without a mental map. He did not know how or why his mind created a map anymore than a singer can explain pitch or Jake Hearenhodoh Venti could tell you how to pound out complex rhythms on a drum and Uncle Pat didn't know why, when they were cartographic simple-tons, the Europeans were so fucking everywhere.

Over a year ago, the Mohawk had bought two Canadian horses in Otonabee.

He, Cap'n and Poco had slashed their way through the upper country and picked up jobs wherever they could. It was not hard to find work. He could swing an axe with accuracy, like Jake Venti could swing a tomahawk, and his all-purpose horses were useful at stump pulling and in drawing heavy logging wagons. The British colony was in frenzy over construction, plank roads, tall buildings, great canals and land-clearance and, although Squire was the dreaded Indian vagrant, he-who-comes-to-steal had the right skills to make himself welcome in any village or town or mill. A young chopper with a strong back cruised through life in the colony and, better, made no female commitments.

Until Jennie. Stuck. Committed.

Committed to Jennet Ferguson. And the idea of her.

He had to sit quiet day after day on the screened-in porch at Nellah's and think about how stuck he was. Polly's orders. He sat under the proverbial apple tree, which, in his case, was a dark-varnished, thin-planked ceiling. He stared at planks all day, every day. He memorized the width of them. He estimated the length of them. He shut his eyes because he couldn't give himself over to studying planks a second longer but they were burned into the back of his eyelids. Over and above the length and width of the boring porch ceiling, and being bored, several things bothered him.

There was a rumour floating in the tavern. There was a serious threat to the security of the Hill folk because someone was set to grab Nellah's land. The threat to the Hill people made him feel sick but what made him feel sicker was the thought of his and Jennet's fending off the entire Western world.

If a miracle happened and they got together, where would they live?

Still, even worse than a couple of sticky adult problems, and the thing that was the most plaguing, was the little problem right in front of him. Every time Pommie brought Squire food and drink, he wondered about the children. What the hell's gonna become of you and your little sister, kid? Munny kids. Poor Nellah. Himself. All their futures were ripe for doubts.

His mind kept circling around the problem of him and Jennet. The voice of the Fergusons' Loyalist associate, a certain Jeffrey Amherst Pickle, boomed in Squire's ears. An Indian at table? What next? Shall we set a place for Rover? Squire should let it go. He should let thoughts of Jennet and him and their union fly out the window of the screened porch.

She had abandoned the Hill.

Why should he worry about where they would live?

Why should he go after her?

But he did worry. He did imagine himself going after her. He wondered what would happen afterward. Where could a so-called mixed couple live?

What open-minded society would have them? Jennet hailed from the sermonizing folk. Squire had no reason to believe that Uxbridge Presbyterians were any different from the locals. Busybodies, the likes of Pommie's Baptist Ladies' Knitting Circle, poked their pointy noses into the parlour, the kitchen and the bedroom. Into the closet and up the flue. A busybody could smell a sin at fifty paces. A busybody sniffed into everybody's nooks and crannies and knew when the Devil farted and Jennet Ferguson was at home among them.

Could he live among her people?

It would be difficult.

Could she live among his people, the Vinegar Hill people? Why would she want to? The glorious, stressed, motley and dappled Hill folks, what were they to her? She needed none of their inclusive camaraderie. Sure, Nellah's place offered him a settled community and a life away from pure red and *pure* white settlements where he was surely unwanted but what about Jennet? What would the Hill offer her, other than the memory of Meatface?

Nellah was blunt.

She would tell him the truth.

Polly had told him he had but a few convalescing days left. After those long days were over he was allowed to join the others, apparently they were always working in or near the dining room, and he decided he would speak to Teacher. He would put to her the question, the bothersome question. What chance did Jennet and Squire have? He wanted to hear Nellah say it. *You best forgit that l'il ol' gal.*

CHAPTER
thirty-four

"Pon my word, hon," Nellah raised her kaleidoscope eyes, "foller yer own lights."

She had her head bent low over the ledger and she chewed her pink lip. Next to the ledger, Nellah had spread out her book of days, on the side near the kitchen. At the far end of the table, Squire was gutting the Lake Erie walleye Pommie had just purchased at the village market. Underneath the stinking fish bowels Squire had put a newspaper and he spied yet another follow-up Seeum Johnston column about Mrs. Octavius Millburn and her stolen Wedgwood. He flipped another batch of innards and bladders and scales onto the paper.

Nellah's homespun bandages were slipping again.

She looked rakish, like a Bahamian buccaneer.

Her sherry-brown eye was covered. Her hazel eye was peeping out from under the gingham bandanna and she brushed away droopy cloths to concentrate on the post-robbery economic realities of the inn. Polly was going to remove the dressing tomorrow and Squire wondered whether Teacher would continue to wear the colourful headscarves she had worn over the homespun. She seemed to want to hide her scar. They had heard nothing from the horsemen. It had been over three weeks and Nellah said she was expecting them. Shortly. Anytime.

The men had covered a lot of ground and they had a lot to do. Just the same, tonight or tomorrow night, she reckoned they should be home on the Hill and she hoped Jeddah had collected on her markers.

Local farmers owed her plenty. They drank up her whisky like the walleye fish and it was time for everyone to pay up. Nellah was in a mood. She wasn't buying excuses. Squire had asked about going after Jennie. He had said he suspected he likely wouldn't do it.

She'd said something like, do what you want.

He half-raised a raven-wing brow because she was so damn pert. "I ask for your help but it's not much. A little advice is all."

Nellah relented. All right. Advice. "You fuss and fuss, Squire. Fret too much. Tsk."

Did Nellah *tsk* at the numbers she ciphered or at him? He could be spiny. "I fret. Yeah. So would any man. I put myself in an embarrassing situation, Nellah, if it's me she runs from."

The fire in the dining room's hearth sputtered and sank into itself and dying coals glowed friendly and warm. Embers snuggled in a radiant bed of powdery ash. It was early on the crisp autumn evening and the adults had things to do in all the buildings and in the course of doing them they met at the cross-paths. They liked to work and be busy and chit-chatted and joked and enjoyed sliding back into normalcy. Nellah was better and Squire was back working.

Aughguaga Polly was outside sitting in the weedy yard. She sat in the dirt, sorted through herbs and leaves and fretted over the potency of bark and berry. She was fed up with Vinegar Hill's apparent complacency in the face of the threat from the greedy villagers and she'd let everyone know it. The villagers should hear from her. That would give them reason to back off.

Lizzie pushed drinks in the Cave and she showed travellers to their rooms. Ann too. The Cave was bouncing. So was the inn. The women had to hustle over from the brick house to the tavern with hard-boiled eggs and more smoked pigeon pie and beet-beer and more ale pitchers to stay on top of things because, and it frightened them all, they were suffering financially. They needed the coin. Real coin was tight for Nellah and a good night at the Cave helped, provided of course there were no Fowlers to move in and destroy the place. Bride was occupied. With Tacks. Pommie and Chrisinny were already abed and notwithstanding a feeble protest they had been ready for sleep and fallen dead to the world.

For the first time, Squire had mentioned Jennet's name to someone.

He had told Nellah he felt troubled. He and Jennie were, well, poles apart. Irreconcilable. He said Jennie misunderstood things. All in all, he said, he should listen to Aughguaga Polly and pay better attention to Maggie Walker.

Nellah did not look up again. She did not appear to have a module for gauging the potential embarrassment of a philosophical man, especially when she did not believe him. She shook her head, pointed to an entry in the ledger and shouted in the direction of the kitchen. "Alfie, come on in here. What in hell would be a-goin' on? How many barrels of whisky did disappear? Where'd be the Gooderham? My supplies is nearly out and they was thicker'n warts on a pickle." The volume of spirits the Cave had sopped up astounded her and she shook her head and frowned at the Mohawk. "Yer gal would be a treasure. Man oughter seek her. Find the treasure." Teacher glared at the kitchen and she barked at Alfie.

Squire muttered. "This aint a treasure hunt, Nellah."

"She aint a-runnin' from you, Squire, 'n you goldern well a-knowed it. You got to go find 'er, hon, an' I 'spect you would best be gittin' a move on."

Alfie shouted back. He was kneading bread dough for break-fast. *'E didn't know wha' whisky dee 'ad used. 'E couldn't be everywhuz.*

Squire cleared his throat. He said, "Cook, he don't know what's goin' on with the whisky." He gave a trenchant whack with his knife and sliced off a fish head. His wrist did not beak at him. "The Fowlers help themselves."

"Jehoshaphat! Mind table, uh? Golderned cockers. Grifters."

"Yeah."

"I will remember that thievin' bit of business, West Fowler." Nellah returned to musing and tapped the quill-pen feather against her lips. "Unh, Squire. Lush, she come after yer?"

The Mohawk was cool. "I handle her."

Nellah gave him the disbelieving half-eyelid and unmindful she stroked her injured head and crossed her eyes to be funny to soften her nosiness. "Hmmm. I knowed all about her."

"No surprise about that, Teacher." He stretched his shoulders. "Pommie tells you. Hard to miss her Indian hair cut."

"Pah. Fer lice, I will wager. Some lady. Why pay her?" Nellah turned a page of the ledger. "Cheap as dirt that one."

He shrugged. "She is gone, anyways."

"You be too purdy fer yer own good, hon."

Squire was mystified. "What? I ask for it?"

Nellah was quick. "No, no. Laws, no. I misspoke myself. I apol-ogize. I see what she would be after. She likes to git hersel cozy with a good-lookin' feller. No offence to you."

"No offence."

"Hmm. Reckon I should have warned you." Her expression was remorseful. "About her lice. And her impertinence."

"Lush is a dark shadow. *Onyare.* Snake. I am prey. I see her in action. She slips and slides. She attracts me, though, and—makes me sick." Squire flicked a fish tail with his knife. "The whisky. I was drunk. Feelin' too sorry for myself. It is my own fault."

"Taint hardly."

"Well, I—"

Despite her disgust at the skinflint Fowlers and the missing barrel of Gooderham, Nellah dimpled. "Well, nothin', hon. Sickly feelin' will pass. Lookit me. Like an ox. Boy Hewson and the sickly feelin's? Git a-gone, I says to them. Git away from me, sickly feelin's! I got lots of folks a-leanin' on me."

"The Goldens are strong."

"Unh-huh. My mammy towl me facts of life. She declared, 'Dry yer eyes, child. Yestiday be fer a-learnin' and tomorrow be fer a-reckonin'. But right now is for a-doin'. If'n you aint a-doin', it would be real bad.'" Nellah leaned over to study the grocery invoices. "Keep a-doin'. Keep a-movin'. Yer gal would be worth it. Go and get her, hon. You are philosophical? Didn't I heerd yer say it? Awrighty. Keep yown tail in the water. Do not spend time a-foolin' yerself, Sky Walker. Time is nigh. Girl waits for y'all. So. Git!"

CHAPTER
thirty-five

H e had no time to fool himself.

Or argue the point or ask Nellah for an explanation and that was unfortunate. He would have liked to talk more about Jennet and how he should proceed with his courtship but there was a rampaging and a wailing and a stomping coming from the Cyclops Inn and, like a cyclone on heeled boots, it moved closer.

Clippity-clop. The sound came through the yard and up the steps to the dining hall.

In a minute, Bride Munny pounded on the knocker and showed her crumpled face through the side window and cried for help. Nellah opened the door and there she was, Irish, large as life, and she was in a state. Her skin, soft poached, her nightwear, all a-fluff, and she, all a-flutter. Her under-attire was no more than a satiny buttercup ribbon.

Bride tumbled into the room and, as was her custom, she fell to her knees and folded her dishevelled hands together in prayer. "All the dear saints and Grace O'Malley, help me."

"What would be a-wrong, missy? Tacks?" Nellah was relaxed. She cast a dimple at Squire. "Is it Tacks? He do not pay?"

Squire thought Nellah was rather jolly, considering Bride's distraught condition, but he knew Teacher was an old hand at dealing with upsets and, sure enough, Nellah's tone permeated Bride's wall of sobbing and induced a midge of sense to crawl to the surface. In a minute, Bride was cogent, but trembling, and her voice, like always, was weedy and unsteady. She said, "It's not Tacks, sir. It's my brother. My brother is on his way. To here. Tonight. Listen, sir. Within the hour. To get hisself the Indian woman."

The Indian woman?

Squire was startled. He said, "Hold on, Miz Munny. How do you know this?"

She said, "Why, Tacks, he towl me, sir."

The question, being obvious, followed fast.

Nellah and Squire looked at each other and Squire said, "Tacks? Bride, how does Tacks know your brother?"

Nellah peered closer at Bride. "Irish. Tell me true. Who would be this brother of yours?"

Bride did not look at Teacher and she shuddered with the chill in the room and directed her answer to Squire. "Tacks ran into Shiner Paddy Connelly, sir, a few days back, maybe a week or so after the cockfight. Lordy, we're some lucky Tacks got a hold of me." Bride almost giggled at the double entendre but her word play did not enchant the Mohawk and, seeing that, her face fell. She started to cry.

Squire pressed. "Why? What does Tacks know? From Paddy?"

"Paddy is a real good Shiner, sir. Smart. Paddy's in the Grand River Valley gang. You know. The one what's got up for smugglin' out the army's deserters and stealing Indian timber. I told you about them poachers and deserters and smugglers, sir. Remember? Remember how I told you? Remember, I told you they are bad folks."

Yeah. He remembered. Very well. Too well.

Bride rubbed her eyes with her fists, just like a tired baby, and she turned a nervous glance to Nellah. "My brother wants a particular Indian woman for cleaning the cabin where they hole up near Whiteman's Creek because it is a disaster there and they need a cook, too, to warm their bedrolls. Paddy tells Tacks that my brother, er, Boy, Boy Hewson—"

Straightaway Nellah lost her natural self-possession.

She turned grey and swayed on her feet.

Squire thought maybe she had got over the sickly feelin's. Maybe not. In any case, there was one thing her sherry eye and her hazel eye shouted like a clarion. For the love of God. No. She had taken in the destitute Irish woman. Bride Munny lived under her roof. Bride existed under her protection. Boy Hewson? Boy Hewson were the brother? Nellah said, "No, no, taint possible. Bride Munny and Boy Hewson be kin? Squire! Goldern it. Taint so! Squire! Say taint."

"It is so." Squire took her hand but it wasn't enough to calm her. Nellah shook worse than Bride. He put his arms around her and held her. He held her tight until she moved a little to catch her breath and he said, "You can handle this?"

Nellah nodded. "I reckon."

She stayed in his arms. She did not push him away but her shoulders stiffened. She was angry. "Goldern Jeddah and goldern you. Youns would a-knowed it? No, I sure am not all right. Irish is Boy Hewson's kin? His sister?"

Squire did not answer. He didn't want to see himself in the middle of a fight. There was no time to defend the Snowman and explain to Teacher about the foul way Hewson had abused Bride and the kids. He would sound defensive and now was not the moment to fuel the flames of the Goldens' explosive relationship. He felt Nellah's temperature cool, as though she knew it was not the time to fight, and he continued trying to get Bride to talk sense. Earlier Nellah had pointed out the facts. She had people leaning on her and they needed the rest of Bride's story to understand the predicament. He directed Nellah to a Windsor chair and sat her down.

He turned back to Bride. "Miz Munny. Bride. Stop the crying, I beg you. Your brother, does he know you're here?"

Bride did not move. She flooded her brand-new lace handkerchief with tears and she said she was that upset, she was done talking.

Squire grabbed her arms and hauled her to her feet. "I tell you, stop it. Does Boy know you are here? Boy means big trouble for us if he knows."

"Well, Paddy Connelly saw me, sir. With Mister Farr."

"Mmm. I remember. Does Connelly recognize you, though?" Squire almost didn't. There was no need for the Mohawk to rub prickly-nettle salve on an open wound by informing her of the obvious. She was a different woman. When the horsemen had found her she had been an emaciated reed, lacquered with oily filth. Overnight, she was a sparkling beauty.

Food, showerbaths, money and days of shopping had transformed her. Perhaps her old friends might not recognize her with her shining morning face and gleaming hair and her furbelow and coin-filled reticule.

Bride pulled herself up short. "Recognize me? I don't know, sir. Paddy never said, *Hey, Bride.* Come to think of it, sir, I can't say he acted like he knew me. Mister Farr, he didn't introduce me. Not to anyone. We avoided the men, sir, especially the plain man with the pink gunk on his cheeks. That man stared at us."

"I notice." Squire returned to Nellah. He put his hand on her shoulder and she nodded her thanks for the comforting and patted his hand.

Nellah said, "So what about Tacks? Tacks tell Paddy you be here?"

"No, ma'am. That I can say for certain. Tacks aint tellin'. You know Tacks wants me for hisself." Bride looked strangely modest, all things considered. "Tacks declares he is upset about Boy comin' over here seekin' the Indian woman because Boy might spot me hereabouts and take me away from the Cyclops. Tacks wouldn't like to tell Paddy. No sir. Tacks knows Paddy would tell Boy."

Squire said, "Where is the heroic Mister Tacks?"

"Tacks, he leaves for Brantford, sir. He says he don't want to be in the vicinity when Boy Hewson shows up. Ohhhh, sir, help me. I aint able go back to bein' what I was with Boy, nuthin' but dirt on a stick."

The very thought of Boy made her weak, Bride said. She surrendered to another bout of sobs and slithered to the floor like an egg yolk sliding from its broken shell.

Frissons of irritation sparked in Squire's head and he grabbed a cedar log and added it to the fire. He waited a minute as the fire caught hold and tried again to get through to her.

He whistled. He clapped. Nothing. "Miz Munny." He wanted to shake her until her teeth rattled. "Bride!"

In the end, she responded. "Yes, sir."

Her tear-soaked lacy hankie wasn't up to the job and Squire handed down the thin clean square of cotton that Nellah had pressed on him. "Here. Blow!"

There was no point in dragging her to her feet again. Bride seemed to be as rational when she was kneeling as she was when she was standing and only getting ready to fall on her knees to hear the angel voices. Her hands remained folded against her cheek.

Squire poked at the logs and the fire burst into bright flames and the room warmed up. "Now tell us. What Indian woman? Who?"

More sniffles and no answer.

He tried again. "Aughguaga Polly?"

Bride kept her hands folded in prayer and she looked up and shook her head. She met his eyes. "Lord knows, sir. I do not."

Squire turned to Nellah. "Boy wants Polly?"

"Reckon not." Nellah was tranquil. She was bleached to grey around the mouth but she was a realist and she said she was ready to protect baby Pearl at any cost. She had rallied her wits and even half-laughed at the dismayed expression on the Mohawk's face because he imagined Boy Hewson was hot after Polly. "Reckon he would have Maggie Walker. Don't you think?"

There was a silence.

The fire cackled.

There was a moment for consideration.

"Yes sir," Bride said with a vivid eye. "Yes sir. It could be Maggie. She was in the Cave. She was serving whisky to Paddy. I—I seen her. Yes, Paddy knows about Maggie, sir. Paddy liked Maggie."

"I dunno."

Bride looked injured. Was her logic in question? "Why not?"

"Man needs encouragement. Maggie aint the encouraging kind."

Bride held up her boots. Squire looked at them. Bride saw him look and she said she would put them new suede boots to that serious misconception. "Oh yes, sir. Yes, yes, she is so. She's the encouraging kind, aint she, Nellah? Encouraging Paddy. Oh, yes, sir. I seen her, sir. Encouraging him. She's the one."

Squire was not sure. "Maybe it's Polly."

Nellah dimpled. She said she could not he'p it. Squire was being obtuse. She said she had perked up some at the thought of a man seeking out Polly for housekeeping, let alone a bedroll-warmer. "Taint Polly, my friend. Polly would be more'n willin' t'snap a man's neck for him as keep his house. Face it. Tiz Maggie, Squire."

Squire grunted. All right. Say it was Maggie. He calculated the circumstances and imagined what might have happened to introduce Boy's man Paddy Connelly to Maggie Walker in the tavern but not alert him to the presence of Bride Munny. The one person outside of Vinegar Hill who knew what had transpired with the Munnys was Missus Lucille Goosay. Say the Cayuga woman was missing when Boy Hewson showed up. Say she had made it out of Mohawk in time. She had paddled downstream to new Caledonia, she and her sons. Say she had disappeared and she had told Boy nothing about Bride. No useful information about the whereabouts of the Munnys had come from her lips, just as promised, and the riverside marketplaces were silent. Say Boy had searched in vain for Bride but he couldn't locate his sister because she was a changed woman and, for consolation, on the recommendation of a certain Shiner named Patrick Connelly, it was Maggie Walker Boy sought.

Of course, the kids would have been a dead giveaway but neither Paddy nor anyone else seemed to take notice of the kids. It was possible Paddy missed them.

That was what Squire hoped.

Did he believe in coincidence?

No. But what choice was there?

Poor little Maggie. Of course it was Maggie.

It made horrible sense.

Nellah sat up and straightened her turban. "Well, there tiz. We would be goldern lucky Maggie aint here. That would be a mess."

Bride yelped.

On her knees, she bounced like a yellow retriever along the high-varnished plank floor, confronted Squire, and reached up to touch his shirt, just as she had done in the way station. "Oh no. No, sir. You don't think that's it, do you sir?"

Squire air washed his hands. He was done.

Where was Polly? Polly should get Bride out of here. He shook his head and bit his lip. "What do you mean, Miz Munny?"

In the instant Bride's sweet face was tender.

You could eat that look, as delectable as Cook's smoked pigeon pie. She wanted to win him over. He knew it. She knew he knew it. She wasn't wheedling a favour from a distracted but benevolent Jeddah Golden. It was the smart and sceptical Mohawk and the offended Teacher she persuaded. She swore she carried no wiles under her fuzzy buttercup peignoir. Only her candour.

She said, "I aint cracked, sir. Please listen, sir. We are in trouble. I am skairt."

"I see that, Bride. Of what?"

"I tell you the honest-to-God truth, sir. Boy has to have a woman. I know this, sir. He used to have me." The peignoir slipped. There was the bare white shoulder that had captivated Farr. Squire was still disturbed about Maggie Walker's encouraging Paddy Connelly and in no mood for Bride's white shoulder, however enticing.

Bride realized she needed persuasion.

He distrusted her.

She realized she would have to cajole him with the panoply of the Munny charms. She was the eternal feminine trader and, for once, the facts made a start. She whispered. "I tell the truth, sir."

Squire shrugged. The truth? Bride was nothing if not savvy and she was a survivor and a liar. He said, "You mean your brother don't search for Ginger Sorley Munny, like you said?"

"No, sir. My brother already knows the whereabouts of Ginger Munny. My Sorley aint a canaller. Work's too tough for him. He is a low grocer. In Welland. Ginger starves and he starves us. I ran away. Boy don't give a fig about my poor Ginger. Or kids." Like the saddest Madonna, Bride placed her praying hands on the side of her cheek. "He would search for me, sir."

"Maybe not,"

"You saw the choking marks on my neck, sir? Boy did that. He uses me and sells me. He likes me. He don't want to lose me."

Squire knew she was playing on his sympathy. He also knew she was telling him the truth and he gave her a kinder look. "Bride, I guess that. You are abused. Brother don't find you here. So what then?"

"He has his needs, sir. Them peculiar eyes of his would like t'set on Maggie, I suppose, sir. Paddy would paint him a grand picture of her, I think. Maggie is pretty."

"Nellah says it, Miz Munny." Squire could feel prickliness creeping up his spine like the kids' inky spider. The woman was not wholly forthcoming yet. "Maggie aint here. Neither are you, if we hide you. There we are. Boy leaves empty-handed."

"You don't get what I am telling you, sir."

"Guess not."

"I spell it out then. Aint Maggie, sir, a-course it's someone else. It'd be Lizzie. Or Ann." Bride gave Nellah a speculative frown. "Or you."

Squire didn't have the nerve to turn to catch Nellah's expression. He leaned against the mantle, more casual than he felt. "You don't lie? Swear it?"

Bride's prayer was answered. He believed her. "Yes, sir. I do swear it. On the grave of my ma and by all the saints—"

"Right. Right." Squire turned to Nellah but he remained impassive for her sake. "Well, we are in big trouble, then."

Bride answered with more assurances. "Oh yes, sir. Big, big trouble. The biggest. Boy will search. Here, there, everywhere. The barn and the Cave and the inn. You know what's the worst part, sir?"

He scratched his head. What could be worse?

"No." He felt the woman had suffocated him but he had to ask her anyway. "What is it?"

"It's like I towl you, sir. He will burn the place down if he don't find what he wants."

Nellah could not listen and keep herself upright. She folded her arms, graceful, on the table, put her wrapped head down, and murmured, "Jesu! Jeddah Golden. Jeddah. Where would youns be at this time? Come home, come home at once, my dear lover. We do want youns right here. All hell is set to break loose."

Squire groaned. "You lie, Bride. Say it."

"No, sir, I aint a liar. Not this time."

"Your brother, really, is he a blazer?"

"Oh, yes, sir. Sure an' he is. I do know my brother. He is a blazer. He has torched farms. I beg you to believe me, sir." Bride looked to Squire and she waved her hands like two twirling shuttlecocks and moved the air like she wanted to move the Mohawk. She wanted him to start the exodus now if not sooner. "Someone tries to stop Boy from druggin' a woman, any woman, outa here tonight—and, and someone is dead. I promise you. He will kill horses and burn the barn, sir, burn it to the ground. Listen to me, sir."

"I listen."

"No one, but no one, leaves Boy Hewson. I must be loyal to him and stay loyal to him. He is my master." And so, she said, they must all run away. They must pack and git. They must wake the children. Grab the inmates. Warn the canallers. Abandon the structures. Right now, this minute, and this here prediction Bride would positively warrant, because she knew Boy and, yes, she knew his tricks. Tonight the Cave, the inn, the barn and Nellah's solid brick house, they would burn to the ground. It's all gone if Boy caint get hisself ahold of Maggie Walker or some other poor soul.

Squire shifted his stance.

He did not dare disbelieve. Not for a second.

Drying her eyes, Bride must have felt she had done her job. She had a bitter edge. "Guess what, sir. We may burn to a crisp and no one gives a shit! Damn them villagers. They want us gone. It's the plan. For the Christian men's sportin' clubhouse."

Squire nodded. Right. He had heard.

So had Teacher. The gentlemen's sporting club loomed on the horizon but Filkin and James Wilkes and their plan to take over the Hill were one thing. Immediate danger was another. Squire was plenty annoyed with Tacks. Tacks got word from everywhere. Every man and his dog delivered messages to Tacks but in truth the Mohawk felt incensed about the latest development and the last message that Tacks had given to Bride, the one about her brother. How could Boy Hewson possibly imagine a return to Nellah's place? Farr was right. Boy was a buzzard with a heart of marble. Boy took what he wanted. He did what he wanted. He was a gangster, pure and simple. He had tortured Nellah. Raped her. He had harmed her household and, so far, he had done it with insolence. Doubtless, Boy knew Jeddah Golden was away hunting down Bobby John. Teacher was vulnerable. Maggie was vulnerable. Boy would make his move tonight. Squire believed it. He felt his sore ribcage beaking at him. He felt the warning bolt of pain run through his instep. He ran a hand through his hair. He folded his arms. His face fell into severe lines. Bride looked at him, looked scared, as though she had forgotten the dynamism of the Indian's quick smile because he looked as though he would never smile again. He was grim-faced and fixed his black eyes down at her and put a moccasined foot on the top rung of a Windsor chair and rubbed his chin.

Christ, he thought, there were problems.

He had to get the Hill folks away from Teacher's place and he had to find another woman to satisfy Boy. Boy needed a woman. He got himself a new woman and they had a chance. He might forget about blazing the place. The Hill people, and barn and buildings, might see tomorrow. Squire had to think.

He shouted for Aughguaga Polly.

Where was she? Why didn't she hurry?

He shouted again for Polly but turned to Nellah.

"Was Mahlon Joe still drinking in the Cave?"

Nellah said yes.

Squire told Bride to fetch Joe.

Polly trunked herself upward on the steps from the yard and she stuck her wrinkled waffle face around the corner of the dining room door and glared at the grandson, the light of her life. In Mohawk, Squire explained the situation and he asked Polly to help him capture Nellah's assailant, to snare Hewson for good and all.

Tonight? It had to be tonight?

Tonight! Yes, he was certain it would be that soon. He had, he said, devised a plan. Compared to Squire's plan, Lawrence Filkin and James Wilkes had absolutely nothing. The real sport was afoot. Tehawennihárhos was about to cool some hot heads and Polly was the mainstay. He needed her and he made it clear with an appealing look that, occasionally, he did appreciate her daunting skills with the magic herbs.

She didn't hesitate. Hesitation wasn't *her* name.

He described the powerful medicine he wanted and the effect he was after.

Locoweed. Decocted.

Got it, Polly said.

She grasped the grandson's intention.

The fat grandmother rolled her old silver braids into circles around her ears. Like iron beehives, Jennie had called them. It was time to get to work. Polly knew she was a genius, well and good, and they all knew that, uh?

And so the famous healer, one Aughguaga Polly, huffed toward the kitchen to boil her potions. Things were heating up, she said over her shoulder, because finally someone would listen to her about the white vipers.

thirty-six

"Jehoshaphat, Squire. Them eyebrows!"

"What's wrong with 'em?"

Nellah said, "Too bushy, hon." She held her hands to her face in mock horror and called to Mahlon Joe. "Hey, Joe. Tweezers."

Teacher leaned in for a better look at Squire's face and she spit on her finger for a dab to try to get the pointed brow hairs to settle into a manicured arc and shook her head and adjusted the gingham scarf covering Squire's manly décolletage. "Dead giveaway, them big black brows. No womern would have them. Best trim them close. Tell you what I think, Joe. Shave 'em off. I kin draw them on."

The night was nippy. It was mid-November and Nellah had wrapped up warm in a cloudy-coloured fringed paisley shawl. She and baby Pearl were set to flee with the Delaware barber, Mahlon Joe. The Munnys and Lizzie Bosson were going as well.

Joe was a knight in shining armour. He was generous and on side and had offered the poor gals use of the Joe family's hideaway on the riverbank, upstream and far into the bush, until the crisis was well and done. Pshaw, he said, why not? Hill folks had to stick together. He had the bathhouse and it was just down the road from Nellah's. He could live there, easy as pie, at least for the time being. On behalf of Lizzie Bosson and the Munny children, Nellah and

Bride had accepted. Nellah was known to be a strict commander but she had clung to the Delaware until he was the reddest of men.

Ann Bergin had already altered her costume to suit Squire's grand plan. She was a wee Highlander lad but she was in a sour temper, dressed in Lizzie's wearing pants and a plain shirt and Pommie's cap and suspenders, and serving drinks in the tavern like a newbie. None of the men had noticed her before, when she was female. They'd not notice her tonight. Ann should be going with the women and children but she said she could not leave because Cook couldn't run the entire operation alone and, if things went according to the plan, Squire would be some busy. He would do what was needed to catch the bugger and everything could get back to normal. They would have to chance it with Ann in the tavern. Everything must seem more or less normal. They couldn't appear too short-handed, at least, not without a plausible reason. Polly insisted she would stay behind too. No argument from any quarter. Squire needed her.

Cook and Joe and Pommie had hitched Cap'n to Nellah's antiquated buckboard. Teacher did not have an open four-wheel carriage and pony. Buy a buggy? Feed a horse? With what? She didn't have enough oats to feed her people, let alone a pony. Boy Hewson's reputation with horses had preceded him and Squire was contented to send Cap'n with them. The patient stallion and rickety buckboard were waiting in front of Nellah's house. The wagon was a tenuous affair and he was relieved to hear that Joe would ride along as escort, stay with them till they were safe. Protection took several forms, especially when and if one of the buckboard's wood axles split on them, as seemed likely. The last thing the women had to do before they left was make sure a feminine Squire was convincing enough to satisfy Boy. They had been packing their necessaries in hampers and, as apprehensive as they were, they had not lost their sense of the ridiculous. Transforming Squire into a woman gave them pause.

Everyone had a comment.

First, there was Lizzie.

Lizzie said that Squire stunk. Male-like. She said he'd best take a showerbath, right quick, after which she offered to dab her fabulous and expensive French perfume on his secret warm parts. She said it was a surefire done-deal that the fresh, sweet grassy fragrance of her heavenly Guerlain would drive the fiend mad.

Alfie told him it wouldn't hurt the cause to run a paddle-brush once or twice through the wet and messed-up hair or maybe put it into a plait or two. At that, Joe got defensive. He swore to Alfie that he had barbered the Mohawk, good and proper, with elixirs, lavenders and a haircut, not a month past. Mess was none of his doing.

Ann worried about Squire's height. He was too tall. Ann was well under five feet. Squire's five-feet-eight-inches was too tall to make a feminine figure. It would never work.

Bride worried about Squire's jaw. Too square. His neck. Too thick. Too bumpy. Definitely too masculine. He was too much man for the job. She rewound the gingham scarf over his collar. Tight. It was enough to throttle him.

Squire obeyed directions and he submitted to the complicated beauty regimen but, after Nellah's suggestion about the brow shaving, he called a halt. There was a limit. He leapt to his feet. "No shavin'. No beard pluckin'. Boy goes to the gaolhouse. *Onen*. I aint a pin cushion."

Anxiety had set Nellah to trembling like Bride but she managed to release the parentheses around her mouth. "No eyebrow shaving."

Bride felt for him, she said.

Brows were ticklish.

Bride offered her expertise. She made the Mohawk sit right back down and grabbed her pots and potions and applied paint and powder to lighten his cheek and offered to sprinkle lemon juice in his eyes for brightening. "I have to darken my eyebrows with burnt hairpins.

I would love it, sir. What I mean is, sir, I would love to have them brows. You have fine thick brows, sir. The admiration of every man."

Joe said, "I don't admire 'em."

Nellah said, "Taint the time, Joe."

The artists worked fast.

It was remarkable they way they could lose and recapture an identity.

Squire said, "Let's have a look-see."

He had put his trust in fate and the women and he was destined to follow the bizarre plan to the end but he should like to take a gander. What did he have to work with? He grunted, unladylike, and stood up slow and stiff, like someone's arthritic great-granny. Concerned but resigned, he clapped eyes on himself in Nellah's long seamstress's glass. He was bewildered. He was transformed. What was he, though? Other than the oddest creature ever born. He was shocked at the horrible image and, for once, he looked what he felt. Teacher had stuffed an old chemise with scraps of cotton. He'd put it on. Instant bosom. She had given him her plain grey-cotton maternity smock and he'd put that on. With a starched petticoat underneath. She had taken a black elasticized broadcloth belt and gathered the copious material tight at the waist. Instant female. He smelled like roses. He had sparkling eyes. He had pale cheeks with spots rouged on them. He had tweezed, arched brows. He looked like a doll, a large grotesque doll, a Maggie Walker clown-doll wearing a gingham bandana around his neck. It was distressing. It was atrocious. What on earth had he agreed to?

Pommie and Chrisinny were frightened. They held hands and stood in the hallway, as silent as mice. Pommie looked as though he might cry and Squire could think of a dozen reasons why crying would be appropriate but he managed to wave at the kid. "What the hell, eh?" Gave the chin-up motion. Keep your fingers crossed. A please-understand appeal.

Pommie returned it with an infinitesimal nod and he regarded his friend Sky Walker with solemn blue eyes and sighed a tiny sigh.

Lizzie saw the youngster's misery and she felt impelled to sketch out for him the fact of the operation's being very tricky. "But promising. Let's not forget that." Squire, she counselled the children, was the daring one to think of the plan. The plan would catch a terrible villain. Pommie and Chrisinny's villainous and wicked uncle. They oughtn't to make Squire feel uncertain about his appearance. They should be pleased, she said, because, for their sakes, someone was ready and willing to make a fool of hisself.

Squire overheard Lizzie's practical views and he wondered what it felt like to have a villainous and wicked uncle but it was waste of time to worry about how to spare kids from bad news because they knew it. A family was an unsettling thing and you could go wild trying to make it perfect. He had a cousin who was an unrepentant drunk and a rapist who deserved gaol time. He had a good mother whom he ignored. He couldn't bear to think about it. He would put Nellah's mammy's advice into play. Today was for a-doin'. Tomorrow was for a-reckonin'.

Cook seemed dazed. The wondrous sight he beheld was too much. He grumbled to Squire out of the others' hearing and shook his head. "Ay. Yer da strange turkey. Sorry ter tell yous dat, me owd kidda, but Ay don't see 'ow this plot wul work."

Polly trundled from the kitchen into the dining room. She looked at the transformed grandson. She stopped. "Holy cow," she said. "This a bad thing you gone and done. You dim the lanterns on the bar, hear me? Cut the light." Polly flipped up a birch-wood vial and was near to dropping it but handed it over to him. He asked whether it was potent. She nodded, yes, it was potent all right. It was a decoction of locoweed berries and leaves and rye whisky and in the instant the plan had turned into a possibility.

Squire acknowledged the genius of the grandmother and, with a peaceful and mind-settling satisfaction folding over him, he breathed in the scent of his secret weapon, an intoxicating aroma that smelled like creosote. Good luck to you, Boy.

The fugitives trooped out the front door and Joe turned. His eyes gleamed. "What's the name, sweetie?"

Squire curled his lip.

Polly was quick and she smacked Joe hard on the chest. "Winona, idiot. Maggie's faraway cousin. From enemy Ojibwe. Thanks to the whites, we all love each other now."

"Winona, uh? That's good, Missus Polly." Joe said. "So, where's she living in these days?" *In these days* meant the Great Indigenous Diaspora.

The fat grandmother threw her hands up in a frustrated don't-know, don't-care gesture but with contrition to show she did care, she turned thoughtful. She unwound the beehives. "North of Toronto. Innisfil. Maybe Uxbridge. Manitoulin? Christ, I don't know where the ugly Ojibwe people live."

Joe began to shut the door behind him and gave Squire the wink. "Not up north. How about down south. Nick's café. On the crazy river."

Squire sprinted to the door and he gave Joe a final push and a yeah-yeah nod.

"Time to go, Joe."

Joe said, "Ha. The Mohawk wears petticoats—"

Squire had nothing more to add but, "Hmm."

"—not the Delaware."

"Get out."

"Hidey-ho," Joe said, pinching Squire's rouged cheek. "I'm gone." Joe couldn't help it. He gave a belly laugh. "Them eyebrows is somethin' else. Oy, keep yer pecker up, Winona."

CHAPTER
thirty-seven

O h, yeah. For sure. Teacher had competitors.

There were forty-five saloons near Brantford. Some three thousand citizens could take their pick. Boy Hewson's coming to this particular saloon on this particular night was suspicious but, say what one would about all the choices, business was brisk. For the most part, Nellah Golden had managed to prevail. Nellah had layers of notoriety. Because of this, and, of course, *that*, she had status. It came wrapped in low prices and mellow rye whisky, watered to perfection, and flaky smoked pigeon pie.

The Cave's unflagging popularity was inexplicable, folks said, but the daring sons of professionals felt an irresistible urge to fraternize with the enemy on the Hill. Also present and accounted for were farmers, soldiers, remittance men, gangsters and Indians. At some time or another, capitalists of every hue and creed were bound to show up at Teacher's to further the cause of building a liberal economy, where individuals and corporate citizens controlled the production, distribution and exchange of wealth and goods in the united province of Canada. It was Progress. Independence was its own reward. Independent drinkers got immediate recognition. The exhausted Alfie generally told the clientele, "Yous stable own blewdy 'orses."

By type, Squire would recognize the clientele. From habit, he knew the drill.

He hooked Nellah's grey skirt high over his arm. He wasn't quite the earth's noblest thing, a woman perfected, but his femininity was suitable, if agonizing, and he was ready to tackle the event, ready for womanhood, all but his feet. His own moccasins took the steps to the Cave, typically, two at a time.

On the landing, he dropped the hem.

A long cold inhalation dampened his roiling guts. He shuddered at the memory of his image. *Ro'niha*, his late father should forgive him for what he was about to do. He opened the door and entered the small sooty-panelled barroom. With a faint pop, the door lock clicked shut.

CHAPTER
thirty-eight

The shadowed men looked up and squinted at the disturbance. A draught of frigid air had caught their attention. Snow was imminent.

It was almost dark inside, as dark in as out.

Squire looked around. From end to end, the room was about thirty feet. Maybe twenty, twenty-five feet wide. Farthest away was the windowless dining area. It was west of the interior staircase that led to the inn's sleeping quarters. Behind the bar, lined up in front of the glass mirror, there were alcohol and camphene hand-lamps with pewter tuques clipped to the side. The lamps burned bright and the heated mix gave off a faint sweet scent of pine and nutmeg but Nellah kept them off the varnished tables because flare-ups were possible. Teacher wanted the lamps under control and, in any case, it wasn't a bad thing to have a clean mirror gleaming expectantly in a rundown shack.

The glass pulled on the camphene radiance and refracted it into the darkness like white knives. The candles on the round tables, struggling, gave out variegated shades of gloom. Globs of mellow buttery lard lit feeble spheres and the fat dribbled and pooled into piles of grease and trickled onto the tabletops.

As a form of discouragement, hoping patrons would mosey along home, or mosey on upstairs, Ann had neglected the fire in the grate, which was right next to the bar. The fire burned low and barely glowed in the stone hearth. Corners were dim but men's spirits were commensurate with the spirits they had consumed and the senses needed time to digest it all. It took a minute for Squire to sort out shapes and co-conspirators and the general population.

Co-conspirators were one. That was Cook.

General population, shy of a dozen.

The barkeep's entry-slot was close to Squire, near the outside stairs. There was a corn-broom hanging with precarious hope on the swinging door. Black eyes half-closed like a lazy frog, he zapped up the wooden handle with his left hand. He slipped into a servant's impassive pose. He bent to look for spills, waggled the broom and appeared as though he had been fussing for hours. He crept into the hub, sweeping, tidying, wiping.

Cook watched the performance.

Squire figured he might give Miss Ince dramatic lessons but no, maybe not.

Alfie shook his head. Muttered, whadda git-up. "Let's git at 'er, dun." He beckoned to Squire and pointed to a dozen glasses, steins and tin plates ready for washing. He changed his mind. Business could wait. It seemed he wanted to talk to the Mohawk. In private.

CHAPTER
thirty-nine

Squire had put on Nellah's dress and, strange to tell, he said to Cook, he experienced highs and lows. He was charting a new emotional topography. "Let's get the men out of the bar before Boy gets here—" but Cook had nabbed Squire's grey shoulder and herded the Mohawk into the small humid nook of a kitchen. They backed into the rough wall next to the scorching cast-iron woodstove, a gift last year from a certain Octavius Millburn. Squire stood the new corn broom in the corner.

Alfie lowered his bristly beard into his bib. He said, "Wa' 're we expect'n ter git outta all the female dressin'?"

"Hopes for the best, Alfie. Hopes for the best. We make a snare. Boynton gets caught." He dipped his hand into a cooling pot on the counter and extracted, cracked, peeled and downed a couple of hardboiled eggs. His stomach rumbled. He prepared another egg. He drew a ladle through the lyed corn soup bubbling on the woodstove and made sure he nabbed a few hunks of salt pork and a pile of kidney beans for his bowl.

Cook persisted. "Say yous kep him, Ay am not say'n yous wul, but say, wa' dun?" He was hungry and, from a leftover plate, he removed a cold potato and a Spanish-onion sandwich, which made the Mohawk shudder. To avoid looking at what the other one was eating, Squire tilted back his head and fiddled with the tight bandana and sucked down the last drops of the soup. Full bellied, he felt, well, kind of cheery. "Brother, Boy goes on long journey."

"Whuz? Wa' kind o' a long jorney?"

"He won't leave but—he travels far."

Ready to move, Squire picked up the broom and tapped it on his moccasin and he noticed the handle was a means of advertising. It had the maker's name and occupation branded on it. *Nathaniel Burr, carpenter/joiner.* He whapped the whisk hard and it banged on the larder shelf on the wall opposite the stove. The flour tin shook. The raisin tin tipped over. Dried raisins and pungent sticky plums rolled out. His ribs ached, particularly on the injured side. Nathaniel Burr. Bah. To hell with him. Burr took Jennie back to Uxbridge when he should have just minded his own business.

"Sonofabitch, that hurts. Brother, you believe me. Hewson goes to the gaolhouse. He pays the price. Goes to the gallows."

"Yous aint 'ealthy blewdy-nuff, Squire. We wait fe da man."

"No." Let Alfie worry. Squire was stubborn. He tapped Burr's broom handle on the floor. "No. We leave Jeddah bloody Golden out of this. You hear me, Alf? No Jeddah. You, me, Polly, we handle it."

"Yous and Polly 'ave cooked up poison fe Boy ter swaller?"

Squire's expression was foxy. "Poison? Nope. Not really. It'll slow him down some, is all. He'll wanna pluck the fleas offa the dog. He's greedy, eh, Alfie? I hear he drinks."

Liar. You are a liar, Squire thought. A crummy liar. The decoction *was* poison. He was up for murder. Just like Peter Johnson had been when he had killed Ziggy. The Frenchman was a good man, though, and so was Alfie. Their way was direct. They confronted their enemies. To what lengths would he go for money or vengeance? There was no purpose in weighing down Nellah's trusted right-hand man with the truth about datura. Squire was responsible for the plan if Boy swallowed a lot of the poison, there was no telling what damage it would do.

"Greedy?" Cook growled. He retied his apron tighter than usual to spite their situation and he girded his loins. "Ah, yis. Boy is greedy. 'E is 'at."

Cook was all for imagining pandemonium breaking out at Teacher's place and Squire could not say it wouldn't but he promised he would hogtie Boy. The Mohawk raised the smoothed-out tweezed eyebrow. "And if he aint happy hogtied, well, lookit us, jackrabbits. Trouble. Lots of trouble. We're up shit creek."

Alfie blew out his cheeks. "Us, uh?"

"Me." Squire showed his white teeth, which changed the entire set of his serious face. "How do women wear this stuff and do anything?" He fluffed up the petticoat. "Me, Alfie. Me. Up shit creek. Without my pants."

"Kidd'n yous. All fe one, one fe all."

"Brother, we see how it goes. Polly's clever. She makes infallibles. We trust her. Boy drinks. Maybe he don't know what's up. One way or other, he leaves the Cave. Like you say. De bee's knees."

"De bee's knees?" Cook allowed himself the spirit of a laugh at the way Squire picked up expressions. "Nowt is ever de bee's knees, we 'opes fe de best."

Alfie was not one to expect the perfect plan to go perfectly. Well, Squire wasn't either. Brave talk was the warm-up.

"Annie says canallers 'ave gone ter flock. Ay dunno quite who's all left. We'll 'uv ter see. We 'uv ter get rid o' dem. Fas'."

"Brother, I do it. I sweep them out. We empty the place." Squire waved the broom over his head.

"Er, laddah—" The man in white assumed the casual pose, one hand on his aproned hip, one tattooed forearm over his heart. Heart and tattoo belonged to the Royal Navy. The large brown eyes were soft. A lock of ashen hair drifted over one eye. He was in selfless mode, the martyr of the merchant marine. Squire knew knew what was coming and steeled himself to agree to the favour about to land on him, whatever it was, because he had no choice and would never be able to repay Alfie for his help if he lived a hundred years, and old Alfie was pushing sixty. Jeddah was something else. Jeddah was tough, disturbing and Squire respected him, feared him a little, he guessed, and resented him a lot, but Alfie was simply a friend. The Scouser was the big soul. A goddam Englishman.

Alfie laid it out. "Nellah says yer leav'n quick as sticks fe de North. Ter get yer girwl."

"Uh, Nellah says that, does she?"

"Yous won't think Ay am bold, uh? Yous girwl 'as soft skin and plump sweet bubbies. Ay know yous cannot wait ter be wi' 'er. It is righ', laddah. Anyone wi' a girwl so tender would long ter touch 'er and put 'imself next ter 'er. She 'as fine-smell'n long 'air. 'Er figure is de bee's knees. Yous feel the ragin' fe 'er. Mun see 'er. Admire 'er. Envy yous. Sweet round arse an' big bubbies an' all. Ripe fe de lovin'." Cook gave him an elbow dig, man to man. "An' from wa' Ay 'ear, yous 'ave de big lovin' 'andle, right fe de job—"

Squire was plenty uncomfortable. His dress was unhelpful. He acted sharp and smacked at the front of the skirt and straightened the cinched belt and inhaled. "Get to the point, Alfie."

"Before yous go, do me a favo? Ay 'ave bags o' fresh salmon juss came in wi' farmers, yous wul see 'em fellas dere at table in corner yonder, an' it all needs smokin'. Ay 'uv traded de fish fe rewm and board, eh? Fish's in Nellah's cold-cellar. Gi' youse some smoked fish fe present fe Fergusons, 'ow 'bout 'at?"

Smoke the fish? Easy. "I am happy to dry the fish. Don't know about needing presents, though." He felt positively woozy at the prospect of going north. Maybe he wouldn't go. Jennie may hate him.

He was at it again. Liar. He was a liar. He knew she did not hate him.

"Ta. Dere's me sound laddah, uh, lady." Cook regarded him and brightened. "Presents be fine. Shure. Smoked fish. Presents wul win a fair maidun. You need presents fe goin' a-courtin'. Woman'll let you into 'er heart, if'n you bring 'er presents."

Smoked fish would let him into her heart?

Squire was amused but he did not say anything. He was touchy about disposing of Hewson but Cook had made him feel light again and he made a plan to go to Uxbridge soon and for a few seconds he whistled "Jimmy Crack Corn" to prove it. He was ready to clear out the tavern and bring a certain Boy Hewson to heel.

~

Wiping their mouths on their cuffs, Alfie and Winona eased back into the undercover business and tended to chores. They left the larder shelves to miraculously reorder themselves, as Ann Bergin, now a certain Anders, was wont to accuse them, and sauntered through the door of the main room. Alfie was the barkeep. The boss. Winona was the minion and she shuffled along behind him, head down, with her corn broom at the ready.

Ann, Anders, was in charge of keeping the liquor supply steady in the tavern. Not too much, in case of robbery or a brawl, but enough to keep from running out. Tonight, when she was not running to the barn for liquor, she was scooting back and forth between the inn's small kitchen and the kitchen in Nellah's house because the Cyclops specialty, smoked pigeon pie, was ready to be baked in Nellah's woodstove. Ann had burned more than one pie in her day but, no matter, Cook had set her once again with the task of watching over his delicacy.

A louche Scotsman who looked as though he was the poster boy for *The Sporting Magazine* posed on the bar counter, drinking, sloshing his blistered feet around in his untied boots and waving around a thick Havana with the distinctive Bock's cigar band.

In intervals an expansive mood hit the Scot like a hot rush hits a geyser and he exhaled clouds of cigar smoke, reeking up the atmosphere. He declared he was Flash Dunlop, not long returned to the Canadas from his estates in Scotland and pleased to visit his uncle up the Minnesetung, near Goderich in the Township of Colborne. Squire sized up the poser with one brutal salient thought: get out.

Flash Dunlop had a pike's snoot, mousey curls and sparse chops. His mouth was pinched into a raspberry but he spoke normal. A mouth like that and the miracle was that he could talk at all. Squire felt his temper sliding into a natural antagonism and his own wide mouth coiled. Winona was nothing but a finishing-school disaster, the shame of those who had created her. He shouldn't let the lofty Scot bring him low and make him into an inferior native bird, a titmouse to a blooming peafowl. Dunlop yapped on. He said he'd do the drop-in to see Uncle Tiger and afterward he would leave from New York, for Jamaica, possibly. He was interested in advising his uncle about estate planning. Wills, he said with a wink and boasted about John Galt.

Squire looked at Cook.

Cook looked at Squire. Alfie raised his cotton-clad arm to scratch his hair. He showed his anchor tattoo on his hairless forearm and he mouthed, *Who is John Galt?*

The Mohawk shrugged.

The gent smoked and he complained about the miles of potholes and muck and po-faced Canadian women. Squire dove under the countertop to finish washing the steins and schooners.

CHAPTER
forty

For some minutes, Flash shone on centre stage.

His hands chopped the air but the tune was griping and the ballad was his journey from Toronto, which had been tedious, as tedious as an old maid, "a being I am obliged to respect but have always detested." Flash planted his tongue in his cheek, let out an exhalation and put down his cigar. The sentiment amused him. His tight mouth crept up and he announced his father was temperance-minded but neither he nor his uncle was so inclined and ordered the barkeep to come up with claret. He wavered his finger along the mirror and pointed to a red bottle. "The pale claret, my man. The Apostle Luke."

Cook sighed.

He had heard it all.

A tab was a tab, though, and Alfie obliged with calculated indifference but he took his own time before he slid a shot-glass of red stuff down the bar. Aside, Alfie caught Squire's ear. "Apostle Luke? Ay. T'as John Scott's finest distilled virgin's piddle wi' some plain ol' beet juice fe de claret."

Meantime, Flash fished deep in his vest pocket. Not for Halifax currency, though. Out came an unsteady, tattered journal and a gnawed lead pencil stub. Dunlop proceeded to record his deucedly bang-on observation about old maids. Satisfied with his unremitting cleverness, he put his journal back. Cigar reek infected every nook and cranny. The smoke circled the spaces but hung suspended like strands of buttermilk.

In the shadows, away from Dunlop at the bar, two tables played at cards but it was hard for Squire to see what they were, or who they were, or where they were from. He put down the flannel and glass, picked up his broom and swept toward the stairs, close to the first table and peered into the darkness. The wheat farmers. Straight folk. The straightest. Indians danced. Mennonites did not. They just ate. Squire moved in. Yes, definitely the wheat farmers, the ones who had traded fish for board. Past the empty tables, at another table, the one pushed into the stale shabby corner, sat three regimental men and one civilian.

CHAPTER
forty-one

The Mohawk poked around the farmers to see what he could do to hurry them along. He rubbed his eyes to encourage them to go to bed but a middle-aged woman in a loose serge dress and an almost-white day cap sat in on the farmers' game and she was not one for hurrying.

She shook her head. No going to bed.

They were at cards. They played something they called Hoss. Flash had said he detested the tedious one and, sure as the great *Rawenniyo*, there she was, Reba Elias they called her, an apparition come to life from the queen of spades. Squire imagined the reaction of Peter Johnson. *"Et voilà! La Sorcière."* The woman's irises were mud and the rims of her eyes were as red as the jar of pickled fig tomatoes on the bar. Her gummy mouth made Squire turn away for fear of staring like Pommie. No wonder the men didn't go upstairs. Stray hairs grew from moles on her chin. She smelled of cat. She tossed out mean glances. Which farmer was hers?

Squire sensed the woman's mind was afloat and nothing much moored her to life in the continuum. Reba Elias was drifting from shore but the men didn't appear bothered. They seemed patient and unsurprised. The dark-garbed farmers said they were Mennonites from a place near Eby, a community upstream on the Grand. The farmers had carted the last bushels of summer wheat to Peter

Green's, or Bunnell's Landing, on the Oxbow at Cayuga Heights to catch the steamer, *The Indian Chief*, most likely the last steamer out. They wanted to get their grain to St. Catharine's before freeze-up. The farmers said the Navigation had transported ninety-four thousand bushels of wheat that year. Modestly, they admitted they'd had a fair to middling yield. This was their third trip.

Cook was astounded. "Ma gawd. Turd!?"

Squire rubbed his forehead, fearful of Cook's accent, but the men nodded.

Cook pounded his fist on the counter. "Satisfy'n ter gerra crop sound as pound."

Wheat famers were reluctant capitalists, persistent scratchers. One productive year was an illusion. Last year, crops were bad. No rain. Farmers were destitute. Next year, seeds may not germinate. Hail may wipe them out. If not hail, something else.

There was another kind of bad news. Trade news.

What trade news? Cook wondered aloud.

The farmers were surprised. Hadn't they heard? Britain verged on repealing the Corn Laws. The Amish in Ohio smuggled wheat to Canada for shipment to Britain. They did it to get an edge on price because of the Canadian preference. It was cheap to ship to London from Montréal. Cheaper than from New York or Chicago. The Amish in Ohio were sure to be out-of-sorts about Britain's repealing the Corn Laws, no matter who was starving to death.

The Mennonite brothers shrugged heavy shoulders and shifted position. It was a modest exchange but their size made the floorboards tremble.

With the possibility of the Imperial preference disappearing into thin air, they said they should never mind smuggling American Amish. What about them? What would the Elias and Fink families do? What would Canada West's wheat farmers do? Find American markets? Turn their grain into spirituous liquors. Booze was an answer, sure. The three farmers looked at each other and laughed. Reba Elias glared but they disregarded the warning. They could sell their grain to distillers, like John Scott, but that was dishonourable and they would not wish it. The scraggly woman broke in. She spoke with a raspy throat, which she clutched, and Squire felt sympathy until she rasped on Alfie. "Beshrew thy whorehouse, Mister Williams."

White-haired, white-garbed Alfie looked mild enough, disconcerted, and the woman pointed at him as though he had tried to argue; but he had not moved from behind the bar and did not exert himself to refute the charge or, indeed, say a word in his own defence.

She said, "We want nothing. We hope for nothing. We look forward to nothing. We follow the model of Lord Jesus Christ and live in expectation of scarcity."

"Scarcity of a decent pick-up." The oldest Mennonite slapped down his cards. The players fell silent. Concentrated on the game. Guilt also must have been in play because the woman had reminded them they were not supposed to be there. Not on the Sabbath. They rested on Sunday. They prayed and they meditated. They were thankful for their lot in life. The woman won the game and she crabbed. About Alfie, the whorehouse, the profanity of a busy day.

"Thy mouth is busy," her card partner observed in a placid accent.

"And it is for us to socialize fine and so vhat? Ve vork," the first man said, irritated. "Don't vork. Don't eat. Trapped here, dat's fer sure." They couldn't make the trip to the landing and back in one day. They had to overnight. They had picked the Cyclops Inn, a pure mistake, but the man in white, that nice fellow, Cook, he had accepted their line of salmon in trade, whereas other innkeepers had mocked them. The man nodded at Alfie and the irritation calmed and he tried for harmony. "Smoked pigeon pie schmecks, Reba Elias."

Reba Elias was in a tizzy. She pinched the upper arm of the speaker, pinched hard. "A blasphemer, Franz Fink. And a fiend for food."

Squire was appalled.

Woman should be thankful.

She had an unsoiled bed for the night. As far as Squire was concerned, Flash Dunlop had made his point. The upper country was hard on European women. It twisted their pretty mouths into spruce needles. The Mohawk was confounded. Seeing male gentleness aimed toward such a poor creature was something new. He swept up clay boot marks, wiped the tabletop and replaced the lard candle. The scraggly messy one had the eyes of the attacking badger. Her menfolk were over six-feet-four but they appeared as dull-edged as his friend Jake Venti's toothpick and as dry as Jake's corncakes. They did not smoke more than they inhaled from the general miasma and occasionally they tapped the table. They did not drink. Brave, patient, non-violent men who had to stand watch over Reba Elias deserved a proper belt of the good stuff. With tee-totallers, Nellah was brusque but, with the Mennonite giants, Squire noticed Cook had let it all slide and, within minutes, the enormous, dour foursome quit socializing and the farmers, trailed by the diminutive Reba Elias, trudged up to their rooms with bone-tired steps. No argument.

Squire understood why. Alfie, being male, couldn't bring himself to fuss at Goliath over a puny bar tab. He had let it go. Cook did not expect them to pony up. Men with thighs like *schenken* naturally claimed a wide berth.

Yoh. So long.

One table remained in the far corner: the four men who played poker.

Squire swept toward them.

Three men in uniform claimed they were from a Toronto regiment. The man on Squire's right, the odd-man out, was a tubby,
bald, hairy-chopped fellow and the Mohawk strained to see him.
Yes, it was he. Mr. Walter Winter, the half-breed politician. Squire
was sure it was the Tory, Whiskers, and he wondered whether he
could dredge up a sweet-tempered Winona to fool his friend, old
man Winter, but Winter was not a bad fellow. About two months
past, Whiskers had taken a shine to the Mohawk, was real nice at
one of Nellah's midnight dinner parties in September, just before
the robbery. His solid presence offered comfort, for all it was worth.

Where was the bastard, though?

Where was Boy Hewson?

CHAPTER
forty-two

Britrish Lieutenant Horatio Needles was the ranking officer. His lean wrists, which were hanging inches below the frayed cuffs of his uniform, made him seem like a child playing a man's game and it was likely he bluffed and blustered to hide his timidity. Needles was the thinnest, most nervous man Squire had ever seen.

Sergeant Jimmy Nelson, sitting next to Needles, was a grizzled veteran. Jimmy Nelson said he was curious about things. His eyes had deep crow's feet around them and patches of white stubble covered his cheeks. Nelson's opposite across the table was Corporal Bing, another veteran with straight brown hair and nothing to mark him but boredom and lack of curiosity. Jimmy Nelson was upset. He was pretty obvious. Lieutenant Needles, the commanding officer, damn his eyes, he was too busy concentrating on his cards to read deep into a man's needy soul and the sergeant smuggled out a leer to Winona. Jimmy Nelson said out loud, "Sweetie. Yo! You native of this place?"

Was it a trick question? A joke?

After a pause, Winona shook her broom. No.

The sergeant turned to Cook, who was tinkering with the lamps on the bar. He asked Alfie how long he had been working in the upper country.

Alfie was curt. "Too long."

Squire was annoyed. That Needles was an impatient stick.

Needles was annoyed too, with Jimmy Nelson's chit-chat. He told the veteran to shut up and crooked a bony index finger and clucked in Squire's direction. Squire resisted the urge to point at his own chest. "You mean me?" Who else? Anders was still in the barn chasing down a barrel of spirits. After the horrifying Fowler experience, Nellah was smart. She had hidden her stash of Scotch with cunning.

Behind the bar, Cook was advising Flash Dunlop, now full of the Apostle Luke, contempt for the lower orders, an unshakeable sense of entitlement and a pigeon pie, that he were aboot ter make hisself sick fer eat'n an oole mincer.

Dunlop said to Cook, "My dear fellow, Alfie, is that it? Say, would you be so kind? Please do repeat." He had found a specimen, an infamous publican. A brute.

Alfie said, "Bibulous berd oughter be in bed."

Dunlop was delighted. He made an oversized sweep and removed his journal again, and the pencil stub. He acted like an ethnologist logging the grunts of a yeti and he scratched away on a dog-eared page. Squire banged the whisk end of the broom against the bar to clear the gunk. Dunlop was obnoxious, a barbarian, a Comanche.

Flash sensed an element of contrariness. His head popped up like a flusher. In a murmur, clear and meant for all, he gave his expert opinion. Neither romantic nor classic, the Indigenous were like Scythians, not Romans. "The Indian is now a degraded being."

The only Indian in view dropped her broom.

Squire reached down to his moccasin and felt for the bone handle of the *àshare*, the faithful toothpick. With an ominous rumble, Cook warned Winona. He tapped the Mohawk on the back of his crouched padded shoulder and caught his eye. He pressed his lips

239

and shook his head and said, "Nope," and with a silent gesture, warned the minion to freeze. Alfie tilted his thumb to direct him to the last table. "'Ogs is 'ogs! So, you git ter work, uh?" He flapped his big wet bar-rag at him. "See ter Horatio Needless, Winona." Squire was reluctant but he backed down and the Indian servant woman, with an unbecoming knot in her jaw, straightened her back, glowered at Dunlop and stood, empty-handed.

But a servant's life is one distraction after another, one insult after another.

The regiment had grown impatient.

"'Oy!" Lieutenant Horatio Needles snapped his long fingers at Squire. "You. Winona, I say. Are you all right?" He tapped his skull making the rude suggestion about innate competence. "Do you understand the Queen's English? Look sharp. Three rye whisky. What'll ya have, Mister Winter? Queen's payin'. You, girl! Three schooners of ale."

For about ten minutes, Squire kept a hectic pace. Back and forth, from bar to table. The military wanted more pie. More drinks.

Sergeant Jimmy Nelson did a loud *pssst* for Squire's attention. Jimmy looked straight at the Mohawk, eye to eye, and asked if there were any women, "You know, for whorin'. Fer the wee Bing, here, and me too, awright? We're desperate, Winona." T'were bad, he admitted. They hadn't seen a gal in weeks.

Squire didn't know whether to feel relieved or insulted but he answered in an airy whisper. "No," he said. "No gals."

He sounded like someone had garrotted him.

He could not quite believe his voice. Bride had coached him. Quick inhaled breaths made his throat hurt but kept him from saying too much. Lieutenant Needles' lean cheeks puckered and released. Sergeant Jimmy Nelson's request for a woman was offensive. Needles returned to his topic. He was an officer of the Royal Canadian Rifle Regiment. The RCRR. The militiamen were there in the village on a delicate mission, Needles said. They were not there to cavort. They had time off in Toronto for that. At this, Jimmy Nelson's eyes curdled. Squire thought Jimmy Nelson had a face like a snotty old ewe but Winona was not quite as invisible as Squire had imagined. He was not going to find cover in whisking and scrubbing and serving ale and spirits.

Walter Winter shrilled. Without looking up from his cards, Whiskers said, "I do not recall you. New, eh, Winona?"

Squire placed a schooner of ale in front of the politician and at the same time he gulped air into his throat. "Yes. Sir. New."

"Ah-hah. No whores? Where's Teacher, then?"

"Megrim."

"So? She's ill? Getting better, I heard."

"Maybe not. Door locked. Nobody sees her."

"Where's Lizzie?"

"Megrim."

"Lizzie too? Terrible."

"Yessir."

"Both ill? Odd, aint it?"

"Not—odd, sir. Ague. Epidemic. They have ague. Even baby Pearl." Squire's voice cracked. He pinched his thumb.

The rotund Whiskers posed for his companions. He knew the place, didn't he? "What about Ann?"

"Her as well. Shakes. Shakes like leaf."

"My God. Must be a quite a bug. I myself am vulnerable to bugs. Glad you are here to help out, Winona."

"Yeah." Squire wondered whether Ann had returned from the barn. "Lad helps."

"What lad?"

"Farm lad. Anders."

Whiskers did not care about farm lads. The rotund politician's enormous navy woollen greatcoat had an equally enormous collar, which was cosseting. He made a moue. "I wouldn't wish to catch the ague."

Winona looked sympathetic. "No, sir. You would not. Fever goes high. Sweats. Bad sweats." In a second's pause, Squire said, "Medicine is bitter."

Shit. Did Whiskers recognize him? No. He didn't think so. Winter did not want to catch a chill but that was it. The man's expression was bland. For Winona, a moment of grace was on the horizon. Abrupt but welcome.

The politician's attention had wandered. Whiskers stopped talking to the Indian girl because the Scottish cigar-smoker was set to retire. Everyone stopped what he was doing to watch Flash Dunlop stagger to bed, hauling at the iron railing to pull himself up, step by step. Flash was irrepressible, though, a man of tremendous *jeu d'esprit*. He cursed at every step. *Great Roddy Slattery, the dissipated natives, the ugly women! None rife for market. Yeh, and the cheeky publican! Oh, the countryside! Hideous, like the ugly women. Responsible government, mes amis? A trap set by knaves to catch fools.* Snorting like a truffler, joking about the wretchedness of the wretched colony that had cost the lives of so many noble Romans, ah, noble Britons, Flash wriggled his herringboned ego up the stairs.

The room watched his back until the Ciminian darkness of the second storey swallowed him up and, at that very second, everyone guffawed.

Squire waved the broom like a wand to sweep away the cigar stink. It didn't work but mockery did not fail as he fluffed his skirt. He folded his hands in prayer and laid them aside his cheek. He was the image of the devout Miz Munny. In a rendition of Bride's trembling voice, he said, "Tweed do make a fat arse, sir."

Alfie snorted. Good riddance. Cheeky publican indeed. The Apostle Luke? Woll, the Apostle Luke would give the bugger t'runs for his money. To Squire, Cook wiggled digits. Four blokes and one woman down. Mennonites were gone. Flash Dunlop was gone. Four to go.

The four-to-go were wide awake and not about to retire to the second storey. Old Sergeant Jimmy Nelson wanted to go in for bigger stakes. Needles said, no. Jimmy Nelson and wee Bing felt goaded. They both scowled. Winter pretended he did not know what was going on in the regimental family and he focused on his draw and hunkered down.

On a whim, Whiskers grinned up at Winona.

Winona nodded back. He could read Whiskers' thoughts.

A ghost of a servant. Almost invisible but not quite. Best kind.

Winter lost the next round.

Lieutenant Needles dawdled in play but he picked the five of hearts he needed to fill in a double-ended straight. Cheered by the win, the boyish Needles opened up about a "secret mission." Squire was puzzled. For some reason, an odd reason, the lieutenant was revealing military business to Whiskers, a civilian. Why?

And where was Boy Hewson?

forty-three

Lieutenant Horatio Needles was built like Squire's frayed rope. He was thin. The big black mop of bear-hair on the top of his head sparked and shook. The hair had personality. More than the man himself, Squire thought. Walter Winter was no rope. He was squat and plump and bald, with hairy chops and dirty fingernails. With their heads together, plotting, Needles and Winter looked like exclamation and horror. Needles explained to Whiskers that he would convey a confidential report to the government leader, one William Henry Draper and, in due time, to the British Commander, General Cathcart. The report was meant to go direct to Governor General Lord Metcalfe but (and here Needles heaved his narrow chest and lowered the hoods of his currant-sized eyes in homage to the ill Metcalfe) it was not possible. Poor Metcalfe.

"What confidential report?" Winter stretched. The untrimmed salt-and-pepper chops tickled his jaws like an ostrich duster. "Speak up, Horatio. I'm ready to call it a night."

Winona cleaned and swept and swept some more and scrubbed. How she scrubbed. She scrubbed the chair legs and the tabletops. She was a busy cleaner but never obtrusive. Always ready to fetch more drinks, the poor simple drudge cleaned the small tavern room like a Cinderella; and she listened to every word they said.

Needles said, "Operation deserter."

"Operation deserter?"

Winter's expression was cool. Disbelieving, indeed. He had not heard about the operation. He had not heard about it and it must not be.

On the contrary, mister, it was real.

Winter gently patted his own mile-high forehead. It was burning up. "What is this nonsense, lieutenant?

"No nonsense."

"What then?"

"It's about smugglers, Mister Winter."

"Y'mean them go-getting Amish wheat smugglers?"

"No, sir," Needles said. "The worst kind. Horse smugglers. Maybe human smugglers."

"Oh, good grief, that is a dreadful thing."

THE CANADAS: COMPREHENDING

Topographical Information

CONCERNING THE QUALITY OF THE LAND,
IN DIFFERENT DISTRICTS; AND THE FULLEST
GENERAL INFORMATION: FOR THE USE OF
EMIGRANTS AND CAPITALISTS

COMPILED FROM ORIGINAL DOCUMENTS
FURNISHED BY JOHN GALT, Esq.,
Late of the Canada Company, and of the
British American Land Association

by Andrew Picken

Second edition

London: Published by Effingham Wilson
Royal Exchange
1836

CHAPTER
forty-four

Squire dredged up Bride's last order. *What was it?* He was not to lope down the inside set of steps like a wolf. He was to mince like Bride did. He came down to the tavern tripping like a Christmas angel. He had just returned from delivering Flash Dunlop's book, *The Canadas*. The Mohawk's world didn't welcome land-hungry immigrants, insolvent capitalists or journal-writing remittance men, and he had wanted to toss the book into the dustbin behind the bar except that Flash might return inconveniently in search of his mislaid property. The fix was simple. It was best to take the volume back to Flash's room. No problem. Squire had banged on Dunlop's door. The door had opened a crack and Squire had shoved the book inside. Intoxicated and impulsive, Dunlop had stuck out his tongue. It was a sweet little thing, the size of a squirrel dick, and the Mohawk, who had never before laughed in another man's face, let it roar. He got the door slammed in his. Not bad. There were no fisticuffs exchanged. Derision was all. Smiling, he gathered his skirt and returned to the tavern. He found a surprising freedom of spirit in the dress, that is, when it was not a hindrance. You did not have to ready yourself for a fight at every turn, although fights, when they did come, must have been wholly unfair to the trussed-up one.

At least two hours had passed since Squire had entered the bar-room and Ann, or Anders, had let the fire in the grate burn out. The Cave was sinking into a freeze and, outside, the temperature was dropping even faster. Winona scowled at the last table. Time to go. Smugglers were commonplace in the upper country. Smugglers were no reason to avoid bedtime. Squire could not catch Needles' attention to treat him to a big, get-out yawn, the kind that servants give to dull-witted, insensitive masters, but Lieutenant Needles had eyes only for Winter. Needles took no hints from the cold room, either. He swallowed a mouthful of watery rye whisky and started to talk. He wanted to explode and the enormous static bush of dark hair fanned out over his narrow head like Spanish lace. He looked part stunned by his job and part up to administering the indelible mark of the RCRR on the colony but it was certain his dry eyes were worried. He put down his glass. "Things go pretty good with the well-paid and well-tended veterans in the RCRR, of course," the lieutenant said, "but the other regiments have a chronic problem."

forty-five

Winter was tired. Maybe ill, he offered with defiance. But not too tired or ill to be inquiring. "Pray tell, what it is? What is the chronic problem, Horatio? Are your soldiers smugglers?"

"Not smugglers, Walter. Worse, I'm afraid."

"Worse?"

"Yes, yes, sir. Worse. They are deserters."

"Oh my." Whiskers' stomach rumbled like springtime thunder.

"I told you it was dreadful."

"I had no idea."

It was all Canada's fault, Needles said, tapping his fingers. Sure, sure, Mister Flash Dunlop was a sophomoric boob. No doubt about it, Dunlop was a remittance man wandering about the backwoods. But he was right. Life here in the upper province was awful. Awful as the black hole of Calcutta. Impassable bush. This fortress built by Nature against infection and the hand of war carried malaria, for God's sake, and back flies homing in to carve steaks from your hide. Needles gonged his fist on the table to emphasize his reluctant sympathy with deserters. The backcountry broke backs as easy as a man might split a twig. Did Walter not know that? Clearing the bush had cleared Mennonite Reba Elias, all right. Cleared the sense straight out of her. Made her as mad as a March hare, couldn't he see that? Canada affronted Needles and he wasn't finished.

Take Reba Elias. Poor strange gal. Always riding shotgun on the moral wagon, beaking about how she knew the right path for everybody, how she knew the Lord and how she was a proponent of voluntaryism, all that kind of stuff. Horatio Needles declared he was indignant on her behalf. Settlers like Reba chumped a few miles to plant a seed or two. Land would obsess them. Kill them, maybe. If not land, then bandits. Rebel gangs and horse thieves roamed the trails and they were hell-bent on treason. Micks and Shiners beat the shit out of anyone, anyone at all. The sullen native despised the sight of a British lobsterback. The lobsterback returned the favour. Battle tactics of Indians were just plain sneaky. They took one by surprise. No proper formation. No honour. Appalling really. Needles sneered. "Canada. Oh. Oh no. Don't be surprised, sir. Soldiers beg for something else, another posting, anywhere. Most would prefer the black hole of Calcutta to this godforsaken frog pond. Villages aren't worth rat spit. So what does our Toby do?" Needles' fists rose from the table and beat the air. "He deserts."

Mr. Winter straightened his collar and he held his fat, cramping stomach. "Pardon if I aint falling head over heels with sympathy, Horatio, but this here's my home."

"I apologize."

"S'all right—" Winter was a man among men and he burped green bell peppers. Oh, boy, he felt sick, he said. Cook and Winona raised their brows, made no comment, and Winona backed away a foot or two from the table and he put his broom on the bar counter. He had to do something. Behind the bar he started to wash glasses and steins.

Winter said, "Though I do not see myself sailing to—where is it that were you born, Lieutenant?"

"Shropshire."

"Fine, Shropshire. Sailing to Shropshire to whine about your women looking like goats and curse the damp or something similar."

"Your point is well taken, Walter. However, you are not in Shropshire. And I am here. I do not wish to insult you. I don't wish to be here and that's not even the point. There is a problem. I am simply trying to explain it. And the complication. The Queen wants to get it, the misconduct, under control. But by being careful."

"Smugglers, you say. Deserters? I'm not sure I understand. Spit it out, for Christ's sake. I am ill." Ten plump fingers with ten dirty fingernails lay planted on the wooden tabletop like a duck's webbed feet. Whiskers so badly wanted to leave.

Needles made a sour, contracted, disgruntled, church-lady face and lifted his shoulders. His black hair crested like a rooster's collar. "The complication, sir, is Indians. Six Nations. They are the smugglers. There. You see?"

"Heh?"

"Now you understand. Tact is important."

"Oh my." Winter signalled Winona and Cook.

From behind the bar they pretended not to see him. Winter seemed pleased. Squire figured Winona and Alfie should not appear to see, nor listen.

"The British Army's weak-kneed deserters flee stateside and the Americans don't deport them. No sir, they do not. They welcome them. Yes, by God, they welcome them." But Indians were the real culprits. They were the means of escape. Indians smuggled deserters stateside. Draper had sent Needles to investigate. Yes, Needles said, even William Henry Draper had heard the troubling rumour about the Six Nations but the government worried about tightening the torque of the Indigenous, who had lived on the continent for thousands of years. Some would remain defiant, ready to rebel against Her Majesty. The lieutenant was dismissive about the one who remained defiant. Those Indians thought even the Jay Treaty was insulting and, damnation, they crossed at will, wherever and however, over the sixty-year-old border.

"Frankly," Winter responded, blowing out cheeks and sending the tips of the ostrich-feather whiskers into a flutter, "I am stumped." He said Needles must be clear. British soldiers were deserters. Indians were smugglers. Indians took the Queen's runaways and delivered them safe and sound to the enemy republic and got money for the horses. True?

Needles nodded. True. His frame seemed to shrivel into a single strand. His wee brown eyes filled with tears. It was true. Army deserters floated over Lake Erie and alighted like goddam seagulls in Buffalo. Or Sandusky.

Winter raised his eyes. They were as sharp as quills. He took an even closer look at the new girl who was stacking glasses on the single shelf in front of the mirror and tapped his nose as though he smelled a burned piecrust. "Ah-hah. You look—like someone. You say you are not from here?"

"No."

"Not Six Nations, eh, Winona?"

"No." Squire gagged on the surreptitious shot Cook had just handed him. "No." He wheezed. "Not Six Nations. No. Ojibwe."

"Hmm." Winter hesitated and he peered hard at Winona and asked the clincher. "Ojibwe, eh? From where?"

"North." Winona kept her head down and picked up her broom and the bar rag from the counter. "Far. North."

"Ah-hah. North?" Whiskers had found a worm in the apple. "So, Winona? From where, far north?"

Winona spoke with her back turned to the regiment. "Why, Manitoulin," she said over her shoulder. "It's a—"

"Oh. Long ways from home, eh? Don't give me the song and dance. Beautiful Manitoulin. I know. I seen it. Coupla times."

Squire remembered that Whiskers' elderly mother was Cherokee, living at Muncey with the Oneida. Winter had travelled and he made something of tribal distinctions but you could say he was not a genius on cross-dressing, not at all. He gave not a second glance to the neck or the jaw or the eyebrows of Winona. Winter was satisfied. The new girl was Ojibwe, from Manitoulin. Not Six Nations, not from hereabouts. Squire sucked an uneven breath and wandered over to Alfie, who handed him another wee dram for courage.

Squire pinched the broom under his arm, took the shot and tossed back the whisky.

This night was fucking endless.

CHAPTER
forty-six

With agitated fingers, Needles fidgeted with his short uniform cuff. He resented the interruption. He narrowed his eyes to dashes. Did Mr. Winter, a renowned Tory and a Loyalist, well look here, did he know any Indians other than the Mohawk Johnsons? Needles had already spoken to the Johnsons. The Anglican Johnsons found the whole smuggling racket distasteful but they were without a clue about the names of the perpetrators.

Did Walter Winter know more than the Johnsons?

The lieutenant demanded an answer. It was important to get at the truth. How were the deserters escaping? Exactly who helped them?

Winter was flummoxed.

He swore he didn't know. His plump upper torso vibrated with candour.

Needles asked the big question.

Did Warriors harbour the army's fugitives and did he, Walter, take money to arrange passage of said persons to Buffalo City? What was the word? Needles forgot to whisper. His rising voice was hoarse. "Come now, Walter. Tell me. Is it Warriors? If you know, you must tell me." Needles said that Montréal worried about maintaining the peace and quiet and loyalty of Indian Loyalists. Did not want to raise the flag, as it were.

Squire had an awkward moment. He was back at the small iron tub, washing glasses. He held a rinsed glass. It slipped but he caught it. Peace? Quiet? Loyalty? Where are you, Missus Goosay? Ignoring Six Nations sovereignty, Draper's government, and all colonial governments before it, had been liberal in awarding British veterans, the likes of snotty old Sergeant Jimmy Nelson, and skinny, bushy-tailed, inquisitive Lieutenant Horatio Needles, enormous chunks of land. If Missus Goosay were listening to that flagpole Needles and his desire for peace, quiet and loyalty among the people, her own flag would be up.

Needles seem to sense negative vibrations. The officer juddered a schooner to his lips and his little jowls stayed tight. He said, "Now, now," to the round-jowled Winter, who was not particularly alarmed about the Loyalists or in need of *now-nowing*. Needles spoke with clipped tones, to remind them of the number one consideration, to keep calm. "Calm. Calm, I tell you. Nobody is to get upset, Walter. We cannot deal with restless natives. Not now. We are stretched. We have limited resources. We have the Columbia district boundary dispute and the Americans and their manifest bloody destiny and the Western Indians to worry about. Keep local Indian smugglers off balance. It's 'forgive and forget,' you see, but terms are clear. You know how things work."

The spin.

Walter Winter may have been a chubby no-account ground-pecking bird, a plump, gossiping birdbrain. But he knew one thing. He knew how things worked.

So did Winona.

CHAPTER
forty-seven

Needles smacked a royal flush in clubs on the table.

"That's it, Walter. Hand over your chips."

Silhouettes and shadows and smoke had drawn circles around the panelled room and the men's faces took on a grave, other-worldly aspect. One of the camphene lamps on the bar suddenly snuffed out. The lard candles on the tables faded to dots and wicks were limpid lavender balls. The Cave was silent, freezing cold, a shining spot for hatching a conspiracy and Walter Winter and Lieutenant Needles had caught the mood but the hypochondriac Winter seemed as ill as he feared he was and his nose dripped like a leaky yard-pump. Narrow-faced Needles looked around for spies but there were just the servants, going about their business. Cook had gone back to the main house to fetch more eggs, beans and salt pork for the canallers' breakfast. Anders scrubbed sticky ale from the chairs on the other side of the room. Winona swept, swept, washed, and swept and swept. The middle of the Cave was clean, swept bare. Active little drudges. Needles' expression revealed his opinion. Drudges were simple. Not bright, not bright enough to understand the complications that his army must face down and conquer.

Winter appeared indifferent to wins and losses at cards. He had dismissed the poker game to hear about operation deserter. "So, the plan, Horatio? You cannot march up to the Confederacy's Council House and demand culprits. It won't happen."

"Not at all, Walter, not at all."

"Humph."

"I have an idea."

"Excellent." Winter was doubtful. "An idea, Lieutenant. Yes, that's excellent. I shall be happy to hear it."

Over his beard, Needles' prominent cheekbones shone like brass doorknobs. His wild hair had settled to a sleek pelt. "Hear it? You will see it, sir."

"See it?" Winter was jumpy. He spoke harsh and shivered. "See what, Horatio? I fear I'm catching the ague that's infected the tavern. Home for me—"

"Wait." Needles was earnest. "Within the hour my man will bring me a guilty Indian."

Winter whistled. "What? By Jove, what's this?"

Needles had the habit of looking seraphic when something was going well, which was why he often lost at cards. "Yes, Walter. You will see. My man has agreed to find me a smuggler. And bring him here. We shall have a one-to-one. A very serious one-to-one."

Whiskers leaned in front of Sergeant Jimmy Nelson to speak to Needles.

Jimmy Nelson eyed the lieutenant with distaste. Bing nodded at Nelson in agreement with the unspoken assessment.

Winter sneezed. "What do you mean? Your man brings an Indian here? What man? Who is this man of yours?"

Lieutenant Needles played the government's game close to his chest. His eyes got smaller than currants. They were pemmican currants. He sized up his military companions. He was the commander, wasn't he? Yes, he was. He acted. Lieutenant Needles ordered Bing and Nelson out. They ought to keep watch for the expected or, perhaps, the unexpected guest.

The old veteran Jimmy Nelson nodded.

Both Nelson and Bing shuffled back their chairs and acted as though they were subordinates to the cause, content to let a superior fellow take command of the investigation. They stood and turned from the table. They walked by the bar, grabbed their uniform jackets from the coat tree, put them on, and headed to the door. With backs turned to their officer, opinions surfaced. Each gave the other a derogatory snort. They hated him, the emaciated beanpole. "Old pins and Needles."

"Stick 'im," Jimmy Nelson said. "We're outa here, mister."

Bing said, "Yeah. We're gone. Hey, I mean it, Jimmy, I mean it, we are really gone."

Squire wondered whether Needles had heard.

Veterans or not, Needles' men must have hoped so. In case their superior had missed the comment, the soldiers made extra-loud stomps going down the steps and they disappeared into the night, heading for Sandusky, no doubt.

"My men wait—" Needles leaned in to look deep into Winter's eyes. "Or maybe not. The chap who helps me, Walter. By name—"

Whiskers puckered his full mouth; he hunkered his neck into his ostrich-feathered chops and bit the horrible dirty fingernail. "Yes? Who is he?"

"His involvement with Draper must not pass your lips."

"I agree. It will not pass my lips." Winter picked up his chin and widened his weary lids and he repeated, "Won't pass my lips."

"Very well, sir." Lieutenant Needles of the RCRR was prepared to give over a little. "His name is Richard Boynton Hewson."

~

That name. Damn if it didn't keep popping up at the most unexpected times.

The new corn broom flew over the bar like a javelin. On the way over, it bounced on the counter and hit the milk-glass jar of chilled fig tomatoes. Container and contents flew high into the air. The pickles splattered on the plank floor like clotted blood and Nellah's display bowl smashed into smithereens. Shards caught a smidgeon of light from the lanterns on the bar and through a mess of acrid tomato pulp Squire could follow glass pieces jabbing into the baseboard. Winona whispered that she was real sorry for the commotion and she begged the forgiveness of the lieutenant. She ran to the disaster. She picked up the broom. She squatted over the muddle to sweep up the broken pieces and squished tomatoes. She was energetic in spite of a few troubles with her skirt and she dumped gunk into her waiting dustbin.

"Dense. Even for one of them," Needles said.

He apparently remembered something. He remembered Walter Winter's mother was Cherokee and Needles' face took on a horrified expression. He apologized. For shame, he said. He was forever forgetting. Some people liked the Indians. Respected them. Were even related to 'em. The sudden sound of breaking glass had shivered his timbers, is all. He apologized again.

Winter said, "Well, whaddaya know—" He made no acknowledgment of the military man's insult or apology. He had a hangnail on his thumb and started to peck on it again like it was suet. "A sage plan. And you're right, by the way. Boy Hewson has a big name. He's a robber and, I hate to say it, sir, he's a horrible ruffian. I have heard things about his ways with women. And horses. Why, I heard even Nellah Golden's got a big problem with him." Walter Winter's tone was nuanced but, of course, Winter knew how it was. He, like Needles, suspected the drudges were not very smart but they had ears like African elephants. "Will it work, do you think, Horatio? Will Boy deliver you a 'savage'?"

"Yes, yes, Walter, I am sure he will."

"How can you be sure? I hear bad things."

"He wants something."

"Ah, hmm, I see, I see. A trade, then."

"Precisely. He says he wants a trade. He probably wants to trade his information for Crown land. He wants Draper to get the government, or the Canada Company, either one or the other, to grant him a section. Freehold. You know how generous the Crown is to allies. Poor in money. Rich in land. Always offering to give you land." Needles opened his palms as though, for services performed, the agreeable Winter might find an acre or two buried there.

Offering to give you something that belongs to someone else, thought Squire, as Winona scraped up the heap of clotted tomato.

Winter cast his eyes to the job Winona was doing and, without hiding his distaste for her and the mess she was cleaning, he said, "So it seems, Horatio. I myself must apply."

Needles' thin face fell hard and his eyes glowed like red beads but his words were brave. "Funny you say that. Do something for us, Walter, and you will get a reward. You may yet consider yourself a western settler."

"I am joking. Don't worry, Horatio. I like village life. I do not need a reward. What does Boy want? Don't tell me he wants social respectability. If he does want social respectability, I dare say it will be difficult. With his reputation, you know—"

"Possibly. He is eyeing the Huron tract. Say, do you think that gruesome creature, that Winona, is she listening to us?"

Whiskers' eyes sought out the Indian woman, who had picked up the pace of her sweeping. He shook his head in the negative and mouthed, "She's a blockhead." As to tracts, Whiskers was knowledgeable. "Ah-hah, Huron tract. Remote, though, aint it?"

"Mmm. Honestly, Hewson isn't sure where to go. You said it. He needs to be careful. Perhaps Elora. An informer's life, Walter, you know how it is."

Winter knew. He knew the Englishmen's so-called Canada Company was big. Too big to be scrupulous but, really, who would expect perfect honesty in a Crown company that was too big to fail? Nearly twenty years ago, an act of the British parliament had incorporated the organization, which was to assist emigrants by providing them with sound ships, reasonable fares, farm tools and, all things considered, cheap land. The company claimed it owned almost one-and-a-half million acres. Vast Indian territory fell under the control of absentee landlords, private enterprise and whining shareholders and the company's directors and commissioners were an ocean apart but so what? The company tried to fulfill its mandate. Clergy reserves aside, charges of corruption didn't excite an unflappable politician.

"Elora?" Winter said. "Where is that again?"

"Not too far. Day's travel. Old William Gilkinson's settlement. Near where them oversized Mennonites hail from. And that poor March hare, Reba Elias."

"Well, that's first-rate, Lieutenant." Whiskers stood to give his cramping limbs a good shake. He rearranged his enormous coat tails and sat down with a heavy smack and the room shuddered. "I guess Hewson is a valuable commodity."

"He is, indeed."

"May I ask you? How valuable?"

"Well—"

"What's his role?"

"He is an informer."

"I understand that."

Needles was sharp. "What's your point?"

"Why him? Why Hewson? Can't you find a better man?"

"Oh, for God's sake, sir. Don't turn squeamish. It is the spy game. Types like Hewson infiltrate oppositionists."

"It works?"

"Sure it works." Needles was blunt. "As long as his cover holds, yes. Bounty hunter catches him. Hewson goes to gaol. Manages to escape. Unlike Bobby John." Needles inhaled to his hair tips, "whom, I am told, is caught. Ahem. Yes, I am told this on authority, by the way. Yes, sir. Good authority. Warriors' head honcho Bobby John is caught. He has been brought in. Turned over to magistrate in Hamilton. If you wanna talk about rough sorts, the bounty hunters, they caught Bobby John and turned him in. Today. They are set to collect a private purse, I hear. A colossal reward, by all counts."

"Bobby John has been caught? That so? I had not heard. It's that wealthy sonofabitch Octavius Millburn what posted the purse, you know. Millburn gets away with bloody murder. Ah, the rich—"

Lieutenant Needles looked at the ceiling. His expression was bleak. He hated this cheerless country and his feelings were writ large on his worried forehead but his black hair stood straight at attention to countermand anyone's getting the notion of *his* mutiny. "Yeah. Millburn still has his filthy lucre, though. So my sources say. They say nobody has collected the purse, as yet."

"Well—" Winter's amazement lit up the room. "Well, if Bobby John has been captured, why the hell don't you go to the Hamilton gaolhouse and talk to him about deserters and smugglers and such things?"

"I would love to, sir. But we cannot get close to him. The Crown has charged him with the rape of the lady that owns this here tavern. There is a problem of jurisdiction. And proof. Evidence, you see. We need someone to give us evidence; we need someone to squeal on Bobby John and the Warriors and give us details of the whole smuggling operation. Bobby John aint talking to us. That is a for-sure. This is all hush-hush, like I said."

CHAPTER
forty-eight

"All right." Winter rubbed tired eyes. "All right. 'When the goodman mends his armour,' eh, Horatio? So, what d'ya want from me?"

"Draper wants you to get the word out. In the district."

"Word? What word? I thought you said 'operation deserter' was supposed to be *hush-hush*." Whiskers made to stand. "You know what? I need to get to bed."

"It is hush-hush, Walter. Good God! Nothing about deserters."

"No mention of deserters. All right, Horatio. What'm I to say?" Winter hunched back down into his greatcoat.

Needles spoke to Whiskers' ear-tips and the top of his head. The lieutenant steamed ahead, full throttle, and he practically shouted at the man across from him. "Just say this, Walter. Great Mother is sad to hear her red children have taken to horse smuggling."

Muffled into his woollen collar, Winter's beak instantly emerged. He beat his arms to start the circulation. "It's frigging freezing. There's no light. Bring that bar lamp over here, Winona! I'm feverish. I've caught the ague. Do I got it all straight then, Lieutenant?"

"Well, Wally, do you?"

"Stuff the Wally, will you? I said I am feverish, you know. I must be dreaming." Winter must have started to run a fever.

His bald dome pearled with beads. "You and your RCRR boys hold tight. I know what you do not want. You don't want a smart Indian."

"Don't be absurd." Needles' eyes took on the same rare tinge as the devil-knowing eyes of Reba Elias.

"I get it Horatio. I do."

Needles' hair sparked in the dry room.

He spoke through scrunched lips. "Get what, Wally?"

This time, Whiskers waved off the slur. He said, "I get the rhetoric but in my opinion, Lieutenant, a good Indian, that is to say, a doctor or a lawyer, a *good* Indian, you see, he makes a helluva lot more trouble for you boys than a smuggler. Indians? Why, sir, you boys want a little cluster of happy hoeing market gardeners, working their little plots, not selling extra produce, just feeding themselves, so's you don't hafta feel guilty about starving 'em. You boys want a red-skinned subsistence farmer more than a smart-alecky red-skinned lawyer facing you in a courtroom. But a day of change is on the horizon." Whiskers pointed the gnawed finger an inch from Needles' slanted eyes. "Enough. I really am tired. Feeling more ill by the second. No more putting lipstick on a pig. I know what's shit and what aint. Just give me the scoop. What is the Great Mother's word? For publication, I mean."

Whiskers' neck had emerged out of his coat and he looked so much like a miserable, ill and hungry bird that Needles found the grace to relent. "My boys, as you call them, the RCRR, the Rifles, that's us, we'll catch the smugglers and bring them to justice. Gaol, in other words. No. No. No. Not true, sir. Do not get ruffled. We go hard on the fella that Hewson brings us tonight. Gaol time for him! We make an example of one. Throw the book at him. Lock him up and toss away the key. That is it, though. We will stop the Warriors with one incisive blow. One Indian takes the fall. Right, Wally?"

"Last time. It is *Walter*. Why only one?"

"Draper aint about to open a can of jurisdictional worms. Too tricky for that. Six Nations Indians do not know it, though, do they? Best to keep them divided. At loggerheads. Keep them jittery. Arguing in Council about the Navigation. Let them fear retribution. Great Mother is angry at 'em, eh? What do you say, Wally?"

"I say, *Walter*, goddamit!"

Needles waved his skinny arms around like maybe he gave a shit. "Sorry. What help, sir, with the word?"

"Hmm. Well, I can chat with a few people. There's one kid who might help. For a few coins, I expect. Tehawennihárhos—"

"Who?"

"A kid I know. Squire Davis. He's Six Nations. He's agreeable enough, I guess. Seems intelligent. Literate. Poor as St. Barty's rat, I can tell you."

"Wonderful. A redskin loves his presents."

"Humph. Careful there, Lieutenant."

"Sorry, oh, oh, so sorry, Walter. Shame on me. I keep forgetting about your mother."

"S'all right, Horatio. She is a Loyalist. Collects an annuity. Anyway, as I was saying. For a modest number of shekels I expect Davis will spill the beans about the horse smuggling. He is into the Indian shell game. Steals horses, sells them back to the owner. He could be a smuggler. Or even a timber poacher. So I have heard."

"Heard? From whom?"

"Coupla fellas. The chiefs, in fact."

"Who? Men of standing?"

"I would say so. George Johnson and Fairmont Hill. They say the Davises are a scurvy lot. Racketeers. Young Squire Davis is naught but a ruffian. A troublemaker, y'know?"

Squire stopped sweeping and stood with an open mouth. His mother Margaret Riley had told him earwigging was bad. She said it brought trouble. He had admired the politician Walter Winter and he applauded what Winter had just said about Indian lawyers and hoped Winter would fare well in the game he was playing. The Mohawk imagined that the feeling he had for Winter was reciprocated. He had no idea that the politician had no respect. Squire Davis was a racketeer? No. An accomplice to murder after the fact? Yes, indeed. He thought of Ziggy mouldering under Ruthven Hall at Indiana. But who said he was a ruffian and a troublemaker? Johnson? Well, fine. Bad weather from that front was anticipated. Chief Fairmont Hill? He had never met Fairmont Hill but he was in no position to speak out and Winona resumed sweeping, but slowly.

The lieutenant's face showed hope. "Squire Davis. Sounds a perfect contact. You'll have a chat with the fellow?"

"Sure, I will. We will see what he says."

"Excellent, Walter. Excellent. You are a good man, sir. Good man, indeed. Resourceful. Glad you're with us. Rewards will come—"

"Hello, Horatio, speaking of—yeah, speaking of come—Boy Hewson is here. I'd say your timing was fine." Winter pecked with vigour at the grubby hangnail. "Yup, here he is."

CHAPTER
forty-nine

Not fifty minutes past, Squire had put a candle on the regimental table. The wick had burned to an icy-blue dot. Cigar fug hung in woolly wisps over the bar. Because of the lack of light and the grey ashes in the fireplace, it was not surprising that the atmosphere of the room had turned arctic, but cold or not, the men wiped their moist brows with large calico handkerchiefs. Squire swore to himself he could smell Needles' sweat, or maybe his own, but the peppery stink of nerves pinched his nostrils.

Squire faced the mirror. His future, unseen, stretched out behind him. He saw his past straight ahead. His rouged cheeks had faded to the colour of weak tea and the bloom was off the rose, as Jennie would say. He felt like a man, weird though, a man in a dress, but there was no time to feel sorry for Winona because in the reflection he saw not only the travesty of Maggie Walker but also a certain Hewson, who had come into the Cave through the south bar entrance and was just crossing over the threshold. From the corner of his eye Squire got a vision, saw the mysterious one and saw what Winter had seen, although in reverse.

Boy wore glasses, chunky lenses in gold-wire frames, same as the Fergusons' girl, Ann Auld. For the pleasure of wardens everywhere, the gangster appeared penitent. He stood, eyes half-closed, not unlike his sister Bride. He beheld vinegary tomato clots at his

boot tips. It took the thud of a fluttering heart, a mere second made
to seem like an hour, before he raised his head. He sniffed the pickle
juice. He squinted. He surveyed the Cave, deliberate, left to right,
corner to corner. His vision seemed defective but Squire could guess
his purpose. Mischief.

Boy Hewson was alone.

Where was the sample smuggler? Where was the red man
doomed to have the one-to-one with the lieutenant and "take the
fall"? And where were Boy's bodyguards? Of course, they were outside. Waiting. Maybe they were wondering why they had taken the
job on such an inclement evening but too bad for them. Boy wanted
to be alone. He was there to deal. The government's dealmaker was
ready, in the grungy corner of the pitch-dark dining room, home of
the Hanover rat, just the spot where the good Lieutenant Needles
belonged.

Boy Hewson spotted the officer of the Crown, the man whom
William Henry Draper had sent, the man who was ready to trade.
Squire thought the gangster's face instantly assumed satisfaction.
Aside from the drudges, nobody was about. The disposition was right
because the inn was as dozy as an opium den and the tavern was as
empty as last month's whisky barrel. One camphene lantern burned
on the bar, which meant Boy had also seen Winona. Squire felt no
need to cower or preen and fluff the grey dress. It was immaterial.
Miss Ince was dead. He wanted to confront the man and he turned
slow, away from the glass and light, and brought his dark, unsmiling
and unreflected Indian image into the cold and dangerous tavern.

Still, a maid was a maid. Winona had refills of whisky for Needles and Walter Winter and, with a smooth gesture, a modest feminine gesture, she reached below the bar for a round-bottomed
tumbler and poured a special drink. Next to the greasy-fingered
schooners, the new glass glittered clean and bright on the tray.

Hewson took a tentative step toward the two men who had remained seated at his arrival and who sat motionless, pending his approach. All the while Boy moved toward them, he held his head canted, as though he expected to dash outside or, at any second, fall down and paste his ear to the ground to listen for a thundering posse. He did not fall. He trotted dainty, like a mountain goat, as though his hamstrings were unyielding after years of wearing boots with heels. Squire was by far the taller of the two. The Snowman, he would tower over Boy Hewson. The Frenchman could squish a furry little caterpillar just as easy. Old Fox Bart Farr would walk into a barroom with more confidence. Boy caused big trouble but he cast a shadow no farther than the icy-blue tick on the candlewick.

Boy Hewson and Winona stood face to face.

~

"Rye whisky?" Winona held up the tray.

"Yeah. Rye. Ale chaser." Boynton Hewson accepted the drink. Behind the glasses, his eyes shone like china marbles. "Hey, get a schooner for me." He squinted. He could not see well or else couldn't believe what he saw.

"What's your name old girl? Aint Maggie—" He grunted. "I hope."

Alfie had not yet returned from the main house. Do not lose focus, Squire warned himself. Be female, act female. The tuneless refrain ticked like a pendulum. Male and female emotions clashed and, for a terrifying minute, he could not tell which was which but in truth it didn't matter. He must be servile.

Boy said, "Wha'd you say your name was?"

"Winona." Squire scratched his neck and he tried not to appear to overstep the mark but not being used to this business he reckoned he did not know where the mark was.

Hewson shrugged his right shoulder. "Winona? Win-on-a? Hey, what kind of name is that?" He ignored the spittoon and hawked on the floor. He canted his head another degree. "Say, you know what? You know John Norton? Yup, you look something like him. If I looked like John Norton, old girl, I'd be pissed. But, so what, you don't care about being pretty, hey?"

"Aint I pretty?" Winona had a defeated expression.

Dead silence.

"Soooo. Win-noooo-na. Win-on-ahhh." Boy tilted his head like he would shake water out of his ear. "Nope. Never heard of it."

"Is that right, mister? Well, Ma, she tells Pa, she says, yup, Pa, I tell you what. Her name's Winona." Squire breathed into his throat and he kept the edge out of his voice but from his seat Whiskers looked up at him and frowned and the Mohawk knew he had made a false start. He would have to watch it.

Boy appeared thoughtful. He stayed in the middle of the room and he stared ahead and twisted his lip. "Hey—" He sniffed. "Place stinks. I smell rotten women and dead daisies. Is that you, old girl?" He wrinkled his nose. He did not seem to care much for Winona and her unsmiling face and her square jaw and her French perfume and her apron stained with mashed tomato figs. "Hey, old girl, where is the lovely Maggie, anyway?"

The Mohawk lowered his gaze. He feared he could not wait. For the mere price of a moment's pleasure, he would flatten the whoreson. He realized he was balling his fist and muttering but he wasn't able to stop and there he was, stuck, explaining Maggie. "Gone to the Territory, I guess." Last words welled up enough to strangle him.

"Hey, speak up, old girl. Where? To Caledonia?"

"Maybe north territory. Innisfil."

"Innisfil?" Boy was disbelieving. The gold frames had turned to black. "Hey? Way up there, Win-on-a?"

"She visits Auntie. Ye-up, way up there."

Hewson shifted from one foot to the other. He appeared doubtful. He gave the impression that he usually was not the one to get things wrong. "Hey, do I believe you?" He shrugged. "Not what I heard. Paddy said Maggie's Auntie Polly lives at Oneida village near the Navigation's new place. Caledonia."

Boy looked down at Walter Winter, who merely shrugged.

In the corner, moon-faced Winter was tense and exhausted. His left eyelid had a tic. His corvid brain was depleted and the salt-and-pepper muttonchops sagged even as he drew his greatcoat tighter around him. Maggie? Auntie? Caledonia? Who cared?

Squire tried to keep a casual conversation in spite of the way he felt. "Auntie Polly is not Maggie's clan. Many clan relatives in Innisfil." There were at least five cracks running across the floorboards. Squire counted them. Counted them again. *Hey, how about I gut you like a walleye.*

"Too bad, Win-on-ahhh. I like target practice. You kin shoot an Injun in the tail-feathers down in Caledonia. On Her Majesty's Service. Hey, military man, you hear me?"

Needles frowned and he pretended he didn't.

Still face to face with Boy, Squire kept his shoulders and back straight. He felt as stiff as a wooden statue, ready for the cigar store.

Boy turned his peculiar eyes upwards. "Hey, I would like to see Maggie. Yessir, I hear she's a beauty. You know what, I hoped she'd be here. I will find her. But, how?" He grinned from ear to ear showing none of his teeth and his tone was as flat as Winona's bare chest. "You Indian people have relatives too numerous to count. Like fly eggs."

"Yes—" Squire bit his lip until he tasted iron. No move, though, he thought. Not yet. "Yes, sir." *Tail-feathers? Fly eggs?* "I'll get you— get your ale."

"Hey, you do that, old girl. Shit. No Maggie, eh? I'd sure like to meet that little beauty."

Boy caught Winona's arm as she moved to the bar. "Say, old girl, where's the boss? Nellah? Is that her name? She around some-wheres? We are buddies. I'd like to catch up."

Squire did not have any guidelines for this. *Catch up your arse. Make a move, you bastard, and I crack your skull.*

Slinking down further into his greatcoat, Winter piped up. "No sir! No siree, Bob. She is in bed. Got the ague. High fever. Running rampant around these parts. Epidemic. I myself am coming down with it. I know it. I can feel it. I can smell it."

"Hey, that's a pity. Yessir, that's a pity." Boy Hewson grinned again.

His expression said nothing was a pity, not really, not when there were people to frighten or there was money on the table. At last he appeared ready for commerce and sauntered direct to Needles and Winter's table and pulled up a Windsor chair, flipped it front to back, and sat down.

Needles and Winter shuffled in their chairs and soaked up their guest's confidence with a fleeting nod. They both seemed edgy; well, Needles was.

"Lieutenant Horatio Needles, sir, at your service, sir." The lieutenant ran and re-ran his hands through his hair. His mane was up, as fluffy as a coon-tail hat. Fingers beat the tabletop as though he did not want anyone, him included, forgetting who was in charge. He was in charge. He, Needles. The boss man.

"One thing, y'hear," Boy said with leisure, looking from Whis-kers to the officer. "It is important, Mister Needles."

"What's that? What is so important?" Needles inhaled and exhaled, noisy like. He appeared slightly relieved because the gang-ster was small and frail. The loss of paralyzing fear must have been unexpected.

"Yes, I want to know." Winter had said he wanted to depart but he added he was not going anywhere until he heard what Boy had to say. Rolls of hairy neck emerged from the greatcoat. "What is so important, Mister Hewson?"

Boy said, "Hey, not to you two. Who cares about you?" There was a snort from Needles. "Important to me. Hey, I am gonna take that back. Important to you too, maybe, if there is gonna be a trade here. No land, though. I don't want to trade for land."

Needles' nose sucked the air. "You don't?"

"Nope. You help me. Something I gotta know."

"What would that be, pray tell?" Lieutenant Needles said, thinning his thin mouth and tapping out reveille with his fingertips.

Boy spoke soft. "My sister, Bride. Bride Munny. Where is she? And more important, where is them kids of hers?"

~

Squire heard the question he had dreaded and, while he lingered in the background, waiting in the musty corner for the answer, he put down the crimped tin tray on the closest unlit table and fooled with his apron like the quintessential worry-wart and, so far as anyone could tell, paid little mind to the white men.

Needles scoffed. "C'mon, now, Mister Hewson. Bride Munny? Where is she?" He looked for a brief second at Walter Winter in the hope of an answer. "I ask you, sir, *who* is she?"

Boy made a show of being sad. "Hey, that's not the answer I am after, Needles."

"Tut, tut, Mister, er, Boynton. I do not know your sister." Needles was offended and his hair sparked in indignation. "And we can't have her inserted into our deal. You see—"

"Well, now, now, now." Winter interrupted. His watery chirruping and high collar spoke to smoky hills. "You should ask me, Boy. I might know her. What's she look like?"

273

Winona looked like a priestess.

She had positioned herself two feet behind Walter Winter. She pretended to pick up something from the floor but reached into the moccasin sheath and held the bone handle of the *àshare* in a firm grip. If the politician started to say he had heard Bride was a resident of the inn, Squire would act and act fast and let the devil take the hindmost.

Winter fought for Boy's regard and repeated, "I ask you, sir, what does she look like?"

Boy was sunk into his own crypt. He ignored one question and answered another. "She's got a couple of brats. She neglects them, a'course. Can't say I used to mind but of late I have decided I do mind. Hey, I hear the Magdalene nuns have a place for female miscreants. I am gonna find them kids and take them away from her." Boy's china eyes rolled in derision. Squire did not doubt that taking away the children was solely meant to punish Bride for running out on him. "Get them raised up proper, you know? With the nuns. Rear them like good Catholics." Boy shook his head and he heaved a sigh, long and sad. With a lazy up-and-down gesture to indicate a woman, he said, "What does Bride look like? Hey, to be frank with you, mister, she's a skinny dirty bitch."

"Oh, that's so?" Winter was crestfallen. "I dunno her. I dunno any skinny dirty bitches."

Boy was pleasant but nothing warmed the porcelain eyes. "No matter, Mister Winter. I will find her. She pays for her sins."

Winter said, "Well, then, sir, I am glad—"

Boy laughed. "Glad? Oh, mister—don't be glad. Aint gonna be a happy time. Not for one Bride Munny."

"Well, I mean, I am glad for the sake of the Christian community, but I don't envy her, of course, not with the Magdalenes—"

Boy fingered the tabletop as though years of wax drippings held a message from Louis Braille. "No, sir. You are right, hey, because I don't envy her neither."

Squire retrieved the tray. He moved around the table, stepped in leisure, and he was sure no one dreamed that the drudge with the faint five-o'clock shadow had a knife at the ready, prepared to plunge it into a man's neck. He loitered. He loitered longer than he should have, afraid to get drinks in case Winter or Needles declared he had seen Bride or wanted to search the brick house but neither man did.

Boy said he was a patient sort. He would find his kinfolk, indeed he would, come hell or high water. He would find them if he had to turn over every rock in the united province but, he would confess it, he could use help. "You see, Mister Needles," Boy directed himself to the officer, "it's like this. You find the kids for me and I find a smuggler for you."

Needles feigned a sucked-cheeked, shocked look but everyone at the table knew the lieutenant's game. "A bribe? Good grief. I can't do that. I am an officer."

"I will even take your word on good account, Mister Needles." The china eyes rolled to the ceiling to give Lieutenant Needles some thinking room. Suddenly, English pounds materialized. Squire could not tell how many but it was a lot of money. "Tell me you'll help me as soon as you leave this rundown shack. That is all I need to hear."

Needles had an epiphany. He understood. His tone was agreeable. "Do you mean, sir?" He should not mistake Boy's solemnity for seriousness. "You mean—?"

"Hey, I mean, don't give me land yet. Don't need it momentarily. I aint motivated by monetary gain in this here trade. I got family feelings. Strong family feelings. I will give you a squealin' smuggler tonight if you keep a lookout for Pomeroy and Christina Munny."

"Oh, oh. Hmmm. I see." Needles pocketed the money.

No land? A substantial gift of money for a hardworking officer who suffered the vagaries of life in Upper Canada? That must have been unexpected. Squire dawdled. He filled their drink orders and he listened, careful not to make a sound, but no one paid Winona any mind.

Needles looked seraphic and he made excuses and took what was offered. "Here's the country for playing hide-and-seek, Boynton."

"Hey, I know that. Better than you."

"Of course. Of course. You know we can hardly keep a lookout for our own soldiers."

"You would be doing the new colony a service, Mister Needles, herding a few wayward Munnys into a confessional. Them youngsters will get goodness." Boy's look was cunning. "Or at least respectability. Mister Needles, listen here. Place a modern kid in a cathedral and the light of opportunity will blind him. He will learn to adapt foul means to fair ends. I tell you so, sir, because I believe it. Past experience." Boy's cynicism turned sober and there was no mistaking his seriousness. "You keep an eye out for my kinfolk and I will hand over what you need, temporarily free of charge and, hey, I will tell you about Bobby John's Warriors and deserters and smugglers and such and so forth. Don't know where on the river they meet, is all. I will find out. Help me, lads, and I swear to help you nab a British deserter and an Indian horse thief."

"I can promise you nothing, nothing concrete, that is, but, fine. Fine. We'll post a bill for the Munnys." Needles turned in the expectation of addressing an order to Sergeant Jimmy Nelson but found only curious Walter Winter. "Wally, make a note."

Walter Winter capitulated. No offence. He was a politician. News was what he lived for, what he lived on. Secrets too. In the end, he was the Devil's own. He did not correct Needles on the *Wally* business. He only said, "Righty-ho."

Lieutenant Needles was beaming. He flattened the hair sparks and smacked the table. "Yes, Boynton. The Crown will send out a missing person's bill to post offices, if you like."

Boy Hewson clapped his hands. Once. "I do like. Bride will get a damn good fright when she spies a poster naming her as a harlot and a derelict mother and her kids as delinquents. Flush her out, hey?"

Winter said, "About the bill. Shall I have informers contact you, sir? Where do you live?"

"Me? God no. Have them write to the postmaster at Paris in care of Brown. Mister Brown, if you please. Direct all inquiries to a certain gentleman, Mister Brown, who lives in Paris. Make sure you state the price—five dollars for a sighting, twenty for a napping. Mister Brown will mail out a reward upon receipt of kids' arrival with the nuns." Boy sat straight. He clapped both hands flat on the table. "Gentlemen, go forward on this thing. I got friends in White-man's Creek and they will look after it, sending out the reward, no matter where I am or what happens to me."

Needles agreed. Fine, fine.

Winter asked what the Munnys looked like and he wrote down the particulars and at times he seemed disturbed but he didn't stop. He said he wondered whether it would be worth the energy to create such a questionable bill but Needles *shhhed* him. He, Lieutenant Horatio Needles, would see to it. It was the least he could do.

And why not? Squire thought. He had just taken a big bribe. Slack-jawed Needles had thought he was going to have to part with heaps of Crown land and instead he had received a payout. What a mouth-watering turn of events.

The officer and Hewson shook an abrupt hand. Boy Hewson hunkered over the back of his Windsor chair. He was satisfied. He was ready to discuss smugglers. Whiskers cracked a couple of peanuts he'd cached in his pocket. Before leaving the vicinity to refill Hewson's order for more ale, Squire pointed to the officer's empty glass.

Needles nodded. Yeah. More. More of everything.

Boy Hewson drank only ale. He did not need a refill of whisky.

He had not touched a drop of datura. His gleaming tumbler remained untouched. The blue flame of the expiring candle danced in the reflection of the full glass. Polly had gone to a lot of trouble. It would be a shame if her divine cleverness with the locoweed went unrewarded. *Good Boy, good Boy, hey to you, old Boy, a certain gentleman like you, Mister Brown, you shouldn't be reluctant to drink.* Squire was desperate and his desperate brain cooed. Dose and overdose ran a pretty tight line but blurred vision probably would not bother a man who couldn't see anything anyway. Polly's hallucinogen would not likely kill him. A hallucination or two might even be pleasant.

Drink, you bastard.

CHAPTER
fifty

Polly's potion continued to sit. Idle, intact and unproven.
Squire shivered. It sure was chilly. He looked at his hands,
proverbially tied, helpless, masculine and numb. He had
a moment of intense longing for Jennet. He dreamed about her a lot.
Sex dreams. He knew it was Jennie. He made a connection with Jennie but sometimes she had Nellah's smooth face and loving Nellah
made him crazy because he wanted Jennie. He was letting his concentration wander. He had to keep sharp. You looked at folks and
thought about them and you saw they weren't much good and, well,
goddam, maybe neither was he, but the plan to capture Boy was
creeping away and creeping him out. At the bar, his mind whirled.

So what now?

Boy was not taking the bait.

In a moment of madness, Squire wondered whether he could
simply open Boy's jaws to pour Polly's infusion down his throat.

Boy was slight. Wiry. Blond. A towhead, Jeddah had called his
type. Bespectacled. A prim schoolmaster. Boy favoured Bride, all
right, but he was not what Squire had expected. He had expected
Boy, the truculent and muscular navvy, and not Boy, the abrasive,
overripe professor. Squire thought Nellah Golden could have arm-wrestled him into the dust and he had to shake his head to get rid of
the notion that Hewson was not dangerous. Bride had said he was

fearsome. A blazer. Missus Goosay had allowed he was wanton. He killed horses. Needles had described him as a wily informer and he should know. In any case, Hewson and Needles were alike. Both had problems with deserters. You joined in with their group and they demanded your loyalty, no matter what, except they did not keep their side of the bargain. They gave nothing back. No defence, no prestige, no safety. Loyalty to a bad master required many regulators to stop desertion and Squire was stumped. If locoweed did not work, what should he do?

Old tricks of seduction would not help.

He was used to approval from the opposite sex but he realized he made a contemptible female, not even close to being attractive enough to lure a blind sailor to a drunken sloop. Where was Lush? She could give lessons. She would have her dogie roped and tied and deflowered before you could pick up your cock or place your bet. The onset of physical ugliness was a mysterious but decisive phenomenon, like the crazy river changing currents, and it required new strategies. Alfie was right. If Boy were one-half as bad as everybody said, it was nuts to be wandering around the Cave in a skirt and petticoat. Cook came through the kitchen door and he stood next to Squire in front of the bar countertop where he was pouring ale into a schooner. Alfie's large, sad, brown eyes were questioning. "Devil is e'yer, dun? Ay feel sick, laddah. Eez a little tyke dough, aint 'e?" He tied his white apron around his middle. "Ale? That's good, un?"

"Yup, Needles wants more ale."

"Tsk. Bugger." Cook was a contrarian but he was worried, see. So worried he thought he could not think straight. "Woll?"

"Well what?"

"Is Boy drinkin' Polly's concoction?"

"Nope."

"Damn. Mention ar Maggie?"

"Yup."

"Ar Nellah?"

"Oh yeah."

"Huh. Fuck 'im." Alfie picked up the bar rag. "Ay expect yous 'uv saved as womun from bad troubles wi' Boy Hewson, any road." He polished the bar. He wiped away the rainbow suds on the counter, he reached for the claret bottle, forgot about it, faltered, left the bottle, and decided he had to speak his piece and ask the big question. "Wha' abou' ar Bride, laddah? 'E ask about 'er t'all?"

"He covers the ground, Alfie. Yeah, he does." Squire thought his own voice sounded far-off, hazy. "Mentions all the women." He made the pour. He did not add that Boy wanted to find Pommie and Chrisinny and take them from Bride to place with Christian do-gooders. He and Cook had trouble enough, over yonder. Potential iniquities could wait. "I'm glad the women are hidden. Thanks to Joe we get this far." He rubbed his jaw. "Brother, what I wanna know—?"

"Woll, say dun."

"Can't say. Half of me wants to fight. The other half feels—"

"Feels wha'?"

"Feels, like—I feel hunted. I know Boy. From the Oxbow. I remember Smoke Johnson and his men had the same fixed look. Like right or wrong they would do what they wanted. Yeah. I know it. I know what Boy is thinking. It is act and be damned."

How had Margaret Riley Davis coped with six children, all less than eight years of age? Squire had always taken the sudden loss of the father and the grandfather personally. He wasn't reasonable. He realized that. He was young and selfish. It was his mother's tragedy. He should have been a better son, even when she farmed him out to Polly. She could have handed over her children to eager Europeans, evangelical do-gooders, and no one would have blamed her, but she got her job with Jacob Decker and she kept the other kids. He had not been grateful. He had resented her for not doing better. Normal attitude for kids, he supposed, but you gotta grow up. He wanted to tell her he was proud to belong to her. He wanted it so bad he ached but he was paralyzed because he felt heavy-hearted, under the old shadow.

"Oy. Yer all right, dun?" Using the wet bar rag, Alfie patted Squire on the shoulder. "D'ya want me ter fetch Polly from de 'ouse?"

"Brother, why? What does Polly do here?"

Alfie stroked his apron and he snorted and moved toward the last camphene lantern, burning low. "What do Polly do? Woll—" He scratched his bristly chin and tightened his apron strings for the fiftieth time and picked up the camphene tin to refill the glowing pewter bulb. "Woll, she do make yous look good, fe starts."

CHAPTER
fifty-one

Shaaaa-BOOM. There was an explosion.

Out of thin air, out of nowhere. They say that the unexpected catches you short. The explosion was unexpected. Alfie filled the lantern with the pine oil and alcohol mixture and—BOOM—just like that, the lantern flew out of Alfie's hand and blew up. In the particles of a second, while the brain engaged with catastrophe, Squire stood amazed because he had estimated Hewson was the blazer to fear. On their own steam, they had done it. Cook never would have filled the lantern's glowing bulb if he hadn't been upset. Alfie and Squire both knew better than to monkey around pouring camphene on a burning wick.

Radiant white knives shot into the air in one furious effort and expired like Chinese fireworks. Dry wood behind the bar burst into tiny fire-buds and at the same time Alfie fell to his knees and howled. He held up his fry-pan hand. It was burned, burned bad. His greasy apron had caught on fire. Cook looked down. He saw the flame-burner on his chest and, most unhelpfully, tipped over hard, like a bunged barrel of whisky, and he sprawled out, fainting, at Squire's feet.

fifty-two

"Fire!" Squire shouted for Ann Bergin, who was making tomorrow's meals in the little kitchen. "Jesus Christ! Ann! Get Polly! Tell her, tell her, bring the honey! In the root cellar!"

He tugged at Alfie and covered his front with the wet flannel towel he had used for drying glasses. He was sure he had smothered the flames but rolled Cook several times back and forth for good measure.

"Help!"

Squire unclasped his elasticized belt and ripped at the top buttons on the cotton dress and pulled down the petticoat and hopped on one foot, nearly losing his balance, and he half-ran, half-jumped to the kitchen to get more sand buckets, which Nellah kept here and there around the premises for emergencies. He remembered there were three buckets next to the cook-stove. He wanted to put out the burning licks that had started to spread along the bar but the first thing he had to do was keep the sparks around Alfie controlled, or killed, until he could lift him up and get him outside.

"Fire!" Ann boomed as loud as the explosion.

She had a big voice for a little person. She cried out another warning. She tore upstairs. Someone might not believe her and she cried louder, "Fire!"

Squire could hear her as she pounded on the bedroom doors. In seconds, stomping and rushing came from the second storey as people took themselves in hand or out of hand and jumped from their beds in their sleeping gear to run for the inside stairs, the one way down to the main floor. From the main floor, you could get to the open yard in three ways: by the barroom entrance, by the dining-room entrance and, if you ran down the corridor that was behind the bar, by the kitchen. People jammed, they moved *à l'écart*, and tried for command of the top landing. The canallers won. They were first. They were on guard. They habitually jumped out of harm's way and asked questions later. They thudded down the ten planks of the inside steps and, clomping like wild mares after a savvy leader, they turned in unison, off to their right, right away from the smoke. They dove for the dining-room door and politely shut it on their way out. Squire was yelling at them. He needed their help. They were gone.

Help!

Help from where?

He looked to the corner of the dining room.

Lieutenant Needles and Walter Winter were gone.

They might live to re-imagine their unseemly haste in running out of the dining-room door after the canallers but run they did. For the honour of Crown and colony, they held their noses and abandoned everyone to his fate. In particular, they abandoned their precious, indispensible ally and informer, Richard Boynton Hewson.

Boy was drunk on datura at last.

He was left alone, weak, out of it, standing on their table. He raised his empty, greasy-fingered, stemless glass and fixed his nearly sightless china eyes on the flickering ceiling. He tapped a soft shoe and stumbled and nearly fell off his stage. He chuckled. He was hallucinating. He was as out of control as the flames. A certain gentleman, Mister Brown, was as high as a flying squirrel and he looked ready to parachute to another table but he did not.

As addled as Boy was, he recognized malevolence in the air and shrieked to his men. "Hey, shitheads! Get yourselves in here!"

Boy's bodyguards were on the outside landing, awaiting his signal to enter but they must have wondered about a camphene explosion as they kicked at the bar-entrance door, which none of the inn's escapees had yet dared to use. Frenzied, Hewson's two men fractured the door, booted the thing into slivers and knocked it aside. A whoosh of oxygen blew into the room and two lumbermen, without doubt Irish Shiners, being built like caldrons if caldrons had full black beards, followed the fire-feeding air.

They were blinking and confused.

They were half-supporting but mostly dragging an Indian. Their forearms bulged under their coats as they lifted the body of the limp, perverse and wilfully collapsed man. The captive was taller than his captors, longer from tip to toe. At least that was what Squire could see as he worked furiously dumping the sand on the fire-flaps. The man was taller, yes, but not as old or as heavily built. The Indian looked Mohawk. Like Jake Hearenhodoh Venti. My God. It was Jake.

"Jake!" Squire yelled at his friend.

"Lady? *Oh nahòten yesayats*? What is your name?"

"Winona. No. Jake. It's me. Squire."

"Holy Christ. Tehawennihárhos?"

Squire switched to Mohawk. "*Hen'en*. It's me. Careful what you say! *Se'nikònrarak*! I need help. It's Cook. It's Alfie. Alfie Williams. The old man from Liverpool. He's unconscious. Dead weight. He's goddam heavy. We gotta get him out."

"Brother, what's happened to you?"

"Speak Mohawk, Jake. Later, brother—"

Jake spoke Mohawk but there was no later for him in terms of worrying about or commenting on an old pal. "Your dress, brother, your buttons is undone."

They met the first time in many moons.

They met on a day when they could both perish and Squire was ready to kill him.

Jake was in earnest. From under the arms of his captors he was ready to probe his friend's aberrant psychology. "I mean, why the get-up? Tehawennihárhos? You aint a good-lookin' sorta gal. You look, uh, you look like John Norton. Why you don't tell me? Sex? Is it sex? You have big problems? What kind?"

On the hunt for sand buckets, Squire was puffing, "Help me, you donkey. We both have big problems."

"Uh?"

"You are about to get arrested for smuggling." Squire jiggled his ear to the right and looked over at Boy, who was still shuffling on the tabletop. A brass band played in Hewson's head and his hands beat his knees to solipsistic rhythms. In another time, in another place, one would call his antics droll. Tehawennihárhos pointed. "That guy, you know him? He is a snitch. He knows everything, Jake, everything. The why, the when, the how. One thing left for him, the where? He plans to find out where you meet, where you cross. He knows all about you guys and Bobby John and Sandusky. And Buffalo—"

"Brother, shuddup. I know him. He is mean. Wolverine mean. Leave him there. Let 'im roast. Problem solved. Everybody happy."

"Aint that easy, brother."

Jake disagreed. "Oh, yeah, yeah, it is."

Squire was doing the stomp step. "You oughta know it aint. Snitches love to talk. Damage is done."

"Talk? He will be dead. What talk?"

Squire was dripping sweat as bad as Whiskers. "Double agents go to the highest bidder, Jake. They turn up everywhere." He wiped his forehead with his arm.

"Brother, you sayin'—"

"Aint saying nothin', Jake." Squire was livid. "Nothin' to no one. Just get over here, Hearenhodoh, and help me, will you!"

CHAPTER
fifty-three

Squire bounced aside an empty sand bucket. It landed against the wall and clattered like a steel drum. The music faded and the flames underneath the sand spluttered with a fitful, uncertain light and for half a breath he had hope as he watched fiery purple crocuses grow up, wither and turn into nothingness but in less time than it takes a burning log to snap and crackle and pop, there were crimson tongues wagging along the sideboard. There was enough air to give flame an ovation and the fire caught on, and caught on well. It rushed up the wall. The thickly varnished panelling peeled and spit. He was coughing and rubbing his eyes but he kept stomping the floor planks and whipping the corn broom on the burning sideboards. He kept at it and shouted. His friend must help him. He was desperate. He needed the sulky hostage. "I need help. Drop him, you guys. C'mere, Jake!"

"Nope, Brother, not a chance." Jake spoke English and he twisted up and sneered at the Shiners. "I am gone. Squire, I am runnin'."

Squire answered in Mohawk. His voice, if not threatening, was not forthcoming. "Hearenhodoh. Brother. Jake. I said I know all about you and Bobby John and the smuggling operation. I guess where you meet. I put my mind to it and I figure out the sacred circle, where you cross the river. Look down here! Alfie's a good man. He's hurt bad."

"You let me down, Squire. You really did."

"What indulging d'you need? I did not—"

"Oh yes, you did. I get you an honest job. At Ruthven Hall, and you get us fired. My ma's destitute. Because of you, I got no money. People starve in the territory but you are fuckin' useless, brother. You run away. Bobby John and the Warriors help us."

A spark flew to Squire's forehead and sizzled. He yelped and brushed it away. He was burned like a fricasseed squirrel but angrier than he'd been before and he'd already been worked up. "Get a proper job, eh, Jake? You turn being Indian into a calling."

"So? Aint it? What's your calling, red boy? Lawyer? Doctor? Bookkeeper? Diamond merchant? Industrialist? Or bloody market gardener? Like the rest of us. Aint a pretty boy, like you, Tehawen-nihárhos. Being a pretty boy takes time. You wear a dress. Wicked git-up. Horrible. Aint got time to be a pretty boy—"

"Shut up! Brother, you get over yourself." Squire hopped on a bucket to slam the high wall. "And get yourself over here."

"Tehawennihárhos, brother, you are a hard man. You think you need nobody. You ashamed of bein' Indian? You play every hand on the table. Always working an angle. That's it! You ashamed. I think so. You think you are too good, too good for us red boys starvin' by the river, but you think you need me now, eh?"

"I think? What do I think? Hearenhodoh, brother, I think you get jealous. Jealous of everybody. Jealous, brother. A jealous man who drinks. You need way too much comfortin'."

"Comfortin'? Me? Good one. You don't care—"

"I don't care? Hah. I don't care, Jake? I do not care, then. Like always, I back down."

"You are perfect. I forget. I stand up for you all the time. For you and your family. Your name's crap. You know that, brother? Never mind your old man's lineage. Polly is Oneida. Lowlife Aughguaga crap. The loyal chiefs think you and your family are lowlife crap. Your mother is half-breed. You never say 'Sorry,' Squire. I never heard you say sorry."

Raw heat in the room and emotional heat from the wrangling with Jake blew Squire's fever to the rafters and he felt near panic as the licks got closer but Jake made him enraged, too enraged to give up. "You, Jake? You don't say shit, brother, and your mouth is full of it."

Ratiksa'okonha. Bad boys. Squire could hear the grandmother saying it as she had pulled him and Jake apart. She would flat-hand both of them on the side of the head. It was a fact. Polly's frequent smacks on his head had never endeared her to Jake Hearenhodoh Venti. Most grandparents in the villages were indulgent. Not Polly. She expected things. He and Jake had bonded over the bitchiness and the heavy-handedness and they hated her slaps. She must be a Lutheran, they had told each other, a goddam Lutheran.

The smoke was gasping, in clouds, black and thick, and it was covering the wall and spurting across the ceiling. Squire had bucketsful lined up and he tossed a fifth and a sixth and a seventh one at the blaze trying to keep the fire down and away from the unconscious Alfie but stopping a raging conflagration with a corn broom and a bunch of sand piles was futile. Everyone on the scene saw and knew it. Jake screwed around again to face the Shiners. His body was awkward and uncomfortable in their grasp and his big wide mouth was leaden, real sulky, but his black eyes were beseeching, *Aw c'mon.*

The Shiners looked down. They looked at each other. What the hell?

They dropped their shoulders and released their hold. They dropped the Indian because they clearly did not know what else to do with him in an inferno, especially when the head honcho was dancing on a table and jigging like a two-bit vaudevillian hoping for an encore. Jake crashed like lumber. The men air-washed their hands. They were tired. Done with hauling around a dumb, collapsible Indian. Done with the whole military charade.

Lying flat on the floor, Jake Hearenhodoh Venti pulled his tattered, chequered bandana from his neck and he tied it over his mouth. He scrambled on his elbows and knees toward Squire, stood up, and grabbed Alfie's white and worn-out baker's boots and started to pull him. Squire threw down the last sand bucket and leaned over and grabbed Cook under his armpits and hoisted him up. The two old friends stopped quarrelling and worked together but they encountered a block, another obstacle, a boulder over the door of the burning crypt. Boy's bodyguards had no desire to move past the billowing smoke, not even to pull their intoxicated and hallucinating commander off the table. To their credit, they were undecided. To their shame, they stood fixed in the doorway, watching Boy, watching the flames move closer to Alfie, and they jutted out their jaws with stubborn grit and refused to move.

·They were tenacious. Fascinated with the fire. They blocked the vestibule to freedom.

By now other guests at the inn had clomped down the inside stairs and turned left instead of right and wanted to use the bar exit to escape but the bodyguards were like prison guards. Two mutinous prisoners, Flash Dunlop and Reba Elias, elbows at shoulder height, made ready to tackle them. The two guards repulsed the attack and one of them, the shortest one, he socked Reba, because nothing would persuade him to move. Nothing, that is, until the Mennonite boys showed up. Peaceable Franz Fink proved Reba was right about something. Franz was a fiend. Not only for food. He was a fiend for action, dressed in white-and-red-striped pyjamas.

With an irresistible touch, Fink turned one lumberman toward the door and grabbed him first on the back by his heavy coat and floppy suspenders and then picked him up by the seat of his navy broadcloth trousers and threw him outside, whooo-haaa, like he was nothing bigger than the stuffed pigskin they tossed around at home for a little fun. His giant brother-in-law, also in his striped pyjamas and night-robe, grabbed the other lumberman and roared it was time for a change and gave him the same treatment, *Don't stand in the doorway, don't block up the hall*, and he jettisoned the man into the air like a hay-stook so that his sister, the badger-eyed Reba Elias, could lower her elbows from tackle height.

Now she could leave the burning building and leave it properly; she could hold to the rickety railing and sashay down the slushy plank steps with the poise of Queen Victoria.

With the claret bottle in hand, Flash Dunlop, also with the poise of a parading queen, sashayed after her.

CHAPTER
fifty-four

I n the meantime, outside, the Mennonite farmers and the Irish canallers, directed by one sympathetic John Fennessy, formed a line-up and a bucket brigade to soak the brick wall and, out of the blue-black night, an Irishman shouted at them that it had started to snow. "Jesus, Mary and Joseph, byes. Lookadat, will yas. Snowin', eh? Comin' down, tun atta time."

Everyone who had been in bed upstairs was outside in the yard.

Some folks hung around to help the Hill people put out the fire. Others sought the remote barn, some distance at the back of the house, and they found their ponies and took off for parts unknown. Ann directed three canallers to the showerbath barrel. Maybe the water was not yet frozen solid. They hustled to the barrel with their tin pails clanking. The Elias brothers and Franz Fink ran along-side. Reba Elias, however, had lost her crown. She perched on the front steps of Nellah's house like a carrion crow. She stuffed herself between the white spindles on the lower veranda and shouted oaths to the runners, mostly things about grog or gag or some such nonsense and the imminent arrival of the apocalypse.

Flash Dunlop was on the move. In his slippers. Yelling to the heavens, he more or less concurred with the detestable woman Reba Elias. Damn the Canadas. God Bless England. God Bless Queen Victoria. Long Live Britannia. Flash swore the world would end here. He, however, intended to get himself away. Fast. He rolled up the hem of his flannel *coureur-de-bois* nightshirt, plowed his way through the muck and aimed straight for the barn and right to the hideous nag that cheating hostler, a certain Norby, had called a horse and, just like that, Flash was gone. Gone from the fire. Gone from the Hill. Dunlop had whisked the Apostle Luke from the bar countertop and he had carried the bottle with him into the barn and waved it over his head as he rode away. The bottle was a trophy. Flash screamed into the air that the whole country was a violent mess. Hell. Hell on Earth.

Over the commotion, Ann screamed to the Mohawk from the yard. "Squire! You guys get out of there, you hear me! The roof is burning! It's coming down!"

CHAPTER
fifty-five

"Tehawennihárhos!"

Squire was choking on smoke as thick as flannel but he heard Aughguaga Polly, just as she demanded, "Hear me good, grandson! I got the honey you want. Got it right here."

The exasperating yet reassuring shadow of Polly called to him from the stoop outside the bar exit. "I'm ordering you. Get yerself and other fellas, get yourselves outa there. Get out. Now!" Polly was mad at him again. She was saying something bossy but Squire heard the universal balm of an order in the line of fire and, thanks to the fat grandmother, somewhere, underneath all the dread and vacillation, he was a man of action. Squire and Jake carried Cook outside and lowered him down the plank steps where Polly was waiting in the yard to submerge Alfie's burned hand in a bucket of honey.

As soon as Alfie was in Polly's custody the Mohawk turned around and went up the plank steps and back into the building though the bar entrance. Sprinting into the flames and hiking up his skirt and covering his mouth and nose with the bandana Bride had tied around his neck and jumping over a blazing beam, Winona managed to save the life of a certain misbegotten Englishman who, no doubt about it, should either hang until dead or burn. Boy was tap dancing. His wire spectacles were askew. One lens had smashed.

His other refracted the orange flames. His head was canted to listen to the beat. The round table he stood on was clunky, solid enough for the occasional dance, but the real fright was behind him. The farthest dining-room panel was blazing and it burned like a lighthouse bonfire. Ships at sea might know Squire had less than three seconds before both he and Boy met the devil at home.

He grabbed Boy's buckskin belt and his silver belt buckle and pulled the unresisting man down from his high performance perch and slung him like a sack of flour over his right shoulder, relieved he was not hauling a heavier man over those few last paces to the dining-room door, and, straight ahead, he scooted to freedom with more zip than a Hanover rat.

The Mohawk ripped the buttons off the grey bodice and threw Nellah's petticoat and cinch belt onto the pyre. What choice did he have? Winona was dead. Disguising himself as a woman was a brainless thing to do. For sure, Squire was a disgrace to the female race and he had endured enough mood swings to last a lifetime.

CHAPTER
fifty-six

I t had been a long night.

Boy Hewson had missed most of it. He sat nice and snug in Nellah's barn.

Squire roped him to a crib but he had a hard time of it because Boy was kissing and pawing a brindled barn cat and the animal was huffy. Cat hissed and arched its back in warning.

Boy Hewson laughed.

Cat scratched.

Boy laughed harder and tapped his feet on the barn floor and the old brindle with the mangy coat escaped his grasp and scampered off. Squire roped the man's arms behind the slats. Saved the poor creature from certain torture. Boy fixed his good eye on a black cat. He coaxed him. "Here, puss, puss, puss."

As huffy as his predecessor, Squire said, "I aint no cat, mister," and behind the man's back he tightened the Appalachian double-loop knot. There he was. Boy Hewson. Snared he was, Missus Goosay. Tricked he was, Missus Goosay. Caught dead to rights, ma'am. Boy was as mean as a boggy rattler and here he was, defeated, exchanging political views with a barn cat. The Mohawk said *meow* to Hewson and stood up on creaky joints. Squire was exhausted. He blew on his cold hands and surveyed his handiwork. Looked good enough. He pulled on his leather gloves and started to walk down the ramp of the homely barn, the horsey-smelling hideaway, to check on Alfie and see what was happening in the night.

His forehead burned. Shame was at work.

Had Nellah's brick house caught fire? Was Cook doing all right? Was he dead? Couldn't be. The thought of Nellah and Alfie made him feel sicker with every step. What would they do if Nellah had lost her home? His fault. She would have nothing and he would carry the excruciating shame of it for the rest of his life. What would he do if Cook never again picked up his fry pan? He touched his brow. There was nothing there, nothing but raw soreness and bristles. The fire had singed off his pointy eyebrows. He started to laugh at the utter folly of Winona but he could not do it. He was the idiot, the donkey, not Jake. He slipped into self-reproach. He had been daft to keep quiet when he should have yelled at Alfie to stop, stop pouring the camphene. Jake was wrong. Sorry was Squire's mantra. He was a sorry fool but a sorry fool or not he had to face the music. Fool or not, he was a fighter. And a dreamer. He dreamed Cook was all right.

CHAPTER
fifty-seven

Like the Irishman had said, snow fell a ton at a time. Here and there, the wind played tricks. It was a mad broom. It was a beating whisk. It whirled and it spun. It threw sloppy flakes into a protective bowl around the wide doors of the barn. The night air was sugary, alive with light. From the barn's ramp Squire could see how the snow held fast. The red currant and sumac bushes disdained yesterday's burnt-out fashion and took on a fresh, white winter appearance. They donned meringue tuques. Cedar branches glowed with crystals. Sugar sifted over cocoa dips. In a frozen wink of windy caprice, the wind had changed directions. The fitful blizzard blew away but it left a welcome memento. Snow and more snow, a silent heavy snowfall. Flakes sifted like flour, down to a spongy earth. Squire got to the bottom of the ramp and he headed toward Nellah's yard but he stopped short. He saw a couple of galloping canallers taking off. He called after them, "What about Teacher's place? Did it burn down?"

One of the canallers waved back at him but Squire did not understand whether it was farewell or a good-news wave.

A claw raked his guts.

The man yelled but it was muffled. "Off to Luckey's."

Was Nellah lucky? Or did the canaller mean he was off to the disorderly house in Hamilton? Squire felt the nausea lash up. What if the entire establishment had burned down?

CHAPTER
fifty-eight

"Oranges and lemons say the bells of St. Clemons." While Squire was walking the fifty yards from the barn to Nellah's yard he heard harmonizing tenors and something more familiar, a rhythm. The beat was coming toward him in the voice of Jake Venti, a nasal, husky and low-pitched mumble. His friend Hearenhodoh was doing *Nyagwai*, ear dance, *we ga-yo we-he*. The clipped, emphatic and earthy syncopation of the Longhouse emerged from underneath an English fruit stand. Squire wondered whether the English song about oranges was political. Maybe William of Orange had written it.

He heard a woman. Loud. Not tuneful. Ah. Ann.

She was not holding the music. Or the rhythm. She jumped from point to counterpoint.

He blinked. Snow droplets melted into his eyes. He touched his forehead and felt the raw burn, sure, but cold water ran down his hot cheeks and his vision cleared and he saw before him the strangest thing.

It was a winter mirage.

It was a magic lantern show.

The air, ashy and filtered, limned the scene. People were dancing. They danced in a circle and moved in a limelight blur, like a child's water-colour fantasy glowing on the wall of a European parlour. He squinted. It was a party. He had heard Ann singing all right. She was hard not to hear, the way she wailed. He tried to force his eyes to see her through the dots of snow, to pick her out, to make sense of the pointillism. At first, he saw Mennonites and Jake Venti. He spotted small Ann in her canvas shirt and brown suspenders. She looked fine, happier than she had looked in a long time. Ann and the four men flapped around, Jake leading the duple beat, not too fast, and their blue-cold faces grimaced like Doorkeepers. They were jubilant. They raised their arms to the sky and then lowered them and, there you go, Jake pounded on a small sand bucket and lumbered like the bear. The Mennonites sang, "You owe me five farthings, say the bells of St. Martin's." Their melody, strange to his ears, floated upward and soared pure as a bird in flight, higher and higher over the rhythm of Jake's syncopated bear. Franz Fink and the Elias brothers were as big as bears and one of the brothers wore a red flannel nightshirt under his hooded robe. Squire would have rubbed his eyes but the stinging from the smoke was bad. Never had he felt the assault of so many physical sensations at one time. Snow. Smoke. Steam. Wet wood. Music. Music? Fire. Ice. Lots of ice.

Ghostlike, he walked toward them and passed mystically through the white scrim. The folks in the yard were not too iced-up to be overjoyed and, he discovered, they were overjoyed with cause. A powerful relief shot into him. Nellah's house had been doomed and yet it was saved. He could not quite believe it.

There, as sound as a pound, was Teacher's brick home. Squire stepped into their circle to meet the celebrants but declined the offer to dance with Jake. He had a headache, he said, politely, and his coolness to Jake lowered the exhilarated tone of the *fête*. Squire said he was sorry to dampen spirits but he had a prisoner and there was Alfie to bother him too.

He had forgotten about the female disguise.

Franz gave him a manly back slap. "Winona? You are man, then? Goot man, goot man."

Squire said, "Ahh, yeah. Not Winona, I am afraid. Squire Davis. Pleased to meet you, mister." He felt he had to apologize for the rude scam. "It seemed like the reasonable thing—"

Franz was a heavyset farmer, used to hard work and solitude, and he hefted himself and his bathrobe into a more comfortable stance to give the shoulder raise. The upstanding gentleman was too compassionate to ask, what made you think so?

The younger of the Elias brothers was apologetic as well. You know, about the singing. He said they did not know how else to celebrate God's wonder. Nellah's house should have caught fire but it did not. It didn't burn down and it sure should have, he muttered, and he scanned his scarlet-and-white-striped pyjamas for burn holes. It was true, he said, that he and his brothers broke with tradition. They should not sing without their congregation and certainly not something that was not represented in their songbook, *Neu-Vermehrt und Vollständiges Gesangbuch*. He and Franz did not know why they liked the old English tune. They just did. One day, they were scything and they heard a couple of children singing "Oranges and Lemons." Kids sang and walked the dusty mile to their log schoolhouse. The song was simply right for the scythe. If you pounced on it, why, you cut a wide swath and, anyway, what could they do? They were helpless. They were born with music in their hearts.

Franz shuffled into the conversation and admitted, yah, it took a hard effort to suppress the music. Linking arms, the men gave up the effort and sang together in three-part harmony. "When will you pay me, say the bells of Old Bailey." They sang it again, chapter and verse, and everyone made music, everyone but Squire, who was too worried to sing, and God knew it, he was too worried about everything to do much more than stare at the whiteness of the snowy surroundings but he was the only one in the dumps. The Mennonite

boys liked Ann's promising enthusiasm. They liked Jake Hearenhodoh's sense of rhythm. The Mennonites gave Jake a round of
applause at the end. Venti, as usual, gave Squire the arrogant eye,
which, as usual, Squire refused to acknowledge. Jake was a thorn.
Always had been. They met. They fought. Cooled off. It was a tradition. They could not help it.

The bizarre world of snow had turned everything upside down
but Squire figured his world was probably due for an upturn. Weary
firefighters received the answer to their prayers and the righteous
folks doing a good deed got a hand from above, and so, goddam it,
mark it down, thought Squire. The day of celestial help. Get out the
axe and mark a chip on the Thunderbird oak. They had done their
puny best to save Teacher's brick home on Vinegar Hill but they
had needed help. It had turned out all right because what they could
not do for themselves was done naturally. Thank the Creator for the
simpler miracles, for snow. Snow had saved his life. Nellah's house
was still there, a squared marker rising from the floor of the clearing, smack in the middle of the cedar bush. With trepidation, Squire
asked Jake about Alfie.

Jake looked like the gangly Cornstalk next to the bulk of Franz
Fink but he was almost six-foot-two, a good half-foot taller than
Squire and, at all times domineering, he tended to stand straight to
make sure their height difference was apparent. Jake's boiled wool
coat had a big tear in the back. He had cut his wiry hair short as
a horsehair brush and his head was bare. His hands were bare. He
must have been cold but did not appear to notice. "Alfie? He is in the
house. He's awake." Jake pointed to the upstairs window. "He is with
Polly. She fixes him, she says. He says, go away, and she says, shut
up." Jake made the familiar rattle-shaking motion.

"Where is he?"

"In Lizzie's room. He asks for you."

"Ah."

"Alfie wants—" Jake stuck his thumbs in his cord belt and stuck out his long fat tongue for flakes. He showed his missing front tooth. Lacrosse was a rough game. "He wants you to rescue him and call off Polly."

"That'll be the day."

"No kidding. Poor Alfie." Jake twisted his wide mouth into amusement and pity. "She calls him Effie." Jake gazed down and kicked a drift. A spray of light snow dusted his leggings.

Squire lightly touched the sore place where his eyebrows used to be and laughed. "Polly makes you better but she sure don't make it easy, Jake. You know her. Alfie is gonna be all right then? Is he comfortable?"

"Yep. Quite. Fair—yeah, I think so. He's got his hand plunked in a sticky honey bucket, which don't help."

"Brother, he gets good care."

Jake gazed up again to the second-storey window, to Lizzie's room. "Polly rubs flax-seed oil all over him, you know, all over, everywhere, and he can't make a move to stop her." Jake caught more flakes. "Yup. He gets good care. I hope he can stand it."

Alfie must have burns all over, everywhere, to get the flax-oil treatment. Squire bit his lip to avoid rushing to the grandmother's defence. He eyed the slushy path that wound around the front drive to Nellah's house. He hated to think of Alfie being in a bad way but felt an enormous, almost dizzying sense of reprieve. Cook was well enough to complain about the medicine woman. "Polly aint going to take nicely to me interfering."

"You do it, though, brother. She's takin' liberties with that old man." Jake's pock scars had purpled in the cold and, hands up, he backed into the drift as though Squire had given notice that he wanted to commit a robbery. "She is your Oneida grandmother."

"Yup." Squire's eyes skittered from Jake to the second-floor window. "Yup. That she is."

Jake's hot gaze bore into Squire's departing back but Tehawen-nihárhos did not turn around to get into the argument Hearen-hodoh wanted to start. The twinge in Squire's back subsided. Jake had returned to making the music. His friend would calm down. So would he. Always happened. He inhaled to block out Ann's ear-splitting singing voice and appreciated Jake's delicate precision with rhythm. Hearenhodoh would hate Ann's enthusiasm. Too intense. Too loud. Unmusical, so unmusical. He could almost hear it. Jake would complain about Ann. Jake would be happy. Complaining made Alfie and Jake happy.

Squire plodded along the path and climbed up Nellah's front steps. He realized he was not alone. Sitting on the lower veranda was Reba Elias, and her face wore enough caustic to lye the corn. Reba was not a trickster crow. She was a starling, a mean little bird with a mean yellow beak. She had moved from the spindles.

She had wrapped herself in an unbleached homespun blanket and balanced on a rickety cane-wicker chair with half a seat.

Squire was courteous and he avoided her eyes and asked her whether she was warm and invited her into the house but she declined.

"No." She clutched a leather sack tight to her bosom. "It is the end of the world," she said. "My bag. I guard it. With my life. This here is our money. It is from top-grade wheat and, yay, it is the end of the world. It is the rapture."

She was a funny old toot for a young woman. Did she imagine admission to her heaven required a toll? "End of the world?" he said. He was so tired. "That's so?"

"Yay. That is so."

"Naw. Taint so, Miz Reba. We avoid the end of the world. Thanks to your kin."

"The horsemen are nigh."

"Ma'am? You get warm, eh? How bout it?" He was coaxing. He felt sorry for her. "Be reasonable. Come on inside."

305

Reba Elias' eyes glowed in the dark. "I stay put. I stay put, you red heathen." She croaked, *"Herr Jesu Christ, dich zu uns wend—* Jesus loves me."

Sing away, lady. I aint Herr Jesus.

Shit, what a disaster. No Cyclops Inn. No Cave.

Maybe it *was* the beginning of the end of the world.

The pewter box that was the board-and-batten hostelry had burned to the ground, leaving a blackened stone chimney to mark the gravesite. The second-storey bedrooms and the entire tavern and the shards of the mirror behind the bar and the memories of people playing at cards, all were misted into yesterday. They sizzled prettily under a fresh layer of snow.

Nellah's brick house had stood, fine, but the wall facing the inn was sooty and, inside the house, the linens and furniture covers smelled acrid and campfire smoky. Whitewash and vinegar and a shot or two of cheap vodka would cleanse the odour.

The Elias brothers sang on.

They harmonized in creamy voices, "Here comes a candle to light you to bed."

From her chair on the veranda, Reba Elias beaked to the snow-flakes piling up on the rail, "Here comes a chopper to chop off your head."

As if by appointment, three horsemen galloped into the yard.

Bart Farr, Peter Johnson and Jedidiah Golden had come home to the Hill. On a signal, in unison, they reined in and leaned forward in their saddles, almost over the pommel horns. They were soaked through, woebegone, and maybe that's why it took them a long, hard minute to appreciate the miracle of the standing brick house when all they saw was a bear in a red flannel robe and all they heard was three-fourths of a barbershop quartet accompanied by an eerie-sounding, nasal staccato.

Jeddah called, "Squire!" And he sounded none too sociable.

PART III

THE EMIGRANT O'HERLIHY

CHAPTER
fifty-nine

The Millburns' new girl, Danielle O'Herlihy, was from County Wexford. She carried a tea tray into the library. It seemed cumbersome but she managed to hold it steady. Lawrie Filkin could see bits of parsley stuck to the bowl of the clay teapot. There'd be the devil to pay for careless dishwashing but steam soared from the teapot's stained spout. Tea was boiling hot. That was fine but Filkin could sense a chill. Something was amiss. Millburn was giving Filkin the cold shoulder and Filkin had noticed it, most certainly he had noticed it, but he was warm and snug, too comfy in his new chair to ask what was wrong. He was unprepared for the outburst.

"Who?!" Millburn sat up in his armchair and bawled. He leaned toward the butt-filled clown-head ashtray that Fannie had bought at the Saturday market and mashed his cigar ash and said it again. "Who?"

Filkin jumped. "Hello? Who what?"

O'Herlihy dropped a cup. It was not the Wedgwood, but, still, it was quality.

The jagged pop of broken porcelain had an effect, just as it had before. Two days ago, O'Herlihy had broken the handles off *three* Wedgwood cups. She had been dusting the front parlour. She had turned to see Octavius Millburn, the manor's lord and master, standing just inside the grand double-door entranceway and he was looking at her. He had been staring. *That way*. It was the I-want-you way. She had been frightened to see him materialize in front of her, *tsk*, no, that wasn't true. She had been distressed and the wooden hand-grip on her soft rag had caught the trolley knob and it had jiggled the stacked cups and they had spilled over the wagon like translucent globs of lard and, pop, pop, pop, the cups' handles had broken off. Millburn had said, "Don't worry, my dear. I'll tell Fannie I broke them—I'll gladly tell her, if—" O'Herlihy had simply nodded. She had known it. She had known it all along. It would happen. The sex. She and the master would seal a deal, intimacy in exchange for protection. She was scared stiff about losing her maid's job before she could get a regular position in James Wilkes' white mill. She was willing to abide the goat in her bed but would a happy Octavius make a happy Fannie? Or would a happy Octavius make a wary Fannie? Whatever else she was, Fannie was their adversary. From this day forward, that was so, and O'Herlihy had prayed with great fervour since the moment the cups had fallen. Maybe Millburn liked her. Maybe he liked her a lot. Maybe he liked her more than he feared his wife. The missus was not a regular in O'Herlihy's prayers, may the saints forgive. At that precise moment, she had said to him, "Why don't you trim—ah, yes, trim the beard then, master? Yer some distinguished man, sir, with all them clothes. You would be refined wi' trimmed beard, sir." Less like a goat, she had thought. Millburn had nodded. He was in the anticipatory mood and had gone straightaway to get the shears and razor. O'Herlihy was satisfied. He wanted to please her, she had thought. As long as he wanted that, she had her own kind of power.

Now, instead of comforting the girl, Millburn comforted himself. He rubbed his tin ear like it was Aladdin's lamp. "Who told Fannie, Lawrie? I ask you, who told Fannie about me and Nellah in the first place?"

~

Filkin reached over and tugged the other man's sleeve. "No one. It was your face, O.G. Your face gave it away. Everyone knew about your buttered bun."

"Horseshit!"

"Humph. Look at you! You should see yourself. Get to the hall mirror and take a look."

Millburn waved off the suggestion. He said to O'Herlihy, "Pour me tea, girl. Sugar! Two teaspoons. Two, I say. Maybe three."

A fusty picture of a hairy-chopped old man was pinned on the wall and Filkin wondered whether Millburn's father, a certain Eliakim Millburn, had been as dependent on women as his wealthy son.

O'Herlihy needed two hands to hold the clay teapot. Filkin noticed how nervous she was. Nerves were understandable. She was far from home and far from her mama. She was a skeletal figure and, for the sake of her starving stomach, she made sure she did not comprehend household conversations. The financial decline in Canada West had turned around and indictors showed a slow upswing. The infant economy painfully crawled to redemption but jobs in service were as scarce as impotent masters. The Millburns scraped more hash and eggs off the trencher in one night than the girl had eaten in a year. Filkin believed servants should be invisible but one more time, one last time, he made an exception. He felt inclined to notice O'Herlihy.

She had thick hair. Curly brown hair.

She was pretty.

Except for her eyes. She had tiny, filmy eyes.

Her eyes spoke of deprivation.

"You don't know women, O.G. No sir," Filkin said, casting a just-you-and-me dart at O'Herlihy, who affected not to feel it.

"Women? Really! Listen here, young man. I can't let women turn me into a bloody spendthrift." Millburn took a gulp of Scotch.

He had his hand dug deep in the ceramic dish. One sugared almond dropped on the Wilton carpet. It shone like a white egg on blue indigo.

Hah, thought Filkin, Millburn wanted to renege on the reward, skinflint that he was. Too late. Filkin said, "Spendthrift? What claptrap. You were brilliant to offer a large reward. You are forgetting something—the village loves you."

"Humph. Well, that's so."

"Yes, O.G., St. George, remember?"

Without warning, Millburn's face crumpled. "What has happened to me, Lawrie?" Too tipsy to think straight, the older man leaned forward in the Moroccan armchair to whisper to the brother-in-law, lest the walls had tin ears. "Fuck it," he said. "I hate Nellah."

Filkin, ever so pleased with the turnaround in Millburn, was anxious nonetheless about how it might affect him. "What do you mean?"

Millburn shrugged. What did he mean? He said he meant he felt culpable. For the behaviour of the Warriors. For their assault on the woman. That wasn't what bothered him so much, though, said the owner of the emporium. "How is it possible?"

"How is what possible?"

Millburn said, "How is it possible to experience an utter change of heart? Guilt has flipped my feelings. Guilt had flipped them *volte-face*. I owe her plenty and I hate her."

"Hate whom?"

"Aint you listening, boy? Nellah. I hate Nellah."

Millburn beat the battered tin ear on the arm of the chair.

"O.G., stop. You owe her nothing. Not a bean."

"I do, though. I do, Lawrie. She's a smart gal. Real good in business. Got a head for it. Saved my bacon. A few years back. She helped me out. Receivables were crushing. Tavern was her idea.

Cash business. She runs it. Runs it good. Midnight dinners are for my prospects. But," Millburn rubbed his ear, "I hate her because—"

Filkin was a plain man but he had a gift for the social contest. He could handle multiple sensations. He did not believe in the concept of race—under the skin he figured people were pretty much the same—but he believed in competition. He was a segregationist. Proud to be so. He nodded as he chewed sugared almonds, drank spirits and thought about how much he himself hated Nellah. In duplicity, Filkin suspected he was the reigning champion. "So. I'm surprised. You hate her. Because?"

"She wanted too much, Lawrie. She wanted in. She wanted to be on my side. She shouldn't have wanted it." Millburn was getting royally intoxicated. He slurred. He sniffed. He wiped his nose with his linen handkerchief. He said he was not a beast. He knew it wasn't fair to hate her. He couldn't help it. He had tried.

Filkin balanced high on the cushion of Fannie's recent acquisition, a special-ordered easy chair. It was a beauty. A scallop shell divided the leafy carved top rail and the channelled, down-swept arms turned into gadrooned, tapered front legs. The material was burgundy and yellow, threaded in a Gobelin stitch. The dizzy pattern complemented the thick pile on the carpet and it rather nicely picked up the ochre grain of the library's walnut furniture. Fannie had insisted upon buying the chair for their guest, her brother, who presently crossed his limbs and dangled the lead-crystal glass. "It is business," said the young man. "You are not meant to worry about business. Listen here, you may assure yourself—" and it was Filkin who leaned forward to make a point. "Yes, sir, on this, Octavius, you are right. Who does Nellah think she is?"

"Hicaghh—" Millburn listened to dilute the pain, to find solace, and for dear life he clung to the ear trumpet.

Filkin pressed. "A cunning whore. A liability, am I right?"

"She is that—" his brother-in-law said. "She's suffering finan-cially. After the fire. She's in a bad way. Very bad."

"Oh, no, not her. Not in a bad way, I am sorry to report."

Filkin admired the Cuban cigars packed in the cedar-wood humidor. They were in silver cases. They were like neat sardines, shiny sardines, and he wondered whether he might try one. "The inn burned down but Tacks says Nellah has recovered. It took the Hill men a week. They erected a log cabin, other side of the brick house. It's the New Cave. She still operates the doggery she calls a tavern. Operates it under the sign of the eye for every beard-splitter in the territory. They even made a shingle. She's back." But not for long, old boy, Filkin thought. Sometimes Filkin was as good as a ventrilo-quist. He barely moved his upper lip. He actually said it aloud, as though he could throw his voice to the humidor, "Not for long."

Millburn did not seem to heed or even hear the warning but Filkin was glad to have said it. Filkin really should help himself to a Cuban. With a sleek adjustment, one of renewed hope for uphol-stering their relationship, he eased himself back into his chair. "She is not the only one who can take a stack of straw and spin it into a skein of gold. Now, sir. You just write to General Charlie Cathcart. He will lend you a hand. Mother will sort it out."

Millburn snorted. "I will. If I have a farthing left to my name after the reward business."

Filkin said, "Ah, well, that is certainly true."

Millburn said, "What d'ya mean?"

"Look here, Octavius, there has been a development. You are short one hundred pounds."

CHAPTER
sixty

"What's that you say?" Millburn was sober. He sat up straight, like an elderly bearded schoolboy. "Is it gone? Is my money gone? Has someone collected it?"

At table, immediately after Millburn's impetuous gesture in posting the reward, the tortured boss of the emporium had mashed the headcheese and corned beef on his plate into a big clump and he had declared he could not afford to part with a hundred pounds. Fannie and Lawrie had had to remind him more than a dozen times, almost to the point of desperation, that he was a civic figure and he could not back out. To end the misery, Millburn had given up. He had turned a blind eye to the financial machinations of capture-and-reward and surrendered the banknotes and distribution to Lawrie Filkin.

"Yes, sir. Gone." Filkin answered and O'Herlihy leaned over him with the tea tray.

The man from New Glasgow felt obliged to admire her breasts and he did it, dutifully, and took a teacup. She was an automaton. Through those rheumy eyes of hers, she stared straight ahead and he had to look away first. With one hand, he held the hot teacup. With the other he tweezed a goose feather from the sleeve of his buff smoking jacket. He shook it free from his fingers. "Yes. Your money is gone."

Millburn put down his tin ear. Money talk made his hearing acute. "To that sonofabitch Jeddah Golden, I'll bet my arse."

"Yes, him. And Barton Farr."

"Pah. Like either of 'em needs it."

Filkin shrugged. What could he do to stop it? They captured the savage and claimed reward for bringing him in. "They earned it."

"Is Bobby John dead?" For a second, Millburn looked as though he dared to hope. The steel in his eyes melted as he imagined Fannie's secret shame might have gone to the grave.

Filkin said, "No."

Millburn let his chest fall. He breathed heavily. "Too bad."

"Do cheer up, O.G. There is a sunny side to this mess. You, sir, have received extra benefit for your money."

"What d'ya mean?"

"They brought in Boynton Hewson with Bobby John. You got two felons for the price of one." Filkin had joined up with the bounty hunters on Colborne Street. They met by the river, close to the ford. The hunters did not dismount. On foot, standing knee-deep in wet snow, which was about to cover his black boots and dribble inside the leather tops to dampen his factory-knit woollen socks, Filkin was humbled. He was forced to look skyward. He squinted into the daylight. They loomed over him. They did not linger to kibbutz, only collected their money. *Bobby John's in gaol*, was about all they had said. And, *Pay up, mister.* Farr had showed him a receipt for the prisoners, locked up on the bench warrant signed by the Justice of the Peace, Alex Roxborough. Sheriff Cartwright-Thomas had drawn up a document for the horsemen. It was plain enough. It referred to the arrest and detention of Richard Boynton Hewson and Paulus Bobby John on the charge of rape. Filkin had accepted the note as proof. He'd had to. Millburn's poster read, *Wanted Dead or Alive.* Both Bobby John and Boy Hewson had been incarcerated until quarter assizes because Roxborough had charged them with sexual assault and battery and theft over fifty dollars. John and Hewson awaited trial. They might hang.

"Still alive. Both. Shit," Millburn said and slammed his hand on the chair. "Where?"

"Hamilton."

"Why not here? I could get them sold off to the American army. What's the matter with our goddam JP? It's still magistrate Nathan Gage, uh?"

"Yes, Gage. Be serious, Octavius. Have you seen the state of the gaolhouse? Crowded with navvies and drunk Indians. Julia Good, she holds a permanent pew. She's Bobby John's girlfriend, did you know? By gad, sir, she drinks like a fish."

"Julia Good? Who cares about her? My money's gone, then?"

"Indeed it is. In a snap like that—" Filkin snapped his fingers to be humorous, hoping Millburn would lighten up and stop spoiling his digestion, "Farr tossed his share of the reward to the Frenchman. Black Peter Johnson."

There was a creaking behind the library wall and both men looked to see whether O'Herlihy was listening. It appeared she was not. She swept and swept. She drudged in silence. She was sweeping up the last of the china splinters. Strange noises plagued Dumfries House, most particularly in the bedrooms, unexplained squeaks from the beds and from between the walls. Fannie complained about it but Filkin had said, "Nay, you hear the house. It settles," and he had told her to forget it. For the moment. Surely, Dumfries House was not haunted. Perhaps they had mice. O'Herlihy was a mouse.

"Fine. Fine. Good riddance. Three of them?"

O'Herlihy offered tea.

Millburn turned her down with lordly dispensation. The girl scuttled out of the library. Her tight curls bounced under her tiny cap.

Filkin thought she should cover her entire head. Who could resist her? No one. No one could resist those glorious brown curls. Angels would love her hair. And so would the ghost of Dumfries House. Filkin had a sour thought. O'Herlihy was irresistible but she was a woman. If a man had long hair like a savage Indian it was a shame unto him. Filkin was sure he saw her expression as she walked away. It was one of relief. "No. Not just three men." In the instant, Filkin's tone took a different timbre, disagreeable. "There was one more, O.G. And Golden tossed him his own purse. You should perhaps know it. Farr and Golden did not take a pound of your money."

Millburn tapped the padded arm of his chair. "Told ya. Don't need it then, do they? A fourth man? So? Tell me. Who was he?"

"A savage."

"A savage? Hunting down one of his own?"

"Bobby John's cousin."

Millburn was slow to nod. "I am surprised."

"Tacks says they went to the river and through Mohawk, the decrepit Indian village, and scoured the bush at the edge and caught up with Bobby John near his sister's place."

"That's funny." Millburn was not amused. He would not laugh about the manhunt, not for all the pig iron in the colony. "John couldn't get lost in his own backyard. He could not hide from his own, eh? Well, there's something. So, the savage, d'ya know him?"

"His name is Squire Davis."

"Squire Davis, uh?"

"He was at Nellah's dinner. End of September."

"Ah, yes, right you are. Got him." Millburn reached into the humidor for another cigar and snipped the end and lit it from the lamp. "Used to work for me. At the emporium. Knows old Smoke. Good-looking kid."

Filkin demurred. "Good looking? I should say not. A bushman. A longhaired bushman. A Hottentot. Black and white and red." His voice was so astringent it stung the air.

Millburn frowned at the cigar scissors in his hands, puzzled, clearly running through the facts. "He seemed intelligent."

"You jest, sir. Not so, O.G. Likely a by-blow. A longhaired by-blow. A breed."

"Hmmm." Millburn turned to give Filkin a look. "So you say. That's not what I heard."

Filkin knew his cheeks burned. He hated it. He wanted to appear cool, pale and detached, not a podgy June bride. This time, this night, he wanted things to be different. He wanted to be the boss. He was the boss. Filkin raised his voice to levels of command but he was shrill. He said, "A thug. A racketeer. Takes horses to Buffalo City. He sells them to the American army. Have you heard of rotten behaviour to equal it?" The last was almost a cry.

"Father Flanagan thought he was swell."

To cool his boiling tea, Filkin had poured the dark liquid from the cup into the white saucer. "I certainly do not trust him."

"Who? Flanagan?"

"No." Patience. Filkin again thought of the country and sporting club, coming soon to Vinegar Hill. What a surprise Octavius was going to get. O.G. would sign the petition of clearance, which he had yet to do, and Wilkes and Filkin could take over Nellah's property. "No, no. Not Flanagan. I don't trust the Indian. Davis."

"Why not? He brought in Bobby John—" Millburn relighted his cigar, puffed, and blew a smoke ring. The smoke ring curled like a blue garter over Filkin's head. "And Boy Hewson. People seemed to like Davis, as I recollect."

Filkin said, "Like you said. Who cares about Julia Good?"

Millburn was alarmed. "What? Make sense. What are you on to?"

Filkin said, "I mean who cares about Davis? Who likes him? Women do. Julia Good would like him. Lizzie Bosson likes him. Good heavens, I bet O'Herlihy would like him, had she the misfortune to meet him. He's quite satisfied with himself around women."

"What!? What folderol—"

Filkin read an incredulous expression starting to spread across the other man's face. Filkin spoke fast. "Davis has his eye on our women. Not just servants."

Without his host's permission, Filkin reached into the humidor. His tapered nails fumbled around on the protective glass of the walnut table as he felt for the cutter scissors. "Breeds are the worst, Octavius. Freaks of nature."

O.G. Millburn seemed far too relaxed about freaks of nature. His body language spoke to his indifference and he combed his neatly trimmed, old-fashioned forked beard and he gave his waxed moustaches a twirl. "Oh, come on," Millburn said. "Walter Winter's mother is Cherokee. Everyone opts to overlook origins when folks get of a mind to pass. I think nothin' of it, myself. No, I aint got nothin' against primitive man except he don't know the value of his land."

~

"You may have nothing against primitive man—" Filkin raised the hurricane glass and leaned into the lamp to light his cigar. The flame parched the colour from his pink cheeks. "But the half-caste is detestable. He sneaks into the hen house when nobody's looking—" The man was a believer and he moistened the cigar between his lips and appeared rapturous. "And the weasel contaminates the lot." Filkin used the rhetoric of America. It pleased him to express his loathing in the form of a principle.

Millburn chuckled at a private joke. "*Tsk, tsk*. There you go, Lawrence. Thanks to you and your scheming sister, the weasel's got himself some money."

Offhand, Millburn glanced at the gilt clock snuggled on the mantle and, out loud, he reminded himself about books. The shelves he had built needed a few books, something more than the Holy Bible and English sporting magazines. He stood and gave all the usual signs of retiring, the stretch and the yawn and the last cigar inhalations and, with a mouth full of stale library air, he said, "And so what's to stop him?"

"What's that you say?" Filkin said.

"Davis has money," Millburn said. "Women want money. What's to stop him sneakin' into the hen house?"

Millburn stood there smoking and he waited for Filkin to rise to join him in the trek through the library to the parlour and up the winding stairs at the front of the house but Filkin sat.

Filkin's bottom clung to the chair.

So Millburn waited.

For a few puffs, the two men smoked in thoughtful silence. Filkin sat and ruminated. He was reliving the kicks he had given Squire Davis at the cockfight. His boot-tip twitched with gratification, as though it had a mind of its own.

Millburn stood in the room he loved and he looked about and dallied. He saw a poster on his square walnut desk, the corner desk with the fancy marble drawer pulls, knife boxes and cellaret. The desk was piled high with papers, neatly stacked, but one page had caught his attention, ah, it was the poster, yes, it was that poster. Yappy Walter Winter had dropped it off yesterday. Too preoccupied to mind Walter and his eternal politicking and his embarrassing disclosures about the villagers, Millburn had tossed the poster on the low magazine rack and he had forgotten about it, just as he had intended.

O'Herlihy cleaned the library on Tuesdays. She must have picked up the bill, put it back on his desk. The curling yellow corner beckoned him and this time he responded. He tottered to the desk and placed his hands on the desktop and leaned over to read it.

It offered a reward for a "rescue."

Even tipsy, Millburn wasn't fooled so easy. A kidnapping, it sounded like. He brooded over the state of the modern world. A certain gentleman, one Mister Brown, must have a few extra shillings tucked in his vest pocket to pay for the recovery of a harlot, even a derelict mama. "Lookit here, Lawrie. Someone's offering money for finding a coupla ragamuffins and saving them from their ma, an adventuress. Good luck. Money supposed to be mailed to 'saviour' on notice of kids' arrival at orphanage in Toronto. Orphanage's better'n a brothel but why bother? Where's the payback? With Catholic riff-raff, I mean? An Irishwoman is low, you know. Very much a pariah. Low as the goddam Julia Good. No. The Irishwoman, why, I hear she holds the lowest rung on the social ladder. The least likely member to pay a goddam fine."

Silent as the Castle Fyvie ghost, O'Herlihy had popped her cascading brown curls into the library door to ask the master what she might do for him before she retired for the evening but Millburn was too drunk for service.

He had his back bowed and his head bent down, way down over the poster, and he waved her off with a curt, "Nothing." He added, "Goo' night, missy."

O'Herlihy bit her lip and blinked her eyes as though she would cry. She vanished from the room like a mouse through a baseboard knot but, really, she fled to the servants' stairs at the back of the house. She ran up to the second floor.

Filkin knew precisely where. He could hear the pitter-patter of her feet.

She had scurried to her hole under the stairs of the east turret. Filkin stretched his arms above his head and he prepared to stand. "The riff-raff, you say, I mean the ones in question. They are around here? Or in Toronto?"

Millburn pulled up the silk cord of his pince-nez and put the small glasses on his nose and muttered as he read, as though he did not read often. "'Round here, would be my guess. 'Wanted persons last spotted in Mohawk village.'"

"What does the woman look like?"

Millburn followed his finger to the bottom of the poster and read the fine print. "It says here she's 'white blonde. Hair, like corn silk.' C'mon, Lawrie, don't pull a face. It says that. Right here. Madness, though. Who would actually post this drivel? Says she's 'thin.' Really. What a load of crap. Who gives a shit about her weight, eh?"

"And the children?"

"Red hair. Pomeroy and Christina."

Filkin was struck with the unpleasant image of a couple sashaying around the cockpit ring. "The last time I was at the Cave, I spied a blonde woman and a boy. I wonder whether—"

"Wonder what?"

"Not a big thing. I shall speak to Tacks. No. No, on second thought, I shall have a word with Patrick Connelly. He was there. After all, there is a reward."

"You need money, Lawrie?"

"Good heavens, no. You are very generous. Does it appear unseemly? To ask around about these people?"

"Yep. It sure as hell do." Millburn's scowl penetrated the blue smoke. He threw his tin ear into the air. More sober by the second, he caught it with his left hand. "Bounty hunters are overpaid scum. We need professionals, Lawrie. Yes, indeed. A proper, trained constabulary. In the villages, not just in the cities. One that don't charge you the price of the goddam moon for doing the right thing."

Filkin was indifferent to a professional constabulary. His mind was winging to a tangent. "I shall speak to Fannie."

"What about?"

"A sleuthing job. Fannie and her potholder circle have dedicated themselves to doing good, modelled on the Upper Canada Religious Tract and Book Society. Fannie says Episcopal governance bothers the Calvinists but all the folks on the moral path have the same mission. They want to smarten up the locals. Christians are on the offensive. Christian values unify us. They eradicate social instability. Fannie hounds the man—Nathan Gage?—about the evils of vagabondage. I believe the Vagrancy Act is for moral purpose."

Millburn nodded. "Vagrancy Act, fine. But what about Fannie? What the hell kind of sleuthing has she got to do?"

"Mrs. Hart and Fannie can ride out there—to Teacher's, on Vinegar Hill—to see about the vagabonds. Look, it is easy. No trouble. They check the premises to catch a vagrant. I swear Fannie will box the boy's ears if he's a truant. He has flaming red hair."

"When do you say you saw him?"

"When? Why, of late. You asked me to entertain that chuff from Cavan, that, that boat-licker Mr. Peel. He was properly entertained, indeed he was, and that's when I spotted the boy."

"I see." Millburn gave Filkin a contemplative look. "I see." He let his pince-nez fall. "Lots of Irish are ginger, Lawrie. Don't know that Fannie will particularly want to see yon Nellah, you know, not after—"

"Fannie can handle *yon* Nellah any day of the week. Hands tied behind her back. Has she not proven that, O.G.?"

Millburn put down the poster.

The land jobber drew himself to full height to stretch his back but, after some thoughtful seconds, he walked over to Filkin and leaned forward and poked his index finger into Filkin's satin lapel.

Filkin tried to shrink into the chair to avoid the finger-tapping annoyance, which grated him, grated him right down his spine, but he was stuck.

"Listen here, Lawrie. Let me tell you something. Fannie, she aint going to Nellah's place. No, sir, she is not. You got that? If there's sleuthing to be done, you do it. I say you do it yourself. Leave Fannie be. You hear me? Leave her be. I warn you. No more of your tittle-tattle. Needs must, I myself will go with you to the Hill." Millburn attempted to straighten the cord of his pince-nez. He appeared to concentrate on what he was doing. "By the by, Lawrie, I'd be most pleased to know when you're plannin' your return to New Glasgow. It's been fine to have you here, of course, but we can't count on the pleasure of your company interminably."

PART IV

HANG A HORSESHOE

Uxbridge Township

The Ferguson Stock Farm

21 December 1845

CHAPTER
sixty-one

My parents tapped on the bedroom door and asked whether we were dressed and decent. I was dressed, never decent, at least never decent enough. My smooth-pressed woollen jacket was grey and smartly tailored, if I do say so. It had a clever detachable collar. The collar matched the black velvet trim and the velvet-covered front buttons and I confess my indulgence. A velvet collar instead of the starched white-cotton collar was a bit of fancy I had picked up from Nellah Golden when I was staying on Vinegar Hill but, gracious, it was Christmas, the season to fuss. We were in mourning, though, and I may have pushed the bounds. I was glad the snug shirtwaist with its slim sleeves was separate from the skirt because I was quick as lightning to button up and I had time to part and knot my hair, tight. Yes, to the naked eye, I was decent.

No corset, though. Corsets were anathema.

Rebecca's sea-green one-piece gown was cumbersome but she rushed into it because neither of us bothered with a corset unless we had to, say, for instance, attend a public event at the Quaker Hill School. That being the case, we did wear our corsets and we laced them as tight as paint to amaze the boys. During my stint, my very brief stint, as a teacher in Onondaga, I had felt obliged to corset myself. A crisp young educator must do her best to intimidate.

A formidable bosom was the perfect weapon, as unyielding to tears as a banker. In Uxbridge the corset was a beast of burden, especially on lonely days when no one passed by your front door and the activity of note was the trip to the root cellar to gather snow apples stored in sawdust or to shake out cabbages packed with damp moss. Anyway, Becky and I were too thin to achieve the hourglass figure. Minnie Pickle said her corsets helped her with lifting milk pails and I said I never saw them lift anything. Mam was displeased with sass, as you would expect, but she never made me lace up. I assure you Father was of a different mind. He would have had us locked up and corseted twenty-four hours. He did his level best to make us hate our bodies, our vessels of lust, but Mam said you could not bend your corseted vessel of lust to pick radishes and gather onions. A daughter's hands were busy. A daughter's hands weeded the garden and gathered the berries and scrubbed the floors and held the reins that plowed the fields and made the cakes and used the washboard. Mr. William Ferguson's daughters rewarded themselves with hidden indulgences. We indulged our embarrassing full breasts with rose-petal quilted flannel halters, front-buttoned, no busk, and we wore soft blush fine-woollen pantalets. Even on the Sabbath, God forgive. Perhaps God, who sees all, could see my pink underwear. Father said lascivious thoughts shamed the genteel and devout Presbyterian and Father believed *our Father* was chaste. My fingers went to my throat to feel the silver bob on the leather thong, my most precious possession. It was from him. The Mohawk. Where was he? I was turning cynical and I was getting tired of me. I could not look in the mirror and love myself on his behalf much longer. I had read that somewhere.

Becky and I were ready to greet our parents.

My sister tied the ends of her *fichu-pelerine* and she bent down and spoke her piece under the door. "Uh-huh. Sure. Enter."

And then Father and Mam came into the bedroom.

They were almost shy.

Each carried a holiday box.

The boxes were stunning, I must say. Vivid satin red ribbons and large red bows added the finishing touches. December this year had been warm and sleety, same as November, and by winter solstice we were long overdue for the big snowfall, which had started last night. The wind rattled and whistled, kicking up drifts like lava peaks around the windowpane. Out my window, lonesome and far away, I could see how the sleet had scratched the naked uplands. The landscape looked bleak, the earth's distant undulations under the far horizon were grey and gritty, but the scarlet ribbons on the parcels were bright, as bright as the berries on a holly wreath, and we clapped our hands in a spirited outburst. Father gave Becky her gift.

He said, "Special-ordered, Rebecca."

Mam gave me mine. "Here you are, dear Jennet. Special-ordered for you too."

~

Becky opened her package and lifted up a gold chain. In her palm she held a gold pendant with a cross inlay made of enamel. The locket was exquisite. The Amsterdam design was braided, intricate, the pride and joy of somebody's Dutch uncle. Holding the gold chain around her neck, Rebecca fastened the clasp and turned to watch me open my package. It was what I had expressly wanted, a leather-bound edition of Charles Dickens' new novella, *A Christmas Carol in Prose, Being a Ghost Story of Christmas*. We couldn't move and looked down at our parents, who were hovering on a precarious perch at the very end of my counterpane. Their bottoms made wrinkles. Lavender violets, cross-stitched on the borders of the homespun bedcover, got squished. Their generosity had us tongue-tied. I was some pleased with the precious book but the book was bigger than itself. Let me assure you, it was a memento of something wild and unexpected like, oh, lavender violets blooming in the snow. We were admiring the gifts and, plain as you please, we heard a hammering at the front entrance.

It was early, too early for the Free Kirk members who lived close by, who might brave the winter weather to worship in our parlour. In such a blizzard, who else would venture outside? We were secluded. In winter, our farmstead was largely cut off from distant neighbours and, oh God, I wanted to escape my velvet cage but I loved my parents and they needed me, and now, I could do nothing anyway. We had visitors. I was trapped in the black mud of Uxbridge and could not *fly the coop*, as the boys at the Quaker Hill School were wont to do. We had guests, visiting from Toronto. A Presbyterian minister, Asahel Filbert, and his wife, Pinky Filbert. Guests should please me, Mam had said. "We have new people to talk to." But they had made my heart sink more often than an anchor on the Great Lakes and I assure you my father was sick of Filberts. The Filberteen cloud above me was impenetrable. The Filberts did this. The Filberts did that. The Filberts thought the deadliest sin was disobedience. Asahel Filbert was trained in the secret thoughts of our Lord and Pinky was, she said, almost certain about the sinfulness of disobedience because, why, she had the best connection. Her dear husband. As a man of the cloth Asahel ought to know about disobedience. What could I say to that? Pinky was nervous. Her nervousness had an ill effect on all of us. Asahel Filbert might ask me to pinch his good wife to bring her to her senses and I would obey. For remedy and silence, I would cheerfully administer the medicine.

The hammering on our entrance continued.

We four looked at each other, mystified.

Rebecca left me toying with the book's tissue-thin pages and admiring the prose to sprint downstairs to answer the door.

In a heartbeat, she shouted, "Jennie, it's the Mohawk."

Dear merciful Lord, I cried to Mam, who seemed more put out than surprised by the indecorous commotion downstairs and Rebecca's ill-mannered screaming, was it possible?

~

My parents did not hold with detesting folks because of shades and hues but let me admit it. They had their prejudices. Last June, my fashious pater had stated his: "No daughter of mine shall wed a man who is naught but chopper. He works on plank roads. Bunks in camps. Ye need someone t'other. Ye need the mature man. I will say it, Jennet, ye need the mature man to watch o'er ye. A widower. Someone like Jeddah Golden. Good old Jeddah."

Father was wrong but persistent.

Even as recent as last week, Father had said it. Good old Jeddah, he was the one for me. Did I know Jeddah was back in Uxbridge? He had arrived home for Christmas. He wanted to be with his horses and his daughters. His horses I understood. His daughters were as dull as Sunday and as rude as Monday morning. Miss Hattie and Miss Hedy were sixteen and fourteen. They were desperate for parenting but their travelling father didn't have a clue where to begin and he had left discipline to Mister Jordan, the horse trainer. Can you imagine? Mister Jordan had had no success, I can assure you. I knew green horses better mannered than the Golden girls. I was four years older than Hattie but it was Hedy-the-younger who hated me. Hedy was vulgar, right to my face. She said I had devil eyes. I wanted to straight-arm slap her and perhaps bring a touch of colour to those sallow cheeks. In the event, I told Father that Jedidiah Golden was not the one. Jeddah knew it and I knew it. I would not marry him. I would marry a chopper. An axeman. An Indian. I promised Father: I would marry Squire Davis.

In writing, Squire had asked me.

I had replied and said yes.

But I had not seen the Mohawk for two and a half months. He had written me. Proposed. Sent a pressed, delicate white trout lily in his letter and mentioned the Brothers Grimm and, rather sly, he said he remembered where to find me among the flowers. It was a love letter. I had never before received a love letter and I expected I would never get another and I got a dry mouth reading it. I sat down at my desk. My heart was pounding. I wrote back to him. A proper letter. No sweet rubbishy things and I sent nothing pressed in return. Who pressed things? No Presbyterian I knew. My mind tumbled. I had no confidence. I was torn, pulled between Father's disdain for everything that engaged that frivolous entity, the human heart, and my own crazed heart. I had accepted Squire. Yes, I had said. I will marry you. That was that.

Rebecca would have sliced my skinny wrists if I had said no. I didn't imagine for an instant Becky wanted to see me happy. I was a useless housekeeper. I suspected she wanted to remove my fumbling fingers and sharp tongue from her kitchen.

In each of our letters, neither Squire nor I referred to a broken promise, my broken promise. I had promised to wait for him at Nellah Golden's establishment on Vinegar Hill. I did not. I wondered whether he understood why I had not kept my word but my sister Mary, my poor sick angel, had passed over and my family had needed me. Squire's grandmother, the fearsome medicine woman, Aughguaga Polly, gnashed her pointy tobacco-stained teeth because Squire refused to marry Maggie Walker of the Turtle clan. I could not imagine old Polly giving Squire a sympathetic rendition of my hurried departure. She had been there when Mr. Nathaniel Burr arrived. Mr. Burr had interrupted one tragedy with the tale of another and Polly knew full well I was obliged to go home. My father had demanded it. My mam needed me.

My letter from Squire was dated 22 November and it was sent from Hamilton. That is the last word I had from him. I did not know whether he had received my answer. I did not know where he was. I did not know whether Polly had thumped my beloved over the head and tied him up. A thousand malevolent ideas tormented me. We were ready for the final Advent Sunday service before Christmas and, I confess, I had been gloomy all week. Squire had vanished. He was either chasing Bobby John or clearing bush or Polly had coshed him with her half-empty teakettle. I was helpless. Maybe Squire was a dream. If he were nothing but a dream, I was determined to feel nothing but a ferocious bitterness, forever and ever. Amen.

~

He was no dream.

There he was.

He and his canvas coat filled the doorway.

Rebecca saw me and said, *Oh my lord*, and she skipped off to the pantry to leave us alone and, I was quite sure, to mock us from afar.

Squire Davis. Tehawennihárhos. What did his Indian name mean? Better late than never? I was stunned. He had found me. I had been falling into a chasm. Abandoned, I had thought. My own fault, I had thought. Promise-breaker. Liar. Was he lost? Was he found? There he was. Standing before me was the one person in the world I wanted. No one else made me feel like a spinning midge. His appearance bubbled in my brain like frazil ice. Snow powder clung to his eyelashes but his eyes were the same. A white scar, a curlicue, severed his left eyebrow but the black eyes glistened like anthracite and his coat was as wet as the water dripping from icicles on our roof and his cheek was as warm as my flannel halter and there he was. As sweet as pinesap. As smooth as rubbed leather. I knew all this because I broke with our custom and ran to him and held him. Love made me do it but sanity made me quick. My parents were prepared to heal the weakling who believed heightened feelings were normal. I stepped back, out of breath. "Squire. You're here. Do you forgive me for not waiting? I wanted to but—"

He grinned in that crooked way and the scarred eyebrow rose into mockery and he hugged me tight but the hug was brief. "I return Poco," he said. His expression was proud and modest. I understood it must have been quite the trip. My face flooded with the colour I had wished upon Hedy Golden. I was embarrassed and he touched my wet cheek. "The woman who turns to cinnamon." His look was soft, intimate. "Happy Christmas, Karihwénhawe."

I felt the familiar marimba of naked desire zip up and down my spine. Not cinnamon. A stick. As rigid as an andiron and, Lo, I might faint. No, I would not. The remedy for lust had descended from the clouds. Father. His sparse hairs were brushed forward to a point on his balding pate. He was a unicorn with his forehead's horn at the ready to neutralize the poison that coursed through my veins.

"What in God's name are ye doing here?" Father had galloped along the narrow hallway and he crowded my shoulder. He sounded cross but, if you knew him, startled. That is what I told myself and that is what I hoped. Startled, is all. Father would act the gentleman. He would. I had faith in him. His boisterous greeting might cow a lesser mortal, me, I should think, but Squire was ready and he was not in the least cowed and acted as congenial as good old Jeddah himself. The Mohawk did not hesitate to answer. "I deliver the mail."

Father said, "What? Mail! What? Do ye jest wi' me?"

"No," said Squire. "I got caught."

"Caught? How?" Father stamped his foot. I shut my eyes.

Why did this curmudgeon not vanish?

Squire remained easy, though, and he showed my parent to poor benefit, which made me feel sicker. The Mohawk gave a rather nonchalant explanation, "Caught for mail duty. The stage driver at Stouffville throws bags to the postmaster and one of them splits. Letters and poster bills fly. Postmaster Boyer asks me if I come this way. I say, yes, I help, because letters is paid for and I don't wait around to collect postage but one family is hard to find." The Mohawk grinned. "The Fergusons. Something for you, I think."

Squire showed us the letter.

It was addressed to "Mr. William Ferguson Esq. and family, who is settled near Goodwood and Stouffville in Uxbridge Township."

The Mohawk said, "So? Is that you?"

"Yes." I took the letter. "I believe so. It's from my Auntie Maudie McMurdo." You would have thought Squire had handed me the golden pear. I held the letter close to my beating breast.

Father was neither poetic nor cosmic. He said, "Gi't over here, Jennet." In two seconds, as though I held a long-awaited summons from the British sovereign, the young Victoria, he repeated the order. "I say, young lady, do as you're told. Gi't over."

I handed Father the letter.

My unruly parent said to Squire, "Ye do not come all the way, my good fellow, all th' way up here—to deliver mail."

Squire was amiable. "No, sir."

Did I smell violets? Lemons? Lavender?

"Aye?" Father had his hands on his hips and I felt he suspected the reason for Squire's appearance but barefaced discourtesy was humiliating. I thought I might throw up or run away if Father did not start to act better. His bullying Squire was beneath him.

Father said again, "Aye?"

"I come to marry your daughter, Mr. Ferguson."

"I bloody thought so," Father said. He had recovered somewhat and gathered wits because he was being an utter fool and knew it.

335

In any case, there must be someone else to blame. He turned his fire upon my mother. "Jesu, Mother Mary, did ye expect it?"

"Don't blaspheme, William. You set a poor example for the young people." That message was for me. My devout mam held out a limp hand for a wee shake. "Well, Squire. Best come in, there's the good lad. Hungry, aye? Come then. I sense that schemes are afoot. So, tell us. What schemes have ye two cooked up?"

"Cooked up!? I'll say." Father was flustered and he hated it. He shouted at Will. "See to the horses!" He waved his arm to scoot Rebecca away from her listening post behind the pantry door. He pointed at the Mohawk. "See ye to the parlour!"

The Sabbath service would begin in less than an hour. We Fergusons were expected to show Scotch piety. We bowed our heads in sorrow, mostly on account of the Original Sin, and we let our hearts fill with pity for those who had fallen from Grace—not us, thank the dear Lord above. Father had been sure it was not us, until now.

He took Squire's canvas duster-coat and he flung it on a peg on the hall coat-rack, crying out as he scurried to take his seat in our Holy parlour. "Schemes? I'll bloody say."

CHAPTER
sixty-two

I t was just so sickening.

Becky had whispered into my ear, "You and Squire are sickening, mooning over each other. Imagine people looking at you." We made her deuced uncomfortable, she said, and she left the suffocating parlour and returned in a few minutes, dressed in layers of worsted stuff, and with a backward wave she slipped out of the house in search of Davy Kidd. They were headed to the pond to skate. So, here we were, fresh after the Advent service and noon dinner, four days before the annual feast of Christmas Day, sitting in our parlour as though we had nothing better to do and nothing at all of import to discuss.

Apparently our betrothal had no bearing on the moment.

The women were having tea.

That was Mam and I and, of course, Mrs. Minnie Pickles' closest friend from the city, Pinky Filbert. Father and the Reverend Asahel Filbert and Squire sipped whisky to aid digestion.

With unsuspected success Jeffrey Amherst Pickle had commended the Asahel Filberts to Father. Reverend Filbert hailed from our native Dumfriesshire but at present Filbert and his wife lived in York and, when it came down to it, Father was pleased to ask a man of lapidary prose to preach in our remote neck of the woods and we had scheduled them to stay over for two nights. Reverend Filbert delivered his wisdom to our small flock on the last Sabbath of Advent. In the aftermath of the service, my family was dealing with inelegant, store-bought crumbly biscuits.

"Cookies," Pinky posited.

Mam thanked the Filberts for their gifts. She said she couldn't get over them.

From Toronto, Pinky had bought old and dry American cookies. From Dumfriesshire, Filbert had bought old and dry Scotch whisky. There was a difference. Mam could be polite about the "cookies" but about the spirits Father expressed a heartbreaking sincerity. A bonneted and calico-garbed Pinky Filbert, whose costume came with a virginal apron, laughed at nothing. She laughed at nothing to make us feel like rustics, like, aye, like hayseeds. Like we did not get it, Rebecca had said. Admirably put. We did not.

My younger brother certainly didn't. William, our gangly mathematician, was not amused. Will wanted to go rabbit hunting and soon after Becky had gone to find Davy he left the parlour. He stomped into the kitchen to polish his squirrel gun. It was his Christmas gift and he could not wait to try it and on his way out the door he gave Pinky the lifted lip. She ignored him. She flagrantly missed his disrespect because she was busy. She was busy and up to no good. She was busy admiring *A Christmas Carol*. She had found it, picked it up and touched it with her square cookie-greasy thumbs. I fumed. I wanted to grab my book. It should have been tucked safe and sound under my mattress. The Filberts had a fire blazing in the hearth and to Father's growing agitation Asahel was on the move. The Reverend Filbert hefted his bulk from the armchair to add log after log to the roaring flames, which at this point were growing maniacal, and he returned to his seat.

Squire and I did not say much.

Puckering his brow, the Mohawk intermittently glanced at Filbert's bonfire, which was cackling and howling on account of the back draft, but he was on the nod because the room was blistering. I was dazed. Blistering or not, it was a wonder to breathe the same air. I held my knees to my chest and sat tight on the low-legged chesterfield. I wore the blank-eyed look of the Greek woman sculpted in marble and Father and Filbert chatted about Toronto. Filbert said, "All is well." He referred to the situation of Knox Church, separated a few years past by the great disruption from St. Andrews, the home church. "Dr. Robert Burns is in charge."

"Glad to hear it," said Father. He had the delicate lips, which sipped on the spirits in his glass. "The Free Kirk has an active role to play in the betterment of society."

Filbert said, "The minister would agree." He rattled the ice in his Auchentoshan. *The Narrative of Arthur Gordon Pym of Nantucket* was lying on his lap, facedown, and ready for an afternoon's read. He said, "Dr. Burns abhors ardent spirits that heat the blood."

Heat the blood? Father turned to the fireplace and he sighed and bit his lip. "Is that so?"

"He's for total abstinence, Burns is. But I have no wish for it. Temperance is for some, maybe. Not for me."

"Nor me." Father agreed with the assessment and he took another reassuring sip and settled into the old Windsor chair and smart as a whip he leaned forward because his Sunday shirt had glued itself to the sticky varnish.

Filbert was oblivious. He had not noticed or, indeed, he cared little about Father's sweating back and handed up his splotchy-fingered tumbler for a spot more of the good stuff. "Burns stands against the church's being self-funded. What does he call it? Voluntaryism? Yes. He stands against that."

The lines were pinched tight and deep around Father's nose and mouth but he acted agreeable. He poured a refill. The mantle could have fried eggs. "That fellow Burns has a quick temper. I do not know him, of course, but that is what is bruited about here in Uxbridge."

Mam heard Father sound virtuous about someone else's quick temper and she made a wry face and gathered and dropped her skirts with a deft swirl and left us.

She went into the kitchen.

Asahel Filbert did not miss her. I am sure Mam did not miss him either.

Filbert was a sight to make sore eyes.

He was beefy and bald. He had red wiry hairs poking out of his ears. His beard, unfashionable in our modern era, was as unappetizing as wrinkled carrots. His few teeth looked like walnuts and they rattled hopelessly in his mouth. Squire, the picture of youthful smooth-faced self-possession, provided sharp contrast.

I relaxed into the comparison and remembered the leather scent of sins as Squire's hand swept past my hair when he reached for the tipple Father handed him.

Father loved discussing politics.

Even so, Asahel Filbert and his penchant for tossing more and more dry wood on a roaring fire challenged Father's humour and politics and soon he seemed to change his mind about wanting news from the city. Fine old spirits or no, perhaps Toronto was not worth the trouble. The men muttered some more about Dr. Burns and I planned how to get Squire to myself but I did not find a way to manage it until after Filbert had insulted him.

~

"Oh, aye. Doctor Burns has his method, that's certain. 'It's guid to be merry and wise' but he has a bite to him, does our Burns. No merry muse. Not like the other wee Rabbie. Speakin' so, I believe a wee drop might do wonders for the Toronto man."

Father nodded. "Despises Papists, I am told."

Father was himself a dedicated anti-Papist but I prayed he would display forbearance because we had read the letter Squire had delivered and learned that Auntie Maudie and her family were planning to immigrate to Peterborough. The McMurdos were Highlanders. They were Catholic. Like Irish families, the Scotch had complicated religious affiliations and the devil made our different sects squabble, world without end. Whose side were you on? The Pope's or the State's? What did it matter, I wondered? A sin was a sin. I could not take much more of Filbert but before I knew it I was deep in the social quicksand. It was total idiocy of me to speak. "It is not a sin to worship God in one's own way, is it?" I made my tone as dry as Pinky's cookies. The empty wood box sat there dumbly. A model I had failed to heed.

Filbert lurched forward in the easy chair and he opened and clacked his false teeth shut in a manner disturbingly like the Pickles' cranky coarse-haired Shetland pony. "Don't you believe in sin, my girl?"

What opinion did I have?

Men of philosophy did not expect a woman or a Shetland pony to speak about sinning, neither a *Yea* nor a *Nay*, and to please Father I bowed my head and lapsed into silence. In seconds, Filbert and Father had resumed their dialogue as though I did not exist or I was a mite too small to see and I decided to forgo the Greek statue thing and be a house-angel of virtuous mien. As before, I sat clutching my knees. This time I was desirable but unavailable in body and soul and the Reverend Filbert was content. Father knew better. He eschewed the poet's deep feelings but slipped me the poet's shrewd eye. He knew me. He was a tough one, Father. He was a rebel fighter for civil and human rights but he was a realist. He was a follower of Lyon Mackenzie, not, alas, Mary Wollstonecraft.

Filbert, insensible of undertones, soldiered on. "Yes, Ferguson. Dr. Burns loathes Papists. Admires *Negroes*, though. And, of course, *red Indians.*"

Filbert had an instant effect on his dozy audience and not merely me. I could tell Father was alert to looming offence and he did not dare look over at the chopper. It was one thing for a father to offer the strident interview to a man his daughter wanted to marry but it was quite another for a stranger to take liberties in his parlour and sally forth with quaint opinions. Father said, "What on airth? What is that you say, Asahel? Perhaps we should change the—"

"Loves 'em. Burns wants a native clergy."

Filbert had no qualms whatsoever about addressing Squire on the subject and with effort he turned a measure in his chair and disrupted the purple points of his nubby vest. "Young man, do sit up! What are your thoughts on Indians as clergymen? Do you have the brains for it? Or, by Heaven, I should ask whether you have the temperament?"

I sat frozen.

It was a ridiculous catechism.

Despite Squire's sleepy position he had been vigilant but he did not sit up, not so's you'd notice. "Hard to tell you that, sir. Some Indians I know are stubborn. And stupid, I guess. Brother—ah, Reverend Filbert—say, is it possible for a Scotchman—"

Father was clucking like a Banty hen. *Bkk, bkk.*

"—to be stupid?" Filbert was pensive. "I suppose," he said. "It is possible. Old McGuinty, now—"

Squire said, "Indians are amicable, sir. Take Desagondensta, now, he is a preacher."

Filbert cleaned his reading glasses with his starched shirttail. "Desa—?"

"The Reverend Peter Jones."

Filbert knew the name. "Right. Right. Another teetotaller. Methodist. Methodism don't count, my good young sir. No sir. I'm afraid not. I speak for the Free Kirk Presbyterian clergy, as you might suspect. Well? What say you?"

Squire turned to me. His eyes wobbled but his wide mouth was set in a hard line. His hair was parted in the middle and it was pulled back and knotted with a deer sinew. He'd had a trim. Who had trimmed his hair? I wondered. Mahlon Joe? I looked at the plastered ceiling. The Filberts should go. They should go soon. Squire hesitated but he answered, "I have Anglican and Methodists in my family but I cannot say who's brainy enough to be a Presbyterian."

Filbert leaned over the arm of his straight-backed chair to examine Squire and he immediately decided there was no harm in the tone. "Are you an iconoclast?"

"A what?"

"You aren't a pagan, uh?"

"Me? No, sir." Squire raised his finger and intoned. "Once, there were God-like beings and they lived in a Longhouse in the sky above and they didn't know how to cry. Or what it is to feel sorrow and die." He cheered up. "I know sorrow and death, Reverend. I am seven years old and I am baptized Church of England."

"Church of England? Good heavens. Do you understand the liturgy?" Filbert removed his reading glasses from his knob of a nose and put them on his lumpy forehead. He looked across the room to peer even harder at the Mohawk. He wanted a better glimpse at the man who was a member of the colony's competition, the Establishment's church. Bishop John Strachan was a proponent of the clergy reserves in the province, reserved, of course, for Anglicans and not Presbyterians. Filbert picked up his linen napkin, which had taken Becky and me hours to blue and iron, and patted the sweat on his forehead. He dropped the napkin to his lap and adopted a serious expression. He waited for a response and began to stroke his wiry, carroty beard like it was his pet ferret.

Squire was slow to answer, even slower than before. At last he said, "I suppose I do. More or less. Wine and bread turn into human blood and human flesh. We drink. We eat. We receive God."

Being under scrutiny and knowing it, the Mohawk was pleased with himself and raised his eyebrow. "Not savage, uh?"

Filbert shook his head. He was quite empathic. "Not a bit of it. No, sir. No, it is not savage. It is our salvation."

Squire said, "Well and good. I am not a *limikkin*."

"Beg pardon?"

"A skin-walker, a hide-behind, a windigo, a werewolf—"

Filbert turned to my father for help.

Father was bland. But—*limikkin*? Hide-behind? Who knew what kind of codswallop the Indigenous could dream up? I could almost hear him.

Lord save us, I felt fizziness in my fingertips. I knew Squire was teasing Filbert and feared he might keep it up. He might keep playing cat-and-mouse with Filbert and Filbert would know it and get angry and then Father would be more furious than ever and we'd never wed. This had to stop but I had no idea how to stop it.

"Presbyterians and Anglicans," Squire said, knowing full well he should shove Filbert back to the safe track, "I believe we share the Apostles' Creed." He crossed his buckskin-covered legs in a relaxed and unthreatening way, one of the undamned, as though he did not believe Hell was the most sadistic creation that had ever emerged from the mind of man.

Filbert took encouragement. He rode on the safe track with authority and pressed onward. His lips bowed over his beard like a Roman arch. "That's not surprising, boy."

Squire looked pleasant. "Your field, sir. Your history. I wouldn't know." He said he for one would take no pleasure in watching the damned writhe in agony for all eternity.

Filbert leered at Father and he rubbed his arthritic fingers and said, "Of course you wouldn't. Say, young man. Call me Asahel."

A man who could rise to the occasion, the Mohawk was as serene and gracious as any visitor ought to be. Soft-spoken.

Despite his fringed leather leggings, he himself looked like a sad-dlebag preacher. He wore a loose-sleeved, high-collar linen shirt and a tight, front buttoned, black broadcloth waistcoat. His hair was blue-black wavy and shone like Maggie Walker's burnished plaits. I felt a mental flutter because Filbert's sticky unctuousness could have whitewashed the walls but the Mohawk appeared altogether unconcerned. No offence. He waved away his own naivety. "You lead the flock, Asahel. I follow. It don't do for me to make sense of super-natural fantasies. I treat my religion with the respect it deserves."

Father burst in. He clapped his hands to bring us to order. "Hear! Hear! There's the spirit. The Free Kirk is independent."

Filbert huffed up from his armchair and he stood tall and threw another log on the fire. "Say, I have an idea."

Ever expectant there would be a miracle to give him good rea-son to forget about the greedy fire snapping angrily for more wood, Father said, "Ha. Do you think responsible government is on the horizon? Right you are. An idea, sir? What about? About politics?"

Also expectant, Squire said, "About religion, Asahel?"

"No," Filbert sat and he hunkered back into position and pointed a tapered index at Squire. "No." His gesture was direct. His finger was level with Squire's nose. "About you."

Governance over citizens or churchgoers, what difference did it make to a silent woman? I was prepared to dismiss Asahel's idea on politics or religion but not his idea about Squire. Father and I felt the line had been crossed and we dropped our jaws and knew we gave Reverend Filbert what William had called the Ferguson dead-fish look.

"What about me?" The Mohawk's tone had been affable but there was a rapid downturn.

Filbert was in earnest. "Here is good advice."

"What is good advice?"

"You might cut that long hair of yours, young fellah. Short. Short like mine." Filbert, being bald, declared he had to laugh. He stroked his beard with enthusiasm. It was disquieting and the rudeness of his proposal tore at my chest. I was breathless. Winded, like I had been kicked, and I felt my eyes glaze. Filbert's lack of respect deserved a bloody whacking rejoinder but what bonnie lad needs a woman to act up, to be unladylike, to take his defence like he were naught but a helpless wee blue Manx cat?

I bit my lip. I turned toward the kitchen as though I were expecting Mam to return straightaway into the parlour with a pot of tea to soothe the nerves.

Squire seemed amazed but by nature he was too much of a stoic to drop his jaw like a dead fish or even look stern at the old fool. He was upset, though. He twisted a bone button on his waistcoat. He twisted another one. "I see. Yes, brother. Ha, ha. Your hair is very short."

"And for heaven's sakes, young man, do ye not be foolish. Put on some trousers. Not those leather-stocking things. And try real boots. Real boots, made in America."

Squire's head popped up. "Real boots? What for?"

"You could pass."

"Pass what?"

"Pass for white."

Squire hesitated. This time, when he answered, he was as focused as a foxhound under a treed coon. "Soooo, Asahel—" He looked straight at me and drawled. "You reckon?"

Filbert misread Squire's polite contempt. Indians could be robbed, beaten up, murdered, expelled from their territory and defamed intellectually but the good reverend seemed to feel Indians must have done something very bad simply because Europeans treated them so bad and he reiterated. "Sure you can, boy. Cast off the Indigenous yoke. You speak slow and deliberate. Like a for-eigner. You, my fine young sir, are a man just arrived. Yes, you're newly arrived on our fresh green shores and you have come from one of the crowded swarthy nations. You can be Greek. Better, Ital-ian. From Sicilia."

"Italian? Newly arrived?" At this, Squire's response was all but inaudible and he took a sip of the Scotch, which he had left warming on the table because he was not fond of it. I knew he preferred gin. I did not know how he preferred his insults. Watered, perhaps. He said to me, "What is swarthy?"

Filbert rubbed his beard, perhaps to free the inner jinni, and he dashed in with a definition, something simple for the boy. "Swar-thy? It means tanned. Dark. You are remarkable. Yes, indeed, you are. Remarkable. You are tanned but you have pleasant features. You need to capitalize on those pleasant features, young fellow. You are Italian."

Enough was enough.

Woman or no, invisible or no, I stood.

My hands went to my hips. I felt it. I was as tall as a white pine. The schoolmarm was back but the goddess of the classroom failed to reprimand the man because Squire had jumped up to erase the board. He locked my arm in his arm as though we'd planned to promenade on the city's boardwalk. I wore my heeled boots, laced to my calf, and we must have looked like masts on a swaying ship to the seated men but only one of us was in full sail and on her way to committing an extravagant faux pas. Squire had known it and so had my father.

As sprung as a bobbin, Father leapt up. "We will call him Cicero." He banged down his glass and he looked at us in apology and said he had not meant to do that and he hollered after Mam. When was supper? He had to see to the stock and if *God Saved Scot-land*, why, he and Will might go rabbit hunting. Snapping his arms to his sides like a pair of scissors, Father said he hoped he snuffed out the Italian question for good and all. It was ludicrous, harebrained.

White teeth flashed as Squire choked back a derisive laugh and he said he had to agree with Father. *Swarthy*, he repeated. He admitted he had never heard of such a word, *swarthy*, and it did strike him as a funny word but he would make a vow to avoid sunshine and stay in moon glow. He shrugged and whispered into my ear, "You and your pa, Karihwénhawe. You are alike. Let us not make a big issue of the bald one's advice. I am swarthy one. Let it go."

I crunched my polished boot on his soft moccasin and he winced with a fake grimace but arm-in-arm we ambled to the front window. I drew aside the heavy drapes and we looked out on the pretty picket fence and searched up and down the desolate Scotch road for strangers travelling our way, there were none, and watched the silver sun float into view from behind a snow cloud. The weather had calmed since morning. Our chestnut tree was hoary and behind us, in the very hot parlour, my father was horrified. He stood like the bellows beside the hearth, puffed up and ready to erupt. He held his breath for so long I considered it must have taken enormous effort on his part not to blow his guest back to the gates of sinful Toronto.

Filbert acted indulgent but remained unmoved. He said, "Well, sorry, Ferguson. I tried to help. As it stands, the future for the half-breed is bleak in this world. I said he could pass and I believe he can. It is only a suggestion. After all, the boy need not look inferior."

Father said, "Asahel, my good man, what hath possessed ye? Italy is not the answer."

In the eye of the hurricane, Pinky was a glaring non sequitur. She held up *A Christmas Carol*. My precious book. My new gift. She had a rusty voice and croaked out something unintelligible and went about clearing her throat. "May I read it?"

I faltered.

Once again, Father leapt to cover the moment. "Yes, yes, of course, my dear Mrs. Filbert." Father did not wait for Mam's answer about suppertime. He bounded out of the parlour and tore off his silk ascot, new for Christmas, and hopped to the coat-rack at the front entrance and grabbed his Nordic jumper and stuck his head back into the overheated room. "Ye are guests." He was inclusive. He flung both of his arms around the room and waggled his digits like a wizard casting a spell on dozens of guests. "Read what ye like."

Pinky laughed. "Why, bless your soul," she said. She spoke to her husband. "Ace, I'm about to tackle Dickens." Trying to get her mate's attention, she made her voice sound high and girlish, like she was about to tackle leapfrog.

Filbert, already engrossed in reading *Arthur Gordon Pym of Nantucket*, raised a glass and did not acknowledge his wife's existence.

I touched my fingertips to my forehead. I prayed to the merciful fates to make the Filberts leave. Get them out of our parlour, our house, our lives. Where could we live, Squire and I, to avoid people like them?

~

Our guests, according to Father, were "in the process of burning up every available stick of wood in the place." The household had abandoned the two relaxed Filberts after the one o'clock chime. As far as Squire and I knew, they were still roasting by an open fire. No one was surprised when we left the parlour. We wanted to be alone and we went outside. We leaned on each other and the old yard-pump and spoke in low voices.

Father and William approached. They marched over and both looked upset. Father's narrowed eyes radiated menace. My forehead tightened but I knew he was not angry with us. The Filberts were set to receive his wrath. Father was a God-fearing man but he was diligent. A farmstead needed workers, even on the Sabbath, God forgive, and what a stock farm did not need was a couple of loungers lounging about, mid-afternoon, reading by firelight *in the daylight* and burning up every single burnable stick.

William was indignant and he tossed his gun from his left shoulder to his right and back again. "They're wretched, you know. Treatin' us like bumpkins."

Father said, "Those damned people use wood with no consequence." Unlike me, Father did not tend to blaspheme. We had heard him curse in a steady stream throughout the day and on account of it we stood straighter. Squire asked whether he should split logs from the cord piled against the barn and the frowning lines on William's raw-boned face burst into crinkles of pleasure. "Say, yeah. Wow. Great. That'd be great, Squire."

Father continued to grouse non-stop under his breath and Squire said, "What do you say, sir, ah, Mr. Ferguson?"

In a couple of seconds, Father spoke up and he sounded obliged in spite of himself and overdid the zest. "Aye, by God!" He wanted the logs split for burning. He'd be beholden. "It's either split the logs, my lad, or spend a happy evening nestled together with Asahel under quilts."

Nestling under quilts gave us pause.

Father nodded. Right. He had read our minds. "Awful thought." My free-as-a-bird parent pounded the Mohawk on the back and he gathered up his tatty old cap and slapped it on his thin forward-brushed hair and gave a satisfied take-that smirk to the house.

He and Will turned away. They jumped the yard fence, four-poles high, and tromped into the bush. They were gone from sight in seconds, gone like the flash of a bobolink's white rump.

The rascals.

It was a Christmas miracle.

The Mohawk had materialized to help us out and I wondered whether Father might re-evaluate his opinion of choppers.

CHAPTER
sixty-three

"After the feast of celebration I leave."

"Leave? What? You mean, *leave with me*?"

"No. I don't mean that. Not with you." Squire did not stop working and selected the sawn side of the log. He aimed for a gash. He was deft and turned the axe at the last minute and let the wood fall on the blade. The log centre snapped with a crack. He almost split the next log, right off, but ended up picking up the wood by the axe and banging it on the table of a sawed-off oak trunk until he ripped the log clean through. "We stack wood over there. See? By the door. You have enough to burn for a month of Sundays."

"Why?"

"Why what?

"Why do you leave?"

Through gritted teeth, he said, "I got—" The axe fell and there was another crack as the wood split. "I got business to look after. Won't take long—" Axe whirred and landed. "I think."

William was in his debt because without the Mohawk it would have been Will at the chopping block but I was in Will's debt too. My brother had drawn Father to the bush and they had let us be by ourselves instead of skulking around after us, checking, spying and ruining our every minute together. "I am leaving with you, Squire."

"No, Karihwénhawe. I come back. I am brilliant—"

Squire had placed another huge section of cedar on the trunk table. He held his breath. He swung the axe back over his head and swung it forward, whizzing the axe blade through the air until it connected. The violent blade cut deep into the heart of the wood and the log broke wide open, exposing shiny sappy red splinters, and I wondered whether the wood felt the pain I felt. The Mohawk said, "I am brilliant at finding my way around the upper country. I am just not brilliant enough to be a Presbyterian—" He leaned on the axe handle and looked at me. "But maybe I give it a try." He wore the navy jumper I had knitted for him but the sleeves were inches too long and he had to roll them up. In the event, he was over-heated and slipped off the heavy thing and tied the sleeves around his waist. Then he undid the sweater and retied it, higher. He hugged his side and inhaled and held his breath.

"What's wrong?"

"Sore ribs."

"Why? What happened?"

"I get drunk and it's too bad for me. Listen, I come back, Kari-hwénhawe, but I got business on the Grand River first."

He was a handsome, broad-faced man with piercing black eyes and he wanted to take the world for fair value even though he knew better. My heart was shredded, cut into splinters, because he was leaving so soon after he had arrived and I did not know whether I could bear another two or more months of separation. Was he angry about Filbert? I said, "What business? You aren't leaving because of Filbert, are you?"

"No."

"Father?"

"Nope." Pause. A laugh. "Nope, not your pa, neither. But your pa sure fancies it. My leavin', that is."

He would not leave because of Mam. She liked him and made no secret of it. He had dried and smoked a line of Masqinonge over burnt corncobs and brought the fragrant fish to her, and a sack of dried cranberries. We felt lucky because salmon was a delicacy to add to our winter fare of potatoes and root vegetables, endless salted pork and white beans. The cranberries had value for good health and we loved the tang and colour. "Excellent with goose—" Mam had said and tapped her cheek. "Or rabbit, perhaps." She confessed she was as pleased as Paddy with the berries. In fact, Ann Auld and Mam were so pleased with Squire and the treats that they had whisked us from the kitchen. Ann had waved the big brass bell in my direction and I knew what she meant. I was excused. Ann and Mam were soaking and preparing the fish soup and they had made pumpkin pie and boiled the cranberries in honey water and left Squire and me to chop and stack the split wood because idle hands were the devil's tools.

~

We had piled the wood at the door of the summer kitchen.

The stack of ready logs was almost as high as the doorframe.

Mam and Ann Auld were on our side and we were a small team but what did it matter? Squire would leave me again and I would get no help or support from Father. He was a man whose many conflicts drove splinters into his Scotch consciousness. And his conscience too, I supposed. I looked at my man, the brilliant one. In his exotic world of piss-a-bed remittance men and pissed publicans, was he brilliant enough to keep the bigots away? Was he brilliant enough to save me from a life everlasting with Hedy Golden?

"What business? Do you leave because of us, you and me?" We walked toward the barn. I wore my apron. A bunch of tiny snow apples were gathered inside it for Poco and Cap'n. "So, do you? Do you leave because of me?"

The Mohawk's surprise was reassuring but he was ever the wit. "Yeah, that is it. Of course. I leave because of you." I knew he was teasing but feared many would wish to leave a stiff-lipped school-marm-type to her chalk and slate and her own best devices.

Poco's little nose twitched and she neighed when we appeared. She head-butted my apple hand. I gave her one. She was in the same stall as Bonnie, our draught horse. They were crib buddies from last summer. "So, why?"

Squire wandered around to Cap'n's stall, right next to Bonnie's stall, on the far side, to make sure William had taken proper care of his horse. "Has to do with a couple of kids. Name's Munny, Pommie and Chrisinny Munny, and their skinny towhead ma, Bride Munny. I reckon Bride has big trouble about to fall on her head."

The air in the timber-framed barn felt prickly on the back of my knees, likely from the ammonia of animal urine, but the climate inside the barn was moderate and considerably warmer than the yard, probably because it stood on a stone foundation. Counting the high peaked roof and the open loft, the barn was a three-storey affair. In the distant stalls and far away from the horse cribs, Mam's two milch cows lowed. Beef stock was too expensive to winter over whereas, if necessary, horses could fend for themselves. We were down to a few heifers and we had kept our Ayrshire bull, randy old Hector. He was pot bellied, sad-eyed and lonely, penned at the opposite end of the barn. He bellowed like a big old baby. He was a prize-winner, a terrific asset to a stock farm if you did not value your life, but avoiding Hector you could still get lost in our red barn and I was thinking about getting lost and how pleasant it would be, to slip away with the brilliant one, to hide out together, to live beyond the picket gate for a while. "Trouble? What is this then? I don't understand."

Squire said, "I see a poster bill, Jennie. The mail sack breaks and poster jumps out at me. In Stouffville. Boy Hewson wants his niece and nephew to stay clear of their mother, a known harlot. Harlot is Bride Munny, Boy's sister. It aint so simple, Jennie. I think what Boy wants is to punish Bride for disobedience. She left him. He's gonna get even."

He told me the horsemen had discovered the Munnys, an Irish family, living in dreadful circumstances at the Mohawk village, and that is where Squire had met Missus Goosay. Poor Munnys. Poor kids. Missus Goosay fed and kept the kids over the summer months.

"Why?" I asked. "Why not their mother? This Bride."

"Karihwénhawe, you don't know. You have no idea. By *poor*, I don't mean hard-up like the English gentleman who don't do a day's work without his menservants. I mean dirt poor. Famine poor. My people know it, that kind of poor."

"How can you help the Munnys?"

"I do not know how to help. Not yet." He looked apologetic, almost embarrassed. "Missus Goosay charges me with the welfare of the kids. We say it's about avoiding do-gooders. Ah, Jennie, I see that poster and I get scared. It's about avoiding Bride Munny's kinsman. Missus Goosay understands. She understands it better than me."

I gave Poco another apple.

I said nothing.

Who was this Mrs. Goosay?

I leaned back on a bearing post. Squire put his left arm around my waist and pointed to the buckboard. "Here. Jump up. It is a story." It was a dirty old wagon and I feared the loose spring under the plank seat might tip us but we made it. We were agile, like artists of the wire. Dappled Bonnie wanted exercise and she pawed the floor and rumbled in her chest because she expected to be hitched to the wagon but in a minute she gave up hope and flipped her head in disgust after she saw us clamber over the seat.

We stood in the dark green wagon box and then we sunk to our knees in the hay and made ourselves comfortable and used the navy jumper and a ratty bunkhouse blanket to cover us. Squire put his arm around my shoulders and we were as good as nestled under quilts and he told me more about the Irish Munnys and a pale man named Lawrence Filkin and Filkin's plans to acquire Nellah's property for a Christian men's sporting club. He described the cold china eyes of Boy Hewson and the deal Boy had made with a certain Lieutenant Needles of the RCRR for the Munny kids' kidnapping. Squire said he didn't expect Boy Hewson or Bobby John to stay in gaol until the spring assizes. He told me about the fire at Nellah's place and the remains of the Cyclops Inn and the Mennonite singers and the log cabin they had built for Nellah's tavern and the non-stop wrangling between him and his friend Jake Venti. And how Alfie's fry-pan hand had got burned from exploding camphene and he felt it was his fault because he knew better than to fool around with fuel and a lighted lamp and how Polly nursed Cook and stayed with Nellah.

It was a story, just so, and I listened and in a weak moment almost hoped to ask whether he had been upset when he had discovered I had left Vinegar Hill with Mr. Burr but I could not interrupt the narrative because the tale was not for me, or my pleasure. He felt he had a big problem with Pommie and Chrisinny Munny and his feeling of responsibility begged for my understanding. Not only that, and he repeated it, Missus Goosay expected him to see to it. He undid the buttons on his waistcoat and took a drawstring purse from his inside vest pocket and showed me fifty English pounds and said Jeddah had given him twenty-five of the fifty, the Snowman's share of the bounty for bringing in Hewson and John, and the other twenty-five was his. There, before my eyes, was a full half of Octavius Millburn's overgenerous reward and Squire stared at it, clearly he was delighted, disbelieving. He hugged me. "I need this money, Jennie. The money buys land, patented land. Thanks to your friend Jeddah Golden, we get married now, Karihwénhawe."

"When?"

"Soon."

"How soon?"

"Look. Here is forty pounds. You keep it."

"I cannot take your money."

"Yes, you can. It is our money. And my promise to you. I come back before you burn the wood we stacked."

"That is a romantic thought. I will be sure to tell my Father."

"Ha. Watch him go easy on it."

"Who is Missus Goosay, Squire? Tell me about Missus Goosay." Who was Bride Munny? Tell me about her. Why did I feel suspicious? Most of all, I hated the sense I was beholden to the likes of Jedidiah Golden for the forty pounds Squire had shoved at me.

"Missus Goosay is Cayuga woman."

He had shut the barn's double doors but we could hear the occasional wind gust from outside and the wooden joints groaned and rasped like young Mr. Caleb, the eighty-year-old man who worked for the VanBarnums in Onondaga. I shivered but I was not cold, not in the least. "Why does Missus Goosay come to have power over you?" I was close to Squire's neck. Close enough to put my lips there. I wanted to put my lips there. I supposed a droning, dizzy, dumbfounded and dodgy mosquito felt the same way.

"Missus Goosay is a lonely old lady, that's what I think—" Squire looked straight ahead but he must have been imagining something pleasant because he radiated the joy Mam said she had noticed last summer. "But then," he said, "I realize I am wrong, dead wrong. She's remarkable. She is not Cayuga, I reckon. She is Italian. Like me."

Who cared about that old Missus Goosay?

I could barely hear the sound of my own voice. "You Italians."

He smiled into my hair. I felt the warmth of his breath. I had a sweet taste in my mouth and cold fire was dancing on my skin. Under the lavender and lemons he smelled of his own perfume and I knew I was deeply, dizzily a mosquito, and dangerously intoxicated.

He kissed my hair, my ears. "Lady, your swarthy lover—" He kissed my cheeks, my mouth, my neck and he undid my shirtwaist and unbuttoned the quilted flannel halter and he kissed my breasts and my nipples and my warm belly. "—is at your service." He put his hands around my waist and then he ran them up and down my back and down my hips. His penis was hard. I could feel it rising against my thigh. Someone had dipped me into a rushing waterfall, the Horseshoe Falls at Niagara.

Falling. We were falling.

We fell into a rhythm.

Clang. Clang. From the porch, Ann Auld rang the brass bell. She shrieked, a great healthy shriek at the top of her healthy lungs. "Supper! Supper's a-ready!" Clang. Clang.

"Shit." Squire inched away from me and he sank his right elbow into the hay and blew out his cheeks. "Shit. Won't Peaseblossom stop ringin' the goddam bell? What's she screamin' about?"

"Jesus Christ." I choked. "Ann is doing me a favour. She's letting us know Father and Will are home." The rabbit hunt was over. No doubt Father would be hot on the trail of new prey, prey closer to home. We could expect him. He was meant to milk the cows momentarily and that would be it for the ardent world's most recent lovers.

I grabbed the lapels of my open shirtwaist and hopped up to the wagon seat and barely touched the step and jumped down and landed on the floor. Dust powder went poof around the toes of my boots. The Mohawk vaulted over the side of the wagon. We had navy oose to the knees from his woollen sweater and were madly doing up buttons. We understood Father was looking for an excuse, any excuse, to order the exotic chopper off the Fergusons' farm. Poe's Raven knew it. Father's catching us in each other's arms would be just dandy and Squire would be nameless around here for evermore. The Filberts had distracted my parent. So had William. But we had to be level-headed.

Filberts and hunting and a blazing parlour were temporary diversions. There was no doubt in my mind that my devout father would try anything to prevent our union.

Squire tucked a hank of hair behind my ear. I knotted my bun and brushed the pricks of straw from his knitted jumper and his black vest. At the last, I smoothed down my pleated skirt and slapped at grey residue on my boots.

He said, "After we are wed—"

"Mmmm?"

"I been thinkin'—"

"You have got a button undone. There. Go on."

"Yeah, I see it. I build you a cabin. Two bedrooms. A great room. A *proper* fireplace."

"Lovely." I kissed him. "Where will you build it?"

He held a pose with one thumb tucked into his belt and directed his gaze over my shoulder to the roof of the barn and I sensed something, maybe his apprehension. "Ahhhh—" He gave me a lackadaisical shrug, as though an idea had just popped into his head. "What about Vinegar Hill? We could live there, couldn't we?"

"Yes. Surely. I would like to live near Nellah. She's a good woman. Rough in the village, though, you know. I have see it when—"

"Yeah—"

"White-man rough, I meant, pioneer rough, unregulated communities. Politics. Elections. Fair days. Not Indian rough—"

His amusement replaced the severity. "I see."

I said, "So—you think Vinegar Hill is as good as anywhere?"

"Rough for settlers in Uxbridge, Jennie. That is until your family changes it to get what you want." He paused and concluded his appraisal. "The Hill isn't perfect but there's improvements. Wilkes' gristmill, eh? That's good. Railroad comes. Pretty soon too, I guess. We are the modern folk in the Grand River Settlement, Karihwénhawe. The new people."

I did a final tuck with the shirtwaist, one last velvet button on the jacket. "What about the Christian men's sporting club?"

"I think about it. Maybe the Six Nations agrees to sell me a lot on the Hill. I register it. Get the patent. From the Crown. Nellah does the same thing. I go to Toronto. Make sure of it."

"I would live on the moon if it meant we catch a minute."

Clang. Clang. Clang.

"Supper!" Ann's cry came head over heels on the wind. "Suupppp-herrrrr."

I ran. To Poco's stall. I gave my horse a snow apple. I practically shoved the fruit down her throat. Squire had jumped the crib and he was in Cap'n's stall, tying an unexpected feedbag on the pleased stallion and we heard it again. The brass bell. The alarm. The clang.

The barn door flew wide open.

There was the enemy. Father. His arms stood out straight at the shoulder. He knew right where to look. He scanned the buckboard wagon for signs of carnal malfeasance. He was snuffling and snorting like Hector.

Squire and I reared cool heads from our stalls and we gave Father a glimpse of unruffled innocence. Frustration had given me a frowning headache but I said nothing. As usual, I was silent. My thoughts weighed heavy. *You can huff and puff like your prize bull, old man of the Free Kirk, but we are on to you. We are players on your stage and I have chosen a mate. I choose the lowly chopper.* I was a woman. God forgive, but it was an exact thing, being a woman, as exact as Hector's huge scrotum. Jeddah had said Squire had *sticktoitiveness.* The man was willing to live a Christian life to please my Presbyterian family but he was not old Europe and no haircut could make him so. He did not hate his own body. He did not hate mine.

By his own reckoning, Father was the reasonable one. He was the epitome of reasonable. He could not act without proof or just cause and because of it, and not finding us wrapped together like the red and white colours on a barber's pole, he was defeated.

His shoulders sagged. "Supper's near ready. Tidy up whilst I milk cows," was what he could reasonably muster.

I had no doubt Father would continue his search for sexual malfeasance with a magnifier, peering here and there on the farmstead for signs that we were pouring our hearts into our vessels of lust. He would rail against the chopper. He was a bucket of wet sand all set to dampen the ardour of my hot-blooded suitor.

⁓

Supper?

Yes, Father, of course. Supper.

I fussed and shook out my apron.

Why did we not think of it sooner, I said to my parent.

We tripped toward the house, away from the scene of our passion and away from the guilty unhinged barn.

"He is afraid he is losing you," the brilliant one said in undertones. He munched down on the last apple and leaned back into a throw and tossed the core over the fence. "You know what, Jennie? I feel bad for him."

"You do? Why? Believe me, he is not a friend in the matter of our betrothal." My retort was not kindly, not to my own ears.

Squire paused.

He was going to say something but he did not.

After that little exchange, our tempers turned less amiable. A poison spread in our veins, young and passionate and vulnerable as we were then.

Squire was frustrated. I was trapped.

The next few days grew more uncomfortable, even after the Filberts had departed. Christmas and the New Year came and went and on 3 January, Squire and Cap'n left the north. He was going south to the Grand River and, he vowed, he would help the Munnys but I feared the worst about him and the towhead Bride Munny. Squire was done with me. He would not come back. I planned my future. I would give the forty pounds to Jeddah to give back to the Mohawk. Ferguson folkways were Calvinist and, as Squire had pointed out, our ways were inconsistent and self-serving and exclusive, especially as regarded the Elect. The Presbytery confused the Anglican in him and absolutely confounded the Indian. Good heavens, why not? A slavering belief in predestination, and the past glories of a previous lifetime to justify one's current prosperity, all of that nonsense would deter anyone with a jot of the common sense.

On a betrothed couple from diverse lineages, social pressures were horrendous.

The Filberts had given us but a taste of prejudice. I was quite positive that a certain grateful and blue-eyed beautiful Bride Munny would suit the Mohawk very nicely, if only temporarily. He would not marry her, though. I feared he was too smart to marry a white woman.

PART V

SKY WOMAN AND SKY WALKER
LEAVE VINEGAR HILL

JANUARY
1846

*Now in due season Mature Flowers lay beneath the tree
and to her a daughter was born. She was then happy, for
she had a companion.*

–Elisabeth Tooker, Ed.,
Native North American Spirituality of the Eastern Woodlands.
Toronto: Paulist Press, 1979, p. 38

~

*Chief Rickard used two treaties to open the border. The
Jay Treaty of 1794 between the U.S. and Great Britain
had, in Article 3, given Indians the right to cross the
border with their own goods at any time. Article 9 of
the Treaty of Ghent, which closed the War of 1812,
restored these rights to us. For a long time the U.S. said
these treaties were no longer in effect but several court
cases upheld our viewpoint.*

–George Beaver,
A View from an Indian Reserve. Brantford:
Brant Historical Society, 1993, p. 76

~

Former slave Sophia Pooley, Queen's Bush
[Joseph] *Brant was a good-looking man—quite portly.
He was as big as Jim Douglass who lived here in the
bush, and weighed two hundred pounds. He lived in an
Indian village—white men came among them and they
intermarried. They had an English schoolmaster, an
English preacher and an English blacksmith. When
Brant went among the English, he wore the English
dress—when he was among the Indians, he wore the*

Indian dress, broadcloth leggings, blanket, moccasins, fur cap. He had his ears slit with a long loop at the edge, and in these he hung long silver ornaments. He wore a silver half-moon on his breast with the king's name on it, and broad silver bracelets on his arms. He never would paint but his people painted a great deal. Brant was always for making peace among the people; that was the reason of his going about so much. I used to talk Indian better than I could talk English. I have forgotten some of it—there are none to talk it with now.

Brant's third wife, my mistress, was a barbarous creature. She could talk English but she would not. She would tell me in Indian to do things, and then hit me with anything that came to hand, because I did not understand her. I have a scar on my head from a wound she gave me with a hatchet; and this long scar over my eye, is where she cut me with a knife. The skin dropped over my eye; a white woman bound it up. [B.D. The scars spoken of were quite perceptible, but the writer saw many worse looking cicatrices of wound not inflicted by Indian savages, but by civilized (?) men.] *Brant was very angry, when he came home, at what she had done, and punished her as if she had been a child. Said he, "you know I adopted her as one of the family and now you are trying to put all the work on her."*

–Benjamin Drew,
The Refugee: A North-Side View of Slavery.
First published as
The Refugee: or the Narratives of Fugitive Slaves in Canada Related by Themselves, With an Account of the History and Condition of the Colored Population of Upper Canada.

Cutting down the forest is hard labour enough until practice makes you perfect; chopping is hard work also; but logging, logging—nobody likes logging.

–*Canada and the Canadians in 1846*
Sir Richard Henry Bonnycastle, Kt.,
Lieutenant-Colonel Royal Engineers
and Militia of Canada West in Two Volumes,
Vol. II
London: Henry Colburn Publisher, 1846, p. 78

CHAPTER
sixty-four

I n 1791, after the American rebellion and the ensuing flood of displaced persons into the upper country, Great Britain took it upon itself to divide Québec into Lower and Upper Canada. Upper Canada, which the British claimed but did not own and had not conquered (actually, Upper Canada was the *territories-depending-thereon-part* of Québec), held a treasure. Embedded in southern part of the province was woodland, a section of the colossal Carolinian forest. The forest tipped as far north as Toronto, ran through the Carolinas, and dipped as far south as Savannah. It encompassed Tinaatoua (the Grand River), which marked its western beginning. In variety and abundance, the arboreal wilderness must have been breathtaking. There were chestnut, honey locust, nannyberry, sassafras, wild crabapple, willow, witch hazel, black maple, walnut, sweet birch, staghound sumac, beechnut, shagbark hickory, blue ash, sycamore and white pine trees, and many more varieties but perhaps because of the work of clearing and stumping them, the inconvenience to Europeans must have been equally breathtaking. Nonetheless, it took a mere fifty years for the magnificent woodland to give way to meadows, grassland, scrub oak and macadamized roads. Forest gave way to concrete. Towns and cities popped up. And farm after farm after farm.

CHAPTER
sixty-five

The battery of Nellah Golden had left its mark. The woman had a scar gleaming from her forehead to her crown and the disfigurement meandered through her curly hair and up her part like a snowy river cuts into the dark land, an awful reminder of an awful night.

Boy Hewson should rot in hell.

Nellah hated the grudging wound.

She avoided looking at her reflection in the oval glass hanging between the crystal sconces in the great dining room. It was bad enough to have a scar running over your skull but that was not the end of it because Mother Nature was at work too, piling on misfortunes.

Hoary threads framed Nellah's face. She looked like a bronze tabby, like her old brown cat if it had wiped its head gingerly over a frosty pane. Nellah was going grey. She had her ha'penny dimples and her dazzling mismatched eyes but she feared young Nellah was dead and gone. Her lost youth wore a feather crown. Pearl, her infant daughter, didn't care that Mama had stopped looking young because Mama was bountiful, a source of life.

Nellah Blaize Golden was the dark-skinned daughter of an African woman and a Scandinavian man. Her maternal ancestor was a corporal in Butler's Rangers and a Loyalist. After the rebellion, the contrarian great-grand pappy of Nellah and her first cousin, white-skinned Jeddah Golden, opted to remain stateside to live with his multi-hued family in the habitual diversity of the green heart of Appalachia but you cannot control your ambitious progeny. His great-grandchildren moved back to the north.

In 1830, tired of the family's squabbling with the Scots-Ulster clans and the quarrelling between mountain people and low-country elites, the unlikely duo of black Nellah and white Jeddah left the backcountry of West Virginia. They went in search of a pot of gold at the end of the British North American rainbow and the fact and existence of their Loyalist relative gained them official entry into the northern colony. They landed in Niagara.

Right off, Jeddah had up and married Dora Gourlay, kinswoman of Robert Gourlay, and in 1834 he bought a stock farm in Uxbridge, adjacent to the Ferguson farm. Nellah had been the last to know about Jeddah and Dorie. She was astounded. She was betrayed. She never forgave him. Dorie had died of consumption a few years back leaving Jeddah to rear two surly daughters, Miss Hattie, just sixteen, and Miss Hedy, fourteen, and Nellah had softened toward him long enough to get herself pregnant with her own sweet darling Pearl.

In any case, back then, Nellah had moved around some. Jeddah had gone north to Uxbridge. Goldern it, she would make things difficult for her loving man.

She went south.

South to Welland.

Southwest to Ancaster.

Eventually she went west to the village of Brantford and expressly to Vinegar Hill, a notorious, ramshackle, inclusive but small community known for moonshine, manners (none) and mayhem (plenty). It was familiar ground, though. In diversity it was not that different from the Appalachian holler she had known as a child. Nellah borrowed money from the local wealthy entrepreneur, O.G. Millburn, and built the two-storey Cyclops Inn and set up the Cave on the ground floor. She was smart. She ran her business with a straight ledger and some strict rules. Body and soul, she was Teacher.

Beauty is in the eye of the beholder and beholders let Nellah know she had it. She survived because she was bright and she had uncommon good looks, which proved what she had guessed. Being intelligent kept you in the game but being easy-on-the-eye lubricated every kind of intercourse. Having the Golden dimples filled the gravy boat. She had built herself a good life on the Hill and wanted to keep it. Nellah felt like Nellah in her conscious continuum but she fretted about getting older, maybe she looked coarse, altered because of her injury, maybe her sex appeal was diminished. Were changes in appearance bound to damage her status? Did a damaged Nellah mean a damaged enterprise? Could a damaged woman command an income in the body trade? She worried about her baby. The assault had cost her more than her looks.

Her livelihood was at stake. That put her child at risk.

To live the liberated life and fit into a community somewhere, as a tender mother and working citizen, she needed money. Nellah planned a recovery. She was the constant optimist. Right from Nellah's birth, her Mammy had known it and she had said it often. That little Nellah, why, she were not the kind of gal t'ever give up.

CHAPTER
sixty-six

Nellah's property was singular.

Soft swishy maple, saw-toothed beechnut and palm-leafed horse chestnut trees thrived in the loamy, occasionally sandy soil around the New Cave and thick patches of white cedar trees filled the swampy quarter and edged the clumped-out trail nearby, the trail from the downtown that led the way to her house. To the east, a sour creek burbled at the foot of Vinegar Hill, suggesting, some winked, that the creek and not the rotgut moonshine gave the place its name.

Nellah believed shades were the souls of the departed. Tree shades were her favourites. The branches of the deciduous clawed at the sky. They were thin flat gentlemen in pointy jerkins and triangle hats and they cast long shadows. They tinted the snow in haint blue streaks. In contrast, bulbous cedar shadows used a broad brush. They were singing dames in bell skirts with raised arms. Nellah believed in shades and she accounted for them in the way the Irish accounted for the dead saints but, with her, there was considerable leeway. On sunny days she cast her own particular haint shadow and she knew she h'aint departed. Not yet.

But January wasn't usually sunny.

January suited Nellah. It was a month of cold and silver. Skies were overcast. Shadows were few. Days hovered around freezing.

Ann Bergin, all four-foot eleven inches of her, was the little woman who served drinks and smoked passenger-pigeon pie in the New Cave. She was not in the least enthusiastic about the shades of ancestors or the shades of trees. Or walking the dreary route from the tavern to the village market, and in the damp air too.

And what about thieves, drunks and wild animals?

Alfie sympathized with Ann because she was the size of a Georgia peanut but Nellah pooh-poohed the fraidy cats who hated travelling the narrow tree-lined clumped-out trail to her place. The queen of the night had no time for indulgence. So far as she knew there were no thieves, drunks or wild animals in the cedar swamp. Haggard-faced tree bark and souls of dear departed were the worst things she met on the trail and Nellah often to-ed and fro-ed to Colborne and Market streets, the main streets of the village.

CHAPTER
sixty-seven

Running a tavern was expensive.

It was more expensive after October last, after the robbery, after Boy Hewson and Bobby John, among their other assaults, had stolen her silver and gold and paper money and markers.

Nellah sewed for a dozen or so clients but often, too often, they were slow to pay. Octavius Millburn was terrible slow at paying her for the clothes she made him. She tried other means to support the Hill people. She traded local moonshine for black squirrels and a line of whitefish but the barter economy was not enough to keep her people fed and run the tavern and feed the customers.

On Saturdays, snow or shine, she gathered her saleable mélange, knitted gloves and scarves, whitework chemises, surplus brown eggs, fresh cornmeal loaves and, if available, a couple of suet and current puddings, and she loaded her old pull-cart and dragged it behind her and went on foot to the market.

After market, she trotted to Allegro's Dry Goods and Excellent Fasteners. The dry goods store was situated due west of the old school and the tower bell. A signal from the tower was trouble, either a funeral or a fire. In the case of fire an old man tolled the bell. The bell alerted the volunteer firemen, the Goose-Neck Company as they were called, to come hither and stoke up the steam on their curious goose-necked, firefighting contraption. The contraption would take off like a Roman chariot. A house fire was sickening. The speeding rescue machine was also sickening. It was a menace to pedestrians and horses. Everyone prayed as often for the silence of the bell as the old man prayed for an excuse to ring it. Nellah had suffered a fire. Fire had burned down the Cyclops Inn and the old Cave and ol' Irish Munny had been right. Many times since, Bride Munny had assured Nellah that she and the entire population of the Hill could have burned to crisps. The fire bell did not and would not toll for them. The Goose-Neck Company had not come to Nellah's rescue. Heavy snowfall, the redoubtable Mohawk Squire Davis and three intrepid Mennonite men had saved her home but the tower bell in the village centre had not rung, not for her. The bell that tolled, tolled for *thee* but, she wondered with a narrowed eye, what about the silent bell, the bell that did not toll?

What was that?

Teacher was reared on totems.

The bell that did not toll must mean something. Maybe it meant you would be left alone and you could be an island unto yourself and you could manage fine without the landed gentry whinging about being misunderstood while groping at your silky knickers but there was not a hope in Hades for that.

The bell that tolled for thee meant community.

Community meant death. But it also meant trade.

Trade meant money and Nellah needed money, needed it bad. Her business had never been so poor. Saturdays, after the assault, she would hurry to Allegro's and look up at the tower bell as she scurried by.

Ring for *me*, goldern you.

CHAPTER
sixty-eight

It was 3 January and the first Saturday after New Year's and Nellah skirted the odious tower and plowed through gravel, grit and clay. She near to ruined the hem of her serge day-gown because there was no way to avoid the mess where the board-walk lay unfinished under Colborne Street's roof overhang. Seeing her Italian friend, Mr. Casey Allegro, the owner/proprietor of the dry goods store, would be worth the effort. Over years of trade, a rapport had developed. Nellah was born a free woman and she had the poise to prove it. Casey Allegro would offer her the immigrant's wink and say, "*Ciao, Bella.* You welcome to my shop." He did not flirt for sexual favours. No, he did not. She was honest about that but he was flirtatious and willing to give her beauty the respect it deserved and she accepted her due.

Allegro had a sheepdog's head and a heron's wingspan. He got up from behind the counter and positioned himself before his bolts of cherry-warp ginghams and unbleached muslins and transparent silks and, like an orchestra's conductor, he opened his arms, long and slow, and waited for her approval, which was granted with a nod, and she purchased her goods, a yard or two of griege linen or a bit of tan muslin or some costly satin ribbon for trim. He had tried to woo her to his shop as an in-house seamstress. She resisted. It would not work. Being in charge at the forest's edge suited her better than being a drudge on Colborne Street, however bustling the village, but the showman in Allegro was persuasive. The man was exuberant. He esteemed Miz Golden's seams and commended her taste in dry goods and fasteners. He sometimes teased her and said her generosity in stitching for Ann and Lizzie was excellent for his trade.

It was the ritual.

Nellah expected the ritual on this particular Saturday day but Allegro did not look up.

He was busy.

~

Allegro was busy counting bone buttons.

He was busy counting them with a woman whose deep-brimmed bonnet and strawberry curls were inclined toward the buttons and, perforce, near his hand.

Jehoshaphat, it was Permelia Wilkes, which was altogether too bad. Permelia was the elder sister of young George Wilkes, who worked on occasion for Tom Norbert at the livery, and she was the daughter of the wealthy deserving squatter, Mr. James Wilkes.

Nellah gave an infinitesimal snort.

Permelia still owed a half-pound for the skating costume Nellah had made for her before Christmas. How best could someone like black Teacher reckon white Permelia? Permelia was airified, stuck up, absorbed with her whitework chemisette, her cheekbones, her purple wool-twill gaiters with the patent heels and tips. Nellah thought Permelia were a cheap, clap-trappin' kinda gal and a stranger to the world of unassumin' charity. Etiquette and custom was her forte. She customarily aimed a raised shoulder to folks from outskirts.

No one was more outskirted than Nellah, who was by now used to Permelia and the way the porcelain lady acted when they met. Permelia would toss her offended Kashmir scarf around her swan-like neck and swan off through the goose poop.

Not this time.

This day was different.

What was happening?

In Teacher's mind, Permelia was effusive.

Miss Wilkes treated Nellah to a smilet. She offered her a fraction of a kid-glove.

"G'day, Miz Golden," Permelia said.

Never mind she was a critic and jokester. She mocked Nellah's idiom. "Tha've changed, mistress. Oh my Lord, I would not have know'd you-un-zz. So—mature. I do reckon the sweet dimple is still they-ah."

Nellah sniffed and she wiped her nose on the back of her merino mitt and greeted the woman. "Mmmm. How-do, Miss Wilkes."

Allegro, who beamed on Nellah on most days, was as sour as a persimmon. He might even have made a kind of get-lost gesture with his flicking fingers.

Nellah understood.

Allegro had moved on.

Their tune was finis. Done. Fade-out.

Teacher spun on her worn-down heel and marched out of Allegro's Dry Goods and Excellent Fasteners. What else could she do? The scar on her forehead baffled a real frown but that did not mean she was not puzzled. Permelia Wilkes had greeted her socially. Why? Teacher was sensitive. She conjured up a reason. In beauty, Permelia did not consider Nellah Golden fit to be her competition, not anymore.

Casey Allegro had snubbed her, though.

Was he smitten with Permelia?

What was happening?

CHAPTER
sixty-nine

Monday, after the dry goods incident, Nellah was back, early, to the heart of the village. She went straight to the brow of Colborne Street, aiming to get the lid of her cast-iron caldron reforged. Unfortunate it was for her, she had to lug the broken cast-iron lid back home to Vinegar Hill because Tom Norbert, who was a blacksmith and a new livery owner, had removed her and her cracked lid from his stable and he had used the force of his broomstick to do it.

Oh sure, Tom Norbert was a fool and Nellah knew it. Ann said, "You kin spot Norby real quick. Face like a rhubarb pie. Rhubarb stalks for hair." Norby was not pleasing. He was kind of chewed up and spit out and his big spiky hair was beyond crediting but he was a man. For Nellah, that had always counted. Norby came often to the New Cave and he arrived in the early evening with the monkey-faced Tacks, the town chorus, and the two would quarrel and Tacks would leave, sulking, and Norby would stay. And drink. Norby introduced himself to the women in the tavern as "a man to watch," which was a painful spectacle. Nellah knew Norby behaved better on daylight streets when Jeddah was staying with her but so what? She thought, Jeddah warn't there. She had to try her luck. Her lid wanted fixin'.

She had made a miscalculation.

She had never been so wrong in assuming.

Norby was dead sober.

The switch in his character was remarkable.

Dead sober, he loathed her and everything she stood for and wanted to sweep her and a multitude of sins under the carpet or in this case out onto the street. The smithy held a sorghum broom in his hands. The mean sorghum lapper stepped forward and attacked her and pushed her out of the stable. "Git out and stay out. I run decent operation. Y'old harlot."

Old harlot? What was this?

It was a nasty turnabout; that is what it was.

What had happened to the saloon's man to watch?

Nellah was disgusted. She figured Norby was chief angel in the book of moron. He must have found a new watering hole, is all. Good riddance, old gormless, she scowled at him. She would refuse to worry about it, or him, but in a million years she would never tell Cook what had happened. Alfie would be upset. He might go after Norby with his fry pan.

Ann now, she would shake her brown pigtails in disapproval. Squire would rub his chin and beetle his pointy black brows and wonder how to distract her from the memory of her humiliation. Yes, the Mohawk would tease.

Jeddah, now, he would fold his arms and stand back on his boot heels and threaten to shoot the bastard when she told him how Norby raised his broom and aimed it like a musket, right at her temple. Jeddah would want justice. He would hate to hear how Norby had hit her boots, rat-a-tat-tat, with the butt end of the broom and how he looked like a baton twirler. Norby had rotated the broom hand over hand, temple over boot, and with a flourish he swept her out of his livery stable. The pie-faced smithy had given a stellar performance.

And so had she. She landed smack dab in the middle of the street, tits up, and boots up, skirt up, bottom down. She sat with her legs splayed and she choked on a cloud of sand, slushy snow pellets and straw dust. Her gingham bandana slid over her hazel eye. The heavy cast-iron lid got away from her and rolled like a hollow thunder-ball over the crunchy pebbles and landed somewhere across the road.

She was not hurt, not bad anyway.

She felt plumb ridiculous.

It was a beast of a come-off, being tossed out of a stable. She wanted to cry or laugh or throw an iceball at Norby or go back to Allegro's. She would kick Casey in his wooden cods. Ruin them excellent fasteners.

A white boy, head down, was shuffling through the skiff of snow, lagging behind his mother. He was small, perhaps four or five. His galoshes were too big. His breath came out like cigar smoke and he took huge gulps of frosty air and made the cigar smoke happen, again and again, because it was funny. He saw Nellah. A floppy tuque tipped over one blue eye and the other blue eye looked into the sherry eye of the woman. The boy removed his wool-balled mitten and stuck his thumb in his mouth and was prepared to see how the affair played out but his mummy grabbed him by the muffler and marched him away saying, "Chester! Come along. Woman's drunk. Don't look."

Nellah was glad she was alone. Wee dautie Pearl and the Munny kids were home in bed, best place in the world for them in biscuit weather like this but the worst of it was not the little white kid's tight-arsed mammy or even goddam Norbert. Norby was bug shit but, trouble was, he had not been alone in the stable.

Lawrie Filkin was there.

Filkin was the brother-in-law of Millburn. Filkin was profuse, especially with curses and spite. Lizzie Bosson hated him. Lizzie said she was positive she hated the paleface Filkin more than anybody else in the entire upper country and Nellah could not argue. Nellah had nursed Lizzie's bruises after Filkin's last visit in the fall. In a drunken frenzy, black-booted Filkin had come close to murdering Squire but what could they do about it? Filkin was the prince of darkness. Prince of darkness was O.G. Millburn's faithful sidekick. Because of Filkin's relationship to Fannie, no one could dislodge him from the territory. He was a maritime barnacle, stuck fast to the prow of a riverside society. The thing was, Nellah's arrival at the livery had halted the swinging hammer. She had delayed a horse shoeing. Norby and Filkin had been shooting the breeze, which was common, because beating and bending the iron demanded patience from the customer and the horse.

Both men had looked annoyed when she made her request. "Lid here's a-splittin'. Fix it, can ya, hon?"

Right off, broom at the ready, Tom Norbert reacted.

Norby had turned on Nellah and swept her outside.

Filkin had watched. He was amused.

Jehoshaphat, Nellah sighed, Filkin were a frightin' ol' wanker, a-gone back on his raisin', but he had witnessed the sweepin' thing, even the landing.

Casual and cruel, Filkin had smacked his riding crop against the stacked heel of his Jesse Ketchum riding boot. The crack was stunning. Filkin was at his sarcastic best as Nellah sat there moaning in the full light of morning. "Oh, do move along, Mistress Black Cat, Mistress Mary Blaize. Cast iron cannot be forged."

Nellah flipped him the middle third.

Filkin had been leaning on the wooden column next to the smithy's furnace. After Nellah had sassed him, why, the change in him was widdershins and terrible to behold. He had glowed like the red devil. "Strumpet! Harlot! Jezebel! Filthy convenience!"

Strumpet, Harlot, Jezebel. Those words Nellah understood. She had heard them often enough. What in hell was a "filthy convenience"?

Not much about her life was convenient.

Teacher believed if something could be said simply, you said it simply. You said it plain so even a dumbbell like Norby understood. Jeddah believed that anything well understood about human affairs was simple enough but nobody bothered to explain to her the importance of Filkin. He was nothing. He was critical. Who was he? What was his purpose? What, Nellah wondered, other than his bein' a cowardly sonofabitch, a bald-headed bastard and a calculatin' yaller-eyed rat, well, what did Lawrence Filkin bring to the table of earthly delights?

Oh Lord, she moaned.

Rat. Filkin would rat on her to Millburn and he would make her appear foolish and, worse, make her seem like a no-account mountebank and Millburn would find a way to get even. He would find a way to shame her for getting in the way and making herself a target, which was bad for his reputation and the land business.

She knew her place.

She had made the big mistake.

For jabbing Filkin the finger, she would pay.

Disrespect was not allowed. She absorbed the other one's anger. She could not dish it out, never ever not once could dish it out.

In the end, she managed to keep a lock on her lip because she wanted to survive in the village and earn a living to support her child and feed her own little band of loyalists. If she had not wanted that, she thought she could have showed Filkin what a goldern riding crop was for.

But Norby broomed me out, she fumed.

What to do?

She cursed her bad luck. She had to think.

Teacher was nervous.

A dinner party was risky.

It was not wise to jump into the Monday salon. Nellah feared she should simply tighten her belt and wait until Jeddah arrived, but no, she would not do that, could not do it. She could not sit around and wait for a man's indulgence and do nothing to help herself in the meantime. She was so honest-to-God frightened about dwindling resources that any action felt reasonable. She faced a crisis. In the robbery she had lost a sizeable stack of silver and gold coins and all her paper money. The Wedgwood was a material loss, a sentimental loss, but it did not compare to the money. She had no annuity from her Loyalist great grand-pappy. She was on her own with people to support and she needed financial security and she needed it soon. She had to renew her relationship with the men in the township.

So she dove in.

Last week, she had sent out the word.

She would tell Octavius Millburn. There was to be an event. Her place. Midnight. Monday next.

CHAPTER
seventy-one

When Millburn was backed into the corner and he knew precisely well that he could not avoid it, he allowed their exchange but he was gruff. Nellah had approached him on Market Street and he had turned on her, gave her a beat-it shrug with the spine of his new, exquisite, expensive and not-yet-paid-for navy fur-lined overcoat but she knew he had seen her and she ran after him and caught him up and, breathless, told him what she had in mind. Wisely, she did not mention that she had made a mistake. She had stitched the coat too small across the belly. All buttoned up, he looked danged uncomfortable. As it was, she presumed on their partnership, his overcoat and the lucrative alliance they had in the New Cave. Every week the lucrative alliance gave him cash money, and lots of it by her reckoning. The New Cave did not do well by Nellah because of their original deal. Nellah covered costs. Before the fire, the original deal was doable. Nellah paid the overhead on the old Cave but she made money on an active trade in the Cyclops Inn. There was no inn now.

Millburn wore a look of stubborn contempt.

Nellah threw up her hands. Was she not right to expect something from him? Was she not right to ask him a favour because he was powerful? Could he not invite a dozen men to a dinner? It was all up to him. Ten pounds per person would cover expenses.

Nellah was almost too relieved to be surprised when Millburn had agreed. He would do it. Yes, he would. He would do the inviting, he announced, as though the salon had been his idea. It would be the standard gathering of men and a couple of new faces.

Important faces.

He huffed. Yes, he said, there would be one *very* important English gentleman. The VIP wished to partake in an evening of fine food and fine entertainment. The idea of something fine taking place in the backcountry confounded the upper-class gentleman and he had wondered aloud whether such things were possible. Millburn had assured the VIP, yes, a midnight salon was quite possible and he himself would see to it. Millburn's features softened and he said he believed in Nellah. In a wild and forested setting there was a beautiful woman and her salons were legend. She must arrange another do, the perfect party, for the colonial dignitary. Millburn said he expected the entire evening would run as smooth as Cook's blancmange. Millburn did not mention his wife, Fannie, nor her corned beef hash. Nellah was pleased to notice the omission but she was coy. She knew what remained unsaid. Once upon a time, Millburn had complained to her, long and hard, about Fannie and her hash and her cradleboard lovemaking.

But now, in closing, Millburn grew rough.

He told Teacher she should be grateful for his giving her a chance at redemption after she had turned herself into a goddam target last autumn.

CHAPTER seventy-two

Bride Munny was some thrilled. "A party!"

Nellah could not abide the woman, that happy-faced, mornin-spring gal, and she could not say her name without showing the derision she felt for Boy Hewson and his kith and kin and so staff imitated Nellah and took to calling Bride, Irish. They would do what they could to spare Teacher pain and if the sound of *Bride Munny* brought their boss into exhibiting sharpness with them they would turn on Bride and do some correcting, even some harrying, but Irish was unaffected. Irish was irrepressible. She existed in a world beyond them when it came to pleasure. Parties blew her nerves into quaky aspen leaves but she loved parties nonetheless.

Bride concurred with Teacher.

A midnight do was the perfect thing.

They both needed the business. They both needed to establish connections.

Grim finances tallied, Irish was near as worried about economies as Nellah. There was no more Cyclops Inn and no more velvet-draped bedroom, just a tiny room and cot at the rear entrance of the New Cave. Her sign of the Fish was hanged, yes, that was done as quick as Jack be nimble and pull down your pants, but she complained every waking minute that no one had fantasies what included a rickety cot. Even snotty Tacks was not much interested, now there was no red velvet. Bride was short of trade and she said she was willing to throw her back into planning a party, the most festive party ever held in Canada West. She handed over some candles, purchased, she had said, with a few hard-earned coins from her own meagre purse.

CHAPTER
seventy-three

Nellah wanted to toss the candles into the bin. She scowled at an innocent Lizzie and complained that Irish had like to have stolen them tallow tapers, maybe from Casey Allegro, but Teacher could not get over years of prudent husbanding and when the time came she lit them and cursed the unsinkable heart of Irish. In trembling tones, Irish had said she believed trouble was as common as dirt and she had made a dirt sandwich or two in her life and she purely believed a midnight do was a good idea. Nellah thought that was serious and worrisome. Agreeing with Irish on any matter meant she should have her head read. Nellah closed her eyes.

She imagined she was a red robin.

It was mid-winter. What was a red robin doing there? It did not matter. It was her imagination. She could look on her property from a swaying pine-tree top. The hour was twenty minutes before eleven, Monday the 12th, and the roof she saw was snow-covered.

Torpid wisps spiralled from the chimney.

It was her home. Her home was a magic kingdom, a castle circled to earth from the heavens above and landed in the woods as gentle as a robin's egg landed in the nest. There was going to be a party. Candles were in every dining-room window and, here and there, the flickering candlelight reflected blue-gold tinges on the snowcoils outside. At least a half-foot of snow had descended on the hilltop in the last twenty-four hours but the snowfall had stopped around eight o'clock and, at this moment, the sky was as heavy as slate but the clear air was as sheer as an organza scarf. All the guests should be able to make it.

What a sight the place would make for someone riding in the night on a half-hidden trail. What relief would a rider feel, the dreamer in Nellah wondered, as he came around the bend and saw the glowing house, candlelit and snug and agreeable? As he rode forth, would he not imagine the comforts that awaited him, a crystal glass filled with spirituous liquor? A thick slice of venison and a piece of smoked pigeon pie? Nellah had told the girls to spare no expense. Light a tallow candle in each lower-floor window. One candle? Light two. Nellah's midnight salon was back and it was the first one she had held since the birth of Pearl, the first since the robbery, and the first since the assault of Boy Hewson. Nellah kept closing her eyes like she was trying to urge the known world to catch up to her imagination.

~

Once more, one last time, Nellah peeked out her window to check the weather.

Sky, black lustre.

Snow, dead white.

Shades, none.

She turned to check on her baby and, with Lizzie's help, finished her toilette and listened to the young maid, who was clean and sweet and dripping in Guerlain. Lizzie had her aches and pains. Lizzie whimpered about her pregnancy but there was no one around to give sound advice on herbals and whip up soothing decoctions. Aughguaga Polly was in Canboro. She went to help Maggie Walker, who in her pregnancy was further along than Lizzie. The Oneida grandmother must come back. Teacher would ask Squire about the chances of Polly's coming home to the Hill and lending them a hand.

Squire would arrive afore long. He said he would.

Lizzie had other complaints, household complaints, serving complaints. Nellah was preoccupied and she half listened and nodded like a bobbing robin.

Chrisinny Munny was curled around Pearl on the bed and both little ones were near to falling sound asleep. The two were inseparable. Nellah had made Zulie raggedy dolls for them. The Zulie dolls were like the one Nellah's mammy had made for her long, long ago. Chrisinny had never had a doll before and Zulie was her joy. The raggedy creature had wool plaits and a black face and two black shoe-button eyes and a red embroidered mouth with full happy lips and perhaps that is why Chrisinny wanted to be Zulie and she had started to call her own self, Zulie, and made everyone call her Zulie.

No more Chrisinny. She was a Zulie doll.

Nellah had told Alfie she warn't a-reckonin' to like them pathetic little Munnys, considering how she felt about Irish. She said in the main she calculated they was not bad kids.

~

Lizzie said she had long ago learned Nellah was a strange fish. Lizzie had told Ann that Teacher did not seem to care about anything much, except she did. You just could never tell what it was going to be. Anyhow, Lizzie had decided to draw her own line in the sand. She was not going to serve table tonight because she hated Lawrence Filkin. She hated the haughty lecher and more than his yaller eyes she hated his insinuating chit-chat and his violent couplin'.

Nellah said that was all right because there was plenty to do in the kitchen helping Cook. "Ann and Irish can handle the servin' at table—"

A neigh outside caught their attention.

The first of the guests had arrived and it did not escape anyone's notice they were rude, coming to dinner early, early by an hour.

"They hope to catch you wantin'," Lizzie said.

Nellah lowered her eyes. To Lizzie she said, well, good luck. They would have to arrive last Tuesday to do that.

Lizzie laughed for the first time in weeks. She thought Nellah was a pillar of strength and dared to hug Teacher, who dared to look pleased.

seventy-four

Pommie Munny was stationed outside on the circular roadway to receive the guests and stable their horses. It was a big chore for a ten-year-old, even a boy who felt he had a natural way with horses, but Pommie knew he was up to it. He was only disturbed because two hours previous he had learned the awful truth and repeated it over and over to himself. Yeller gobshite were comin' to midnight dinner. Pommie told Nellah he wanted to get 'nother look at the man who had beat up the Sky Walker and maybe he, Pommie, would stick a firecracker up that fella's arse.

Nellah could not help herself. She was impressed. She had grown fond of him. "I would like it, Pommie, but no, not tonight, chil. Business would be on the down-go and we reckon to get ourselves associates. Stickin' a firebomb up a bull rat's arse aint a proper start for the feelin's we would be a-needin' to rekindle."

Pommie was a smart lad. He saw the sense in Teacher's advice but, just the same, he would keep the sharp eye for a feckin' viper.

The guests were on horseback and disadvantaged. Four on two. Four men dismounted from two horses and they looked puffy-faced and irate. No one spoke to the red-haired stable boy and Pommie selected one of the military men. He said, "How do?" Pommie snickered behind his hand. He couldn't help it. Four men riding on two horses, that was funny. Funnier still because they had packages.

A big pot and a long-handled cowhide satchel. He never expected to find himself having a feckin' laugh. Not easy to carry goods ridin' double, awkward, in fact. He pointed to the lathered horses. "You fellas foine? Gimme reins. I take them two, pore critters, frothin' away like dat. *Tsk.*"

"Yeah, here y'are, kiddie." The lieutenant handed him the reins.

The military feller was heaving around the pot and it must of made him feel wretched. From the corner of his eye Pommie saw that Lawrence Filkin, the feckin' gobshite, were holding the satchel and Pommie got his back up.

"Not *kiddie.*" The ginger-haired boy waited to be dismissed. "Name's Pommie."

The French-fork beard, the older man, the one who was so particular 'bout hisself, shook his head, and being a crotchety type, he must have been used to bossiness. He barked like a French poodle. Made Pommie jump.

Man said, "So what? So goddam fine, then. Off y'go, Tommy."

In the dark you could still tell the boy's face was not wind burnt but flushed. He held his legs straight and parallel like he was facing a dreaded schoolmaster but the four riders seemed distracted and they waved him away before he could exchange a word or two with them, which made him feel kind of deflated. In another way, Pommie was relieved. He exhaled and grabbed the proffered leather, skipping off in the direction of the barn with two steaming creatures lolloping along behind him. He planned his next move. The old fart was deaf. His own name was not Tommy and he would have to find a spare minute to let the true fact of it be known.

~

Filkin shouted to be heard.

A gust of fine snow had blown up from a drift and caught him up the nostrils. "Oy! O.G.! Did you get his name? Urchin did declare it. Pomeroy? Is that it?"

Rubbing his inside thighs to relieve a plaguey saddle sore, Millburn squinted into the night and he looked sideways and snarled. "No."

Filkin was persistent. His cheeks reddened. He brushed the snow from his face. "Well, sir. What then? What is his name?"

"It's Thomas, Lawrie. Kid's name is Tommy."

Filkin had to shout louder over the rising wind. "Ah. Tommy. You sure?"

"Yes, Tommy. Sure, I'm sure."

Silence descended.

The gentlemen were reserved. They avoided eye contact with each other. They slapped their gloves on their palms and made no effort to walk toward the solid brick house, flanking the New Cave. The reticence must have been powerful because they were not moving yet and they appeared to be cold, as well as ill at ease. Millburn caught the eye of the others. Well, fair enough. O.G. Millburn was the boss.

He acted brusque and cleared his throat. He signalled with a nod that he would take the lead. He reached for his crotch where he rearranged business and he strode to the house and up the steps and marched across the veranda and lifted and then banged the treble-clef knocker on the white front door. Far away in the swamp a wolf howled, a chilling *ah-ee-ah-ee-ah*. The knocker had "Courtesy Allegro's DG&EF" stamped in tiny letters across the bottom. The agitated fixture set off a series of silver sleigh bells. The bells decorated a leather strap slung around the enamel doorknob. The bells tinkled and the music was sweet but tinny. Male riding boots stamped and made gun-cracking sounds on the cold wooden planks.

Other than that, there was nothing but deep silence all around.

Ann Bergin answered the door.

She had done her plaits, Polly-style, and wound them tight around her ears. She was not prepossessing but in Nellah's magic doorway she developed sudden warmth. The four men took a shallow bow and removed their hats and humbly received her most kind invitation to enter.

~

The men stepped into the main hallway and an air-cloud wanted to follow. With the door shut firm against such ephemeral impudence, the maid directed them down the hall to the great dining room. The fire in the hearth drew them forward. Ann thought Filkin approached it, uplifted, like he was Jesus welcoming the children of Salem.

She was not feeling very damn uplifted herself. Nor, she guessed, were the other three.

Muffled to their necks in woollen scarves, they looked like distressed parish beadles. A bright glow tinted their disagreeable expressions as they bent close to soak up the heat, which the pine logs provided with Christian munificence.

The men looked sour.

Ann felt sour. She chucked another pine log on the flames as though she were the one who had split it, which, in fact, she had done because Squire was not there to do it for her but no one cared. None of the men cared. No one would notice her, or anything about her. They would notice nothing but their own comfort and consolation. Nellah had trained her maids well. Ann knew that she and Lizzie could treat a man the way he thought he deserved.

Ann indicated she would collect overcoats. She would take the hats and outerwear to the scullery and brush off snow into the basin and keep the garments on wooden pegs near the kitchen woodstove for the return ride. It was the way things were always done for the

Monday midnight salon but in normal times, Ann glummed, at least somebody said something. Socially speaking, the four men were as dry as tinder sticks, even the emporium's owner, who, as a rule, held court without a moment's pause, tonight, even he was quiet. No matter. She gathered the coats and the scarves. She had an active inner life, did Ann, but she knew her place and kept all the noisome thoughts to herself. The New Cave made a little money but the profit went to the old goat, Octavius Millburn.

Ann fumed at Millburn.

Saint Nellah.

Nellah must absorb costs and overhead and insult. That was the deal. Never make a deal with O.G. Millburn, Ann told herself. It was the damned so-called secret agreement with the mis'able hornswoggler what boiled Ann's blood. She knew about Millburn and Nellah. Even Jeddah Golden knew about them because Tacks had a tongue as flappy as an oiled garden gate but Nellah never made a squeak. She never ever mentioned it. Ann gave the hearth's grate a stern glance. Bad deal it was. Unfair.

Ann had heard Millburn was a first-rate fellow. Oh, yes, a first-rate penny-pinching chiseller. She did not say a word to her mistress' guests during the ritual disrobing and they returned the favour. She asked for Filkin's satchel, which he refused to surrender, and she showed the lieutenant where to stick his pot and, straightaway, up on the landing of the staircase, she heard someone cough.

~

A dainty look-at-me cough.

Eyes looked up and they saw her.

Nellah Golden.

Gliding down the stairs, Teacher was the dazzling embodiment of womanhood.

She held the banister with a slim hand.

She was as poised as a long-stemmed black rose.

It was her home and making this party work was her duty. The visitors were early but she was ready. In her trade, contingency was a fact of life. She paused on the lower landing to survey the guests. To allow them time to admire her.

The costume was simple but perfect. Her turban was black satin. A pink pearl-topped stickpin held it together. Nellah had combined black satin with wool challis and she had stitched the seams with stunning precision, as though the gown were created from the night sky itself. Sloped shoulder. Silver satin piping. The piping was threaded across the boat collar and down to the dipped waist. Fat pink Japanese pearls glowed on her bare neck. The pearls were as fine and as varied as moons and they were her only jewellery. No rings. No earrings. The pearls and stickpin were special because Jeddah had given them to her. She had never before worn them and wore them now. For courage. She needed her lover's courage, the crazy kind. Her figure was hourglass and voluptuous but that was all right. This year, voluptuousness was fashionable and, really, with men wasn't it always?

Nellah had curves because Lizzie had pulled the bodice tight around the waist, as tight as a shallow breath would allow. Nellah had stuffed her corsets with absorbent snippets of cloth from her sewing basket. She had to. She worried herself sick about milk stains. Milk from leaking bubbies might soak through the bodice and mark her, mark her for shame and motherhood, and in every way she must protect herself and her business. The sex trade had no time for the mama. It was for virgins and the pretend virgins. She could not falter. She thought of her three-month-old, asleep in the upstairs bedroom, and it made her raise her chin. And her arm.

She had put herself on her own stage.

She smiled as shiny as the polished silver and dimpled as though her life were balanced on a silver thread and stepped down from the stair and walked to the hearth. "Hallo, Octavius." She pecked his bristly cheek. "You sportin' a fine Osbaldiston tonight."

She turned to the youngest man and enunciated her words, above all the G's. "Good evening to you, Mister. Filkin. How are you doing on this fine evening?"

Filkin's pink cheek turned as white his waistcoat. He kept looking around the room and at the kitchen door as though he expected to see a hand-wringing goblin under the table or a beavering troll in the pantry.

Who was he looking for?

He gave Nellah the curt nod, the upstairs gentleman's nod, but she was prepared for condescension. She imitated Permelia Wilkes and tilted her head. Good to be good at dissemblin', she thought, and she were better at it than him. He were naught but a sadist. Look at 'em pissy eyes a-givin' my place the onceover. Pissy yaller eyes like a pouncin' cougar.

She twirled her skirts to meet the third man.

Nellah did not know him. Or the fourth.

She did know Millburn was bringing very important guests but the former did not do the courteous thing and make introductions and after an uncomfortable few seconds Nellah said to the third man. "I am called Nellah Golden and I am honoured to meet you, sir."

Behind her, Millburn made a derisive sound.

Nellah understood.

She appreciated Millburn's little ways well enough to guess what he meant. He meant that she had no idea of how honoured she was. Her ignorance about the governance of Canada West, he had told her time and again, was classic. Rough, Millburn grabbed her arm and made an aside. "We've had word that Metcalfe's mortally ill. In effect, this here gentleman's no less than the Governor General. You *are* honoured, Nellah, beyond your wildest fancies and I'll be expectin' ya to act it."

Nellah turned toward the military man who held the high civilian office and her hands gripped the over-stuffed chair and, unaware of herself, she patted the striped green and brown fabric as though it were in need of bolstering. "Honoured to meet you, your Excellency."

He wore the lion and crossed swords. She knew it was the insignia of a General and the bubbies started to spurt milk droplets into the snippets.

He said, "And I you, mistress. Charles Murray Cathcart at your service. My aid-de-camp here is Lieutenant Horatio Needles."

Millburn had no time for Major Needles. He wheezed at the third man. "Earl Cathcart, you, my Lord, are attending Miz Golden's infamous midnight salon. In the backwoods of the upper country. My favourite place of business."

Nellah thinned her lips.

For shame. Octavius was a boat-lick.

Millburn continued to be obsequious. "Yes, and by God, sir, Miz Golden here, she is privileged to have you at this here soiree. For *your* business. Yes indeedy. It is a great privilege."

Cathcart shrugged, if-you-say-so. He was used to bestowing privilege. The Governor General had sleepy eyes and dark brows. He had frosted white hair that he wore in white-icing dollops. He also wore a studied, serious look. Military life had trained him to put people at their ease if he felt so inclined. His courtesy was liable to be more languorous than true but he clicked his heels and bowed, inclined, or so it seemed, to rescue Nellah. "Your privilege, madam? No, no. Not at all. The honour is mine, I assure you. Needles! Sirrah, please find my souvenir for the good lady. For her gracious hospitality and this evening's entertainment."

Like his commander, Lieutenant Needles was in dress uniform. He wore a long belted coat, double-buttoned, and the high striped-red collar of the RCRR. He stepped forward, shook Nellah's hand, leaned down and picked up the pot. He handed the pot to her. It was the size of her cast-iron caldron but much lighter. The lieutenant stepped back as though on inspection parade. His black hair was huge, as big as a bearskin, but he was the thinnest person Nellah had ever seen. He was no wider than her stickpin. One measly square inch of skin was stretched over his bones like a hide on a drum but Lieutenant Needles was no drum. He knew his place. He was as intrusive as the tiny jingle bell on the front-door strap. Nellah thanked him and she inspected her souvenir. It was a tin-glazed earthenware punchbowl. The inscription on the inside of the bowl read, "FREE AND EASEY SOCIETY." She murmured, "Oh, my Lord. Would y'all look at this? Thanks to your Excellency, thanks indeed." She admired the chinoiserie motif and decorative bunches of grapes. How had poor Needles lugged the awkward thing on horseback? Had he worn it on his head? She thought of her heavy cast-iron caldron lid and her spine stiffened. Needles had had a horse. He was not after druggin' rickety old cart. Needles bowed and he shrugged, helpless to disagree, as though he had read her thoughts.

Millburn seemed unable to follow the military's lead. Nothing would deflect the owner of the emporium from his purpose, which, as Nellah suspected, was the public scolding of his host and business partner. "His Lordship is surveying the fortifications of the upper country, Nellah. Primarily, I'm told, because of border trouble with Americans and British in the Columbia District. Notwithstanding our fear of President Polk's manifest destiny, my dear lady, the Governor General's travels have been uneventful. Uneventful, that is, 'til tonight!" Millburn clenched his teeth and to underscore the anger, he gave her arm a punishing push.

Nellah's heart started to thrum. Her limbs started to wobble. She was concerned about Cathcart, though, and, in truth, not that much less about herself. "Wha' happened?"

Millburn spittled into her face and he poked his ear trumpet in his ear like he was boring an ice-hole and, frustrated, banged the trumpet on Nellah's shoulder. "Speak up, woman."

Nellah did not dare. Her words were stuck.

Her shoulder hurt and, worse, she had a lump in her throat. It was a prickly pinecone and she could not trust herself to speak to Millburn or to any of them but Filkin had heard her question and he answered. "We have been beset upon."

"Jesu." Nellah's hands gripped the chair. "Who would a-done the besettin'?"

Millburn got the gist. He straightened the barrel-knotted ascot and scowled at Nellah and the punchbowl until she felt like she had been caught red-handed trying to steal it. She thought Octavius might have a stroke. He might have dipped his head into the contents of the saltcellar; his face was burning bad. He aimed the narrow end of his trumpet at her bodice, ready to tap. By habit she moved out of range. He said, "It was awful, I tell you, woman. We was attacked by thieves, drunks and wild animals."

Nellah gave over the punchbowl to Ann. The maid carried it, free and easy, to the kitchen as though it weighed the same as a Murphy potato. To Nellah it had weighed a ton. She let her fingertips touch her mouth. She shut her eyes and lowered her hands and her knuckles were stark white against the stuffed chair's cover. "Jehoshaphat. I reckon that never happened afore. I caint imagine who would do such a thing—"

Filkin clapped, a vigorous business, as though he loved to encourage the lower classes. "Caint you? Please do continue. However, one can well imagine why you caint, Mistress."

Nellah was set to be sharp with Filkin. In fact, she saw herself stabbing him with her turban pin but no. She needed patience, Squire's disdainful patience. She must mind Jeddah's coaching, be careful, be wise. To impress Charles Murray Cathcart, she would choose wisdom over amusement. She had picked up Filkin's insinuation about honour among thieves but, so help her dear mammy, there was no gesture, not this time. She would shut up. She would be patient. She would be wise. She knew the game. She must find an ally. The drawn faces and the intense expressions of Millburn and Filkin repelled her and she spoke to Cathcart. "Terrible, hon. What did ya'll lose? What would be a-stolen?"

Cathcart said, "From me, not a damn thing, m'dear. Needles here saved your punchbowl. Thief wanted horses. He took Filkin's. And that of the lieutenant."

"Oh, no. Thieves? How many was there?"

Nellah knew as soon as the question left her lips it was the wrong thing to ask, although Governor General Cathcart was more than willing to answer. "One red Indian wearing war paint, I believe, Miz Golden." With stiff square shoulders, Cathcart turned to his cohort and he raised a mild eyebrow. The eyebrow was dark and curly in spite of his white hair and the brow-lift was near a chuckle. "One? Am I right, Lieutenant Needles? Do I count correctly? One?"

Needles had sweat beads forming on his upper lip. His bear hair looked to be a foot high. It stood on end. He did not say anything. He appeared abashed, like a sad overgrown child, with his hairy wrists hanging from his too-short sleeves.

Lawrence Filkin was boyish too. He was a six-year-old brat.

He crossed his arms in a sulk and appeared ready to kick the legs of the chair that Nellah had been gripping. "One. Fine, one. Armed, I should think. Knives everywhere on his person. I saw a Baker rifle. Oh, yes, I'm certain of it, he was armed."

"Oh, yes, I am certain he was. Yes, armed to the teeth." Cathcart was unsuccessful in suppressing an officious smirk. He sounded too cheerful, really, as though he intended to say, "I am certain he was not."

Millburn mounted his high-horse because, he said, something was clear. He did not know how it had happened but Teacher was guilty. She had caused their discomfiture. "Biddy Julia Good held us up too, Nellah. There she was. No better'n a pig. Lyin' in a heap of stinking manure, right on the trail. Drunk as a Lord, er, skunk, yes sir, I say, drunk as a skunk."

Filkin's cat-eyes flashed. "Our horses might have trampled the hag but they did not, thanks to the wild beast. I suspect it carries rabies." His voice turned as cold as an iron pike and it pierced Nellah's heart. The man and his suspicions were too much for her. He must have sensed her revulsion. He said, "Dog was disgusting. Should have killed it. By God, I should."

Cathcart, on the other hand, was gentle. He was a commander. He appreciated loyalty, even in beasts. "The animal wouldn't abandon the trail. Barked like a brute. Yes, it is true, I'm afraid. The poor lady's dog sounded the bell, I'm bound to say."

The general had decided to adopt a cosmic view of the incident but Millburn was taking it all personally as of course he goldern would, Nellah thought.

"A disgrace. An utter disgrace!" Millburn dropped his tin ear. He was rigid, more rigid than his starched, button-popping linen shirt. He stuck his face close to Nellah's with pugnacious effect and his underbite jutted into her dignity.

She knew she was visibly shaking.

She was scared. She had never seen Octavius so angry, not with her. Filkin was always angry, yes, but once Octavius had been very kind. It was this eternal night, she reckoned.

So many things had miscued.

Millburn's fist opened and closed. It seemed he had to do something with his hands besides slap her. He curled his thumbs around his suspenders and cracked them, out and in, out and in. He snorted. "Julia Good? Lady? There's a joke, Charlie. She's the worst drunk around. Has a permanent pew in the gaolhouse. Ask our Magistrate Nathan Gage about the likes of Biddy Julia Good."

Nellah was done with it. Enough of this.

She must rein them in.

She could save the night if they would let her. Wanting from the depths of her mortal soul to be seen the way she felt, benevolent and innocent, she pulled out matched green-and-brown brocaded chairs and pointed to them and begged the men to be seated. She beckoned to Ann. Ann passed around the Calvados. It was a gift to Teacher from the Frenchman, Peter Johnson. Use the liqueur of apples and pears as an aperitif. Whet your appetite with the scent of oceanic Manche. Savour it, *ma chère*, save it for that special moment. She thought kindly on Peter. Goldern it, hon, this would be it.

Inside her four walls, she said to the men, her honoured guests needed to open up and be as good as the punchbowl's sage advice, a *free and easey society*. The great room was fragrant with roasting venison and smoked pigeon pie, the hearth's fire crackled, a serene Ann clucked about the dining-room table straightening the cutlery, the drinking glasses gleamed and Nellah was charming. Nellah thought, she hoped, she prayed to her dear Mammy, maybe there was an ally among them.

Maybe General Cathcart.

She plied the general with profligate shots of brandy. Her conscience was clear, she reckoned. She haint a-done no dirt to nobody.

CHAPTER
seventy-five

I n the kitchen, Ann was gloom.

She shook her head. Too goldern purdy t'shit, Ann told Cook about them holier-than-thou types in the great room. Ann pointed to the low level of the liquid in the Calvados bottle, *Age Inconnu*, and asked Alfie whether he had anything remote similar in the New Cave. For supplementing. Flat apple cider, maybe. Barrel brandy would be best. "Them fellows is too particular. They gotta put mishaps into perspective."

Alfie nodded.

He was busy with the soup, too busy to chat. He was deep in thought.

He was waxing meditative on the subject of fathers and sons. He shooed Nellah's nameless brown tabby off the kitchen table and put down the large soup ladle and with his good hand picked up a lard candle, stuck it hard into a wooden candlestick holder, and put it where the cat had been and lit the wick from tinder. Shadows kicked off. They danced on the rough cedar walls. The truth would out. His father, one Alfie Williams Sr., was also the Cook. On the African slave-ship *Kitty's Amelia*. How ironic that the elder Williams, an employee of the rich Liverpudlian merchants who had brought nothing but misery to the slaver's African passengers, would have a son, a fine son, who was devoted to the likes of African Nellah Golden. Strange how the world turned.

Ann stamped her feet. She wanted Cook's attention.

She wanted the Calvados bottle filled up with a spirituous liquor, God-knows-what, but with something, and Alfie should make it quick.

Cook was going to state his piece. "Take Joseph Brant and Paulus Bobby John, fe instance. Brant wuz coageous. Great-grandson, um, not so much. A thug."

"Right. Right," Ann said. She had better humour him or she would never get it.

"Bobby John wuz a feck'n weasel with Miz Golden but taint no good ta dwell, y'know, Annie, me gal." Alfie returned to stirring the sumptuous consommé. "Taint desirable neither to o'er-stir broth nor o'er-ponder sins o' fathers 'n sons."

"No." Ann said. "Sufficient unto the day is the evil thereof. Can't change the past."

Alfie was worried.

About today.

About tomorrow.

About someday soon.

He was worried sick because he knew something and he did not want to tell the others. His old friend had given him terrible news. His old friend was Jackie Carrick, a Yorkshireman. Jackie worked as a groom and handler for the Mansfield Farms and Stagecoach stop, up the Cayuga Heights way, on Grand River. Couple of weeks ago, Jackie had been passing through the village with fresh horses for the Mansfield's big remuda. He dropped into the New Cave to wet his whistle and have a chat. He had given Cook some mighty bad news. He had told Alfie that Bobby John had busted out of the Hamilton jail.

Bobby John was out? He was free?

Alfie was staggered.

He was not about to tell Nellah. Or Ann or Lizzie.

He would tell Squire, though. Tell him tonight when he came for dinner. He had already told Jeddah, which was damn certain. Quick as sticks after Jackie had left, Alfie put pen to paper and he wrote a letter to Uxbridge. He advised Jeddah to get himself on down to village because Nellah was bound to have trouble.

Cook worried.

Hadn't heard nothin' from Jeddah, nor from scoundrel Bobby John for that matter, not so far. No worries, though, some time soon Snowman would turn up. Squire would roll in later this evening. Alfie had faith in Squire. Squire was smart. Damn clever, thet fella, fe' sure Squire would think of something.

"So, may I have the apple cider, Alfie? Now? Before the evil of today gets outa hand?"

Cook looked desperate. His white outfit was grey. His apron was stained. He was a sad sack. Cook used to be fastidious in the kitchen. His hand must hurt him still.

Ann thought she saw a tear roll down his tough face. Oh, now really, she thought. It was only flat cider or cheap brandy she wanted. She decided to hop over to the tavern herself.

Cook puffed up his chest. "Annie, listen 'ere. Squire seys 'e is com'n ternight. 'E is comin', eh?"

"Place at table set for him."

"Righ'."

"Whasamadder, Alfie?"

"Ay tell yous, me gal, me darlin', dat end of dis night, yah, it wul br'n nah good."

CHAPTER
seventy-six

Nellah was the moon and Bride was the sun.

An hour or so after Nellah, Bride made the same entrance. She wanted to, anyway. It started well. Coming down the stairs, holding the varnished handrail, she paused on the lower landing to survey the room, which was filling fast with the guests.

She made certain everyone saw her.

Her costume sparkled plenty under a cloudy wrapping. The wrapping was the crocheted shawl of Nellah's mammy. Timid, slow, Bride lowered the shawl and then dropped it. It must have fallen to her feet but her hopeful face, to say nothing of the teasing emergent white roundness of her breasts, kept everyone's eyes up. Her gown was a golden muslin affair, yielding and filmy, and she was thrilling in it, a modern woman in a modern creation, with the new short sleeves, low flounce collar and pointed waist. Tiny pleats gathered her gold bell skirt. She wore a tight bodice with a frill. A sugary lace peeped out and tickled her bosoms.

"Me bosoms is what turned Mister Farr t'jelly," she had said, prideful, to Teacher sometime after the cockfight. "And spitty Mister Peel, he told Bart he were punchin' above his weight, havin' me on his arm."

Tonight nothing was stuffed into Bride's corset. She was as purely herself as a holy offering. She had washed and scrubbed her blonde hair. Curls were pulled up and tugged into perfect sugar springs, a Vinegar Hill facelift. Her head shone with firm iridescent gold bubbles. Her eyes shone with lemon juice.

Nellah was shocked.

Gold was firm on her mind. How much had that gown cost? It was special ordered. From Toronto City. Had to be. There was nothing like it in the village. Only one seamstress hereabouts was capable of making a concoction such as this and that was Nellah herself and she knew she did not do it, would never have done it, would never do it for Bride, not for a king's ransom. Gold. Gold. Gold. Irish wore naught but gold. She was froth spun from gold thread and angel hair. Gripped by the madness of efflorescence, Bride had sprinkled glitter dust on the ivy leaves she had tucked into her curls. Glitter dust might rain on the guests.

To block the vision, Nellah shut her eyes.

Bride had turned out good, beautiful, one might say, but poor girl had struggled all day with the stress of the party. She had a sudden bad bout of aspen nerves. Her slippered foot caught in the puddled shawl and she was near to tumbling facedown on the hardwood stairs but she grabbed the railing and saved herself from injury. She sneezed. Lord Jeezus, Mary and Joseph, she cried to the crowd, did she ever get off a good one.

She sneezed again and giggled, a sound on the edge of mania, and she pinched her nose until her skin turned blue.

For what seemed the hundredth time this night, Nellah shut her eyes. Idiot.

Males ogled.

Yes, they were staring.

And admiring. And gentling. And forgiving.

Nellah felt a sharp pang in her side, an unaccustomed, lightning-fast strike. For a couple of seconds she was in real pain. She was jealous. Stop it, she ordered her jealous self. Jehoshaphat, she could not afford to wallow in the luxury. She scolded her hurting pride, *don't be s'foolish*. Too much jealousy would be like too much excitement. Too much suspicion. Too much rage. Too much downcast. It brought on a perpetually offended state of mind, the social sickness. Why bother with the sickness? Nellah was harsh with herself. She whipped up a defence. That Irish, she aint got a brain no bigger'n a ducklin's. She kin catch fella's eye but she would be a small, puny, little old thing what caint talk Lord's simple sense, let alone interpret a ledger account.

"I don't believe I seen that girl before."

Millburn materialized and Nellah started. In the instant, she saw his attraction to the young woman and she gave him a speculative look and saw other things, saw them clear for the first time. Florid face. Maybe the start of a cataract in that milky left eye. Veined nose. Gin dandy of a man. Old but glib. Failing to attract Irish-the-prize into his bed, an aroused old man would dip his ducy into any handy vessel, a woman such as Nellah herself, pregnant Lizzie, or even Ann. A maid, a servant. All lesser female beings would qualify to give the adoration. Huh, goldern old men. Nellah was reflexive, though, when it came to business. She realized she had been spinning straw into gold. She decided Irish was an asset, not just a horse's appetite. "No. Most like you aint a-seed her afore. She is the new gal. Loverly gal, aint she just? Say, Octavius, you would be ready for expandin' the operations? I will put up 'nother inn, 'nother Cyclops, I reckon. Kin we touch hands on that?"

"What about touching hands on this one, the new gal yonder? Where's she from, I ask you, madam. Speak up. What's her name?"

"She is Irish."

"Iris?"

"Irish, I say."

"Yeah. I'll tell you, Nellie. That's an unnerving cackle, Iris has. Over the top. Don't she own a hankie? Jumpy gal too, sneezing like that and holding her nose. Ill-poised for all that she's a pretty little thing." There was a great, resigned Millburn inhalation. "Some horny pipsqueak will enjoy. Hummm. Yup. Nice, flaxen curls. She'll load up the coffers, I dare say."

I dare say, Nellah sighed. Whose coffers, uh? But now taint time or place, as Jeddah would tell her, to get her knickers in a knot.

Filkin strolled over.

She knew he was not about to let Millburn wander about the room and maybe start to get all over-friendly with her, just like before, before the assault, in the good old days. She saw he was more than ever the yaller-eyed whoremonger and his purpose was see-through. A plain lean creature with a pink cheek and a stinger of a nose, he inclined it toward Bride and spoke to Millburn. "She is a good-looking girl."

Millburn nodded, unhappy, downcast, still put out for some reason or other. Lawrie Filkin must depress poor old Octavius. Filkin sure as hell depressed her.

Filkin scratched his tonsure. "I believe I've seen her before. With Barton Farr. Do you know her or know her name, O.G.?" He put his hands in his pockets and he leaned straight forward from his boot heels to stare hard at the woman in gold and peered at her myopically.

"Gad, Lawrie, what's with you, sir? Are you still for going on about that poster bill?"

Nellah let herself into the conversation. "What's that, Octavius?" She felt her interest piqued. "Say wha'? What poster bill?"

Millburn shrugged. "Gentleman, up Paris way, a chap named Brown, as I recall, he wants to pay a whole lot of money, I think, for purely nothing. For a kidnapping. Bah. He wants to trap and punish

411

a certain highfalutin' strumpet, name of Bride Munny, a derelict mama, and grab her fancy-named kids. Wants to send them to an orphanage. Reward to be posted to the 'saviour' on notification of arrival. It's a dumb idea. Crazy to pay out good money after bad on a dumb idea." Millburn said he was mystified. "Who does that?"

Filkin raised his left pinkie and he took a drink of brandy and watched Nellah with interest, no doubt wanting to see whether she flinched at the information. He was a shrewd drunk. He watched her but addressed O.G. "Who does that? Why, my dear sir, you did."

Millburn glowered at the utter gall of the man.

Nellah looked first at Filkin and then Millburn, as though to say, I am innocent. First I ever heard of a poster. And that was the truth. Maybe, she imagined, they read her look different, deeper, like she was innocent to the core and knew nothing about a certain derelict mama, one tarnation, pain-in-the-arse, Bride Munny.

Good to be good at dissemblin'.

O.G. Millburn was furious with brother-in-law. He snapped his suspenders and Nellah could feel her body temperature rise. Millburn said, "Which is why we need a constabulary. I never have condoned orphanages. Even if their ma is a notorious harlot, worst in Toronto. Aint their fault. No more'n it was my fault. You see, there was a time, once, when I was a boy—"

Nellah stretched her back.

God help her.

Not another long-winded when-I-was-a boy story. Someone would have stuffed her ledger down her throat if she had started to recount a when-I-was-a-girl story at every turn. She stood tall, about six feet. She was taller than Filkin. Even in his high-heeled Ketchum boots. That helped, somehow, because the news about the poster bill was bad and she felt unbalanced.

She felt faint.

She wanted to sit down on her brocade chair and put her head between her knees.

Wanted poster for the Munnys? For their kidnapping?

Why was she always the last one to know? Well, not quite the last. She had to get to Bride. Warn her. Order her to keep quiet about them kids a-hers. Goldern. Where was that Squire? She said, "Pardon me, gents—" She hovered, though, wanting to get away from the men but not wanting to miss anything.

Filkin ignored her person and her pardon and he turned to Millburn and spoke with oily insistence. "About the Munnys, I say—"

"Say what, sir? You're the great one for puttin' a handle to every fool." Filkin's erstwhile insolence had been obvious, that was as clear as the veined nose on Millburn' face, but the older man opted for a plea. "Boy outside is Tommy. Girl yonder is Iris. No Munnys. No poster bill. For Christ's sake, let the rest of this bloody night run smooth. Please."

CHAPTER
seventy-seven

"Boy outside is Tommy."

Pshaw. Deaf as mercy, that old man.

The picture was complicated.

And yet it was clear.

They were in trouble, big trouble, and it was an inconvenient trouble, and it was trouble up to their filthy inconvenient necks.

Nellah pried Bride from her corner near the hearth in the great room and she scooted her into the scullery, "Git, git, git," and ran her past a droopy, broth-stirring Cook. "Youns hurry up, Irish," Nellah said, and she shoved her into the washing-up corner, Bride's favourite cranny. "We have got ourselfs a passel of shite, missy."

"All right, all right. Quit pushin'," Bride yelped. "And watch the gown. It's only loaned."

Nellah rubbed her forehead with worry.

Unh-huh, the gown. Gown was trouble too.

Irish was dressed as a guest for the pleasure of the men and not as a server and Nellah did not want to see Annie's face when she got the picture. There was nothing for it, though. Serving must fall to Ann. Lizzie was sick, having herself a lie-down. In a few minutes Nellah would seek out Lizzie and ask her to help but would she? Her Filkin-aversion might make her stubborn. To say nothing of the way Ann and Lizzie's waiting on the lazy feckin' Irish would stick in everyone's craw, Nellah's included.

Why had Bride picked tonight of all nights to reveal her wares?

Instinct, Nellah figured. Like a ducklin's instinct for water.

Aint the time for fussing over arrangements, though, because she had a job to do.

It was urgent and required Teacher to plumb depths of tact with the asinine gal. Nellah warned Bride about the danger they faced, a certain Mr. Brown's poster bill, which offered a reward for a do-gooder kidnapping, and the Munnys being smack dab in the middle of it all, especially the kids. Teacher described Filkin's interest. "Filkin, the arsehole, he has been all over lookin' at things. Tryin' to spot a derelict ma on the premises."

Fine, Bride asked, but why?

Why did Filkin suspect her and the kids were at Nellah's place?

Nellah bit her tongue. She looked at Bride's face, scared ashen, and thought, maybe t'were Tacks or maybe t'were a-cause y'all *are* here or maybe t'were just like him, like he got nothin' a-short of a sixth sense for findin' the weak spots. "Who knows why?"

Bride, typically not one to take her string to the labyrinth, pursued it.

Did Filkin want the reward money? Was it the money? Bride opened her reticule. She could pay, a little, not much, not really. Irish was near collapse. Teacher grabbed her and she held the white shoulders tight and shivered them, ever so light. Her slanted eyes, the sherry and the hazel, locked on Bride's round blue ones and she told Irish to hold firm because Filkin did not know who she was, not for dead certain. No, he would not be paid off. Not tonight, not ever. Blackmail was the road to hell. Blackmail was a sin. Blackmail was as low as you could sink. Bride must have learned a thing or two from Squire about playing cross-culture games. Look world-weary,

415

blasé, she said, and never stop calculating the odds. Millburn's deafness, altogether too frustrating in a conversation, had given them a ready cover. Bride was Iris.

Iris? "I hate that name. Me feckin' Auntie Iris was a right ol' horror. Skinflint, she was." Bride seemed set to shriek but ever the contrarian she turned quiet. "It's Boy's doing, Nellah. Mr. Brown? In Paris, upstream from Brantford? In Whiteman's Creek, I bet. *Pffft*. It's all like I say. It's Boy. He's after me. I'd like to kill him. So help me, Lord Jeezus." She reflected a minute. "I'm Iris, eh? A disguise? Aint our Squire getting here tonight?"

"Our Squire gets here when he gets here. We gotta take this'un on ourselves, Iris, but you do need a protector and it would be a fersure you aint Indian so placin' y'all under the wing of Mohawk do not he'p us none. I reckon Jeddah be the one. Youns would be Jeddah's other cousin. Unh-huh. From t'other side. From Irish side. Get it?"

"You two aint got an Irish side! I heard you. You told Alfie you would be a-thankin' the stars above you, you and Jeddah aint got an Irish side."

Nellah soothed what she purely wanted to shake. "Not now, Irish. *Shhhh*. My mistake. Iris, I recollect."

"You got everything. I got nuthin'."

Nellah felt her blood pressure wanting to rise and blow like a geyser through the roof of her skull. She reckoned she could have spit her teeth out at Bride, one by one. She thought, goldern, Iris, or whatever your name be. You be a derelict mama. I take up tasks. I pay bills. I watch over three kids, feed 'em and so forth. You get to do nothin', not even for yown kin. But with reclaimed calm, Nellah said aloud, "Now, now. You listen up, my gal. Jeddah Golden, why, sure an' begorrah he gots hisself an Irish side. You mention Jeddah's

416

name whenever you can, Iris, wherever you can. That will give pause. Jeddah Golden does the regulatin' in these parts."

Bride was sullen. "Christ, Jeddah, he don't like me none neither. What's my last name?"

No, you are right. He do not like you none. Thank the good Lord above. "Tut, tut. Last name would be Green. Iris Green. Sailed to Montréal, through Liverpool, I guess, from Albert dock, stole away on a cargo ship. Tommy and Zulie, why, they aint yown. Last name would be—what?" Eager for Bride to catch the spirit and come around to thinking clear about the mess, she dimpled and teased. "Green would be for Emerald Isle."

Bride said, "I hate Emerald Isle. I hate everyone in it. I love you, Teacher. And the Mohawk. That's it. Oh, fine, then. And the kids. Say, Nellah, I get it. O'Herlihy. O'Herlihy's name of my friend in village. She loaned me this here gown. She made it. She has a fine stitch, such as yourself. Feckin' desperate too. She hates them Millburns. She is in service. Keeps house for Fannie, the bossy bitch. Hash-up Fannie."

"Whaa—?"

"'Hash-up Fannie.' Fannie is mean. That's what Danielle O'Herlihy says to the bossy bitch behind her back."

Nellah shut her eyes and bit her lip. Jehoshaphat! Let not a certain Octavius Millburn get wind of it. But O'Herlihy? Why not? "Do not much care how you call them kids, gal, so long as y'all a-gonna stick with it." It was a contest played close to the wire and Nellah had to take command. "Quit a-loaferin' now, Iris, and get yown self outside and tell Master Pomeroy—tell him he would be a Tommy O'Herlihy, not a Pommie Munny. We play hard. We play for high stakes, Bride. We plan to take men for possums. I will get to Lizzie and Ann. And Alfie, I guess. Inform 'em 'bout Wanted poster. It would be serious, the name changes."

She took a breath. The Lord of Misrule was in charge tonight, what the Frenchman called the *Prince des Sots*. Her good girls must fabricate tall tales about fancy Iris and court the devil, Lawrence Filkin. Being clever, they might win this thing and get what they wanted, their everlasting freedom in the village and on the Hill. Nellah touched her fingers to her scar. What else could she do? She warn't a broom-lapper like Norby. She could not broom pore Iris and them kids right out the goldern front door.

seventy-eight

T eacher's great room was alive. Tallow candles flickered in the crystal-drop sconces and they hooped gingery, rainbow spheres on the blue-blood walls. There were fledgling capitalists flapping around the room, eager men, men as raucous as crows, and they were tapping each other on the lapels and slapping each other on the back and planning their land deals and discussing advantageous trade tariffs for incoming and outgoing commodities. They had amiable faces, mouths laughing or smoking, either a pipe or a cigar. A general satisfaction shone back at them from the hazy gilt-bordered mirrors.

There was the bald, round, hairy-chopped politician Walter Winter. He was listening to that leafy twig Lieutenant Needles, who appeared to be conducting the inquisition. There was young Wally Ormiston, the bank teller. And Father Flanagan, Father Feel-again, Ann called him, and she turned away from the priest's inquiring touch. Also Magistrate Gage and John Murchison and Dr. Drummond. Last but not least the deserving squatter James Wilkes had blown in. Nellah knew he was a competitor of O.G. Millburn and the father of the precious strawberry-blonde Permelia and young George.

"Jolly sort, old Wilkes—" Filkin said to Millburn in a feigned *sotto voce.* "He arrives complete with his store of boasts. Wilkes hates

Nellah's salon, actually. And Vinegar Hill. Wilkes says he mixes with quite a better class of person than you, O.G. No one from Vinegar Hill is on his Christmas list. He bests you."

Nellah heard and she glanced up at Millburn but he was relaxed, going as soft as clarifying butter. Octavius tipped his tin ear to Cathcart as he spoke to Filkin. "Nope. No, sir, I do not believe it. Wilkes aint besting me on nothing. Not as of now." It seemed as though Millburn would overlook Filkin and the constant jabs and simply allow the whey to settle.

There was sunny *call-me-Iris*, perfection in her role as conspirator.

She shone her appealing beams on every gent who was flirty when he crushed his privates against her or slapped her arse with pent-up longing or winked at her or whispered *boo* to make her bubbies jump.

There was his Excellency Earl Cathcart and he looked privileged, as though he were enjoying the salon in the backwoods.

A partial pink chunk of a Caribbean conch shell wobbled on a glass shelf over the china cabinet, and it appeared ready to crash because the room was crowded and boisterous and vibrating like a hive. The buzz about the stolen horses and the near miss of the crone was splendid enough to tell and retell.

In the candlelight, there she was. Teacher.

She was, as she said to Alfie, planting her taties with the prospect of forthcoming salons. She was dreamy, out-of-this-world Nellah, queen of the Hill, a glory in penumbra, happy to be brave. She heard her mammy's voice, "No chil' a mine a-gown starve on account of I got no ideas." Holding a heavy silver salver, a gift from Father Flanagan, she orbited the room, collecting schooners and seeing to wants and hoping like heck that the dear Mohawk friend of hers were close by and he warn't set to miss the fun.

CHAPTER
seventy-nine

Cap'n stopped short.

Squire tipped forward in the light saddle. He strained to see the trail and grabbed a healthy hunk of Cap'n's thick mane and half-stood in the rope stirrups to see if he could get a look at what had caused the horse to spook.

There was a definite nippiness in the gusts of wind spouting the snow into swirls but he had been warm enough in his new canvas coat. In fact, he had been dozy and he patted Cap'n's firm-muscled neck and thanked him for being a sharp-eyed guide because obstacles could block your way, anytime, anywhere. Thieves, drunks and wild animals.

It looked like a dog. In the gloom. Near the cedars.

Squire had been assessing his position with the Fergusons and wondering what metaphysical shifts were expected in converting to their Calvinist church when Cap'n had pulled up. Rider had not been minding the material world because the material world was nothing but trouble. The poster bill he had seen in Stouffville bothered him, bothered him more every day, bothered him more than he had expected. He told Jennie he feared Boy Hewson, even from his gaol cell, would see to it that someone hunted down the kids like rats just to get even with poor, pitiable wretched Bride.

What does poor, pitiable. wretched Bride look like, Jennie had asked?

Oh, brother. He was not going there. Heart and soul with Jennie, he felt the tie that binds. He liked her toughness and her brains and her aquamarine devil eyes and her agility and her unbound wildness, he had seen that side of her more than once, but he wondered whether she was the kind who found others hard to credit, like she did not want to give people their due. Bride was pleasing to look upon. It was not his fault. It was not his fault he was not blind either. Fact was fact. Squire had said to Jennie he could not figure out how to help the Munnys and he found Jennie's curiosity about Bride's small upturned Irish nose and huge blue eyes and golden curls irrelevant and told her so and for the first time there was a long silence between them. He was fortunate Jennie had not asked how he felt about Nellah. Nellah was old but he reckoned she was a fine woman, maybe, quite possibly, one of the grand ones.

Well, worrying about women, that was the road to nowhere. He went back to the imminent problem. He might ask Aughguaga Polly to hide the kids.

No, that was no good. She was poor, dirt poor.

Polly's future lay with Nellah. Nellah would take care of the fat grandmother, although the two of them could pretend it was the other way around. Polly was real old. She could not keep a couple of fireball kids safe and he would not wish her on them anyway. Kidnappers might be easier to bear than the grandmother.

Missus Goosay, she would welcome the kids to stay with her but she was struggling and she was gone from Mohawk. Over the winter she roosted in Oneida or Seneca, somewhere near Caledonia. He did not know where to find her but he knew it would not take much looking. Missus Goosay was the best possibility. Tomorrow he would ride south; ride on the river if the ice was not thin.

The Fergusons, now, they were thin ice.

Would the Fergusons give the Irish kids a home until the threat died down? They might do, but he could not ask. Pommie and Chrisinny Munny would put a crack in old man Ferguson's thin-ice of a temper.

Maybe the kidnapping threat was not serious.

Who paid attention to poster bills?

Don't be naïve, he thought. Lots of men paid attention to bills when there was a reward. Look at him. Hadn't he paid attention?

He was proud to ride the neat-stepping Canadian stallion and they headed northwest to Brantford from Ohsweken at a steady canter. It was well past eleven-thirty but he was not feeling rushed. He had time to get to Nellah's just after midnight, for sure by half-past.

Cap'n knew the route. The stallion was a navigator with an uncanny homing ability and it was easy for Squire to drift into musing and find company with his own thoughts and problems and return in spite of himself to thoughts of Jennie, Jennie on the floor of the buckboard wagon, Jennie and the tight-arse Presbyterian cosmology.

He was not paying attention to the landmarks.

Rawenniyo, God Almighty, then he was. He had to.

There was this dog sitting on the trail. Tough to see it because it cast no shadow.

Squire urged Cap'n forward.

A St. John's dog, perhaps.

Black with a streak of white starting under the chin and running to mid-chest. Longhaired and matted. Not about to run off in any case.

Cap'n was casting around for a scent.

Squire dismounted because he could not urge the stallion to walk wide to bypass the creature. The dog's tail was thumping, sending off enough curls of snow to make smoke signals.

The man stepped forward.

There was no piss-off growl. The matted old girl sniffed the air and she snuffled at the outstretched hand, got up and shook herself roly-poly, like a string mop, and turned away and trotted a few feet into the grove. Squire was tempted to say, fine, goodbye, yoh, and go back to the main trail and get on Cap'n and ride to Nellah's but he did not.

Something nagged him.

He followed the animal and together they padded farther into the cedar swamp, about twenty paces, and came to a clearing. Winter trunks surrounded the clumped out area but the illumination, reflected from the snow through the lacy branches, was like daylight but daylight under a hazy spell. He saw a shadowy mound in the middle of the blue-white snowcover. He saw what looked like a fragile column of breath. It rose, delicate, through a tiny cleft at the extreme of the heap of leaves, twigs and snow.

Someone was alive.

~

He knelt beside the rime and snow.

From the sheath of his high moccasin, he removed the thin-bladed knife and cut away the ice crystals at the base of the mound. He put the knife down. He used his gloved hands to dig. Dirt and snow piled up beside him.

Not two yards away, the dog whimpered. She howled twice and would not quit fussing and moaned and licked a white-tipped paw with obsessive attention until Squire muttered aloud, "Hai, hai. We get him out, girl, we get him." On his knees, he spent ten minutes clawing around the crystal heap and gave it extra effort and got the fellow rolled out of the snow coffin.

Not a male.

A female. With red ochre clay slashed across her cheeks and long blue-black hair, plaited neat, considering the leaves and gunk. The rest of her was tattered. She stank of wet dog and compost. Not an old woman, perhaps, but well used. Her forehead was creased and her lips had shrunk and gathered into a parlour curtain because she was almost toothless.

"Can you talk, friend?" Squire put his arm behind the woman's head to lift her up. "You need water? I have water here." Water from his leather flask dripped into her mouth. Water overflowed her lips. She was icy to the touch, too frigid to swallow much. "Your name? Friend, can you tell me? What is your name?"

"Julia Katoserotha' Good."

Onkwehonwe. Kanien'kéha. Grand River settlement. From the people, thought Squire. He said, "Julia Katoserotha' Good, well, no, it is no good. You freeze to death."

"Dog is—Yeksa'a." Dog is girl.

The woman's voice sounded as furry as the back of a gypsy moth looks but she was coming around. A brown finger with a red-ochre-stained fingernail protruded through a shabby fur mitten and it was raised to the air. The finger was shiny, with flat, dinted spots, as though the finger fat was sucked out.

She said, "Who are you?"

"Tehawennihárhos. Squire Davis. I make a fire. As soon as you are warm, Julia Katoserotha', we go up yonder, a mile farther, to the New Cave, you, me, and old Yeksa'a here. My friend Nellah Golden helps you."

In a few minutes he got a miniscule flare but wet swamp-cedar twigs were tricky. They had a habit of hissing and smoking and throwing many sparks. So far, he was not making real headway and Julia Katoserotha' was not warmer than she had been when she was tucked under the wild blanket. He gathered fallen twigs and snapped them into tiny bits and poked them underneath the glow and he blew on the single ember and sat down and rubbed Julia Good's hands and feet to stimulate the circulation because her mitts were worn to nothing but sinews and threads and loose beads.

The woman said, "You sweat—"

"I do. And you will too, soon—"

"If fire catches. *Hmff.* I dunno. Luck on that."

He could have used her confidence but she was right and it took a full fifteen minutes to get something going and it was a half-hearted something at that.

In any case, Julia Katoserotha' started to thaw.

She drank more water. She was thirsty and drank again. By the time she had finished the water, she wore Squire's big-collared canvas duster coat. It was a blanket and a cover. He had bought the coat at the emporium, just before Christmas, just before he had gone to Uxbridge.

Squire was fascinated with the grave. "How do you get yourself under a mound?"

"I lie down and sweep stuff over me. So. So."

"Likely saves your life." He figured it was an exceptional and energetic manoeuvre for one near death and fast speeding her way to the other world.

"No. Not the mound. I think you save my life."

"What do you do out here?"

"*Yonontakàronte.*"

"Drink? You mean drink at the tavern? The New Cave?"

"Yes. I drink there."

"Maybe you do, Julia Katoserotha', but it aint open tonight."

"Ah-ha. I remember." She gave him a huge empty grin and the two of them laughed at the ridiculous state of affairs. There she was, caught in the bitter cold. Caught because she wanted a drink of rum to warm her insides. Caught because there was no rum. Caught because the tavern was closed. She and her St. John's dog had ended up stranded in the cedar-wood swamp and the dog was doing her part to keep her mistress warm. Julia sat beside the fire with her legs stretched out in front and the dog wrapped herself around Julia's feet. Julia bent forward, stiff in her joints, like a shutting clamshell, and patted the dog on the crown. "Yeksa'a, she tries to help me. Stops men."

"What men?"

"In the village Henry Yardington gives me rum. Much rum. Maybe I was drunk. Yes, I think maybe I was."

Squire had no doubt.

Heat from the fire made fumes.

The woman smelled unpleasant, acrid from filth, but there was liquor too. He could smell burnt sugar and it was making him lightheaded. Reverend Asahel Filbert believed Indians and Irish were at the mercy of spirituous liquors. "Forever drunk on the fire-water the Fergusons' friend had said with a long sniff, "in my judgment, neither Paddy nor Pocahontas is capable of responsible self-governance." It was an arrogant remark even for one of the Elect, arrogant even for a Scotchman, and more arrogant because Squire had just split at least a month's supply of wood to satisfy the Filberts' democratic but unbridled extravagance of the hearth.

Was that the gist of Calvinism?

He whistled for Cap'n.

The black stallion tramped into the clearing, swished his huge heavy tail in a show of disinterested horsey friendliness and pawed at shoots poking through thin snow patches. The horse lowered his head and he made soft contented neighing sounds and nibbled the grass without much concern for the strange mutt sniffing up and down his foreleg.

Squire patted Cap'n's muzzle.

"What about the men? Tell me."

"Give horse this." The woman fished into a huge pocket on her grubby apron and held up a dried pippin. "*Akohs:tens* likes it a lot."

Squire took the apple. He hiked himself up from his haunches and gave the pippin to Cap'n. "What about the men?"

"Men? Say, you are handsome man. Short hair's no good, though. Where are your long braids? You been scalped, Tehawennihárhos?"

"New haircut. I am a Scotchman. A Calvinist."

"Scotchman, I dunno. Englishman now, he is ugly. No feelings. Stiff neck. Mean."

"Listen to me, friend Julia Katoserotha'." Please hold a thought, Squire begged in silence. It was like talking to Missus Goosay when she was charming. What kept women from sticking to a point? Their busy minds jumped like grasshoppers. "What do you say? Who?"

With a toothless grin, she gave him a short, rueful summary. "Bad man kicks me. I crawl away and prepare to die."

"Why does the bad man kick you?"

"Yeksa'a here barks. She warns the galloping ones I am there. I am asleep, passed out, see. On the trail. They stop. Bad man kicks me off the trail."

Julia Katoserotha' rolled up a leather sleeve, which that had seen better days, and she showed him her arm. It was scraped brown and streaked with dots of blood. Squire reached into his squirrel pouch and pulled out a wooden pot and he rubbed grease on her arm. He poked at the fire and breathed quiet while the woman breathed heavily as she gathered strength. "I tell them they got no feelings but they don't care. Toss me over here and leave me in the middle of the godforsaken bush, leave me for dead."

The corners of Julia's mouth turned down.

Greasy tears filled her eyes.

Squire was alarmed. "Huh. Huh? What's this, Julia? C'mon, now. You talkin' to me, my friend, and you aint dead."

"Not yet, Tehawennihárhos—thanks go to you. Hallo, I remember. Another man jumps out." She indicated the clearing. "From there. Confederacy man. Our man. Six Nations man. A red-ochre man." Like the crow flies, a sly expression flitted over her brows. She twisted away but he had caught it. She said, "Maybe Mohawk, like us. Or Seneca. I cannot tell these days and I do not hear him say nothing." She turned back to him. She was a mask, the spoon mouth. "War cry. Big noise." The woman threw her head back and she screeched and Squire was pleased she could make such a hideous sound.

Yeksa'a was a sport. She joined in.

Squire was feeling chilled and he slapped his arms but, hai, that was funny. He chuckled into his chin and suppressed a shiver. "A noise as bad as that?"

"Yes. Two old men hold their horses' reins. Hold tight. They yell to the red-ochre man, 'You git outa here, goddam Indian.' The skinny Queen's man and the ugly paleface, the one who grows the fuzzies on the back of his head, they let go of their horses' reins. With both hands they pull their scarves down, like this, over their ears, you see." The woman took the collar of the duster and pulled it over her eyes, like a bonnet. "I think they believe the red-ochre man wants scalps. Scares them plenty. They are wrong. The red-ochre man, he don't want scalps, Tehawennihárhos. No, sir."

"So, the red-ochre man, what does he want?"

"Oh, well, you know. He wants ponies. He grabs reins. Takes two critters. Runs swift, a silverheels. White men jump up and down on the trail like rabbits and they cry, 'Come back here, you fucking red whoreson!' They don't follow him, though." Julia Katoserotha' Good held her arm as straight as an arrow and pointed away from the trail and into the depths of the cedar swamp. "He goes there. I cheer, '*Ooo-eee*, for red-ochre man.' Big mistake. Pale one gets mad. He marches into the bush. I sit there. He kicks me again. He wears high black boots. He kicks Julia Katoserotha'. See?"

The woman flipped up her plaits so Squire could take a gander at her neck and see the extent of this wound.

"*Sotsi kowanen*," Squire whistled. "Too many injuries, Julia. That big one there is a mean-looking slash. It's gotta be four, maybe five fingers across. Lots of blood, Julia. Wide-ranging bruising. I try but maybe I cannot do much good for you out here—"

The woman shrugged.

She appeared world-weary, blasé, unconcerned.

Who had ever done much good for Julia Good?

~

The skin was ripped across her shoulder.

The tear was as jagged as a saw-tooth beech leaf and the wound, just plain gory.

A proper mess.

Squire scanned the swamp for birch because he believed the divine bark was unsurpassed for making an ointment or a healing tonic but it was impossible to see anything remotely like what he needed in the dark and he could not wander around the place, getting too far away from her, wasting their time.

He would have to use cedar.

Julia Katoserotha' muttered to her dog and she drifted in and out of sleep and coherence and was patient with preparations. For some minutes Squire boiled needles and twigs and snow water in a tin mug. With one hand on the woman's shoulder he steadied her; with the other he dripped the coniferous decoction over her neck and back to cleanse the wound. He resealed the flap and, with nothing else to hand, pasted down the jagged rip with resin.

He tried to go careful. He even took out the gingham shirt he had planned to wear to Nellah's dinner and wrapped it around her neck and back. She must have been feeling goose bumps after the bitter drips on her skin and he thought to put his canvas coat over her shoulders again. He had a moth-eaten woollen blanket in his bedroll. Blanket would do. If he needed cover, he would wear it the old way, like a cape. He had dabbed and patted and pulled and wrapped up the wound and Julia had not moved, not so much as a muscle. It must have hurt. Plenty. If the white man had kicked her any harder, or higher, he would have killed her. Kicked her head right off her shoulders. Her neck would have snapped.

The woman said, "Both the old ones shout to red-ochre man, 'We're a-partyin' yonder and we aint armed.' There were four men. They ride off, two on a horse. One man, he holds a pot over his head. They are off to Nellah Golden's, off to the midnight dinner, I bet."

He did not answer. Off to the midnight dinner? Ah well, that secret had had its day.

Julia hefted herself to her feet.

She seemed reluctant to return the canvas coat but did the right thing and held the coat out to him. He shook his head. You keep it. You wear it. He reached for Cap'n. "C'mon, Julia Katoserotha'. Let's get you to Nellah's. Like you say, there is a midnight dinner. Men will be up, having a party. Bad wound may need a recalybratin'."

Julia nodded. She said, "The old man, he shouts into the bush, 'Goddam it. You had better stop kicking 'er, Lawrie, or we'll have ourselves a corpse to bury and you never get to catch Teacher off her guard."

Ahhhh-haaaa. Squire held onto Cap'n's mane and he stamped out the fire. "Lawrie. Right. Yeah, I know him. Lawrie. Lawrence Filkin, that's who it would be." So Filkin had attacked Julia Katoserotha'. Kicked her. Kicked her when she was drunk. When she could not defend herself. Wasn't that a familiar scene? Snow made it easy to put the fire out. Twigs, damp earth, it was a miracle he had got the thing going in the first place. Jeddah could not have done it better. A sudden clump of soggy white stuff slid off a cedar branch and landed on his head and he cursed as stone cold water trickled down his own bare neck. Lawrie Filkin, eh?

Was Lawrie Filkin at Nellah's place?

No doubt.

Lawrence Filkin would be a proper society guest and appear *la mode* to the others who wanted to associate with Maritime aristocrats but Filkin was nobody's aristocrat. He was a goddam segregationist who needed a lesson in good manners.

Squire and his woozy, wounded, tippling patient walked out of the clearing and stood on the main trail. Cap'n followed, chewing on some last minute wayward grass tips he had discovered beside the trail. The black dog wandered after them and she trotted up to the man and sat at his feet and seemed willing to wait for her marching orders and he knew it was up to him to command the troops but he was slow.

Filkin needed a good lesson, yup, that he did. A painful lesson.

Dog waited. Good girl. She did not move.

Squire was preoccupied.

Something in his head had snapped like the dry pestering twigs. He was a thoughtful man. As a rule, he dumped all the bad shit that had happened into the laps of the indifferent gods and, like them, he mostly forgot about it. Not this time. This time he was ready to fight. If a lesson were needed, he thought, he would do the instructing. He would punish Lawrence Filkin for the attack on Julia Good. She was the sick one, the one who held the lowest possible status in both the white and red nations. For Julia, he thought, I will see one Lawrie Filkin cut down to size, with black boots shoved up his scrawny arse. Revenge was not Squire's style but then, he reckoned with apologies to Missus Goosay, his fear of the bully, the one who was meaner than him, hah, that fear could not serve him forever as an excuse. The ancient gods thought so little of the people of the Six Nations that they had allowed the European invasion to overrun and overrule the territory and so now and again, naturally, he felt what a philosophical man would call glum. Getting even for a wrong done to Julia Katoserotha' had a different, heavier weight. He could not allow the cruelty to go unpunished. For Julia, he would disobey the Mush-hole's priest. He would change the rules about turning the other cheek.

He would be a bad Christian but a good avenger.

The woman spoke. "I ride with you?"

He shook his head.

The poor soul could barely stand but she was not going to ride with him and that was for absolute certain because his stomach was not his long suit and the smell of her was wicked, worse than a sulphur fart. She smelled as rotten as a couple of American slave-snatching sonsofbitches he had run into last summer and sitting close to her might encourage bad memories to intrude on good ones. This here overripe, battered and not-quite sober lady could straightaway wipe his and Jennie's slate clean of every snatch of glorious erotic inspiration.

He was not a Calvinist yet.

"Naw," he said, cupping his hands for her tiny mucky moccasin. "You been through hell tonight, Julia Katoserotha'. Up you go. You ride on Cap'n. Yeksa'a and I lead the way, eh? We are close to Teacher's. We walk. We get there soon enough."

He was at his nicest, politest best and it was not right that a knife tip was poking into the small of his back and a familiar, very satisfied voice behind him was saying, "I got you. If I wanted to, I could kill you, brother."

CHAPTER
eighty

"Jake, Hearenhodoh." Squire was as indignant as he could be under the circumstances. "What the hell's the matter with you? Get that sticker outa my backbone."

From above Squire, high on Cap'n, Julia said. "You took your own sweet time, Jake. I was almost dead."

From behind him, Jake said. "So, hey, Julia. Wow. How are ya? You looking better, eh? Yeah, yeah, much better. Why, y'know, I come back here as fast as I can."

Squire turned from one to the other. "You two know each other? Jeezus, Jake, what's that crap on your face? You paint now? You are the red-ochre man? I see."

"Brother, you do not see. Tehawennihárhos, my old friend, you do not see nothing."

"Fine, then. Tell me. What is going on?"

Once, when they were boys playing together under Polly's miserable watch, Jake's po-faced indignation had made them both want to belly laugh. Jake was not funny anymore and Squire was not up to teasing him about the lavish application of war paint. They were out of tune, the two of them. Jake's hair had grown longer and Squire's hair was cut short. Last October, things had been different. Jake had had the clipped and tidy locks.

Jake scoffed, no doubt at Squire's ignorance. "We broke Bobby John outa gaol couple weeks back. Your cousin wants to meet, and I can tell you this, brother. He wants to meet with you real bad. On account of a certain posse."

Jake had got him, got him for sure. Squire was caught, surprised, but it was old corn-cob Jake Venti, after all, and he shrugged with guileless unconcern, as though a group of horsemen did not exist and never had existed. "Yeah? What posse?"

Jake said, "Don't be an arsehole, Squire. Bobby John wants a chat. About four bounty hunters and Millburn's big reward. He figures you owe him some of the money. In fact you owe him big. And brother, you be warned. Not just money. Bobby's not happy till he gets your pony. He wants Cap'n."

Squire's heart took a leap. "Tough for Bobby then. He aint gonna be happy."

"So you say. He gets what he wants—"

"Boys—" Julia Katoserotha' hung her head. She was in pain, she said. She had a sick headache from the cedar gum and their quarrelling irritated her, irritated her bad. She shuddered and shook herself all over like Yeksa'a. Bobby was not going to take Cap'n anywhere, she said, and she should know. She was Bobby's girlfriend.

"Brother, don't mind her. You know what Bobby calls her? My old Julia Good-for-Nothing—"

"Shuddup, Jake. I kin hear you," Julia cawed.

~

The sound of Julia's voice seemed to disgust Jake because he made himself look away to grimace before he ignored her. "I tell you again, Tehawennihárhos. Bobby John gets what he wants." Knife up, Jake nudged Squire along on the narrow bush trail through the cedars. Squire and the dog were together; they walked on, straight ahead, just like they were told. Jake came next. Julia followed them on Cap'n.

They turned east at the bottom of Vinegar Hill. They marched over the sour creek, which scrabbled along in summertime, and climbed a forested embankment.

Edgy, mostly about meeting an irate Bobby John, but also curious and stubborn, like always, Squire quizzed Jake. "Julia says, 'Not take him anywhere'? Where does Bobby take horses?"

"Buffalo City."

"Buffalo? Why?" Squire was weary. Jake loved to be in the know. He loved to have the jump. Show him up. Yes, show Squire up for the dumb piece of crap he was and Hearenhodoh could not help but grin.

Jake said, "Sells them stateside, naturally, brother. Steals them up here and sells 'em down there. To American army. Army is grateful and it pays us good coin for horses, yeah, and, better yet, asks no nosy questions. I tell you, brother, Boy nearly ruined the operation with his stuff. Embarrassing stuff. Bad with women—"

"Yeah, yeah. I know that, Jake. From personal experience, remember?"

"I guess. A fucking maniac. Creeps me out."

"Yup, yup. You are right. Boy's a creep. Yup. He sure is that. So Bobby John sells horses as well as deserters to army?"

"Yup, brother, you get it now. You must be a smart Indian. People say you read and write. Pick up things quick, eh? Pick up the warning then. Cap'n's going next. I'm telling ya."

Squire felt the goading like another surge of nausea but he shut down the wave of nastiness rising in his gorge. "Quite the old smuggling racket you guys got."

Jake's facial topography was full of ecstatic bumps and ruts and in the dark he howled. Moon or no moon, Yeksa'a with the white blaze sat down, raised her head and joined in and Jake clammed up.

Jake aimed an air kick at the dog. "Quiet, you." He grabbed Squire's arm. "Brother, name it. We *trade* it. Tobacco. Rum. Runaways. Tea! If there's profit, we're in." With Squire's attention full on him, Jake wrung his fingers like a Midas. He was pleased as Paddy's pig about operations. "Yessir, south market, south market, we trade a fine hog. Home again, home again, jiggety jog. And why not? We are traders since creation. North, south, up and down. No Englishman or Irish Johnny-come-lately's gonna starve us out with the fucking Naviga-tion and tell us we can't trade stateside, except on their goddam say-so."

"Hah." Squire patted the head of Yeksa'a, who had ceased howl-ing as commanded and was tagging along again at his side. "A new verse, Jake. Last summer I tell you the Navigation is bad. You change your tune. Who's on to you guys anyways? Anybody know your game?" He thought about Needles. "Lobsterbacks know you *sell* their horses?"

"Ah, Brits don't know from nothing." Jake spit in derision. "And we keep it like that, eh, brother? RCRR look for deserters going to New York or Ohio and good luck to them. Many deserters go south, voluntarily, aiming to fight Indians. More money in it."

"Mercenaries?"

"Some."

"Some?"

"Mmm. Yeah, some." The red-ochre clay on the pockmarks made Jake's chin and forehead look as though someone had attacked him with a wax seal ring. "Deserters. Mercenaries. Who knows? Who cares? You wanna go stateside? We take you. You want it? We take you to the army. And the army pays us good for the ponies, thanks to Bobby John."

"Yessir, our Bobby's a real enterprising Indian."

"That's right, Tehawennihárhos, he is. Looks after his own, unlike—"

"*Pfft*. Looks after his own dick. So what about Teacher's being raped?"

"Nope. No way, brother. That don't involve him. Not Bobby John. Robbery, yup, for sure. Why not? Nellah's a squatter. She steals our land. We steal her goods. Rape, nuh-unh. Sex stuff was all the doing of Hewson. Unexpected on Bobby's part. I swear it."

~

They trudged onward, mostly uphill, for half a mile. Squire forced a yawn as though Jake tired him to death, which he kind of did. The bush was dense. There were no clearings ahead of them as far as he could see and the trail was a tight squeeze for Cap'n. Like slingshots, branches sprung back sweet-smelling pine needles at Julia's head. How much farther did they have to go? "I am supposed to believe that, Jake?"

"Yup, you are. Bobby thinks maybe you like a funny story. Right now, as we speak, Boy gets his loving in Hamilton gaolhouse. Boy's 'wife' is the biggest goddam Swede Bobby John ever seen, bigger'n me by a foot and I aint speaking lightly."

"Ouch, eh? So why don't you guys break him out?"

"Can't. We break out Bobby John without a hitch but lover-man Swede won't allow Boy Hewson to leave his side. Boy insists to sheriff he knows all kinds of things about Bobby John but who's listening?"

"So, what happens?"

"So what happens is that Boy gets his loving in the nighttime and I tell you, brother, he purely hates it but Bobby John saw no governor or lieutenant or rifleman galloping to Boy Hewson's rescue. Night after night, like Bobby John says, it's the same damn thing. The big Swede loves Boy Hewson but he drives Boy crazy. Not the sex. No. The loving! That's what Boy says. Boy says to Bobby John he's sick to death of it. Ja, it's the loving."

Squire stopped and he turned back to look at Jake and made a choking gesture. The big-Swede image was simply too much. Jake slapped his thigh and snorted. Squire joined in and for a minute they were kids again, whooping and making faces behind Polly's back. Still laughing, he said to Jake, "Brother, Boy Hewson earned it. He earned every minute. He's on his knees praying for help and he gets another meatball but no one gives a shit. I am right, eh, Hearenhodoh? Oh, c'mon, brother, don't tell me. Are the Warriors preparing to bust him out?"

"Tehawennihárhos, brother, listen here. Boy's having a sweet-heart don't bother us none, not one bit. Boy Hewson expects Bobby John to get him out of gaol but Bobby John aint a-gonna do it. You tell me Boy's a snitch and he works for Lieutenant Needles and I tell Bobby what you say and Bobby's glad to be rid of the little bugger but he don't tell Boy that. Huh—" Jake brightened and he dropped the knife, "that's so, aint it? I mean Boy aint the big bugger in the scenario, if you get my drift—"

Squire said, "What drift? With Bobby John busted outa gaol Boy Hewson has new stroke with government men, right? Needles will show up again for sure. He will want to chat with Boy about Bobby John's whereabouts now, you can count on it." The shrunken blanket over his shoulders was not warm. How long had he been wandering around the bush, consoling dogs, digging up ladies, freezing his arse off and listening to the red-ochre-man Jake and his stupid stuff? "Oh, yes. I get it, Hearenhodoh."

"No, I tell you again, Squire, last time. You do not get it. You think you earned Octavius Millburn's reward, fair and square. Hah! You earned blood money, brother. Guilt money. You and your god-dam posse put a Warrior in gaol, charged with a crime he don't commit."

"Ah, shit. Come off it."

Jake jumped up and down on the path and he hit an exposed cedar-root system and stubbed his big toe and hollered and he knew Squire was laughing. It made him madder. Angry and in pain and rubbing his toe Jake yelled, "You arrogant bigheaded redskin. You make a mistake. More fool you. Bobby John's gonna tell you—"

"Gonna tell me what?"

"He's gonna tell you about Fannie Millburn—"

"Nothin' to tell."

Jake was riled and being riled was the perfect lubricant. It greased the wheel of secrets. "Fannie Millburn is it. She plans the whole thing."

With loose lips, Squire snorted like Cap'n. He knew he was annoying Hearenhodoh with his scepticism and waved off the accomplice idea. "She plans it pretty good, then, brother. I don't see her locked in the gaolhouse with a lover man—"

"Brother, you shut up." Jake whapped Squire, caught him on the shoulder with the flat of his *àshare*. "Fannie tells Bobby John that the whore is rich."

"I know it, Jake. The *Courier* says it."

"Yeah? Well, who says this? It was Fannie Millburn. She was the big cheese all along."

"Brother, you keep repeating yourself—"

"So repeat after me. Fannie Millburn—"

"But the *Courier*—"

"The *Courier*? Get real, Squire. You read the *Courier*. You read the *Globe*. Read. Read. Read. You better start to read the people. Who will tell a certain Seeum Johnston that Mrs. *Whot's this then? Look-at-me-garden Millburn!* asked an Indian, a fuckin' outlaw, to pay her a visit, and she paid him gold. Gold, Squire, and I mean real gold, to steal Wedgwood from the whore and deliver it up, right to Fannie. The whore wasn't to know—"

"Stop saying *the whore*, Jake. And I don't believe you. Millburn and Nellah, they own the tavern together. The Millburns aint cutting off their noses—"

"Aint the Millburns, Squire, you bloody fat blockhead. Just the missus."

"You don't make sense—"

It was Jake's turn for expressing the weary cynicism. "Agh. You think about it. You are gullible, brother, and a bad man of the people. Confederacy don't need *you*. You don't understand what I tell you about Fannie Millburn. I say it. You are a bad man of the people."

"Brother, I understand. Jealous of Nellah—"

Julia Katoserotha' broke in.

Her voice was back to normal. It was a ringing bell. It was a ringing bell as urgent as the tower bell in the village. "You are a bad man of the people, Jake Hearenhodoh Venti. You paint my face. In case a poet finds me, you say. Waiting for you I am about to fucking solidify." Jake Hearenhodoh danced the dance of contrition. He rocked back and forth, from sorry foot to hurting toe, but Julia was not finished. "Tehawennihárhos here, he saves me. Count on a reckoning with Bobby, Mister Lazy-Hearenhodoh." Julia pointed her finger like a witch's wand. "You leave me to die."

Jake's expression shifted from frustration to sorrow. "Jeez, Julia. You didn't look so good back there and I had a lot to do. I had to get the horses over to Bobby and I had to get the rum to the rest of the boys, and I had to swing back and I had to run as fast as I could and I—"

From high on her easy seat on Cap'n, Julia listened to a brace of excuses and she glared.

She looked pissed.

And Squire was pissed.

A ranting apology from Jake was worse than useless, he thought. Oh God, it was going to be one of Hearenhodoh's windy treatises on forgiveness and, so help him, not tonight, because he was chilled and exasperated and tired and cold without his coat. And anxious to get going, back to Nellah's warm kitchen. With Cap'n.

~

Finally Squire flat-out grabbed Jake by the jacket. He shook him hard and interrupted the windiness, which he could feel building into a Venti cyclone of ritual and denial and excuses. "Brother, hold on. I got money. I got my share of the reward. Ten pounds—"

Jake was sensible again and aside from his interest at the mention of money he looked relieved to find the conversation spinning back on point, away from the trials of Julia Good. With renewed determination and a surge of confidence in his captive, he stopped flaunting his knife and turned his back to the path and marched ahead of Squire, talking over his shoulder. "Ten pounds? Not too much. You try to buy your freedom, Tehawennihárhos?"

"No. I buy a favour."

"Hmm. Not likely, brother. Bobby don't do favours. You are just darn lucky you aint one of the bounty hunters showing up at his sister's place."

About three feet ahead, the overgrown trail got crunchy with snow and ice chips and the path narrowed. Squire stopped walking. So did Jake. Squire said, "Yeah, I am darn lucky. So here's the deal. I got a man ready for transport. To American army. For personal reasons, Bobby John wants this man. For revenge. Easy money, I tell you so, brother, no, I guarantee it. Easy money. I do the work. You pick up the package. Zachary Taylor will not believe his bad luck when this yeller-eyed corn popper shows up to do battle."

"Who is it? Who's the corn popper?"

"Lawrence Filkin."

"Who's he?"

"Fannie Millburn's brother, see? Her precious kinsman. I reckon Filkin's right in season. In his cups. He's at Nellah's. I bet he is sitting at Teacher's table drinking brandy with his pinkie up. How about it? I meet with Bobby John and we talk about the deal but pretty quick I ride to the brick house and get Filkin outside—"

"Go on—"

"You wait for me. By the barn. In the shadows, eh? Near the beechnut grove. I hand over Filkin, eh? Trussed and ready for the spit."

"I dunno—"

"And I give you guys ten pounds for past injury."

"Hmm. That is it? All you got?" Jake crept along the narrow path and he kept to the single file and they were friends again. Squire answered, with no sassing this time, and Venti listened as his taciturn friend started to rationalize things, to beg for help.

Squire was intense. "You transport Lawrence Filkin to Buffalo City, or Sandusky or, goddam, to fiery hell, wherever. I read there is trouble in Texas. There is trouble for the American army with the Comanche. *Globe* says Polk wants to carry O'Sullivan's type of idealism across the plains to the Pacific and down to the Gulf of Mexico. United States needs soldiers, Jake. So does Mexico, if you come right down to it. You got choices. You can dump Filkin with the Saint Patrick's Battalion. Or right at the feet of Santa Ana if you want. You make a profit somehow." The speech was pleading and he was gasping because of the pleading, which he hated. Especially with a blunderer like Jake Hearenhodoh who was acting more in-the-know than St. Peter the adjudicator.

Julia liked the plan. She bounced in the saddle, although it must have considerably hurt her neck and her back, and she cawed. "Awwwwwwhh right. Bobby sells the bastard Filkin to the Americans, boots and all. He does it for me too, uh, Tehawennihárhos? He sells that mean sonofabitch to army. Yeah. Maybe somebody kicks him in the head."

Jake was solemn. "You're baptized Christian, Tehawennihárhos. Even worse, you wanna link up with a white woman. A bloody-minded Scotchwoman, for Christ's sakes. Bobby John will not like it. He is full over gone to Longhouse religion, the Code of Hand-some Lake and all that. Christian and Longhouse Indians, big ene-mies in the settlement now. Brother, I dunno. Your plan, it might work. I say, might. No guarantee."

Squire puckered to whistle. He decided instead to lay a positive note on his old friend and was strangely pleased to realize he looked forward to meeting his cousin. "Bobby John is family. We grew up close, Jake, like brothers. He'll do it. It will work. I make it work. Around here, a certain Lawrie Filkin is done. Done like dirt." The thought of Filkin's being sold out for a price of a tealeaf or cigarette, or if the Nova Scotian were a man at all, for the price of a pernicious little-head cold, gonorrhoea, was heartwarming. Squire reckoned it was fair justice for poor battered Mohawk woman Julia Good. A good night's work but he felt different. Not much like his old self. There was no joy. He felt impatient. Tougher. Meaner. He had crossed the evil line.

Thanks to Filkin and Bobby John, Squire was turned into an outlaw. He whistled, "And I don't care." He took up "Jimmy Crack Corn" and in the forest the trilling rang out like a hooded warbler. He was not a Shiner or a timber plunderer or a liquor dealer.

He was a racketeer. A pirate.

He had made himself an integral part of organized crime. He would assist Bobby in securing a bounty for procuring enlist-ments in the constantly war-depleted American army. Ha, he laughed. That fat hairy crabby old blue jay, Whiskers, he was right.

The Davises were a scurvy lot. The Davis boys knew it. Squire was English literate. He was proud of himself, far too proud of himself for his own good. His pride made him scurvy.

Asahel Filbert said disobedience was the greatest of the sins. Considering everything he had lately seen, Squire was ready for sinning. He thought, why not disobey the British? To punish a yeller-eyed Lawrence Filkin for acts of cruelty, a Davis stood at the ready, happy to mess up the colonizer's prized military code of honour.

CHAPTER
eighty-one

After the terrible start, things had settled. Nellah was satisfied with the progress of the dinner. Alfie's flaky, tender, tantalizing, delectable smoked pigeon pie was a choice dish at the New Cave and tonight it had been superb. Compliments to Cook. She donned the sweet mantle of the favoured host and sought her place at the head of the white-linen-covered table and reached for her wine glass, thinking before Cook's famous blancmange and the after-dinner brandy to make a flattering speech to please Governor General Cathcart, but no. It was not about to happen. In this simple act of civility she was straightaway thwarted.

Millburn interrupted her.

He was casual about it, not aggressive anymore. In effect, he did not seem to see her.

She wondered how it was possible—was she made of a miraculous substance, there one minute and now invisible?

"Here, here," he said to the air over her head, "I'll sit at head of table now, opposite my dear kinsman Charlie Cathcart. You, hmm, you kin sit down there."

Down there was the empty seat next to Father Flanagan. Squire's place.

Where was the Mohawk?

"Hep, hep, march my girl."

Hep. Hep. March. My girl. My God.

She was fighting for breath and Millburn gave her a fierce poke with his tin ear to make her get a move on. He said he wanted her to hurry. To pick up her wine glass real smart-like and, smart-like, change her seat and be quick, smart, like he had told her.

Nellah could not move, did not move.

She did not care so much as a cracked teacup whether Octavius Millburn lived or died but somewhere in the depths of her soul she had as great a natural-born sense of protocol as the valuable Permelia. A dandy white man sat at her dining-room table and he ate her food and wore clothes she had sewed for him and used their partnership as the home base for his land acquisition business and, that being so, there were rules. There were rules in the village. There were rules here. In her home, she was the one. She was Teacher. As she must honour her guest, he must honour her. Millburn should give her that much respect. Sending her to a seat at the far end of her own table as though she were a naughty child was impossible. It was inappropriate. He had ground her down like a peppercorn. She choked. Contempt from resident Protestants in the village was a regular event. Betrayal, right in this brick house, yet again after the assault, Jehoshaphat, she could not endure it.

First Bride. Now this. Her blood pressure rose. Her breasts filled with spurting milk and liquid started to dribble and dampen her bodice. Nellah surveyed the table. Her glance, wounded and frightened, drifted over the seated men and it met the varnished eyes of Irish and it lingered on Squire's empty place, the place set next to the nimble-fingered, doe-eyed priest, and she shook her head. She would not go there. She had the power. Mammy's veto. She used it.

"No, Octavius. I will not. Not my chair—nunh-uh. Place be set for Squire. He will arrive a-fore long, I expect." She spoke straight at

Millburn and turned and waved to the guests. "Youns be a-wantin' yown tea an' hot water. And a sip o' brandy, also, I reckon." She made a brave go of it. She stiffened her aching back but she knew very well it was a poor, failed effort to save face. She had been shamed.

She left her wine glass where it was. She left the men, who complained about the quality of the clotted cream on the blancmange. It was sour, gummy, off, apparently. Walter Winter complained the loudest. The cream made him sick, he said. She glared at him and scorned his piggy looks and white-splattered ostrich chops and directed her steps to the kitchen to seek a bit of comfort from Alfie or Ann. She remembered. Ann had taken food upstairs to Lizzie. Cook was rooting around the New Cave for more Calvados.

In the event, a second before she reached the swinging kitchen door, Lawrence Filkin overtook her. He was on his way to avail himself of the outdoor privy. He protested. He was blunt. Her food gave him terrible cramps. It was too rich. He was well enough to wave behind him, however, imitating her. "The drama of it, mistress." He seized her. He caught her and hissed. "Yes, Mistress Harlot, I am a happy man. In my satchel I have carried a petition. Oh, yes, Mistress Mary Blaize, I brought a document into your very house. And it has been delivered. To our current Governor General."

Filkin's clutch was tight and painful on her arm and tighter around her waist. Who would imagine his bloodless double-jointed fingers could grip so bloody hard? Who could imagine the beast-like intensity? He would not let her go. She itched to recover her pearl stickpin from her turban. She wanted to stab him in the ear. Kill him dead. She reckoned goldern Filkin ought to be as dead as goldern Meatface and it was all she could do to sound remote and disinterested. "Petition, sirrah? What fer? Have to do with that Munny family youns would be a-seekin'?"

"You might wish it, Mistress Black Cat, but no."

"I have no interest, then, in—"

"O Lord of mercy but you do. Miz Golden, yes, youse do have an interest. It is *your* petition, you see. It's all about you."

"Wha'? Me?"

"Yes. You. You are on your way. The military comes for you tomorrow, to clear you out, to move you off the Hill. You see, I have a formal request, which calls, in this year of our Lord, 1846, for the clearance of the coloured population in the village of Brantford, including and especially the dissolute types on the infamous Vinegar Hill. Governor General Cathcart is here, right in your own dining room. He wants the local colonists to defend themselves militarily so he butters 'em up, pays attention to their wishes. On behalf of the British Crown he has accepted the paper. The Crown claims lands surrounding the village. Ask John Smoke Johnson. Ask David Thompson. Ask William Merritt. The Navigation has no holdback on Indian Territory within the 1833 Burwell survey. So, thanks to the weakness of the natives hereabouts—oh, by the way, where *is* the long-haired Hottentot?—and so, as I say, thanks also to the growing strength of the British colony, you, m'dear, you will vanish. Poof. Gone to Queen's Bush. Gone tomorrow. Good riddance. Say, why don't you sit right down, hmm? Sit right down here, right on your fancy, padded chair, and fine stitch *good riddance* on your handkerchief? Or you might embroider a "H" for *Harlot* on that soaking bodice."

CHAPTER
eighty-two

L ike the impudent plume of cold air Ann had tried to shut
out earlier that evening, Squire drifted into Nellah's
kitchen. Licks of fire, reflected from the woodstove, threw
the devil's pitchforks up the wall. Just as he had imagined it, the
Teacher's kitchen was welcoming, homely, and aromatic, with bread
and corn-soup smells and pigeon pie and venison and gravy. A solitary candle burned on the butcher-block counter. Outside it had
started to snow again. It was wet, sleety and miserable stuff, and
Squire was glad to duck inside.

Eyes closed, Nellah sat on the bench.

He wondered about it.

Teacher's sitting alone? Not mingling with her guests? Not
like her. Not like her at all. She had an elbow propped up on the
sideboard. She held her turbaned head in her hand. Her honey-
coloured hands were thin and ring-less. Her nails were cedar pink.
She was dressed in a fine black gown and her smooth neck, shoulders and upper bosom were bare. Pink moon pearls glowed on her
neck and glowing tears tripped down her cheeks but she was not
making a face. Her face was relaxed. Resigned more than upset, he
would guess. She was calm. Ah, lovely lady, he thought, she was
exhausted. That was it. She was recuperating yet.

He removed his gloves and stepped carefully over the floor toward the stove to rub his cold hands and for half a second he wanted to wring them but, instead, he pampered his empty stomach and grabbed a square of cornbread from the counter. He was walking quiet but she heard him after a floorboard cracked under his weight. She glanced up. She dropped her elbow and waited for him to apologize.

He nodded, sheepish, sorry for being late.

She inhaled. "Jesu, Squire. Where y'all bin?"

"Long story, Nellie. I got no time to give you the lowdown, not here. I tell you later. Filkin? Where's he at? I want him."

"In privy yonder. Wantin' the little prick do not make a speck of sense, hon. Stay clear of him. Dab-arse, Lawrence Filkin, he done his worst a'ready."

Squire moaned. He had hurried down from the north but he was too late, damn the stops and starts and dogs and buried women and red-ochre men and inconveniences. Damn Jake Venti. Damn himself, most of all. He said, "Filkin cottons on to Munnys then, eh? Discovers Pommie? In the barn?" He slid onto the bench and snugged up to her, as familiar as yesterday, as ready to comfort the teary Nellah, as men have been ready to comfort sexual and desirable women since time immemorial.

Nellah made room for him.

With her fingers she dabbed at her eyes and her cheeks and shook her head. "Nuhn-uh, not yet. Filkin do not know about the Munnys. Leastways, I do not think so. But Filkin, he seen the poster. You aint told me, Squire. Why?"

"I seen it myself, first time, in Stouffville. I know I come back here then. Lieutenant Horatio Needles and Walter Winter, they are the culprits, Nellah. And Boy Hewson. Boy is the instigator. He bribes Needles to print the damn thing. With Bobby in gaol—"

Squire stroked the satin smooth flesh between her shoulder blades. "Well, I hoped with Bobby incarcerated maybe Needles lets it go. Maybe Needles forgets the poster. Faint hope—but still—" He put his arms around her. "Anyway, not the Munnys, well, I cannot guess it. What is wrong?"

"Munnys is still safe. What's a-wrong?" Nellah nestled into his compliant body. "Needles, uh? And Winter? Culprits. At my table. Amen and so be it. No, aint Munnys. We covered them up. False names, we give them. Iris. Iris Green. Chrisinny be Zulie O'Herlihy. And Pommie would be Tommy O'Herlihy, the stable boy. Still and all, trouble be here, Squire. For you and me. It would be—" She stalled.

"Be what?" He squeezed her bare shoulder. He had to get to Filkin. He sounded abrupt and he was sorry because Nellah was wounded. More tears gathered until they overflowed. He felt bad and soothed and rocked her.

She said, "They got a petition—"

"What petition?"

She could not speak.

Ahh, damn. He could not leave her, crying, and run after Filkin, could he? Not when she was beside herself, most un-Nellah-like, and he did what he perpetually did. He teased her. "Say—" He reached up to the sideboard and grabbed a clean, pressed and folded table napkin and handed it to her for drying her face and tried to coax out a flicker of the old optimism. "Say, aint you the lusty crabapple they call Teacher? I heard tell o' ya." Months ago, to explain the persecution they felt or at least take away the sting, a self-deprecating, mocking game had sprung up between them, free and easy, especially easy when Nellah was out of sorts.

Nellah lowered her eyes and dimpled and loyally played along. "Unh-huh. I would be that very one. Call me Teacher. Whore with heart o' gold. Say, brother, aint you the redskin they call the savage?"

"Right you are, madam. That's me. The knave. The savage. Don't forget 'noble,' uh? Look, Nellah, I haven't much time but I have something to tell you. It's almost unbelievable. It is about Fannie Millburn."

Squire's eyes were darker than normal, not gentle and not at all noble. He had no debate with himself over telling Nellah Golden the truth about Fannie Millburn. He told her the latest news about what had happened to her last October. Fannie Millburn did it. She set up the Warriors. Warriors claimed they stole the Wedgwood but took no part of the interfering. Nellah nodded. Correct. It was Boy Hewson. But the robbery? A set up? By Fannie Millburn? Was that not a goldern caution? She would not forgive that bit of business. Huh! Fannie Millburn was the mastermind. Why was she not surprised?

Squire inched closer to her.

She relaxed more and said she allowed she wanted to hear him say something funny. "Fannie Millburn, she done me wrong. I will remember. Tonight is bad. Petition be bad, Squire. That Filkin, he b'lieve he hung the moon when it come to schemin'. A petition of clearance, it would be. To get rid of coloureds. Clear us off streets. Off Hill. Tomorrow." But, she said, Squire would make her believe petition of clearance were not a'tall real. Laws a'mighty, Squire were alive and well and real hisself but, Jehoshaphat, that was some awful tatty blanket he wore on his shoulders and the goldern petition, why, it were not a real petition, please, say it were not. Say she could stay in her home.

He shook his head.

He could not say that.

Most likely the petition was real.

Anyway, he understood she meant legitimate and kissed her on the back of her neck. A soft kiss. He expected a whiff of Lizzie's mystical, magical Guerlain but Nellah smelled the same as she always did. Like hope, like soap, like spring cherry blossoms. He felt their connection was strong. He was not altogether surprised but he was not pushing her. For one thing, his mind was racing. A meeting of white villagers had cooked up a petition of clearance. Why wouldn't it be real? Numbers? He was curious. "How many signed?"

"As of tonight, I would say at least twelve men. Octavius, even he signed Filkin's petition. My old partner did betray me. The petition—"

"So where is it?"

She nodded or sighed or groaned. It was hard to tell. "It would be handed to top man. Direct. Governor General Charles Murray Cathcart. In t'other room, Squire. Eatin' my food. Drinkin' my brandy. Flirtin' with Bride. Bein charmin'. He takes it. He takes the cake. Unh-huh. Hill community be done."

Squire agreed.

That was that, he thought. Hill people were certainly done.

Petition was given to the English Crown's top man. At an intimate salon, the top Canadian executive and military man was dining with many of the men who had signed the paper. They were the Sons of Progress. Oh, for sure, this petition of clearance was bound to succeed. A Christian men's sporting and country club had once loomed on the far horizon. It had just tumbled over the offing and landed smack dab in the middle of Vinegar Hill but Squire would get Lawrence Filkin. A certain Filkin would live here no more. Others, though, the homesteaders and the Indigenous, they were losing a home.

Where would Nellah and Pearl live?

With Jeddah, in Uxbridge?

What about devoted Alfie? Annie?

And most important, Jennet Ferguson.

What about her? Where did Jennie fit into the dismal scene? Maybe nowhere. He and Jennie had struggled to get into step.

The Fergusons' self-discipline was clear enough but not the princi-ples. The household walked on eggshells. With his *àshare*, he could have cut the tension into gelatin squares for the omelette. Teacher had rules for the New Cave, lots of them, and they were posted on the tavern's wall. Her rules were dug from reason but in Uxbridge, rules floated into play from the City of God. What to wear, when to eat, when to sit at cards, when to drink, when to couple, how to cou-ple, who could couple. The Elect had rules for everything. He had been dazed in Uxbridge, like someone had slapped him, and he never got over that anxious, disconcerted feeling but he had left the Fer-gusons with undeniable regret.

He felt cheated.

He wanted to make connection with Jennet.

She wanted it.

Did she need him for more than that, though? She was furious because he had left the stock farm without taking her with him but he planned to travel fast. He was wrong, without a doubt, about suggesting they live together on the Hill. How could he bring her to this place? In any case, they had parted on bad terms. Like two starving turkey vultures, they had plucked away at each other's tender spots until everything he said had provoked her into a fum-ing silence. He had not kissed her goodbye. He regretted that.

Nellah and him, they understood each other.

According to legal description, they were coloured, he as much as she. He and Nellah were spiritual but neither of them was a strict this or an orthodox that. Jennie was classified as *white*. In ortho-doxy, she belonged to the Presbyterians. St. Paul and Handsome Lake would say he and Jennet made an unholy mix, as unholy as the *Courier* found life on Vinegar Hill.

The Hill was done. In humanity, inhumanity. Jennie did not need it.

He did not need it either.

Nellah sighed. "Where would be the new canvas coat of yown?"

"Gone." He was worried about having no warm coat for the cold weather but felt it was unmanly to accede to a female's fussing.

And, she added, the short haircut? "You look different. What is with that haircut, hon?"

"Hair grows, eh?"

"Unh-huh. It do." She leaned against him. Her face was buried in his chest. With the back of one hand she touched the smooth part of his cheek and with the other she patted at the tears on her own cheek and she spoke in a voice that sounded far distant from the buoyant take-charge Hill woman she used to be. "What would be wrong? Oh, Mammy. What aint a-wrong with here?"

Nellah's voice got muffled. Her breath was sweet and hot and he felt it tease him through his broadcloth vest and flannel shirt. A sunspot on his chilled skin. She said something more about her heart of gold but he did not catch it. He was not listening. He was weak. Weak in the knees. He kissed her neck again. And again. She leaned harder into his chest.

Hallo, hallo. Thunder in his ears.

More thunder. What now?

A thundering commotion in the dining room shook them. Squire felt feeble-jointed and fixed to the spot on the kitchen bench but Nellah jumped up and skedaddled to the door. She opened up a sliver between the swinging kitchen door and the doorjamb and looked into the great room. She crouched. Someone had stoked the fire in the hearth. The room was dim, candles had burned low, but there was enough light to see.

~

From over Nellah's turbaned head Squire peered at the scene and he caught the gist.

Three newcomers had arrived.

They had entered by the front door. No doubt the tinny bells on the horse strap were still tinkling in alarm. The men had tramped down the main corridor and stepped into the great room, riders fresh from the bush. Squire and Nellah inhaled at the same time.

She said, "Goldern, Squire. Lookit there. Some hideous bad timin', hon."

The horsemen.

Jeddah Golden and Peter Johnson and Barton Farr.

There they stood, each holding his distinctive pose. They were in Teacher's dining room and loaded for trouble. Their interruption had been bizarre and uncomfortable. Nervous diners had clammed up. James Wilkes and Octavius Millburn looked embarrassed as Golden and his cronies crashed into their private land-jobbing talks. On the other side of the coin, Peter Johnson was astounded to see men swigging down precious Calvados like beet beer.

Jeddah and his congenital sense of order had registered an uneasy peace and his feet were planted firm because he was ready to bust a few heads, "a-cause ridin' hard makes a man as savagerous as a meat axe." Against his will, Squire felt the top of his own sweet crown because he imagined the pain of an errant meat axe landing on it. Jeddah Golden was not one to overlook an intruder creeping around his back stairs.

Last and least there was Barton Farr.

Like a beetle in the salad, Bart Farr would make himself known. And so he did. Farr puffed on his two-headed cheroot.

He stubbed the burning end into a delicate pale-shaped and transparent saucer. Saucer cracked. It was a small saucer but when it broke it made a life-sized crack. Farr removed his hat and smacked it on the end of the long white table and, scratching his close-shaved head, looked around him in a great show of manhood, daring any guest to stand up to him. and challenge what he was about to say.

"Goddam it, Bride. You lookin' fine, darlin'. *Ooo-eee.* An' all dollied up to beat the band. How's about you and me goin' upstairs for a little frolic."

~

Christ, Bart. Shuddup.

Squire whispered to Nellah and he grabbed the doorjamb, stunned, while the reality of what had happened struck him like a moving boulder.

The Munnys had been outed.

Innocently done but with profound effect.

Bear-hair and Whiskers sat in plain view, perched right at the far end of the table, smack under Bart's nose. At Bart's shout, "Bride," the skunks who had created the Wanted poster bill narrowed their eyes and mouthed *Bride Munny*.

The Mohawk felt his instep pinch like a bitch. He feared, no, he *knew* Needles and Winter would act. They could have announced their plans and they would not be any less clear than they were now, sitting stiff like ramrods, saying nothing and staring violently at each other. Squire estimated Needles would try to collect the kids tonight, dump them off with the Magdalenes in Toronto and get a receipt notice and head to the Hamilton gaolhouse to meet Boy Hewson. Dealing with Bride would be simpler. She would be singled out to face charges of prostitution before magistrate Nathan Gage in Brantford. Sharp-featured Horatio Needles and Walter Winter had just had an opportunity tossed their way. With Bobby John's having escaped, matters of jurisdiction would be unsettled and Boy Hewson just might have information about a dangerous Indian smuggler. The RCRR would leap on it. Boy would need a gesture of goodwill to tell his tale. With the capture of the Munnys, the RCRR could give him just that.

Lieutenant Needles chawed on a plug of tobacco and the man's mouth smiled into his rum and, *pshaw*, he looked like he was on top again.

But, Squire reckoned, Needles and Winter did not know the lay of the land. The smugglers they had sought on and off for months were close. Laughably close. Jake Hearenhodoh Venti and Paulus Bobby John and a motley few of the Warriors leaned against the bare-branched beechnut trees at the far side of Nellah's barn and they waited for Squire, the man on the inside, to deliver their package. They would not be disappointed. Squire was no snitch. He disliked the RCRR. He had made a bargain with the Warriors and he had made up his mind. Filkin was going down. Even more, the duo of Needles and Winter would be outmanoeuvred *vis-à-vis* the Munnys. Squire would see to it.

In the dining room a general uproar had broken out because the men had digested Bart's challenge. Iris Green was in fact the infamous Bride Munny and *you can bet*, one man had yelled to another, *she's up for grabs.*

Biscuits flew. A schooner sailed into the wall. Cream spilled. A saltcellar was a maple-seed twirler. Brandy and rum tumblers wobbled on heavy bottoms.

Guests roared and threw punches.

Johnson brandished his Bowie knife.

Golden thumped a washboard-sized fist on the table.

At the centre of the masculine melee, glossy Iris pouted and swayed eerily on her chair but her eyes held a steady bead on a wall sconce, as though it, and perhaps she, were well placed in a French museum.

Farr waved his hat in front of her to get her attention.

He had no luck.

Body and soul, she was detached. She pouted and stared. Bride Munny was not up for grabs; it was most evident she was not. Everyone had seen it. She had reached up and grasped Jeddah Golden's hand.

Jeddah could be as prickly as a holly hedge, especially if he did not want to do something, but with Bride he was fine. He held her hand. He was her roving knight. He seemed surprised but not apologetic or annoyed and he struggled to hold her steady on her chair as she sat staring at the wall sconce and he tried not to drop his Brunswick rifle on her pretty gold-dusted head. Squire had seen enough.

Bride had anointed Golden. He was her protector.

That was fine for her but the Mohawk had to get to her kids. Saving the children was up to him. He tapped Nellah on the shoulder. "Go upstairs. Get Chrisinny. Wrap her. Bring her to pantry. If she wakes, tell her it's a game. Hide-and-seek game and she hides. I get Pommie ready to go. I come right back for her. Run, Nellie, please!"

He put his finger to his lips and the shadow of a regretful man retreated from the aura of blossoming enticement and moved toward the back door and, for future consideration, shut it on half-lock, careful to make sure it would open free and easy.

CHAPTER
eighty-three

S quire ran down the path toward the outhouse, pleased with the Segenauck-like moccasins, which Polly had made, because the time-wasting and dangerous shilly-shallying with the lovely Nellah had meant he really had to hustle to catch his cornered prey, catch him in the two-holer, where the prey was raw, exposed and vulnerable and, best of all, sitting pretty. Sitting all alone with nothing to disturb a quick kidnapping, no kicks from the black boots and no booming, *here-here, what do you think you're doing*, from Filkin's brother-in-law.

Next to the New Cave the outhouse was silhouetted on the skyline like a narrow-framed sentry and from a distance the grass-topped privy resembled a certain Lieutenant Needles. Squire ran as far as he could, as fast as he could, until he hit the gravel path. The stones crunched.

He stooped and crept close.

He tiptoed to the outdoor privy's plank door and hunkered down half-a-foot. It was sprinkling. Rain now, not snow. He could feel the drizzle seeping into his flannel shirt and the collar was getting damp. He had left the tatty blanket inside the house because he needed speed, not warmth, and he wanted to set the snare and trap for Filkin. He tapped with urgency under the carved-moon crescent.

He tapped again.

"It's the whore's bad food." From within the privy an irritated voice rose, growing more strident. "Bad food, you hear? You can tell the seat is occupied, sir. I am ill."

Squire crawled to the side of the structure.

He stretched and put his right shoulder to it. He and Jake had knocked over a few of these in their youth and he remembered it was easy once you got the top-heavy thing to start rocking.

He pushed. He pushed again.

The outhouse obliged.

It rocked.

With each roll, the voice got more indignant. "Oy! Oy! Hold on. I'm coming out."

Through the clanks and the pushing, the privy tipped and tee-tered and righted itself. The door burst open. And, lo and behold, there was pale Lawrence Filkin. There he was in the flesh, if not quite the pink, squinting into the dark light of the eastern sky, per-haps anticipating the glorious sunrise of the brand-new day not yet there. He was busy, though. He stamped old *Courier* pages from the soles of his black boots and yanked up his camel cashmere trousers. He hesitated and did not button up the fly front. He looked about him. "Whoever you are, you are rude, sir. I'm not done—"

Squire jumped from the south side of the privy.

Indian surprise tactics came natural. Like Uncle Pat had always said, British army manoeuvres were disastrous, especially in the bush. Lieutenant Needles had said he hated the unsports-manlike conduct of Braves. Screw Needles. Approaching from the back, the Mohawk grabbed the unsuspecting Lawrence Filkin around the neck and twisted him and pulled his arms behind him and bound his wrists with a length of new hemp rope and pushed him forward and let him stumble along the gravel to the barn, which was some distance behind the outhouse.

Squire and Filkin were around the same age. Squire felt he himself was by far the stronger man and he was in better shape, but Filkin might be surprising. He had strength in those fingers. In the village Lawrie Filkin excreted disdain. He trotted along the plank walks of Brantford with his nose in the air, very much like Joker's Breezy, and it surprised Squire that Filkin started to come undone, so soon, so easy, but there it was. Puffery had won. Filkin the spider shrivelled into a shouting exoskeleton.

We go at a snail's pace, Squire worried about the time as he trudged along the path.

He had a rope over his shoulder and lugged a crying man, a man who wailed as loud as the terror-stricken Robespierre before the virtue of the guillotine's inflexible justice. Filkin hollered. He hollered for Octavius and he hollered for his sister, Fannie, and he hollered for Saint Ignatius. Or any saint.

Squire shrugged.

Filkin could holler as loud as he wanted and he could create a regular fireworks kind of hullaballoo. With the excitement of uncloaking Bride's identity, none of the guests seemed in the mood to use the privy.

Captor and captive plodded toward destiny.

Filkin's shrieks took a sudden breather. In the silence, above them, blown on the wind, Squire heard horses' neighing and male voices shushing them. Praise Handsome Lake. The Warriors were there, by the barn as promised. Squire paused to listen.

He heard something else. Steps on the gravel pathway? He hoped no stranger wandered around in the rain and sleet to hinder the Warriors' escape.

Were they being watched?

The captive took a dive on the stones.

Filkin cried out in pain. Worse luck, he ended up shrieking in humiliation because his trousers were flagging around his knees and his bare white arse was visible. Stinking, steaming excrement dripped from his arsehole down his backside and into his expensive undergarments.

Oops.

Squire looked at the privy fiasco and he reeled in disgust as he hauled the man to his feet and prayed they were alone in the yard. Jeezus. What a mess. It was coming fast, like shit out of a goose. He stayed poker-faced. "Bad food, uh? Phew. Willya smell that—"

In a towering rage, Filkin puffed up his cheeks and he howled at the night sky and cried.

Squire paid no mind. He was not the least impressed with the man from New Glasgow. When it came to a howl at the moon, Filkin was neither as sincere as Yeksa'a nor as funny as Jake. Filkin was not funny at all. Squire said, "You just about kill Julia Good."

Filkin's forehead blanched. "She—she—she bloody well asked for it." He was puffing. "She deserved it. She was sleeping on the road—" He was transformed from a blushing sugar almond to a glistening camphor ball. "In the bloody middle of the road." Again he was rendered speechless but he continued to shit. His voice, when it came back, was operatic. "Julia Good?! Sonofabitch! Who cares about Julia fucking Good? General Cathcart will see you hang, you bastard. You fucking Hottentot! Come the next full moon, redskin, you hang! Hang until dead!"

Hang on.

Who was the captor?

Who was the captivated?

The Mohawk had had a bellyful of the *Hottentot* and *redskin*. "You green gobshite, you don't know nuthin'. A full moon is for lovemakin', not hangin'." He dragged Filkin along at arm's length so as not to get splattered with flying feces and, out of the blue or because of the crap, he happened to think of the Fergusons' friend, the Reverend Asahel Filbert.

Filkin's skinny moon was inspiring.

Wouldn't Asahel Filbert love to see Squire take on the role of a swarthy lunar aficionado? He held his nose with his rope hand. With his other hand he yanked at Filkin who, unprepared for a smart whiplash, lurched into space and was hard-pressed to stay steady on his pins. Using a rolling wrist, Squire pointed toward the man's leaky arse. The only Italian immigrant Squire knew was Allegro, the dry-goods proprietor on Colborne Street. The Mohawk was not now or ever going to be Italian but it amused him to use Allegro as a model for the swarthy immigrant, the one who fit in. He opened his arms. "*Ciao*, Mr. Filkin. You welcome to the United States Army."

Asahel would be gratified.

He thought maybe Filkin looked gratified. Or was that petrified?

Squire was no actor but he was thoughtful. He realized he had been thinking about Uxbridge and all along weighing the pluses and minuses of the place and had made up his mind.

He would go back, straight away.

The minute he handed off Filkin to the Warriors he was gone. In the middle of the night, no coat, no provisions, all of that difficulty notwithstanding, he would swoop up Pommie and Chrisinny and leave the Hill and head north.

The Ferguson family would accept and shelter the kids. He knew they would. He had known it all along. Sure, Uxbridge was uncomfortable. Sure, the township was stress incarnate for an old Hottentot like him but it was also home to a bunch of anti-colonial-government types, the rebels of '37, and he had had enough of being the outsider in two worlds. He would be the rebel. Up north. He had had enough of the south's red and white elites and closed societies.

He knew he and Jennie would fare better together than they would apart. They ought to give themselves a fighting chance. They ought to stay put in the Home district and partake in the development of Uxbridge Township.

Squire handed off Filkin. Under the beech trees there followed a shuffling and rustling and then a phewing and a mewing as Filkin got officially transferred to the dark side. Squire did not see Jake. Bobby John was not there, either, only six or seven men, most of them as young as or younger than Squire, wearing the robber bandanas. He might have recognized one or two. He was not sure who they were. He preferred it that way. Someone said, "Ah Gawd, what's this?" Another said, "*Eech*. Smelly pants. Wiping stick." Filkin screamed at them and got a filthy bandana in his gob to keep him quiet for the journey ahead.

Squire left the Warriors to handle Filkin and the clean-up. He left the wheelers and dealers and trading and undercover operations and he dashed back to get Chrisinny. His heart had pounded over reaching her once before, when he had shinnied up Keneun, the Thunderbird oak, and it pounded again as he ran to the house and he prayed he was fast enough and savvy enough for another rescue.

CHAPTER
eighty-four

S quire carried a sleeping Chrisinny up the barn's ramp. Chrisinny wore one of Nellah's heavyweight homespuns and she held her Zulie doll in her arms. She was wrapped up tight, swaddled in the blanket like a pork sausage in Cook's thick pastry, and the small heads of black Zulie and carroty-topped Chrisinny poked out through the confines of the homely cover.

Teacher had left the child, wrapped up so, on the scullery floor but to make sure everything was fine she had popped her head around the door and clapped her hands because Squire had got there, finally, to retrieve the little girl. On impulse, Nellah had entered from the doorway into the maid's workroom, past the warming greatcoats hanging on neat pegs, and she had reached out over the cracked sink and hugged him and whispered, *Ben Franklin, he got it correct. I am grateful, Squire. You fix my soul and I reckon souls caint be forged.*

Polite, he had demurred and hemmed and hah-ed. *Fix your soul? No. How?*

She had said, *Squire, you do have yown fun. For a-wantin' me, a-course.*

Embarrassed, he had felt his ears turn dark.

Shit, what had he done? He ran his hands through his thick short hair. It had started to curl. So had his mind. From his toes.

She had shaken her head. *Pshaw. I aint a-telling nobody. Neither are you, I reckon. I caint choose you and you know it. With old strumpet it do not matter much but, well, I swear it, I know who wants puss and who wants me and it do matter, to my soul, cause you do want me.* She had kissed him, gentle, wet, full on the mouth and every part of him curled but, like she had said, there was no follow-up and there would be no follow-up, not ever, and she had vanished like sweet incense though a keyhole, and all that remained of her was the scent of flowers and a breathtaking tingling in his loins. She had surprised him but he had had to smile.

Yeah, Nellah was grand. Smart too.

He had wanted her. He sure had.

He had wanted her more than he had ever in his life wanted Maggie Walker but that was not the whole picture. He wanted Nellah Golden less than he wanted (and needed) the fierce smouldering Scotchwoman and that was the current state of affairs, as he saw it.

Love drove him to the north.

He loved Jennet Ferguson.

He would try again.

Go back to Uxbridge.

Go back to figure out the Fergusons, their strict principles and their hideous old-country rules. Stay or leave Uxbridge, he would win over the fierce one.

Whatever it meant, Nellah's soul was fixed. He was glad. He could not have explained what he had done to fix her soul other than show his desire. He wanted to touch her smooth tea-and-cream skin. What the hell? She was old, maybe thirty-five, but not age-diminished and he admired her. He respected her strength of character and her inner fire and the goddam, heart-rending optimism of the woman. He would have liked to mull over the whole Nellah and Jeddah thing and enjoy the memory of her sweet face close to his but everywhere he looked there were problems, shitty problems, big problems, elephant-sized.

In the scullery, his quiet conversation with Nellah had taken seconds. A loud exchange was happening in the dining room at the same time. Even as Nellah had kissed him and sweet longing was assailing his senses, the strident drunken voices of the dinner guests had been ringing in his ears.

~

In the dining room, the men had decided to search the brick house for Chrisinny.

Over the din, he had heard Lieutenant Horatio Needles shout he was under orders from William Henry Draper. General Cathcart had responded, just as loud, but tight-lipped and sarcastic, that he was confused. Who was running things in the colony?

Golden, at Nellah's behest, was attempting to collapse a circus into a walnut shell but he had not done it. Not yet. Guests had imbibed freely and drunks were unstable and difficult to collapse. Drunks wanted to save Chrisinny from perdition.

They were ready to hunt her down.

They would help the military. Help the RCRR. Help poor old Needles do his job.

They would turn the girl over to the Magdalenes.

Jesus Christ. Squire had known he held a tight harness, time wise, and it would be mere minutes before some wiseacre had the bright idea to head to the barn to hunt down young Tommy O'Herlihy, the stable boy. He had imagined he could hear them piecing together the puzzle. Why, Tommy O'Herlihy must be Pomeroy Munny.

Yes. The very same.

Hearing them, Squire had been certain: the do-gooders would pack up like wolves and they would lumber to the barn, sooner or later. In one fell swoop he had picked up Chrisinny. He had taken off with her and the back door of Nellah's house slammed shut behind them. He had sprinted. The old red stable had never seemed so far but

469

Chrisinny was light enough to bundle on a cradleboard and he figured his race time must have smashed a few mission-school records.

Inside the barn, standing adjacent to the Fowlers' cockpit,
holding his little lantern aloft, Pommie waited, anxious, pacing, and
ready with news. "Yo, Sky Walker. Jake Venti, he says, give yer this.
Yer t'ave—"

~

Squire put Chrisinny on a hard straw-covered workbench but she
was not disturbed. Her eyelids were thin and blue-veined and they
flickered like blue butterfly wings when he put her down. She breathed
deep and turned her head, still warm and cozy and fast asleep.

He straightened and gave his full attention to Pommie. "Have
what?"

"Yer t'ave back yer very own ten poun's." Pommie handed over
the money and he fastened a peg button on his new navy serge
jacket and looked around the dark barn and puckered his ginger
brows and looked around again and patted Chrisinny on the feet
with quick, concerned, brotherly taps.

Squire was amazed. "What's this money for?"

"Huh? Oh, it's fer you, mister. On account of—"

"Whoa, look at me, Pommie. On account of what?"

"Jake says, account of your bein'—racketeer."

Squire snorted. "C'mon now, sonny. What did the Mohawk
genius really say?"

"Foine den. He says yer a *dumb* racketeer." Pommie yawned. His
freckles were faded.

He was too tired to joke.

Tired or not, the boy looked for something.

His eyes, so much like Bride's, wandered from the Mohawk to
the empty stalls; especially the empty stalls near the barn's entrance
ramp. "Serious, Squire. I towl ya true. Jake, he says Mr. Octavius

Millburn, why, dat nasty old bugger, he awready paid Warriors in gold coin, big stacks of gold coin, real gold, to send a certain stinking package to those United States. So's that's it, yah see? Sure it's bin paid fer, whatever t'is, and you get yer money back. What stinking package, uh, Squire?"

Octavius Millburn had paid for Lawrence Filkin's removal? To the United States Army? Squire did not answer. He rubbed his chin. What the devil?

So the Warriors had been hanging around Vinegar Hill all night at Octavius Millburn's bidding. They had already been on Filkin's trail.

Squire was a stumbling interloper. He had tossed his poker chips into the middle of a game already underway.

Filkin upset Millburn. Everyone who knew them, knew it.

Millburn likely wanted to see the end of his tiresome brother-in-law and he had paid well for the service and Bobby John had known all along he was going to nab the pale-faced arsehole. Bobby John must have been flabbergasted. He must have thought Handsome Lake had dumped his eager, naïve cousin Squire right into his lap. Squire was a sucker.

It made complete sense. The Warriors had used him. They had used him to get to the stinking package. The coincidence of the painted red-ochre man had been over the top and Squire should have twigged to it then. Except the red-ochre man, the fumbling Jake, had messed up earlier on the trail and bungled the first go-round to snatch Filkin. Octavius Millburn? Warriors? Jake? All with a hidden plan. Even Julia Good? Nah.

Julia Good was for real. You could not fake a near mortal gaping wound like that and anyway Filkin had admitted to kicking her.

As for the rest, who knew? You couldn't trust nobody these days.

Squire remained silent.

Pommie seemed to realize he was not going to get an answer. The contents of the stinking package were a mystery and he pegged another button on his coat and changed the subject. "Oy, Squire. Jake left Cap'n."

"What?! Oh, hell, Pommie. Warriors are horse thieves. They take the saddled mounts?" Squire leaned over a crib and he peered into a couple of the wider stalls and growled in dismay, mad at himself. He had not noticed the empty slots when he arrived with Chrisinny because his mind had been occupied with Uxbridge and escape. "Took 'em all?"

"Sure, and they did so. Left Joker's Breezy, I tink, and Cap'n, a-course. Back't the back. And I aint entirely positive but that there's ol' Diablo yonder." Pommie pointed a vague index finger. "Jake says to tell you he don't want any goddam vigilantes followin' 'im outa goddam spite so here's your goddam money. The horsemen posse gets to keep their goddam horses and they have to call it off. No. Yer supposed to call it *quits*, mister, yup, call it *quits*. Tis what Jake says. I am real sorry fer it, Squire. Guest horses are vanished. Gone outa here, faster'n old cockers. Oy. I fell asleep. You leave for Miz Nellah's house to get Chrisinny and I lay meself down. Not watchin' out for hooligans. Nor nobody, see? Pretty goddam fast, them renegades, they snuck in. And quiet. Lordy, they are some quiet. I dunno—"

"Ah, little brother. You sound like Jake. Don't lard it on, eh? We got no time. We gotta git. It purely aint your fault. That's all there is to it. Against the Warriors and Bobby John, you are but one small boy. Like me, apparently." Squire whistled for Cap'n's attention. The Mohawk made it plain to Pommie he wanted to hustle to the far stall to get the horse and get the three of them on the trail but the boy's expression stopped him in his tracks.

"Yes, foine den. We do make a pair, Sky Walker, you and me, eh? Leastways, we got ourselfs some company. This 'ere's 'arold."

"Eh? Harold? Who the hell is Harold?"

"Him. And beside 'im, why, dere's Sam. Oy, Sam! 'ower yer be?" Whoever they were, Pommie Munny was cheerful enough and glad to see them and he smiled from ear to ear, beaming through freckles.

Squire sighed. What now?

He swivelled to face the company Pommie addressed and found himself saying *how-do* to Harold and Sam Goosay.

They were good-looking young men. Unsmiling, straight-featured. Slim, competent Cayuga braves, with enormous ears. And they were dressed warm. Squire noted the warm clothes and he shivered. He saw broadcloth leggings and jackets from deerskin hides, fringed and beaded. Heavy wool blankets draped their broad shoulders, casual-like, in a becoming and efficient manner, as befitted their architectural talents and natural dignity. Their cloaks were perfect for cold or sleety inclement weather.

Excellent sons indeed.

To give himself a little face-saving credit, just because he needed it, Squire was not that surprised. He thought it had been odd he should have imagined someone watching him and Filkin at the privy. There were men wandering in the middle of the night, yes, the Goosays, the untouchables. The men who knew things.

He himself knew nothing. He knew less than Pommie.

As it happened, the Goosays had come to parley.

Courteous, Harold bowed his head and he commenced to deliver his piece to Squire in diplomatic Oneida, the language of Squire's grandmother, Aughguaga Polly.

Sam had faded away somewhere.

It was anybody's guess whether Pommie translated for himself what Harold was saying but Squire sensed the boy understood very well that Pommie and Chrisinny were leaving now with Harold and Sam Goosay and going deep into the forest to stay awhile with Missus Goosay.

Harold explained that his mother, the *wise* Missus Lucille Goosay, had her way of knowing things and she had known there was big trouble for Tehawennihárhos, what with the circulated poster bill and Bobby John's escape, and she had sent her two excellent sons, Harold and Sam, to the rescue. It was a short-term remedy, of course. Anyone interested in seeing the children would find the Goosay family camped in a wigwam on the riverside at Mohawk, after the ice break-up on the crazy river. Until that day, the little ones would be out of the sight of interfering do-gooders and greedy bounty hunters wanting Goodman Brown's payout. They would be secure with their own dear granny. And Missus Goosay's special friend, Tehawennihárhos, he could tell their feckless ma, Bride Munny, that bit of good news.

Relieved by the rightness of Missus Goosay's plan but pained not to have the responsibility of the kids on his shoulders, Squire felt the tears sting his eyes and for one dreadful moment he feared he would laugh and cry at the same time. Under winter ice, the crazy river was upset, flowing both ways, and, goddam, he had come this close himself to being a no-good do-gooder but so what? For the Munny kids he would have been the best no-good do-gooder in the territory but with his back against the wall he had to agree with Harold. Missus Goosay should keep the children. Squire promised to let Bride know.

It was all he had but he gave Harold the ten pounds Pommie had returned.

Harold was full of himself and full of false reluctance but Squire insisted and in the end the dignified Harold almost looked grateful for the money.

Sam reappeared with the swaddled girl.

Harold prepared to take hold of Pommie.

They wanted to get clear away because—and in unison they joggled their oversized ears in the direction of Teacher's brothel house—they knew there was no spare time. On this special and serious occasion there would be no females for the frolicking. They would bundle up the children for a long sleigh ride and depart from the Hill forthwith, if not sooner.

Squire struggled to put the disturbing situation they were in, right for Pommie, to put it right for himself too. "Harold Goosay, Harold here, he says, Pommie, he says, ah, he says Missus Goosay believes Segenauck needs you, eh?"

"I understand, Squire. Kin yer come, Sky Walker, to Mohawk? In spring? I aint goin' wif them if you caint come to Grand River in spring."

Squire was a modest, restrained man, not one for getting keyed up. Not one for hugging. Not in normal times. These were not normal times.

He hugged the boy tight to him for many seconds. Pommie snuffled on his shirt and Squire held him tighter. "Yeah, sure," Squire said. "Pommie, I greet you again. You wait by the Thunderbird oak, eh? In a couple of months, I see you. I promise. You believe me?"

Pomeroy Munny nodded to Squire and to Harold.

He turned back to Squire. He said he agreed he and his little sister would go with the Goosays. It was a deal. It was a deal because Sky Walker would return to the crazy river in the spring. Sky Walker promised.

"Say, little brother." Squire was puzzled. "You are smart fella. When do you pick up Oneida language?"

Tut. Tut. Harold wanted to flee. No time for explanations or the protracted farewell. A pair of sleek jackrabbits, the Goosays were at home in the wilderness. They were runners. They did not like the horses much. They ran through the brambles. They had hauled a small birch sleigh with them and they had made it special for the occasion. They brought wolf skins to hide the Munnys and keep them warm while they travelled to a cozy spot near Cayuga. They ran through the briars. They travelled on the ancient trails. They had secrets. No one would find them. Not the bloody British, they said, that was sure.

Sam pointed to the rear door. *We go.*

Harold dipped his ponderous ear. "Good luck, Tehawenni-hárhos. The geese fly home to Ohsweken and then you visit Tinaat-oua. We are gone now." He dipped his huge ear a fraction lower. "Someone comes."

The Goosays were right.

Squire could hear running steps.

With a final good-luck nod, the excellent sons of Missus Goosay dashed to the barn's side door. Red heads bobbed on their shoulders. Through the door the men ducked and scooted and disappeared into the remaining minutes of the fading winter blackness marking the tail end of an amazing and successful night's work.

Heavy-laden, Nellah Golden ran up the ramp. By mere seconds she had missed catching sight of the excellent sons, Harold and Sam Goosay.

Her turban was loose and about to come undone but that was too bad. Her scar was blazing but she could not help that either. She was not worried about herself or her hair. She was worried about the Munnys and her dear friend Squire because the men, her guests, them yaller rats, they planned to storm the barn and set it on fire and smoke the miscreants out.

She peered over her shoulder. Coast was clear.

No one on the scene. Not yet.

She gave Squire the supplies she had brought. "Jeddah would try but he caint git control of the mob without a-shootin' one of 'em. You'ns would do best to git a-goin'."

Epilogue

~

Very early on Tuesday, 13 January, a handsome swarthy man with short wavy hair and pointy eyebrows aimed his Canadian stallion northward, away from the crazy river. The day was cold but the air smelled of dill weed. The man had coins in his purse. His saddlebags were full of food: cornbread, venison, pickled eggs and chunks of dried salmon. He packed an extra flask, Calvados, he hoped, for warming his belly.

The young man was respectable. Anyone might say so. He wore a navy fur-lined overcoat, previously owned by a certain local, one Octavius Millburn Sr.

Some minutes before the swarthy man's departure, a certain Miz Nellah Blaize Golden had changed his immediate circumstances. For the better, one must say.

It was a switch for the books.

Upon hearing that Nellah Golden had discovered the identity of the mastermind of the October robbery on Vinegar Hill, Octavius Millburn expressed his utter surprise and amazement, both of which he directed with nervous twitches toward acting Governor General Charlie Cathcart, but Nellah, goddammed stubborn, refused to let the matter drop. The mastermind of the robbery, Nellah shouted, why, it was none other than Mrs. Octavius (Fannie) Millburn.

After the fit of temper, Teacher regained herself.

She was as cold as the dawn. She was in her own dining room in her own brick house for the last night and she was not about to act as though she had anything to lose but her baby. Love of Pearl gave her the courage to bargain and it made her fierce, as fierce as Jennet Ferguson. They could take Nellah's house; they would not hurt her child. Octavius was no match for Nellah Blaize Golden's fury. Not after she had been betrayed and scorned.

She said when she got to Montréal she might reveal the name of the guilty party to, say, that nosy Mrs. Hart, ace reporter at the *Courier.* In fact, she would write. Yes, from Montréal. Nellah would write to Mrs. Hart the very minute she, Nellah Golden, originally from Appalachia, arrived there with the Frenchman Peter Johnson. Through the backing of the columnist Mrs. Hart and the editorialist Seeum Johnston, Nellah would enlighten the villagers of Brantford regarding the mastermind of the October robbery on Vinegar Hill and the whereabouts of Teacher's missing Wedgwood. In the Millburns' parlour, of all places!

General Cathcart had expressed majestic astonishment at the untoward allegations against Fannie Millburn but Octavius Millburn had been quick to see the light and quicker yet to exchange his warm coat and some English silver for Nellah's protracted silence.

Millburn had said he thought *Hart to Heart* had turned quite gossipy of late and Major Lemmon could not be trusted. The *Courier*'s publisher might even print the scurrilous stuff Nellah was saying about poor Fannie. Nellah could not agree more. She would send Millburn a post-box number. Or he could simply hand over her weekly allowance to Alfie or Ann or Lizzie and they would post it straight to her. (They were set to stay in the brick house with Darius Davis and the four of them would continue to run the tavern.) Nellah said she looked upon the payment as reparation rather than extortion.

Her mammy had reared a good girl. She would never stoop to blackmail.

But Millburn was horrified.

Lover, he said, how could you? He saw his cajoling was doomed to fail and changed his tone and his tune. He said he was glad she had been cleared out of the village. Good riddance to her and her ilk. He cursed her. He swore. What a goddam awful disorderly half-breed community Vinegar Hill was, why, it was no wonder his brother-in-law, Lawrie Filkin, had tired of it and, earlier in the evening, he had left the village, post-haste, and forever. Millburn said that Filkin had told him that he, Filkin, did not fit in here.

Governor General Cathcart had nodded in agreement. The upper country was rough. Wild. Ill with Irish and Indian fever. A gentleman, such as himself, could well understand why the Nova Scotian had run off.

And so it was.

The optimist in Miz Golden had all this exciting news for the handsome young Mohawk who smiled and told her for the ump-teenth time how grand she was. Nonsense, she dimpled. Best of all, she had said, it seemed her cousin Jeddah Golden had made up his mind. He would take Bride Munny to Uxbridge to meet his teen-aged daughters, Miss Hattie and Miss Hedy, in the hopes of a mater-nal turnaround. Perhaps Bride's getting together with Jeddah's dear spawn would persuade Bride to view her own kin in a more kindly light.

Laws, Nellah said, she had laughed at that.

Teacher assured the handsome swarthy one she would inform the Hill people that the Munny kids were safe and, Jehoshaphat, she said as she waved farewell, she even promised the kindly young man she would warn the ever-harassed Alfie to expect a fresh arrow-killed wild turkey in the spring. Would Cook not just love that?

Appendix

~

The River, the Indians and the Navigation

William Hamilton Merritt and David Thompson (not the map-maker DT) were visionaries and they had caught a bug. They had caught "canal fever," running rampant on this continent in the 1830s, and they saw stars in the skies of Buffalo.

Buffalo was the end of the line for the Erie Canal. How best to get to Buffalo from the upper country? Well, that was the big question. Perhaps the Grand River was the answer. Early on in the 19th century, the river had been dammed at its mouth and a feeder line ending at Dunnville, five miles from Port Maitland, took smallish craft to the Welland Canal. Absalom Shade, a mill owner and a distillery operator who lived upstream on the Grand (in present day Galt/Cambridge), had built and rafted huge arcs downstream. The arcs had demonstrated a "phantasmal" opportunity, something businessmen were quick to notice (see Reville, *History of the County of Brant*). They argued the entire Grand River would make a logical addition to the North American canal waterways system: Brantford to Buffalo, or to St. Catharine's, and onwards. From the upper country, the river could float raw products to Lake Erie—the interior's gypsum of plaster, wheat, sowbellies and timber. Then return the favour. It could paddle luxury imports and manufactured commodities upstream.[1]

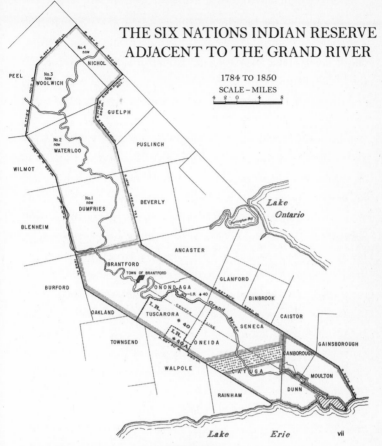

THE SIX NATIONS INDIAN RESERVE
ADJACENT TO THE GRAND RIVER

1784 TO 1850
SCALE – MILES

— LEGEND

—— Boundary of the original grant as described in Simcoe's Patent, January 14, 1793
- - - - Boundary of present day Six Nations Indian Reserve #40 and New Credit Indian Reserve #40A.

SURRENDERS

- 15 January 1798 – Block No's. 1, 2, 3 and 4 now Dumfries, Waterloo, Woolwich and Nichol Townships
- 5 February 1798 – On both sides of the Grand River 352,707 Acres including Blocks 1, 2, 3 and 4
- 19 April 1830 – The site of the Town of Brantford 807⁰ Acres
- 19 April 1831 – The north part of Cayuga Township 20,670 Acres
- 8 February 1834 – The remainder of Cayuga, Dunn, part of Moulton and Canborough Townships
- 26 March 1835 – Confirmation of all surrenders
- 18 January 1841 – "The remainder of the lands on the Grand River," excluding the Bed of the Grand River
- 19 November 1809 – To the Honourble W. Dickson 4000 Acres

Developed from a plan registered with the Surveyor General's Office in Kingston. Ont. 1843
Ministry of Natural Resources – Surveys & Mapping Branch ——————— April, 1982*

*GRNC not referenced in 1986 publication

In any case, for Merritt and Thompson in the 1830s, Buffalo was a main jumping-off point and all eyes were on burgeoning Buffalo as the desirable means of entry from British Upper Canada into the United States.

Brantford was/is located within the Six Nations Haldimand Deed. Buffalo grew apace but, way back in 1822, Brantford was small, less than 100 people, according to James Wilkes, whose memoir is excerpted by Reville. Wilkes recalls, "The principal trade was done with the Indians, but there was some through travel on the way to Detroit. This section was known as the Grand River Swamp, and twenty to thirty miles a day was big travel, so that taverns were, of necessity, numerous" (p. 71). Notwithstanding the joys of the tavern, the roads were notorious for being merely terrible to downright impassable and farmers and producers were desperate to get commodities to and from Buffalo. Reville says many "wide-awake" souls figured it was possible to improve the Grand River's water levels to permit slack-water navigation. It would take tinkering: some locks, dams and maybe a few canals. The Lachine, Rideau and Welland canals were making a go of it, sort of, and settlers of European origin (the white man) imagined the ancient Tinaatoua, with improvements, might compensate them for the province's "detestable" highways and byways.

The timing of canal fever was a perfect front for individual Loyalists, Indian entrepreneurs[2] and land jobbers. After 1830, Great Britain did not consider her erstwhile Six Nations allies useful for military defence. The British felt free to toy with colonial governance. Around this time, the government shifted their Six Nations allies to a civilian instead of a military administration. The Compact's men played their wards like checkers, shoving them around and "claiming" their land for the Crown. White settlers now controlled the homeland and hunting grounds of the Neutral,

Huron, Mississauga and Rotinonhsyonni (Iroquois/Six Nations Confederacy) and the strangers had got right into the farming business and removed considerable chunks of Carolinian forest. Brantford was threatening to transform itself from a cedar swamp into an agricultural centre and Chief Justice John Beverley Robinson, by turning a blind eye to unlawful incursions into Indian Territory, encouraged land jobbers or "deserving squatters"* (like the aforementioned James Wilkes) to put down roots, helter-skelter, and to stay put, wherever, and to "make improvements." Heading to Indian country and the Grand River Settlement, jobbers were on the prowl because nobody wanted or seemed able to stop them and every pioneer, British or oppositionist, knew land was power (see Harring, *White Man's Law*).

The Council of Six Nations Indians did their best to stand guard against endless chicanery. The Six Nations had money. They owned the Tinaatoua, the desirable Grand River, and, despite the sales and surrenders and some individual land-sale shenanigans within their own ranks, they still held gobs of land on either side of the river. The Haldimand Deed, foggy about some matters, was clear enough on that. Nonetheless, in an optimistic mood, Merritt and Thompson and other interested riverside stakeholders got together. They moved on the Grand River canal venture and they made a seminal decision; they would use funds that were not theirs to use. They would use Six Nations' money.

The entrepreneurs had lined up their ducks and with some valuable help from high officials, William Hamilton Merritt and David Thompson formed the Grand River Navigation Company—the Navigation, so called.

---

*A deserving squatter was one who made "improvements" on the Indian land he/she unlawfully occupied. See Harring, *White Man's Law*.

In the beginning, Thompson held 2000 shares; Merritt held 2000 shares; a host of individuals, including a certain Barton Farr, held a nominal number of shares. Last but not least, the Six Nations Indians held 1760 shares but that was all right. Lest the Six Nations Councils worry themselves sick about the stunning investment being made on their behalf, they were told to remember the high officials who helped Merritt and Thompson were canal lovers.

The colonial governor, Sir John Colborne, was a staunch Anglican and he was serious about canals. He had loaned his own money to the Welland Canal Company. John Henry Dunn, the other man, was about to prove himself.

Some (many) said John Henry Dunn was not the sharpest Jack in the box. All work and no play made Jack a dull boy but not a poor boy, from all accounts. He was a Six Nations trustee, a Welland Canal Company president and the Receiver-General of Upper Canada. He blithely ignored such a rarified concept as conflict-of-interest. He knew influential people and, like Governor Colborne, he had canal fever and he believed in a colonial waterways system. It was true Dunn fell out with the canal magnate William Merritt over Dunn's refusal to release the promised 50,000 pounds in debentures for the Welland Canal, against which Merritt had secured loans, but that was for the future. Promoters Dunn and Merritt were cronies at the inception of the Grand River Navigation Company and Governor Colborne had joined in with them. Canal builders had known all along Dunn was a valuable crony to have. He was the one man who had access to the hefty Six Nations funds, accumulated from timber sales and land surrenders, and invested heretofore in British government bonds. After Colborne himself approved of the money grab, the game was afoot. The Grand River venture was monumental and controversial but leaping from the foam like killer whales both Dunn and Colborne rose to the occasion.

There was ongoing resistance to the canal venture and it too was monumental. The Six Nations Indians opposed the Navigation and they had every right to raise a dissenting voice, more than a right. After all, the river, the British bonds and the trust monies in general-revenue and the thousands of unsurrendered acres along the riverbank belonged to them. Six Nations' Tory, Billy Kerr (husband of Elisabeth Brant, daughter of Joseph Thayendanegea Brant and Catharine Adonwentishon Croghan and grandson of Molly Brant and William Johnson), remained on side with the Navigation throughout the early 1840s but the Tekarihogan, Chief John Brant (Catharine and Joseph Brant's son) and, after him, most of the Six Nations' Councils at Ohsweken, worried about dams, flooding, fisheries and a host of other problems becoming apparent with the Welland Canal. They did not want outside promoters, either public or private, to assign town-sites and waterfront lots and towpaths in their Territory.

In the interim, however, and over Six Nations' objections, the Navigation had gone ahead. For the sake of the company, the government created and laid out a new village on a fragment of land between Seneca and Oneida villages. In 1834, the Navigation hired Ranald McKinnon to build a dam in Seneca and a dam in what is now Caledonia. Completed in 1840, the Caledonia dams made waterpower available. Mills popped up everywhere and some settlers made a lot of money but, ever weak and fiscally unaccommodating, the Navigation did not make money. Not a thin white dime. The enterprise remained forever iffy. The canal company had started out on a risky footing and so it continued until it reached the tipping point.

The Navigation's directors were supposed to manage risk. They had a charter to that effect. In most companies, a heavy investor, as you would expect, wants some say on the board of directors. Equally, directors want to hold shares in a company they plan to make profitable. In the case of the Navigation, neither was true. A major shareholder, the Six Nations Confederacy, who provided the river, the money *and* the land, was not on the board at all. Two of the company's directors, Merritt and Thompson, acted with sharp and shady if not criminal intent. In the process of selling their shares high, they dumped stocks—only to buy them back later at a depressed rate. The company was a disaster. Even the Indian Department had started to believe the sucking sound they heard was the Navigation. When it came to money, the canal company was like Mohawk Lake: bottomless.

Where did the money go?

Go it did. The Six Nations purchased 80 percent of the Navigation's stock but it was same old, same old. Council members at Ohsweken had no idea when the last stock purchase had occurred, they had no control over the company's development and they watched in helpless anger as the health of their communities deteriorated. Ohsweken believed, by rights, as it turned out, that the land-patent numbers were not commensurate with occupied lots but that was too bad and it was nothing new because deserving squatters were as thick as locusts. Settlers and canallers and lumberjacks swarmed into Indian Country, into the new Navigation villages by the river and even into the actual Grand River Settlement.

In the event, much of the Navigation's mess was left to Indian Superintendent David Thorburn to sort out. Samuel Peters Jarvis, named Chief Superintendent of Indian Affairs in 1837, had been fired in 1844. He was a man in disgrace for the alleged embezzlement of Indian funds and now Thorburn was in charge of Six Nations' land disputes. Thorburn was also a director of the Navigation and unlucky for him, and everybody else, he was a man in serious conflict. He worked for the flim-flam Indian Department, he felt duty-bound to the government's commitment to waterways, he had an obligation to the company's powerful directors, and he carried a fiduciary responsibility to the company's hapless investors, the Six Nations. For Thorburn and the others ratting about in the Indian Department, the circumstance was all the more complicated because the Navigation was a two-headed creature, a Crown and a public corporation, and whatever else you said to describe the canal company, you said this: it was not thriving. Not even Thorburn could breathe life into it.

The result was that the Navigation had used up the Six Nations' investment capital monies in fifteen years. The company *never* paid the Six Nations out for the non-surrendered expropriated land nor handed them a single penny in dividends. Most remarkable, the Navigation had wrung so much out of Six Nations' trust funds that the Indians actually landed in debt to the Receiver-General in 1843–44, right about the time brand-new salubrious Caledonia, with its very profitable mills, had burst upon the scene.

In his book *The Grand River Navigation Company*, the intrepid Grand River historian Bruce Hill quotes from Reverend W.H. Landon's letter to Lord Stanley. Nothing describes the Six Nations' misery more simply than the following observation: "many of the Six Nations the year before [the post-1837 period] perished from want of food owing to the non-receipt of funds expended by the government on the Grand River Navigation Company" (p. 23). But, Hill tells us, it was William Hamilton Merritt himself, begging the Governor General for yet more money, who was particularly succinct: "The Indians hold ¾ of the stock, they receive no dividend, no income, and can have no prospect of receiving any until the work is in successful operation throughout" (p. 51). Ontario historian David Shanahan[3] insists Samuel Jarvis, a Tory with a history of irascible behaviour, fell afoul of the rising power of Reformers, and it was more likely the Navigation's own William H. Merritt, and not Jarvis, who was responsible for mysterious financial discrepancies and missing monies in the scattered Indian Department.

What can be said about the Navigation's other powerful director, David Thompson?

In 1845, in the midst of the Six Nations' severest financial shortages, Navigation director, mill owner and liquor mogul, a certain David Thompson, was constructing his Greek-revival mansion, Ruthven Hall, at the site of yet another new Navigation village called Indiana. People had heard the train whistle and had seen the light at the end of the tunnel but waterways were still an important means for carrying commodities. Thompson built his estate at the peak of river travel. Shipping by river remained a reasonable option but that happy circumstance changed nothing for the degenerating canal company.

David Thompson, busy as a bee in Indiana, would have known it. In 1845, the Navigation was not performing up to anybody's idea of peak. Sure, the Grand waterway carried a significant level of traffic but the company was touching bottom over and over again. Under the circumstances Thompson was particularly Scroogey. He wanted to ship his own goods on the river toll-free. Worst of all, he must have known he built the colossal Ruthven Hall on Indian land in the midst of the excruciating poverty his company had caused.

No wonder the Navigation seemed rudderless. It whirled in a maelstrom: administrative, financial, structural and moral.

Of course, there were malingering complications with canal fever in and of itself. Not all of the Navigation's drawbacks were systemic. Tolls and revenues did not meet projections because many farmers were doubters and they continued to ship by land in spite of bad roads. Wooden locks were ripe for fast decay and money for necessary repairs and upkeep was in short supply. Further, the ongoing cost of the Navigation was crippling. Debt and deficit in a nascent colony, where economic downturns proved the norm, provided no legitimate follow-up to Indian funds. Public money, the little there was of it, drifted toward the needs of railroads and the entrepreneurs who would build them.

The failure of the Navigation to turn a profit had shocked the powerless Six Nations in the 1840s. By the 1850s, the shock waves reached upstream, to the Brantford citizenry. The Brantford Canal had opened in 1848 but the Navigation was already stressed to breaking. The town of Brantford, although it eyed the railroads with warmth, did indeed support the canal company with debentures and loans throughout the fifties but rail aficionados and the Brantford *Expositor* had got it right. Railroads had won. Trains took the Navigation's stations and commandeered all the tolls but what's a poor town to do? Brantford had put up thousands of dollars and the Navigation had defaulted on the payments. Historian Cheryl MacDonald writes, "Help arrived in the form of the Brantford and Haldimand Company, Ltd. The new company bought the locks and dams that had formerly belonged to the GRNC [the Navigation], with the town of Brantford holding the mortgage…. The Haldimand Navigation Company had sold 75% of its stock, continued to earn revenue from tolls, and had spent most of its money in repairs but still the dams and locks were far from being in a safe and satisfactory condition" (p. 279). Further petitions for government and municipal monies were denied and Brantford's town council was left with no option. It took the last step open to it and foreclosed.

The Navigation and Brantford went to court.

In 1861, one Judge Spragge informed the wide-awake Brantford citizens they were entitled to "some remedy" under their statutory mortgage and he determined that Brantford owned the corporal remains (Hill, p. 70).

Was it a remedy? Citizens expressed dismay and it sounded as though they were shocked and appalled to discover the extent of the mayhem. Hill quotes the *Expositor*, "concealment from the citizens of such an alarming state of affairs [in the Navigation] is absolutely criminal" (p. 70). It was indeed. Criminal tomfoolery had been going on for many years, *vis-à-vis* the Navigation and the Six Nations Confederacy, but when it dared to dump its depredations on Brantford's front doorstep, the newspaper's editor sat up and took notice.

In any case, the editor told it like it was. It was criminal. A proper mess too. Where was the wily Ariadne when you needed her, when it came to finding settlements and offering restitution? Where was the string to show interested parties the way out of the Navigation's labyrinth? Government records and Navigation records were intertwined. Nothing seemed to match up. Land patents (where were they? who held them? when were they registered?), towpaths (how big? in particular, where were they?), right-of-way lands around the dams and locks and towpaths (how large? who sold them? who pocketed the profits from the sales?), about everything incited disagreement and stirred up a court case. Every doubt was substantiated and every question lacked an answer.

One Alfred Watts, being a human dynamo with an Electric Dynamo, paddled the Navigation to the end of the line. Hill writes, "In 1875 Alfred Watts bought the remaining holdings of the upper navigation system for $1.00 from the town of Brantford with the stipulation he keep in good repair the dams, locks and canal banks and afford access over the Grand River Navigation lands for sewer and drains" (p. 131). Of course, that did not happen.

In the mid-1880s, Mr. Watts sold the canal system to the *Brantford Electric and Power Company*, which the power company's president, Watts himself, had formed with G. Wilkes, R. Henry and Watts' two sons, C. Watts and A. Watts. The selling price was $40,000. By anybody's reckoning it was a hefty increase from the original purchase price (Hill, p. 131). Watts and electricity aside, it was the end of the Grand River Navigation Company. The last broken lock was abandoned in 1880.

You may ask, what about stateside? What about the stars in the skies of burgeoning Buffalo? Did exporters-importers from the upper country in Canada get to see them? Yes, they certainly did. Newspaperwoman Jean Waldie writes, "January 13, 1854, was a gala day for Brantford, for it marked the long-awaited opening of the *Buffalo and Brantford Railway*. Notwithstanding inclement weather, 12,000 people are said to have assembled at the little depot to await the arrival of trains conveying invited guests from Buffalo and intermediate points…. Shortly after 2 p.m. the trains pulled in, to be greeted with loud cheers, firing of cannon and other demonstrations of rejoicing." The mayor of Brantford, one George Wilkes, made a congratulatory speech (in Waldie, p. 86; in Reville, p. 184).

The Navigation is extinct but the memory and the lawsuits linger on. Right up to present day. Almost two centuries after the fact, there remain gossamer knots in the money pit, hundreds of them. It was as though a behemoth spider had been at work, spinning a web of truths and secrets and lies. In general, we do know this: economic depressions, shoddy bookkeeping, shuffled bank accounts and shifty entrepreneurs, those whom we might call "the robber barons," plus the gross stupidity and negligence of Dunn, Colborne and the Family Compact and the Reformers, all the aforementioned followed the tried and true recipe for a major Indigenous catastrophe, which left many people dead from starvation and brought unwanted land jobbers into the Grand River territory.

The new Navigation villages performed an economic turnaround because of the railroad but the Six Nations were left broke and angry. They were angry with their leaders and each other; they wondered what had happened to their wealth and their sovereignty. Who could they blame when everyone was at fault? One hopes, despite the tangle of the Navigation's records, a change of attitude about the canal era is afoot.

We all need to know what happened on the Grand River. Tomorrow's students of the Canadian narrative will want to read through, say, David Thompson's collection of ledgers, letters and leaflets to pinch out fine points describing the hope and the glory, the delusions and the hysteria, the thieving and the spending, all brought on by canal fever in North America.

Notes

~

1. For the infant British colony, the most valuable import coming into the upper country walked on two feet: Anglo-Saxon-type farmers and, as necessary, Irish canallers and lumberjacks. Later, after 1844, and in full stream by 1846–48, Irish refugees poured into the British colonies and many of them made the trip upriver on the Grand. Americans were not wanted on the voyage, not on any raft. The dreaded American influx was a worry to loyal British subjects but, like your mother says, that is a whole n'other story.

2. Some believe Joseph Brant, Mohawk chief, was an exotic United Empire Loyalist. He was neither. He, many confederate Indians, and Brant's volunteers were military allies of the British during the American Revolution; they were not British subjects or wards. Upper Canada was under fifty years old when the Navigation was incorporated in 1832. In 1790 York/Toronto was a mud hole of about a hundred people. In fact, the British had no claim to what is now Ontario. They just took it on their grand say so. Nonetheless, in light of the "empty" upper country, Brant had every reason to expect a sovereign territory to replace the Mohawk Valley in New York, which his people lost fighting on side with the British during the revolution; but, sadly, it was great expectations for a hopeless cause. Indian entrepreneurs wanted to buy and sell land as much as Europeans. Within a sovereign nation, land sales would have been possible; requisite taxes turned into the state would support

the communities. That is what Brant wanted. Six Nations historian Barbara Graymont criticizes Brant for not understanding the British and their reluctance to surrender sovereignty over any part of the land they claimed in the upper country. I suggest, after the British/American peace of 1783, when the Indian allies were left out of the Treaty of Versailles, Brant understood all too well the mentality of the Crown. In any case, Graymont knows the issue for the Six Nations was and is and always will be sovereignty.

She writes:

> *Brant was a noble figure who dedicated his whole life to the advancement of his people and who struggled to maintain their freedom and sovereignty. His major failure was his inability to understand the nature of British imperialism and to comprehend the fact that the British would not permit two sovereignties to exist in Upper Canada. The Indians were manipulated and exploited by the British government to serve the purposes of the empire; they were encouraged to cede their land in time of peace, pressured to become military allies in time of war, ignored in the treaty of peace, urged to form an enlarged confederacy as a barrier between the British and the Americans, and coerced to abandon the confederacy when the British had composed their differences with their enemy and growing Indian power threatened to rival their own. British colonial agents were then urged to foster jealousies and divisions among the Indian nations in order to keep them in a state of continual dependency upon the British government.*

> (from *Dictionary of Canadian Biography Online*, www.biographi.ca/009004-119.01-e.php?&id_nbr=2686).

3. See David Shanahan, "Tory Bureaucrat as Victim."

References

~

Harring, Sidney L. *White Man's Law: Native People in Nineteenth-Century Canadian Jurisprudence.* Toronto: published for the Osgoode Society for Canadian Legal History by the University of Toronto Press, 1998.

Hill, Bruce Emerson. *The Grand River Navigation Company.* Brantford: Brant Historical Society, 1994.

MacDonald, Cheryl. *Grand Heritage: A History of Dunnville and the Townships of Canborough, Dunn, Moulton, Sherbrooke and South Cayuga.* Dunnville: Dunnville District Heritage Association, 1992.

Reville, F. Douglas. *History of the County of Brant.* Brantford: Hurley Printing Company. First printing, 1920; Second, 1967, Centennial Edition.

Shanahan, David. "Tory Bureaucrat as Victim: The Removal of Samuel Jarvis, 1842–47." *Ontario History*, Vol. XVC, Number 1, Spring 2003, 38–64.

Waldie, Jean. *Brant County: The Story of Its People, Volume II.* Brantford: Brant Historical Society, 1985.

DR. SUSAN MINSOS, author and retired coordinator of Canadian Studies at the University of Alberta, grew up in Brantford, Ontario, along the Grand River and in the heart of the Haldimand Tract. Minsos is proud to have an ancestor from the Six Nations. In her Sky Walker / Tehawennihárhos stories, she brings the history of mid-19th century Ontario to vivid life and creates a new Canadian hero. Renowned nationalist Mel Hurtig once said of her work: "No one understands culture like Minsos. A great yarn. Entertaining, absorbing, wicked."